THE ZENITH SERIES

THE
SPY'S
NET

DAMEON COX

Lezen Publishing

The Spy's Net

Lezen Publishing, LLC.

Original Cover Concept: Kästle Olson
Map Illustrations: Kästle Olson
Interior Design and Formatting: Deborah J Ledford

Manufactured in the United States of America

Lezen Publishing, LLC, Phoenix, AZ
ISBN 978-0-9960063-6-1

Dedicated to

NEAL E. LOSIER

A true friend

TABLE of CONTENTS

THE ZENITH SERIES
MAP

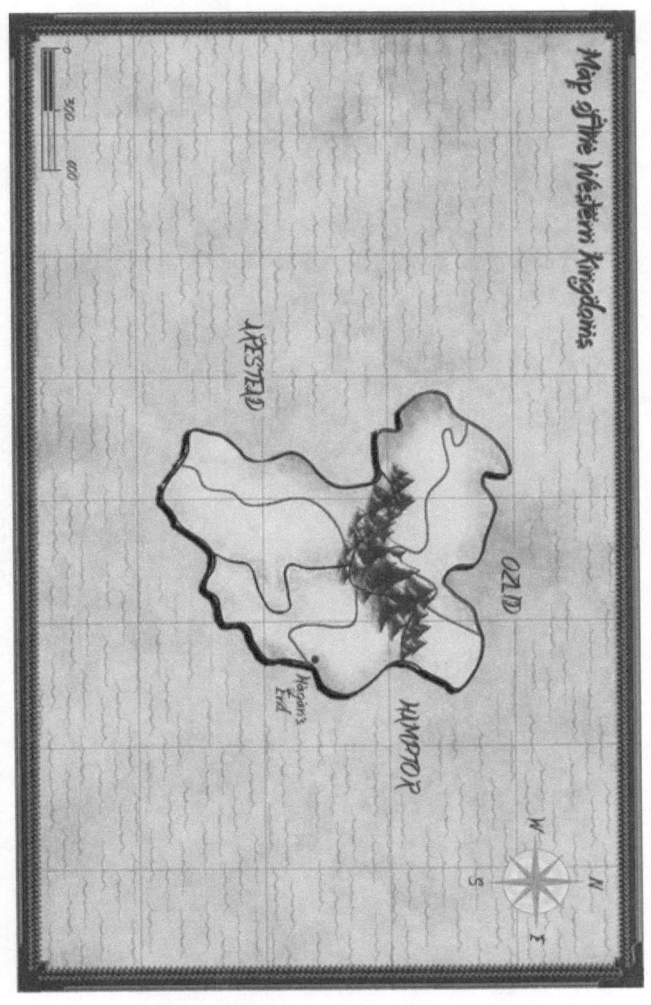

MAP OF THE WESTERN KINGDOMS

THE ZENITH SERIES MAP

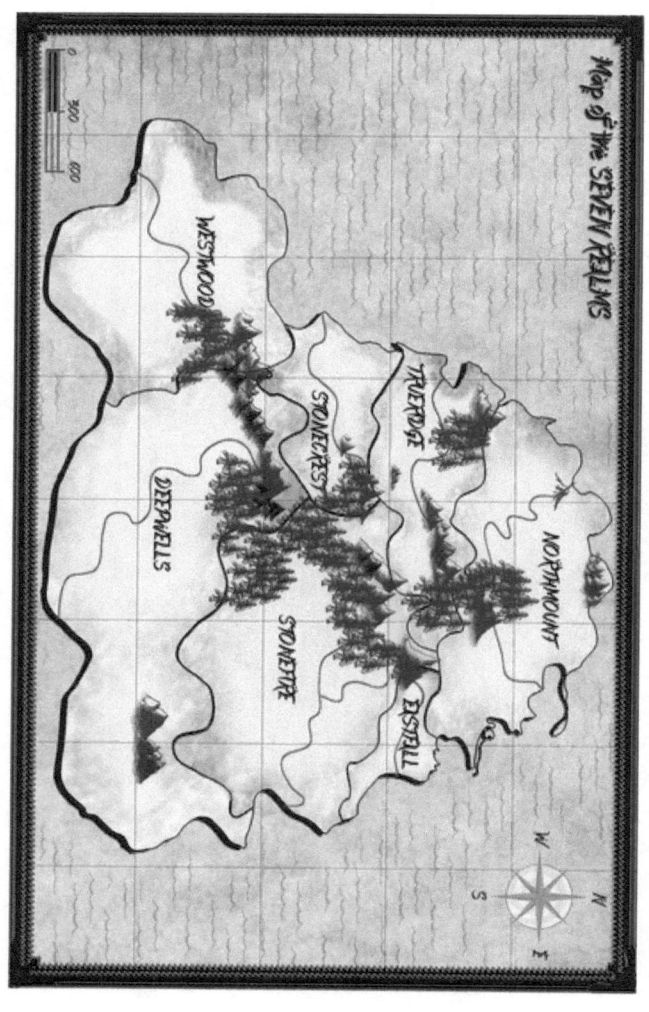

MAP OF THE SEVEN REALMS

THE ZENITH SERIES
MAP

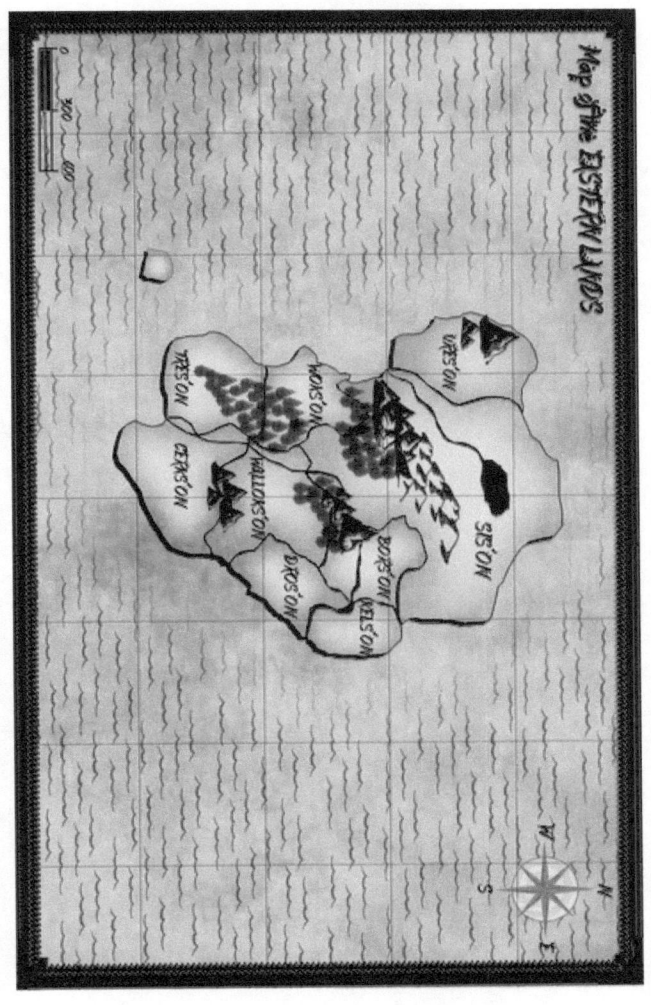

MAP OF THE EASTERN LANDS

PART I

1

THUNK! The arrowhead slammed deep into the tree next to where Zack Stand was hiding from bandits. He jerked his head, pulling out a few hairs that had gotten embedded with the steel bolt head. *Arrows? These idiots don't have archers! I doubt they would know which end to shoot.*

He ducked down, sighting back along the arrow's trajectory, moving back and forth a few inches to see around one tree or another. *There! I thought these bandits were stupid. This one's even wearing a red shirt.* Zack remembered when he'd worn a similar shirt while infiltrating a bandit gang to identify him when the Zenith's Guard attacked. *I don't think this is the same.* He smiled at the thought as he silently crept to deeper cover and closer to Currat, his partner in the service of the Zenith Lord.

Zack sounded a perfect imitation of a wren. Currat answered the signal and met Zack in his new position, eyebrow raised.

"An archer in a red shirt! Almost put an arrow in my head—close enough to pull out hair. He's in a tree, and I don't think he knows I found him. We should take him out before dealing with the bandits. There's only twelve of them, and I think they're as thoughtless as we figured. The way they lounge about, they'll still be here."

Currat nodded. The two spies circled around to approach the archer from behind, their multicolored cloaks hiding them well in the forest trees and brush. Currat took point, as stealthy as a cat. It took longer than expected, the brush and brambles becoming thicker and trees growing closer together. Finally, Zack pointed into the branches overhead.

Currat nodded, and took a position that gave him a reachable knife throw. The archer had built a sling holding a platform braced against the tree he rested against. Currat watched Zack move into a place with equal throwing distance ten yards to his right.

The archer jerked about, raising his bow, arrow nocked and starting to pull back the string. Zack stopped in mid-throw, nearly losing his dagger. The lad steadying his bow into a shooting position overhead couldn't have been more than twelve or thirteen summers.

Zack flashed a hand signal to Currat, then stepped forward, pulled the cowl of his cloak back, and put a finger to his lips. The boy looked confused. Waving at him to come down, Zack stood clear, an easy shot. The boy started to aim.

A throwing dagger thunked into the tree trunk, as close to the archer's head as the arrow had come near Zack. Startled, the youngster looked all around, but maintained enough presence of mind to not loose his arrow. Seeing nothing, he brought his attention back to his first target, who shrugged and put his hands out, palms up, motioning the boy down once more. A few heartbeats passed before another knife sank into the tree, just below the first one.

Looking defeated, the boy started down. Zack held his hand up again, raising his finger to his lips and pointing for him to bring the knives with him. After a few more gestures, the knives landed on a mound of dead foliage. The boy came down to several feet from the ground, jerked the rope, and grabbed the harness before it could crash into the undergrowth. He started to jump off the tree, and Zack again shook his head, holding his arms out to him. He landed in Zack's arms in a cradling position. Zack had to chuckle; the lad was actually smiling.

Currat snuck up behind them. "Thanks for getting my knives down. I don't like climbing trees," he whispered.

The lad twisted around, his eyes widening at the second man. "I didn't hear you and couldn't find you."

Currat smiled and pointed his chin toward Zack. "You wouldn't have seen or heard him if he didn't want you to, either."

The boy looked back and forth between the spies' twin-like appearance in face and powerful body, twice. His shoulders relaxed in Zack's arms and he soon stood on his own. "I guess you both are pretty good hunters."

Zack chuckled again and knelt in front of the youth. "Why are you out here?"

"Those men—" He sniffed. "Those men...killed my family—my da, mom, and older brother. There were six of them. They did it from ambush. My da went down first with two slashes, and then my mom and brother ...stabbed from the back. I was in a tree waiting for game. I cried out, but they couldn't find me. I waited until dark, and tracked them in the moonlight. They don't know how to move in the forest, and their trail's easy to see. I, or you, could have tracked them with no moon! I knew they would have to come back through the forest where you stood. It will be easy enough to pick them off."

"What's you name, son?" Currat asked.

The lad jerked toward him. "I'm not your son!" he hissed.

"Easy lad, easy," Zack said. "He meant nothing by it. Now, tell us your name."

The youngster turned back to Currat. "Sorry, I'm... sorry." The tears came in a rush; he took a deep breath and sobbed. Zack stood with the lad in his arms, resting his head on his shoulder and patting his back. It took several moments for the sobs and tears to stop and then he relaxed in the strong arms holding him. "Sorry—a man shouldn't cry," he squeaked out.

"Whoever told you that?!" Zack said. "I cried when my wife and daughter were killed by bandits. Sometimes, it's good to let your feelings out before they fester into something you don't want eating at you."

Currat took the youth by his shoulders, looked directly into his face. "We work for the Zenith Lord. I've killed many bandits and murderers, and I cried when my da was killed."

Looking between the spies, the lad spoke in a stronger tone with wide eyes. "Really...you work for the Zenith Lord?"

Zack chuckled. "Really."

"My name is Obien Webster. Our...my farm's about a mile northeast of here."

"You're very good with that bow," Zack said.

"My da made me my first, and I can't remember far enough back to when I received it. He told me I was two summers grown." Pride crept in his voice. "I brought a lot of game down for food. I learned how to make the arrows hit so the animal wouldn't suffer. He told me that was important."

"Your da was right," Currat said with an approving nod. "Now, you want to watch us capture or kill some murdering bandits?"

"I...I want to kill them!"

"I tell you what," Zack said. "You'll have our backs. I know how you must feel, but now isn't a good time for you to start killing men. If you wait, I'll see what I can do to put you under the Zenith Lord's care, but only if you promise to wait."

Obien's eyes returned to full roundness. "You...you can do that?"

Currat chuckled. "Yes, he can do that!"

The lad thought for a moment before saying, "To leave, they have to come through here. I'll go back up the tree, and if one gets by you, I'll wound him. I'll try not to kill him, just make him hurt...a lot."

"Fair enough," Zack said. "But no stomach, head, or back wounds. Promise?"

Obien looked deflated, but he nodded.

Before the spies returned to the trees overlooking the bandit's camp, the lad sat back in his harness, up the tree.

"Swords or knives?" Currat whispered.

"Let's take down a couple, and see if the rest will surrender. I don't like the way the boy said these bastards killed his parents. If they won't lay down, we'll kill them."

Currat nodded. "I agree. They're murderers, and it'll save the boy from reliving his ordeal for the Zenith's justice."

* * *

THEY caught their first bandit returning from a badly made latrine, judging by the smell. Zack's thrown blade caught him in the throat, cutting through the hyoid bone and windpipe. He toppled forward, pushing the knife through his spine. Other than slapping the ground, he didn't make a sound.

"Hey, what's wrong with you?" a bandit called out as he walked to the body. "Seven Hells! He's dead!"

As he whirled around and began running toward the rest of the men, a knife slammed into his chest on the left side, the snap of bone cracking in the air. A second knife pierced his throat from the right side.

"Throw your weapons in the fire, walk six paces toward me, and lay down on the ground!" Zack called out.

Confusion and fear ran through the four remaining bandits: "We can take them!"

"Are you an idiot? You can't throw a knife like that!"

"If they take us, we'll hang for killin' that family!"

"They don't know about that—!"

"Yes, we do!" Currat called from other side of the

camp.

"Find them; kill them! I'm not gonna hang!"

The bandits drew long swords and charged at where Zack's voice had sounded. The last man among them gasped in pain as Currat's dagger sliced into his back. Staggering, he fell when Zack eased from the tree line and ran his blade through him. They turned down the trail, putting them out of Currat's line of vision. Zack's knife rammed into one's throat at the base of his neck. He went down. Currat reached Zack as the last bandit ran down the trail.

"Why'd you let him get away?" Disbelief rang in Currat's voice.

"I thought Obien should have some fun."

As if on mark, a cry of joy came from down the trail, followed by wails of pain.

When the spies found Obien, he swung a length of rope across the bandit's back. From the look of the coward's shirt, the boy had been at it a while. The bandit screamed anew as each lash landed, drawing fresh blood. Obien swung again, the rope catching on the ends of the two arrows coming from a thigh and calf. The bandit's answering shriek came full-bodied and long.

"That's enough, lad!" Zack said. "We need something left to hang—"

"Lad?!" the murderer yelled. He flipped over and looked on his attacker for the first time, rage twisting his face. Reaching inside his front trousers, he drew a knife and cocked his arm to throw it.

Zack's short sword chopped through bone and into the ground. The bandit's throwing arm collapsed in two pieces. The blade fell into the dead man's arm, point first, quivered once, and then tumbled to the ground.

Currat looked at the pleasant scene around him—large mature evergreens, blue skies with white clouds, a hawk soaring high above him. The birds had returned after flying from the shouts and sounds of death; their songs seemed surreal to him. Flourishing greenery smelled of the freshness of new life. The contrast to the gore surrounding him made him sad, but the rescue of the lad softened his concern, and he smiled a little.

Zack aligned the bodies in a neat row, except for the last one, and then took their purses and saddlepacks. He gathered their six still frightened horses by lashing the leads together with the picket rope in one long line, and recovered Spellbinder and Snowflake, Currat's and his mounts, respectively. Guiding Spellbinder with his knees, he held the lead for the thieves' horses in one hand and Snowflake's reins in the other, before placing them in Currat's hands. The saddlepacks rode on various horses and the purses rested in his cloak's pocket.

Obien's eyes still held a shadow of disbelief when Zack reached Currat and him. Zack eyed him with concern. His voice, while strong, had a gentle touch. "Obien, do you have a horse?"

"No, she died last week. That's why Da had all our coins in his pouch. He wanted to go into town and buy a mare for plowing and the wagon."

"Well, you're a good hunter. Do you know horseflesh, too?"

The lad shook his head.

"That's all right. Currat knows a lot about them. Go with him and he'll show you some pointers. When he's done, you can pick out the best horse for you. You do know how to ride, I hope?"

The smile on Obien's face answered the question before he said, "Yes!"

By the time they returned, Zack had examined the contents of the thieves' saddlepacks and placed several pieces of parchment aside, throwing lots of dirty, stinking clothing away. Standing, he smiled, recognizing the horse Obien rode as the youngest and strongest the thieves had. He mounted Snowflake and they headed for the nearest garrison, some seven miles away.

Reaching the large fort an hour before lastmeal, Zack and Currat talked with the garrison commander, going over the parchments they'd found, and explaining the need to place the coins in trust for Obien. The commander agreed, and sent ten men, a pebble in the Zenith Lord's Guard out to bury the bodies and to Obien's farm for a more personal ceremony. The commander also agreed to send the lad and Zack's report to the Spires with a detail leaving the next day.

Zack rejoined Obien and explained he would be going to the Spires, the Zenith Lord's seat of power outside the city of Stonefire. The boy's reaction made Zack laugh, as he tried to squeeze the life out of the spy in a joyous bear hug

* * *

THE next morning, Currat and Zack waved to Obien as he struck out with the pebble of men going to the Spires and a new life. Turning to head back to their quarters, a man holding a piece of parchment ran toward them.

"Master Zack," the priest said, slightly out of breath, "I've received a message from Master Gaz for you. It's the strangest one I've ever seen, just a bunch of numbers. I read the bird's mind three times to make sure I got them all and in the right sequence." The graystone—the device allowing him to interpret messages flown in by birds— that usually remained under a priest's shirt, dangled on a gold chain that hung nearly to his waist.

Zack took the message from his superior, the Zenith Lord's spymaster for the Seven Realms, looked at a few of the numbers, nodded, and thanked the priest before Currat and he started off again for their quarters.

Once back inside their chamber, Currat sat by the window and held out his hand. "May I?"

Zack smiled. "Of course." He handed over the parchment and codebook from his saddlepack.

"We are to return to the Spires in all haste." Currat said after a pause. "Do you know someone named

Openhand?"

Zack looked surprised, and nodded. He thought of the enormity of the Spires, the Zenith Lord's seat of power outside the city of Stonefire in the center of the realm with the same name. It was the closest feeling of home he could muster.

2

ZACK and Currat rode abreast on the last day before reaching Elizabethville, expecting to arrive at their destination before the setting sun's rays spread their glory over the sea.

"I read the reports Gaz gave, and I remember what you told me about our ambassadors, but what's so special about Openhand?" Currat asked.

"I heard when he went into service for the Zenith Lord, his surname caused him a great deal of distress by his peers," Zack replied. "As his talents grew, that anguish went away. His fellows began seeking him out for advice, and his name became a badge of honor. He's resolved many disputes between the High Lords, always with an acceptable outcome for all. Jarod pulled him out of retirement to approach Hamptor and Arestead. Not receiving a message from him or the trade delegations in a reasonable time has Gaz and Jarod worried. I'll be distraught if he's not in good health. I've met him, and he's not only talented in his field, he's a good person and wishes well of everyone. If he's injured or dead by nefarious means, we'll take action."

"I didn't read that in the report or hear it in our orders...the take action part," Currat commented.

"I read it in the Zenith Lord's face."

They rode in silence for a while before cresting the hill overlooking Elizabethville and the sparkling blue water beyond. Spellbinder and Snowflake whuffed, probably remembering their displeasure of sea voyages.

Reaching their destination two hours before the sun disappeared into the rolling waves, they rode to the Silver

Tankard Inn. The innkeeper, Franc Horn, a retired Guardsman, ran a tight operation with cleanliness, good food, ale and wine, good service, and no vermin in the beds, which if there were any, would cause the bedclothes to be thrice-washed in boiling water.

After giving the horses to the stable boy for grooming, water, and food, the spies entered the inn's common room. Franc Horn's chipper voice sounded from behind the bar on the north wall. "Welcome back to my custom, my friends."

Zack smiled at the warm greeting. He and Currat found a table in a corner with no one sitting nearby. In moments, Franc set two tall mugs of ale before them "The first round is without cost for fellow Guardsmen," he whispered, glancing at Currat with a raised eyebrow.

"Franc," Zack said. "You well know we are in the Zenith Lord's service, but not in the Guard. This is Currat Duval. Keep his name quiet, and mine too, for that matter."

"Well, my dear spies, may I assume you're on your way to Hagan's End?" he asked, keeping his tone low.

"You certainly may," Zack said ambiguously. "And, where might our smelly friend be?"

Their noses answered the question as Calbris entered and sauntered toward them in a perfect imitation of a drunk. "An...an ale, good...good innkeeper! These good fellows...fellows will stand...stand me a round!" he roared. Several of the other guests looked annoyed, and one table of patrons left.

As Calbris plopped unsteadily into a chair, Franc frowned. "Calbris, you cost me a fortune in lost custom."

"Yes, and the coin I pay you afterward more than covers your losses," Calbris murmured, dropping his drunkard act.

Franc smiled and gave a mock salute before leaving for the bar. A moment later, he returned with Calbris' ale, and then left the table of spies alone.

"I assume you're going to Hamptor," the "drunkard" said in a nearly normal tone. "I recently got a message that you'd be arriving about now."

Franc returned with another tray of ales. "I believe Briggs's *Silver Dolphin* should be in port tomorrow. His new ship has increased his trading abilities a great deal. I swear, that ship looks as new as when he got it." The innkeeper chuckled. "He said he chose the name because *Flying Dolphin* was too plain. I still don't know how he managed the cost, and he won't tell."

There are many things the Zenith Lord does that you'll never hear about, Zack thought before saying, "Yes, we're going on a little journey and, as always, it's privileged knowledge."

"I won't say a word," Franc murmured. "Calbris would kill me if I did."

"I certainly…certainly would," the man said in a somewhat drunken voice.

Franc raised his right fist to his heart in a salute before making his way back to the bar.

"You met Currat when we last came through?" Zack asked.

"No, but I saw that huge coach. You looked quite ill, young spy."

"More than you can imagine," Currat said. "Zack rescued me and saved my life, *again.*"

"We ended up doing that a lot," Zack commented. "What did you speak about with Ambassador Openhand when he came through? I read your report; it didn't say much."

"There wasn't much to write about. Darius and I spoke briefly. He wanted to know the attitude of the Hamptorian and Aresteadian people toward outsiders. I told him the Hamptorians are more trusting than the Aresteadians, but after not receiving much information from Arestead, that's really all I could say. He wished me well, and went to open a window as I left. A lot of folks do that when I visit."

"I think every spy in the Seven Realms knows of your smells," Zack said behind a grin. "And yes, I know how long it took you to master your disguise, but why couldn't you at least be a clean drunk?"

"I thought it best at the time, and I can't change now. I'm as stuck with this as you are, but at least I'm used to it, and it no longer bothers me." Currat's chuckle brought smiles all around.

"Well," Zack said, "what can *you* tell us about what's going on over there and anything you know of Openhand's delegations?"

Calbris frowned. "Not much, recently. When he first made contact with Hamptor's ministers, things seemed to go well from the initial reports. Briggs stated he'd secured more trade goods for over here, and he found wares his people could afford there. The difference in our gold values still hampers most trade items. But about three moons ago, I stopped hearing anything about Openhand or his delegations. I wrote to Gaz, as you're probably aware, and asked Briggs to quietly investigate. He reported back what I put in my report to Stonefire; the delegation's offices and warehouse are abandoned, with no trace of the men to be found."

"Knowing what Currat and I know," Zack replied, "I don't think Wathdure would kill them. He might use necromancy on them, but unless he's improved his abilities a great deal—and I hear they're increasing—Openhand wouldn't pass for someone alive. Spercine would kill them without a second thought. Have you heard if she's still running Ozlid during Wathdure's absences?"

"Getting information from Ozlid is as difficult as when you went there," Calbris replied. "I've had no reports. Hamptor and Arestead are still under Ozlid's yoke over allotments of water. Actually, some word came stating Ozlid may have increased the water to the kingdoms, I imagine simply to keep the populace from starving. From your reports, I don't think either Spercine or Wathdure would care how many died."

"Calbris," Currat asked. "Have you thought of those people being used as a necromantic army?" His direct stare into the spy's eyes sent a chill up Zack's spine.

Calbris choked on a swallow of ale in the middle of his drunkard's act. "No, by the Great Creator, I have not. The men from two whole kingdoms?"

Currat's face twisted deeper into a look of disgust and possibly pain. Zack couldn't tell which. "No, Calbris, not just men, but women and children, too! Wathdure and Spercine are capable of issuing such orders and seeing them through. I believe the only thing stopping them is Wathdure's inability to perfect his capacities that far. We defeated his necromantic army outside Stonefire, losing many less men than he lost creatures. Will he do that in the future? If the thought comes to his or Shadure's mind, they would if they would be more effective than the last time."

Zack could see Currat's anger building. He unseeingly slipped his hand over the other man's, causing Currat to snap his head in his direction, then he took a deep breath as his shoulders relaxed from their strain.

He looked back at Calbris, who wore a dismayed expression. "I'm sorry, Calbris. Those monsters have my people in their grasp, too. They may not know what Wathdure does to others, but someday his control over their minds will come to an end. I know my society; it'll be very hard on them. I think many will not be able to live with the disgrace. They are a proud lot. I once loved my country. Now, I love the Seven Realms more, almost as much as I love a certain brother in all but name." He squeezed his lover's hand, unseen, and relaxed some more, but kept his face somber. *This is not the time to discuss our relationship with any who do not already know. It may not be frowned on in either of our societies, but it very well could be used against us in battle and other situations we find ourselves facing. In fact, I've probably said more than I should!*

Calbris' troubled face twisted around his mouth, not part of his inebriated act. "I just never thought it could come to something so horrible. I'm a cynical man, as you know, Zack, but this is something beyond even my comprehension."

Zack leaned forward. "My friend, we are dealing with the Dark—that will muster all the repulsive horror you can envision, and more!"

Even Calbris shook at the thought.

* * *

ZACK answered Currat's request, massaging his tight muscles until he finally relaxed. It took longer for him to sleep, and even longer for Zack to free his mind of Currat's future imaginings, and to find peace.

All the torture we endured at Wathdure or Spercine's orders, he thought, *all the times we fought side by side, all the times we saved each other's lives, all the despicable men we killed, all the time we spent in the Zenith Lord's service, all the time it took for us to find our true selves; in all those times, I've never watched the lasting torment you've hidden so well. I must help you heal your emotional anguish as you healed mine.*

He managed to sleep for a few fitful hours before dawn.

* * *

ZACK watched Currat enter the common room as the sun tossed morning shadows onto tables, chairs and the floor. Dust motes swirled when he walked through the sunlight. He hid the stress from the previous night well, but Zack knew better than to think it was gone. *I don't know when to bring it up, or even if I should.*

Currat sat beside Zack at the corner table for four,

their backs to the wall, putting his cloak on top of Zack's in an extra chair. Their choice of tables came from too many bad situations in common rooms. It kept them out of fights as much as it gave them an advantage if the fight came to them. The two men had adopted many routines and mores to keep the environment in their favor. Zack didn't like fights, maiming or killing fellow humans; given the choice, they'd decline involvement, something not offered too many times.

"You didn't sleep well," Currat said without preamble.

"Did I wake you?"

"No, I know *you!*"

"Do you want to talk?"

"I do, but not now."

Zack nodded. "I suspect the *Silver Dolphin* will arrive today. If so, we'll probably sail tomorrow, unless Briggs is in a hurry. He doesn't mind leaving port on the night tide."

Currat looked relieved, and Zack wondered if it came from having extra time or not having to discuss his pain. He didn't probe. He wouldn't probe.

Zack had never seen the serving maid who wound her way between tables to reach them. Her white dress, tied at the waist and with a pristine, full bodice, fell nearly to the floor. Long blonde curls reached to her waist. Her smile had a feeling of truthfulness about it.

"Franc said you two are important guests. What may I bring my special brothers?" Her eyes measured them, lingering over hard muscles and finally, she giggled.

The men somehow kept a straight face. "Eggs not runny, ham and fried bread. Oh, and fresh water from the well."

Her smile didn't leave, but her dark brown eyes hardened.

Because they looked so much alike, being called brothers was something they had heard often. The woman's address ran off them like water from a breaching dolphin, without notice. Zack did glance at the maiden's long hair, its curls bouncing near her waist.

After firstmeal, they struck out to see Elizabethville. Zack wanted to see the changes and show Currat the town and what it offered. Trading ships from Trueridge, Westwood, and as far away as Northmount and Deepwells found Elizabethville's port welcoming. Its location resulted in two large markets carrying goods from all the Seven Realms except Eastfall, whose flat lands provided wheat for all the realms, along with the Zenith Lord's fields in Stonefire. Zack had been to the markets many times, and he wanted Currat to see the beautiful carvings from the tusks of sea creatures, one of which supposedly had a horse-like body with a long horn jutting from its head. He wondered about *that* story.

Browsing over tables of carved bone, a merchant approached with an elaborately carved tusk nearly as long as Zack's forearm. "I can tell from the excellence of your cloaks and boots that you're used to the finer things, good sirs. This is a special tusk. The cuttings are ancient runes insuring wealth and safety. But they aren't the main feature; this beautifully worked piece of art harbors a surprise…"

Tugging on the end of the bone, he pulled a blade free with a flourish. He looked from the dagger back to his prospects. Eyes wide, he carefully sheathed the steel, never taking his eyes away from the razor-sharp points of Zack and Currat's swords, both positioned within a few inches from his heart.

"You really shouldn't pull a blade without warning," Zack commented.

Currat matched Zack's cold voice and the hardness in his face. "After all, you never know who you might encounter."

The trader backed away, then whirled around and ran back to his table of goods.

"That was fun," Zack said.

"Fun!" Currat grinned. "It's a good thing he had a stable heart. I never saw color drain from a man's face so quickly."

They moved on, listening to dealers selling their wares in a wide variety of voices and stances. More than a few reminded Zack of pantomimes at a party. *Perhaps that's what they are trying to do, entertain us. They are comical.*

Zack read Currat's expression as well as the man read him; his partner's face contained all the elements of agreement. They drifted in and out of the crowd. Finding a guardsman, Currat pointed out a cutpurse. The guardsman looked bothered, but he did circle behind the man—boy actually—and caught him while scampering away from another victim.

Zack's stomach growled.

"Perhaps it's time for midmeal," Currat said.

"At the Silver Tankard; I wouldn't trust the food here."

The walk back to the inn included a fine view of the sea. Zack pointed out the full sails of Briggs's ship, making fast time cutting through the waves, the spray flying away from the bow in silver streaks.

* * *

ZACK didn't see the serving maid from firstmeal. The one that came to their table moved efficiently through the common room, checking on guests while approaching the same corner table Currat and he had sat at that morning. He and Currat placed their cloaks on the same empty chair and sat with their backs to the wall.

After enjoying a midmeal of roast rabbit and root vegetables, they donned their cloaks and headed to the wharf, watching as the *Silver Dolphin* came in a half-mile away. The air held its crispness from the morning, making the walk enjoyable.

An emaciated-looking passenger disembarked as they approached the ship. Zack recognized something about the man; he didn't quite know what, but he had a familiar look.

"Zack?" the man croaked as they neared, then nearly collapsed.

Currat reached the man first. Catching him before he fell, he eased him onto a piling and held him steady. He looked up at Currat with a blank stare, showing no emotion.

Zack stepped close. "Summerton?"

The man nodded. "I was with Openhand until men captured us. They took him on one wagon and me on another in a different direction. I never saw him after they tied him, hands and feet, covered him in a tarp, and rode away."

"You were cared for on Briggs's ship?"

"Yes, he wanted me to wait until he could have a crewman take me to the garrison. I thought I could make it, and I wanted to send a bird to the Spires. I don't know if I can reach there now."

"We'll see you there and take care of the message to—" Zack stopped as Briggs and two crewmen approached.

"Zack Stand and Master Duval!" Briggs boomed, and then looked abashed. "Seven hells, I forgot myself, assuming you don't want to be noticed. Master Duval, you look much better than I ever expected to see you. You advanced on death until the final day of our crossing. It's good to see you well." The robust, stocky captain looked at the man sitting before him. "Oh yes, Summerton. I told you you'd not reach the garrison in your condition. These fine sailors will see you there."

"No," Zack said. "If you would, see him to the Silver Tankard and tell Franc, the owner, he needs food and a bed. Ask him to send for a healer from the garrison at my request. And Summerton, I'll take care of the message. Do you wish to add anything more than you've already told me?"

The other man shook his head as relief flooded his

face. The two brawny seamen took him from under the arms and slowly headed north toward the inn.

"I got a good bit of broth into him on the voyage over," Briggs said. "It didn't seem to do much good. Perhaps one of your healers can help him. He came to my ship. I hardly recognized him from several months before, when he made the crossing with Ambassador Openhand and several other men. I liked the ambassador. We enjoyed a few meals together and talked long into the night, although he didn't say much about his visit to my lands. I didn't ask, figuring if he wanted me to know, he'd tell me. I suppose you're on the business of *jewels*?"

"Why, Crawford," Zack said. "I do trade in jewels. I'll show them to you tonight when we have lastmeal at the Silver Tankard, and it'll be my pleasure for you to be *my* guest."

"Now, how could I reject such a gracious offer?"

Zack remembered Briggs's smile carrying good cheer. He doubted if Currat recalled much of anything from his last crossing on the *Silver Dolphin*. He smiled at the captain. "We'll see you at six bells?"

"That you will, my friend, and I'll have cabins ready for you and Master Currat by tomorrow," Briggs said.

"Put us in the same cabin," Currat replied.

Briggs gave a questioning look, but only nodded and returned toward his ship.

"Need we explain wanting one cabin?" Currat asked.

"No, I'll mention that it's a safety issue our miners require," Zack replied.

A sailor ran past them with determination in his mien.

A somber mood fell over both spies as they returned to the inn after paying their respects to the garrison commander and seeing the priest to send a message to the Spires. Franc told them Summerton's room number, and they arrived as the healer came from the room. A look of recognition crossed his face as he said, "Zack Stand and Currat Duval, I thought you might be involved when I saw Summerton's condition. He wouldn't say much about where he's been. Did Ozlid do this to him?"

"I don't know for sure," Zack lied. "I think he'll talk to me. He knows me, and I believe he'll trust me."

The healer nodded. "Well, I've done what I can to straighten out his stomach muscles. He's taken much physical abuse, but primarily there. He's not nearly in as bad a condition as you and Master Currat the last time I saw you." The healer lowered his voice to a whisper and looked around before stating, "I wouldn't be one of Gaz's spies for all the gold in Stonefire."

Zack chuckled. "I've had that same thought from time to time."

The healer left them, and Zack tapped lightly on Summerton's door. One of the sailors answered. "I'm glad you're here," he said. "Captain Briggs sent a message for me to stay until you arrived. I've been in my share of brawls, but I've never seen a man in his condition who lived." He gave a sailor's salute and left.

"Are you up to talking?" Zack asked when the door had closed.

"Yes. I'm very tired, but I'll tell you what I can remember. I was unconscious much of the time. I was to stay with the ambassador as one of his assistants. The kings wouldn't open full diplomatic relations with us, but they did allow the trade delegations. We were on our way back from Arestead when ten men, all in black and on black stallions, waylaid us. They took Openhand and me before brutally killing the other three—except for Juston Dowell, whom they seemed to know. They let him go. They tortured the others, seeming to enjoy it. It took a long time for them to die. I've never thought men did that to one another."

"What did the men sound like? Is this the way they talked?" Currat said in a thick Ozlidian accent.

Summerton's eyes widened to their fullest while trying to pull the blanket over his head.

Zack reached out and took his arm, pulling the covering back down to his chest. "It's fine, Summerton. Currat hates the men who did this to you more than you can imagine. He'd like to kill them all."

The envoy relaxed his bunched shoulders as Currat smiled and pulled a chair close to the bed. Zack eased onto the corner of the bed as well, looking around. The room looked much like Currat's and his room, the same pleasing colors in ground tones of sand and white. The yellow and blue in the rug brought a splash of color. The bed linens in a bold blue matched the rug.

He looked back at Summerton, recognizing the remnants of an ordeal best forgotten. *Perhaps some day he can forget...if so, he'll be better off than Currat and me.* "What happened after they took you?"

"We rode for three days, camping in the woods at night. During that time, they pushed me around, but didn't hurt me too badly. On the third night, we rode onto a dirt road that took us to a barn off to the side of a torn-apart house. Another man, also dressed in black, waited there. My captors deferred to him in everything. He had an air of superiority that radiated in all he did. Two other captives were chained to the floor. He selected one and had him put on a steel table and tied down. He spoke to the man with great compassion. What he did showed no compassion, though. He used metal rods—"

Currat stiffened and rushed from the room.

Summerton jerked. "What...what's wrong?"

"You saw what the man did with those rods?"

"I only looked once. I'll always remember the screams... Wait—that happened to Currat?"

"Yes, and he nearly died. It took all the skills of a High Healer to save him. Don't mention it again if he's nearby."

"I...I won't. Oh dear Creator, how does he make it through the day?"

"I help him as much as I can. He needs to rest alone,

now. We work together, and we've been close since that time. How did you escape?"

"The man eventually killed the other two men with his torture, and became very upset when he didn't get the answers he wanted. I've never even thought the cruelty brought on by those men existed. The questions he asked made no sense to me. They were all about where they came from and what they saw when up north. I didn't think he meant Hamptor, and one of the men confirmed they came from Ozlid. The captured men had Hamptorian accents. I spoke with our pronunciation, and he lost interest in me. After both men had died, something came over the torturer, and he went into a trance-like state, kneeling on the floor. The others in black did the same. Coming out of the daze, he rushed out of the barn, and I heard him ride off.

"One man pulled a tarp off three boxes. He opened one; it contained bottles of wine. I lost count of how much they drank. They hit me with the empty wine containers over and over. The one who opened the box did most of the hitting. He was careful not to hit my limbs or bones, and told the others to hit my stomach. One of them kept hitting me in my privates. When I curled up in a ball, the man giving the orders went wild, ordering the others not to hit anywhere but the stomach. When they straightened out my body, they retied the ropes they had loosened to see me jerk around; it seemed to amuse them. They were drunk by then, and didn't fasten me well. The man giving the orders finally passed out; the others laughed and one of them relieved himself on him, saying he would think he pissed himself. It didn't take long for the rest of them to collapse. I worked my ropes loose and stole a horse. I rode back the way we came until I reached Hagan's End."

Summerton leaned back on his pillow, his voice weakening. "Captain Briggs's ship was in port, and he took me on. He and his men tried their best to feed me, but my injured stomach wouldn't allow anything to stay down. I could only manage sips of water and broth without upset or much pain. When we got in port, all I could think of was to get to the healer at the garrison. Then, I met you and Currat."

Zack wiped sweat from his brow. "You're safe now. Franc won't let anyone up here. Currat and I must leave on tomorrow's tide. I'll leave orders with the garrison commander to see to your care and to get you back to the Spires. The Zenith Lord will be informed of what happened. You're sure they took the ambassador north?"

"I assumed so. The roads in that part of Hamptor wind about so much, it's hard to tell where he might end up."

Zack paced the room, gathering his thoughts. Stopping, he looked at Summerton. "We must go. I'm going to see the commander, and I'll try to visit you again before we leave."

Summerton merely nodded as Zack rushed out.

* * *

ZACK found the commander in her office and reported to her, making his requests and giving codes requiring her full cooperation by order of the Zenith Lord, surprising her, by the look she gave him. Nonetheless, she handled it well.

He needed to spend time with Currat before Briggs arrived for lastmeal. He hurried back, leaving a request with Franc. Currat lay curled up in a ball, arms wrapped tightly around himself. He looked at Zack with dead eyes, saying nothing. Zack rested his hand on his shoulder, gently massaging him, bringing a little life back to his face.

"I didn't think it would ever bother me like this again, just hearing about the torture they did to me…"

"I don't think those memories will ever die," Zack replied. "I still have nightmares from when the steel bear claw ripped down my chest. They come less and less frequently, but I still have them." He took Currat's arm, straightened it out and massaged his tight muscles. "Relax and stretch out."

Currat did as asked; Zack chucked his boots, crawled in beside Currat fully clothed, and pulled a light blanket over them. Shortly, they slept wrapped in each others' arms.

The light rap on the door brought both men awake, sitting up with short swords drawn. Franc's voice sounded through the door. "Gentlemen, you asked me to wake you at this time." There came another rap, a little harder, and then the sound of footfalls fading down the hallway.

Zack smiled at Currat. "Feeling better?"

"Yes—not much, but better. We'd best get ready to feed the good captain."

Zack chuckled, and they did just that.

3

THE captain arrived on time with a bottle of expensive wine. Franc acted as if he didn't see it, but brought wine glasses to their table as Crawford pulled the plug. "I opened it earlier to let it breathe. They say it helps the flavors combine, or some such nonsense. Well, perhaps I did have a small sip—just to make sure it would suit, mind you."

Zack enjoyed the fun playing across the captain's face, especially in his eyes. "I asked Franc to prepare something special. I have no idea what it might be, although I'm sure it'll be good."

They were pleased. Seafood chowder, hot, thick, and full of cod, shrimp, lobster and root vegetables, satisfied them all. Next came venison in savory gravy with carrots and mint leaves, followed by chilled cream and berries.

"From the empty platters, I assume you enjoyed my efforts," Franc said as he and a serving maid cleared the platters.

Zack chuckled. "Franc, I know full well your wife did the cooking."

"Yes," Franc replied with a wink. "But who do you think taught her?"

"Her mother!" Zack said as Franc disappeared into the kitchen, bringing laughter to the table. He looked at the captain now. "I suppose you want to hear the tales of the Seven Realms."

"I do!" Crawford replied.

Zack and Currat spent the next hours regaling the captain with gossip from all the realms, leaving out the business of the Zenith Lord and the military training stretching across the continent. He didn't think it would be long before military exercises would increase and new techniques were brought to the front to combat another attack by Wathdure when it happened but that was something no outsider should know.

Zack thanked Franc for a wonderful lastmeal after Crawford had left for his ship. Franc's wife stuck her head around the corner and said, "I heard that, and you both are welcome!" Franc only smiled and went to tend to his guests as the spies climbed to their room. They slept well.

* * *

WAKING in predawn stillness, Zack attended to his morning ritual followed by Currat, who fussed over the cold water in his basin, part of his day breaking routine. Zack smiled where Currat couldn't see him and continued packing freshly laundered clothing.

When they both were fully dressed and wearing their cloaks, Zack piled saddlepacks on their shoulders and they headed for the common room. The firstmeal lacked the finesse from the night before and when Franc brought steaming trenchers of eggs, pork, and toasted bread with cheese, saying, "I *did* make firstmeal," Zack knew why. Still, the food satisfied, and on Franc's return to clear away, Zack paid their bill, thanking their host for good treatment.

"It's what good innkeepers do," Franc said, letting the coins slide into a flapped pocket. His mien turned serious. "Stay safe over there."

Currat put on a questioning face. "Over where?"

Franc chuckled as the two spies, their cloaks concealing a walking armory under bulging saddlepacks, left through the back door to the stable. Spellbinder and Snowflake waited, saddled and fed, coats shining from a good brushing. Zack gave three copper coins to the stable boy who threw them a salute and hurried back to the stables. The men each gave their fidgety mounts some treats: sweetstones for Spellbinder, and an apple for Snowflake.

"Do you think these will calm them when they see the ship?" Currat asked.

Zach shook his head. "Not in the least, but it might make the trip there more pleasant."

Captain Briggs supervised the last preparations with the new hoist. "A little something new, Captain?" Zack called.

"Little!" Briggs answered. "Do you see the size of this contraption? Just wait until you see it in action, lifting Spellbinder up over the ship and down into the space I've set up for him and Snowflake! This hoist cuts loading time by over half and saves the crews' backs. Bronson will show you what to do."

Zack and Currat removed their saddles and tack as the first mate and crewmen carried large, wide straps to the horses. Spellbinder didn't seem to mind being harnessed in a strange new way. Snowflake did, however. With lots of encouragement and quiet whisperings, the big stallion sailed up and down without kicking or snapping. Currat went to aid the crewmen in removing the straps and clearing the harness. For once, the overly excitable warhorse stayed calm, although the nudge he gave Currat nearly pushed him to the floor.

Back on deck, Bronson approached. "Master Stand, it's good to see you and Master Duval again."

"I'm glad to see you again, Bronson. I trust your sailings have been mostly uneventful."

"Mostly, a storm here and there. Nothing like the mutiny you helped put down on the old ship. Some of the men don't believe the stories our cook tells. He does exaggerate a good bit; you would think he captured and killed the mutineers himself as you, the captain, and I looked on. I passed the word around on what really happened back then when we found our usual crew.

Cook makes good meals and the men overlook his stories, but I have heard a few groans when he starts one. It's fun to see what he interjects in the tale that's new."

The sailor nodded at Currat. "I'm quite glad to see you as well, Master Currat. I didn't know if you'd fully recover from all that happened to you."

Zack became instantly alert, watching how Currat would handle the comment. Currat answered with his usual calm remarks, making it clear that Zack needn't have worried.

The captain called the crew to stations. Untied ropes landed on the wharf, and sails began to billow as the big ship glided out with the tide. Zack watched the routine to bring the *Silver Dolphin* into the current, wondering how Currat would feel experiencing a ship once more. As before, he saw no distress in the other man's appearance. Still, he wondered what might be hidden under his cool disposition.

Currat smiled. "Don't fear, Zack, I'm fine."

"How do you always know what I'm thinking?"

"The same way you perceive me. Our bond is forged over how many battles, fights, and brawls we've survived. We anticipate each other's moves, and each knows what to expect from the other. I'm not telling you anything you don't know, I'm just pointing it out."

Zack smiled, slapped Currat on the back, and turned to watch Elizabethville fade into the distance.

* * *

BRIGGS insisted the spies have lastmeals with him. The second night, he got around to hinting that he'd like to identify their purpose in visiting Hamptor. Zack winked at Currat before going to their cabin and returning with the fake jewels. He made a show of unwrapping the container and then, without a single flourish, dumped the glittering paste rocks on Briggs's desk and stepped back.

The color drained from the captain's face. "Great

Creator, just one of those stones would buy this ship and run her for a hundred years or more. Put them away, quickly. Don't let anyone see them. You saw what happened when the mutineers thought you knew of the Black Stone Wathdure sought. That voyage was like a wreck on the shoals with all the fights and plots. I don't want anything like that now. I trust my crew, but praise to all that's holy, there's enough there to buy Hamptor and half of Arestead."

Zack gathered the fake jewels back into the box and secured it. When done, he turned to Briggs. "Don't concern yourself. These are all fake."

"Fake!" The captain looked concerned.

"Yes, to carry this amount of wealth would be ill advised. The real jewels are safely stored away. We show these to prospects, and if they make a selection, we return on the next trip with the real stone. You can see from the lack of trips we make, business is not plentiful. But, it doesn't have to be. One sale a year will earn us money for our time and more to invest in other ventures. It's rare, but some years we sell three stones. Mostly though, only one or two in a year. When I carried news to Wathdure about the Black Stone I knew of, he paid me enough gold to make the trip worthwhile. After Spercine tried to kill us and we escaped, it seemed the whole of Ozlid's forces chased us, and you saw the aftermath."

After another hour of conversation, the spies left for their cabin and a restful night's sleep.

The next day, the *Silver Dolphin* moored at her usual berth. Briggs refused any payment saying Zack's involvement in putting down the mutiny and the Zenith Lord's largess in making the *Silver Dolphin* available and affordable had earned him all the crossings he cared to make.

4

FAREWELLS said and their horses offloaded and made ready, the spies walked them to the street, letting them get their land legs back. They set a leisurely pace to the Tarnished Anchor, a run-down tavern with a quiet entrance to the best stables in Hagan's End through its back. When the spies took Spellbinder and Snowflake through the gate to the paddock, the stable master looked questioningly at the men, but his eyes lit up in recognition upon seeing the horses.

"Ah, I remember the black and the bay. I'm glad to see them, and I'll take excellent care of these beauties."

"As you did before," Zack said. "I'm Zack Stand, and this is Currat Duval. We'll be at the Blue Sail."

The horse master nodded as he took the money for the horses' care. "Ah, *you* are the ones with the coin weighing more than ours. This will cover you for the next few days. If you're here longer, I'll collect when you leave." He turned away, leading the two fine horses to waiting stalls and care.

"Hasn't changed much, has he?" Currat asked.

"Nope."

The walk to the Blue Sail Inn invigorated Zack, and it seemed to do the same for Currat. Upon entering, Yasho, the innkeeper greeted them warmly. He had been instrumental in the spies' escape the last time they had passed through the city. Zack and Currat returned the welcome in kind.

"We need one room with a large bed, and all the privacy we had before." Zack knew the Blue Sail held the reputation as the best and most expensive inn in

Hamptor. All its rooms had big beds.

"I have another room adjoining the one for you—" Yasho began.

Zack cut him off. "It's a safety issue."

Yasho nodded, a wise expression on his face. "I trust you won't be going to Ozlid."

"Only by force, being dragged kicking and screaming!" Currat said.

"I certainly hope *that* won't happen." Yasho shuddered. "I'll show you to your room. The inn is about half full, but we have enough guests to add a few more things to our fare. We'll have veal, partridge, and goat tonight. I don't advise the goat, however—why my buyer bought it, I have no idea. Our usual fare of rabbit, fowl, and venison is always good, of course."

Zack let his mind wonder, as Yasho prattled on the way to the room.

The innkeeper opened the door without his regular flourish, which Zack took for a compliment. The room reminded him of his previous one, done in pleasing browns and golds with contrasting blues on the linens and draperies. Two plush chairs sat before the fireplace, a writing table with a chair stood against the wall to the right of the burning logs, and a painting hanging on the opposite wall depicted a hunting scene. The wide entrance to the sleeping area revealed the expected large bed, with a table on each side. The second fireplace and two more plush chairs, flanking a table large enough to accommodate a lastmeal for two, proved an unexpected sight.

Yasho left them with a stout key and a warm smile. Currat gathered Zack up in a bear hug. "I'm glad we're here." He released him. "I'm ready for whatever we may find."

"Good!" Zack replied, pleased to see Currat more like his usual self. "The trip's uneventful nature is welcoming. I wonder how long it'll last."

Currat's sigh, the only answer Zack got, said a lot.

* * *

THEY freshened up before going down to lastmeal in the main dining room, deciding to take their weapon-laden cloaks.

As they pushed through the big doors with inset glass to a room devoid of smoke, a man dressed completely in black came face-to-face with Currat. His mouth opened, and then snapped shut as he moved around them and through the door. Zack looked at Currat, and both of them frowned.

A beautiful serving maid, dressed in the inn's colors of blue and white, showed them to a seat. Looking around, Zack spotted a table of five men, all dressed in black, with one seat vacant. The men, intent on their food, didn't look in his direction. Nudging Currat, he pointed with his chin at the suspicious table. Currat nodded. Frowning, he sipped his water and looked at a parchment listing the evening's fare.

While giving their order to their maid, the man they'd seen upon entering nearly ran to the table and began speaking to the others. He gestured in Currat's direction. A few of the men looked at the spies.

Neither Zack nor Currat moved their heads toward the table, but both took note of the table's interest.

During the discussion with the Men-in-Black from Ozlid, Yasho approached the table and spoke to them. One of the men answered, and Yasho moved on to seat a new guest. He checked on three more tables before venturing to Zack and Currat's table.

He leaned down and pointed to an item on the parchment. "Those men don't stay here, but they have eaten here almost every night for the past week," he whispered. "Only one of them ever talks when my staff or I come close to them. I passed them a few minutes ago, and one man carried on a heated discussion. I didn't hear what he said, but I heard his Ozlidian accent!"

Currat looked up. "We know, Yasho. Thank you for telling us. We'll be most careful."

Yasho's wry smile didn't hide the concern in his eyes. With a nod, he headed toward the kitchen.

Moments later, two heavily muscled men came through the doors and took the table beside Zack and Currat's table. Yasho didn't allow weapons in the inn's common rooms. Zack couldn't miss the short swords the men wore under their dark burgundy shirts, tucked into dark blue trousers.

The larger of the two leaned close, where no one could see him behind a column to Currat's right. "Yasho sent us. He said the two of you could handle all six of them, but we wanted to have a little fun, too." He smiled and leaned back to his table, within sight of the Ozlidians.

"They want us dead," Zach whispered to Currat, smiling. "I imagine there is a fairly large reward for our heads."

Currat returned the smile. "Yasho is right; you and I can kill them all. Perhaps our new friends would like to take a walk with us along the sea wall after lastmeal? I feel a little stiff, and a good stroll will be just the thing to limber me up. Besides, I want to kill the bastards."

Zack chuckled.

The food, as always, delighted them. They didn't overeat; such practice made killing difficult, as Zack had said many times. As they rose to leave, the men at the next table stood as well. Currat looked over to Yasho's men. "Would you care to join us for an ale?"

The men's smiles lit up the room, easing Zack's mind. As his group walked past the table of death, none of them spared it a glance. Pushing past the glass doors, they walked to the bar and ordered ales all around. The men introduced themselves—the larger one with piercing green eyes and deep brown hair cut shorter then the current style was named Turlas; the slightly smaller one, blond and blue-eyed, was Cerrol. Four mugs of ale appeared before them as the six Ozlidians filed into the room and took an empty table. One man gave an order to a serving maid; the others kept quiet until they looked around and started speaking quietly among themselves. Their attempts at being inconspicuous fell far short, giving Zack's group some amusement.

"Are they that stupid?" Turlas asked.

"No," Currat replied. "The one doing the talking is probably a sergeant or low-ranking officer. He's been trained in Hamptorian accents. The rest probably volunteered to get away from duty inside Ozlid, but outside the city. It's a lousy assignment."

Cerrol's mouth dropped briefly as Currat spoke. "You are the one they hunted and tortured and—" He swung his head over to Zack. "—you must be the one who rescued him. The two of you are renowned here."

Zack smiled. "Actually, Currat rescued me before I rescued him. We are always there for each other, and we fight well together, as you may get a chance to see soon enough. We live in the Seven Realms, the land you call Jewel. If Yasho has talked, what else do you know about us?"

"Not too much more," Turlas said. "We know you send evil men to the Seven Hells, and that you killed thieves who tried to kill a woman and her daughter, and they went with you back to Jewel, uh, the Seven Realms. Yasho said you and Currat tried to warn our king and the king of Arestead."

"We did what we could," Zack said, growing tired of the conversation. He felt uneasy talking about himself and Currat. "Do you have horses?"

"What?" Cerrol asked, and then said, "Oh, yes, we have horses stabled behind the inn. There are only four stalls back there."

"Would your horses be good in a fight with mounted men?" Currat asked.

"We don't know. They've never been in a fight."

"We'll go on foot," Zack decided. "Are those barrels still between the warehouses?"

Cerrol looked surprised. "They were still there last week when I went to Yasho's warehouse to get replacements for broken chairs."

"All right," Zack continued. "Our friends in black will probably be on horseback. That's not as bad as some imagine. You can jump back out of a sword's reach, even roll under the horse, and if you have time, cut the saddle leathers. Also, when a rider passes, his back is usually unprotected. If you're good at throwing knives, that's a good time to practice. If you unhorse a man, he may be hurt or stunned when he hits the ground. Don't lose the advantage; kill him!"

The two young men looked a little shaken as they began to realize the consequences of what they had wished to do.

"We are four and they are six," Zack said. "Nonetheless, I doubt if any but the leader has much fighting experience. He's taller than the rest. Look out for him. If you can get a knife in him, do it. Try not to get in a one-on-one with swords. Also, killing a horse to kill its rider is not a disgrace, contrary to popular belief. If a man is bent on killing you, are you going to die to save a horse you don't own? Watch us and follow our lead. If the fight goes bad, climb to the top of the barrels and fight from there. If I remember, they are lashed together to withstand storms, so they should hold. Have either of you ever killed a man before?"

They both shook their heads.

"Then one last thing: you know these men are evil, and want to do you and your country great harm if they can. You know their death is justified. Still, killing a man, even one as malevolent as these, will shake you to your center. Be ready for that. You can think about it later when we are back here having ale. But during the fight is definitely not the time to go to pieces. This is a fight against men who have orders to kill. Kill them first! Now, if you want to reconsider coming with us, it is not disgraceful or a mark of cowardice. You simply realize that you'd be greatly overmatched, and you'd lose your life and achieve nothing. On the other hand, if you're up to it and want to rid your country of some of the vermin infesting her, let's go kill some Ozlidians!"

The young men looked at each other and nodded, resolve hardening their expressions.

"We are the men protecting an owner's inn," Turlas said. "We are here only when Yasho sends for us. Some of the places we work have rowdy crowds, and we break up a lot of fights, often outnumbered. We don't use knives, although we're good with them. We've both been cut a couple of times, but nothing more than scratches. We've talked about situations like this one and wondered what we would do. Like many, we think Ozlid will eventually invade. If what we do now will weaken those we must fight in the future, it's worth the risk. Besides," he added with a smile, "what chance will we ever have to again learn from real warriors? We want this time to learn how to kill our enemies!"

Currat nodded. "Well said! Zack and I will look out for you as we can. Keep in mind you have only one goal—to learn; one mission for your country—to defeat her enemies; one desire—to remain alive; and one deed to do—kill. What Zack said is true. Bury your emotions for later. Become a killing machine, and you'll win. Let your confidence slide and you're left open for great injury, or probably death."

Zack looked at the two somber men. "Are you ready for a drunken walk? You work in common rooms; you should know what a drunk looks like. Behave like one as we leave. If you remember, we had our arms across your backs in a supporting position when we passed our friends in black. We've been purposely leaning on the bar and you unconsciously followed suit. It won't take much for the scum to believe you're drunk. Follow our lead." Zack and Currat swung their cloaks in place across their shoulders.

Zack put his arm under Turlas's shoulder and Currat under Cerrol's. As they helped the two staggering "drunks" to the door, Zack said, "Come, my friends. A walk along the seaside for the salt air will sober you up. There's nothing like it."

Turlas blubbered something unintelligible and nearly fell over as they stumbled out the door.

* * *

SEAWALL Street faced the Blue Sail on one side, and the low seawall on the other. The four men kept up the act, passing shops and inns until they reached the warehouse district. There, they relaxed in the shadows.

Currat chuckled. "We should sing bawdy songs and walk slowly."

"We know a few," Turlas said, and the two burst into a drunken song.

Currat and Zack pulled them closer to the buildings and slowly walked farther down Seawall Street.

Zack raised his fist, flashing hand signals to Currat. He leaned in toward the men. "They're coming on horseback. Keep singing, and I'll place you about five feet apart, stop singing when they come into view, and stay out of sight. Have your knives and swords ready before they pass, and remember what we said about swords on horseback; get out of their way and attack after they pass. If they're bunched up, stay out of sight and take the one at the end. Fight well and live!"

Horses came into view three streets away. The men sang even louder.

Zack saw moonlight glisten on bare steel and signaled Currat. The men continued singing.

A horse cleared the intersection one street away.

Turlas and Cerrol stopped singing.

The horsemen stopped, giving Zack and Currat the chance they wanted. Reaching back to draw hidden blades, they threw in one continuous, smooth motion. The first two men fell forward, pushing daggers deeper inside them. Their horses reared and bolted, dragging the dead men toward the city proper. The leader was not one of them; Zack cursed.

Currat barely made out the tallest man with one horseman behind, one in front, and one on the side closest to the buildings. The first horse became spooked, reared, and then galloped forward, its rider fighting to regain control. Cerrol rushed in front of the horse, causing it to lock its legs and throw its rider over its head. The man in black landed hard. Before he could recover, Cerrol slashed his throat with a large dagger, sending a large arc of blood spraying upward. Currat watched the young man dive back into the deep shadows behind some barrels and start heading east, waiting for the next rider.

Currat threw his knife, the point slicing into the soft tissue at the base of the last man's neck when he passed. He fell backward, sliding off the rear of his horse and hitting the ground headfirst. Currat heard the man's neck snap. It lolled to one side, dead eyes open.

The moon made an unexpected appearance through overcast skies. The leader stopped, reining his horse toward the seawall. Zack shook his head and reappraised the man's training, wondering why he'd make such a dumb move.

Turlas's sword thrust skewered the side of the horseman closest to the buildings. He screamed and tried to bring his sword around, but twisted into the cut. He shrieked louder. Turlas pulled his sword free and, as the horseman slumped forward, he pulled his head back by the hair and slit his throat. He must not have heard the leader approach after regaining control of his mount.

"Jump back!" Zack cried out.

Turlas hesitated for half a heartbeat before jumping. The pause cost him as the leader's sword arced down and slashed into his right thigh. Turlas went down, clenching the bloody wound in his leg.

"You're nothing but an untrained boy!" the leader snarled.

"That may be, but I killed your man," the youth said through gritted teeth. "Who've you killed today?"

Rage twisted the leader's face. "I'll kill you!"

"No you won't!" Zack yelled. His knife flashed through the air, catching the stallion in the throat. With a gurgling scream, it collapsed. The leader cried out, his leg bent at an angle, caught under the horse's body.

The leader's sounds stopped when the point of Turlas's sword pierced the back of his neck.

Currat ran to Turlas's side and sliced through his shirtsleeve, ripping it off. Turlas groaned as the spy bound his wound.

Zack looked down on the injured man. "It's not bad. If it were serious, you'd be losing a lot more blood."

"It hurts like the Seven Hells!" Turlas whispered.

Zack chuckled. "How do you know how any hell hurts? Besides, just think of the fun you'll have afterward."

"Fun?"

"Yes, all the women will want to see the scar, and well, it *is* on your thigh. How much more fun would it be if he'd cut your inner thigh?" He grinned. "I could put one there for you if you wish."

Turlas managed to laugh between moans. "No, thank you. The ladies will have to make do with this one."

Currat and Cerrol went through the dead men's clothes, taking everything of interest to examine later. The leader had a fat purse with more gold than silver. Zack recovered knives and returned them to the rightful owners, cleaning off the blood first, while Currat bundled everything together in one of the dead's empty saddlepacks. Ending with three full, smaller bags, much heavier than the others, with double stitching around the seams, he placed one on Spellbinder and two heavy ones on Snowflake. He clearly didn't want to open them there and thus hid the weight, handling them as if they only contained clothing. They rounded up the horses, mounted four and led the fifth back to the Blue Sail.

Yasho rushed to the street when they were a half block away. At the sight of Turlas's leg, he sent a boy running. Zack liked the innkeeper, and wished the Guard were as efficient; *perhaps I should bring that up to the Zenith Lord.*

Yasho led them to the back of the inn and through a private entrance with a key. A kitchen boy stuck his head out, and the innkeeper ordered him to take the horses to the stables and put the saddlepacks in Zack's room. The lad scurried off, taking two horses at a time farther back into the alley.

They placed Turlas on a table, and Yasho uncere-moniously ripped his trousers off, exposing the cut and probably more than the young man wanted to show. His face turned bright red.

"He'll need stitches," Currat said.

Yasho sent another kitchen boy to the healer. "Tell him to hurry!"

The first kitchen boy entered and trotted to the table. "I placed the saddlepacks in your room. Three were very heavy. I had to get help for those."

Zack gave the boy five coppers. "Three for you, two for your helper." The boy smiled as he turned and headed out the kitchen door.

Zack motioned Cerrol over. "See what you missed." The young man smiled. Zack got the impression both of them had aged a few years in maturity tonight. He took out the leader's purse. "This belongs to Turlas, but it's quite full with more than enough for two. I suggest you split it between you." Zack looked around and waved the kitchen onlookers out. When he was sure the room had cleared of bystanders, he dumped the gold and silver on Turlas's bare stomach. Both young men's eyes bulged. "See what I mean about enough to share?"

Turlas nodded dumbly. Cerrol just kept staring at the coins.

"Yasho is trustworthy. I suggest you allow him to handle the coins for you. There's enough to buy or build a business and home for each of you. I suspect neither of you know much about running a successful trade." Cerrol came out of his trance and shook his head the same time Turlas did. "Yasho, would you care to take these two under your wing and guide them until they can fly on their own?"

"If the boys…I guess I should say men…want my help, I'll give it to them, but it has to be fair to me also. I *am* a proprietor. What would you think of opening an inn, a nice inn, on the other side of the city in the hills? I've been thinking of the project for some time. You each would have forty-five parts ownership and I would take ten parts. That way, I have an interest in your enterprise, and I will plan for you as I planned for me. I even have a backup idea if the inn should fail for lack of clientele; I could easily restructure the building for a cheese factory. There's not one nearby, and the cost of getting it here is high. The inns all the way to Ozlid would be your customers. It's a lot to think about. If you wish, I'll put your coins in my safe place and give you a receipt for them. I've held much more than this. Zack has stored at least twice this much on previous trips. It's a lot to think about, and you don't have to make a decision soon. In fact, I'd suggest you wait a month or so for all of us to sit down with clear heads and see where this goes."

Zack saw the uncertainty in the men's faces. "Yasho's last statement makes a great deal of sense. I would heed his advice until you find your path. I'd be very upset if you threw this opportunity away on frivolous things."

Both young men looked stunned. Finally, Cerrol

spoke, "Yasho, I'm glad you called us in tonight."

Turlas burst out in laughter, bringing smiles to the others.

Yasho left to safely place the coins away, returning with a count and receipts for Turlas and Cerrol. The young men looked at the amounts of the receipts and their eyes bulged once more.

"Turlas, we've been friends for many years, Cerrol said. "Are you sure you want to share this with me? Zack said, by tradition, the coins belong to you."

Turlas laughed again. "Cerrol, I'm way too wild-headed to have even half this gold and silver. It would go through my hands like sand through a grate. With you and Yasho to set some goals and limits, I might make it to old age, with coins to spare and beautiful women all around me. Yes, I'm in favor of giving you forty-five parts and Yasho ten parts of a business we'd start together."

"Turlas, you may be a spendthrift," Zack said, "but you're a wise one. Not many men your age have the maturity you just voiced."

A round of discussion began, basically stating the same things. When the healer arrived, the conversation stopped. Zack and Currat eased out to their rooms when the healer gave Turlas a little syrup of the flower to stop the pain and started stitching.

The spies pulled off their cloaks, shirts, and boots. Bones popped as they stretched. A bottle of wine and two mugs sat on the table in the front room. Currat padded to it, opened the wax seal, and poured dark wine for them. He drank. "It's good. I wouldn't mind drinking the whole bottle—with you, of course—and sleeping until midday tomorrow."

"That *would* be nice, but I'm anxious to see what we can find in these saddlepacks."

Currat rolled his eyes. "You work too much."

"And, you're spoiled rotten!"

"You can't blame me; it's my upbringing. And, you might have something to do with it."

Zack smiled. "I can fix that."

"Give me a saddlepack and I'll start over here."

Zack traded a saddlepack for a mug of wine and emptied the leather pouch across the bed. There was little inside; no clothes, no weapons, and no food, only several lengths of string looped around to make a design. *Perhaps some kind of wall hanging,* Zack thought.

Currat found much the same thing, incidentals having no meaning to the outside world.

Zack called for Currat to join him. They took the contents of the five and loaded them in one. "This is the leader's," he said. "It's heavy." He dumped the contents of several parchments, some keys, and another purse containing gold—a lot of gold, worth twice what the young men had recovered. Equal amounts of gold fell from two other saddlepacks.

Zack whistled.

"Great Creator!" Currat exclaimed.

The parchments contained copies of orders for a great quantity of weapons. "It makes sense," Zack said. "Ozlid has limited resources. Wathdure can't get weapons from here or Arestead. Look at these markings. Have you seen them before?"

"Mmm," Currat murmured. "Yes, I have. They are location marks for sea and land. You have to coordinate them to a map."

"You mean this?" Zack raised a parchment with a drawing of Hamptor, Arestead, and Ozlid. Another sheet pictured the Seven Realms in small but detailed lines. A third sheet pictured the Eastern Kingdoms. They started comparing marks. One location pointed to a place up the coast from Hagan's End. The second showed a spot at the north end of the Eastern Kingdoms. The spies had never seen that map, and knew next to nothing about the Eastern Kingdoms listed there. "We should send the maps and weapons orders to Stonefire, and we should capture or sink the ship. None of the Men-in-Black or Wathdure's creatures can escape. Does that mean he won't know we killed them? I don't know."

Currat shook his head. "What should we do with the gold?"

"I have an idea. Hamptor, or at least the men we've met so far, want to fight Ozlid. They can't in the open, but behind the scenes, they could be quite hurtful to Wathdure's plans."

"How so?"

"Well, for one, Ozlid sends soldiers and raiders over the border," Zack answered. "No one has ever fought them, mainly due to a lack of training and weapons. With these kinds of resources, they could get both. I know retired Arms Masters in the Guard who would love an assignment like this; there must be *some* Hamptorian Masters somewhere near here. If we capture the ship, its cargo would supply the weapons, and the gold would fund operations.

"Ursel fought well," Zack continued, "and practically carried me the length of Hamptor, although I traveled in the coach most of the time. He's always wanted to fight Ozlid. Jarod has been training him, and I hear he's done well, mastering weapons, becoming a spy, and learning fighting techniques. I don't think there would be a problem bringing him back here to lead a group of fighters.

"But, before I say anything to anyone here, I need to report to our Zenith Lord. This is something only Jarod can decide. Now, let's clear away this mess and get some sleep."

"Are you really that tired?"

"No, not really." Zack cleared the parchments and remaining saddlepack from the bed.

* * *

BRYAN Daven looked around the tavern's common room as the last customers left, some staggering, some being helped, some smirking at the others. It wasn't the best tavern in Hagan's End, but certainly not the worse.

I like working here. I like the Blue Sail better, but here's not bad. He straightened up as the barman sauntered over and placed a silver in his hand. "Not too bad a night," he said. "I only saw you eject one guy, but he looked a hard one. Sure caused a ruckus."

"That he did. He might have been in for a more serious battle. The two thieves that frequent the Iron Lady went after him. If they meant him harm, we might not see him for quite a while, if ever. I suspect they've killed before."

"You may be right. You going home to your lady?"

Bryan's crooked smile beamed. "I hope so."

"You need to bring her by some night."

"It's hard; we don't work the same hours."

"Be careful getting home."

"I will; you too," Bryan said.

The tavern master walked him to the door, locking and barring it after Bryan left.

The walk home was uneventful and for that he was glad. He climbed the stairs to his small room above the Crystal Wine Inn, and put the silver coin in his special hiding place. He had three of them, the first two fairly easy to find, the third, nearly impossible to discover. He let the room for working one night every two weeks and the other taverns and inns usually fed him when he worked those. Saving most of his coins over the past three years, he would soon have enough to buy a small home, his dream.

He shed his clothes and washed using the basin on the nightstand. Although the room was small, it didn't lack for comfort, with a good bed, a small table and two chairs, and a chest of drawers he would never fill. Most of the clothing in it belonged to Synithy. Over the last year, she'd slept with him three or four nights a week, resulting in an accumulation of her shifts and dresses. The room's walls, plastered white, had blue trim around the window and door. She had painted a picture of sunflowers that hung above the dresser. It wasn't too realistic, but added color, and he liked it because it came from her. He doubted she would come that evening; she rarely did at the first of the week. In a way, he was glad. He treasured the time alone as much as the time with her. She worked at the Blue Sail Inn during different hours than he normally performed his duties, more and more at the Blue Sail. He liked the innkeeper, Yasho, who treated Synithy and him well, and paid a good wage.

He opened the window a few inches and stretched out on the bed atop the covers. He would wake in the morning completely covered, wondering how he had gotten under them.

5

ZACK woke first and watched Currat sleeping for a few moments before getting up to wash, shave, and dress. As he did, Currat's voice slipped through a half yawn. "You let me sleep late."

"After yesterday and last night, I thought you needed some rest."

"You're most kind, good sir, but now we'll be late for firstmeal."

"It's not that late, but it will be if you don't get started soon."

While Currat did his morning routine, Zack took the parchments, packed them back into the leader's saddlepack, and added it to the pile of others. He wondered what to do with them. The gold was too heavy to give to Yasho, and he had already decided to send the maps and its keys to Jarod. There seemed to be only one workable answer and he didn't like it; burying their find until the right time came to use the gold. He needed to write a lengthy report and get a packet ready for Briggs to take to Elizabethville with instructions for the garrison commander to forward it to Jarod in all haste. As he prepared for the day, the idea of burying the gold still nagged at Zack.

Currat finished and looked completely refreshed, as if nothing much had happened the previous day and night. They left for the dining area and selected a table far from other guests. While waiting for their food, Zack ran down his plan's good and bad points, with Currat listening with his usual rapt attention. He cited a few things Zack hadn't thought of and added ideas during the discussion. Zack asked him to write them down and add them to the information going to the Zenith Lord.

Firstmeal came and the spies ate like the activities from the previous day had caught up with them. When finished, Zack leaned back in his chair, watching as Yasho meandered across the floor, talking to guests and giving orders to staff on his way to them. Reaching them, Zack pushed out a chair. Yasho sat and started to speak, until Zack raised his hand.

"Do you and the boys have an agreement you all are pleased with?"

Yasho nodded.

"Good, that's all I need to know. Do you remember Ursel?"

"How could I forget him? He's the man I would wish for a son, but then, people would think my wife cheated on me, may the Light's Source comfort her soul." Yasho's smile became infectious.

Zack smiled as well, but sobered just as quickly. "Yasho, no one—and I mean *no one*—must know what we're about to discuss. You were or are the mayor of this city, and as such you're the man I should come to."

"Alas, I'm still mayor, but I'd gladly hand it over to someone else."

"Maybe not when you hear what Zack has to say," Currat cut in.

Yasho looked surprised as much as he ever did, which was not much or often.

"Ursel wanted to fight Ozlid here, in Hamptor," Zack stated. "What would you say if that where to happen in say, six months to a year from now?"

Yasho's face became perplexed, his lips drawn. "What could he possibly do?"

"Quite a lot. He's been training with the Zenith Lord's Guard in fighting techniques. He would be trained in other, more clandestine stratagems of warfare to augment what he'd learned before he arrived. There's much he could accomplish to cripple Ozlid's incursions inside Hamptor, and possibly Arestead. This venture must remain highly secretive, and the men he recruits must be completely investigated. The gold for such a venture would be provided. What do you think?"

"Why would your Zenith Lord pay for this?"

Currat frowned. "Do you actually think Wathdure will stop with the kingdoms here? The Zenith Lord doesn't, and neither do we. Don't forget, I've met Wathdure and felt his wrath, seen the monsters he creates, watched his assassins, know of Spercine's perversions and murder, and suffered under their torture. I know more than anyone in Hamptor and Arestead, with the exception of Zack, about what a monster he is—and the monstrosities he creates will grow with the continued rise of the Dark. Based on the last war, the Dark's goal is the Seven Realms' lands, wealth, and people. It was the first Zenith Lord who defeated the Dark two millennia ago. It wants vengeance!"

Yasho sat with his mouth open for a moment. "Yes, I'm afraid you're right. Hamptorians tend to think our woes from Ozlid are confined here. It's all they see and know. Even I forget until reawakened by something like your thoughts. Is the Dark growing quickly?"

"I don't know," Zack replied. "I don't think anyone knows but the Dark's minions. At some point, Ursel and his men would have to disband or find greater power to protect themselves. Back to my original question: would you sanction such an effort and work with Ursel? You are the only man I can trust to take on such an operation. Not to run it, but to help coordinate and give advice. You would be Ursel's only resource when he arrives. The two of you would have to build a group of dedicated men whose resolve cannot be shaken. What say you?"

"I say, I think I need a glass of wine—no, brandy, even if the sun did just rise." He flagged a serving maid and soon, a very old, dusty bottle and three glass goblets graced the table.

Zack and Currat didn't say anything while sipping brandy with Yasho, letting him ponder. His facial expressions told a story of tossing ideas from side to side and possibly back again. It was all Zack could do to keep from laughing, even with the gravity of the proposal. Finally, Yasho finished his drink in one gulp.

"I agree! Great Creator help me, but I'm in favor of what you describe." He stood, looking down at the spies' half full glasses before placing the wax back into the old bottle. "Keep the brandy; you'll have need of it." Turning, he walked around and through the tables, talking with guests and staff as if he'd not just made such a decision.

* * *

ZACK and Currat sat in the plush chairs in their room, facing the fireplace; their glasses still one-fourth full. Currat held his glass up, watching the flames dance through the amber liquid in the glass. "This is a fine brandy. I wonder what it cost?"

"Probably more than we'd want to pay," Zack said. "Come, we'd best get started; it's going to be a long report."

They set their glasses on the table, pulled parchment, glass pen, and ink from a saddlepack and placed them on the writing table. Currat sat next to Zack and watched him begin. They had midmeal delivered and set up in the front room and ate sparingly.

Watching Zack's fine penmanship flow across the page in highly organized thoughts, he wondered—*How does he do it? I have trouble just writing a letter.* As he watched, Currat thought he recognized a pattern. Zack wrote on a timeframe, placing thoughts and conclusions that became clear later at the point in the report when the first event happened. *I've got to learn how to do that, like so much else he's taught me.*

Finished, Zack signed, sealed, and wrapped the

writings. He and Currat donned their cloaks and headed for the door, the missive tucked into the back of Zack's trousers.

* * *

THEY were lucky, the *Silver Dolphin* gently rocked proudly at the end of the quay. Briggs saw them coming and walked down to meet them.

"Mmm, I can see from your demeanor this is important," the captain said after they greeted each other.

Zack laughed. "I'll need to work on that. It's not good to be so easily discovered in my business."

Briggs grinned. "What can I do for you?"

Zack brought out the report. "Lock this away, and deliver it only by your hand to the commander at the garrison. All you need say is that it's from me and it's vital that it reach the Spires in the fastest way possible." Zack reached in his purse and handed Briggs a gold.

Briggs recoiled with a scowl. "Are you trying to insult me? I don't want your coin."

Zack smiled. "This is different, my friend. I'm giving you the gold to express the importance of the actions I request of you, nothing more. You are my friend and, I hope, always shall be. The gold is well within my operational cost. It's yours, more as a gift than payment for a request."

Briggs seemed deep in thought and, after a few moments, glanced at Currat. "Do you ever win an argument with him? He makes everything he says sound like it was my proposition."

Currat shook his head.

"Oh, all right; give me the gold and I'll spend it on the ship."

"Now," Zack said. "If we can discuss something in private, perhaps your cabin."

Briggs raised an eyebrow and led the way. Once inside, he seated his guests and poured each a goblet of wine.

Zack explained some of the things in the captured orders.

"A ship carrying weapons and landing an hour up the coast," Briggs said. "I've sailed the coastline of Hamptor for years. The water there is over ten fathoms deep. Keep that in mind. When she delivers her cargo, I suspect you'll want to sink her. You might also consider more of these Men-in-Black showing up with wagons. I can supply men to handle the ship if you want to try and capture her. Some of them are good fighters, too."

"That's an interesting point," Zack said. "If she's a good ship, and I think she will be, we could send her to Deepwells for reconditioning and renaming. How would you like her when we're done? Is Bronson able to captain another ship in your growing line of cargo vessels?"

Briggs sputtered, spitting a small spray of wine across his desk, and quickly wiped it up with a cloth. "Light's Source, bless me!" he barked. "These men are going to make me wealthy! Zack, it's more than an interesting point. I've never seen an Eastern Kingdom's ship that wasn't big and well kept. Don't see them often, and they tend to avoid other ships, but they're hard to miss when you do. They probably have a minimum crew of twelve to sixteen, plus the captain and mates. How in the Seven Hells are you going to take her?"

"When you're outnumbered and in unfamiliar circumstances, you improvise. In this case, I think poison will work fine," Zack said. "What would you say as a ship's captain, if someone showed you gold, but said the wagons are late and won't arrive until morning—and knowing that, brought some grog for you and your men?"

"After a long voyage and a crew that heard your statements, I'd have it brought aboard. The captain and mates may not drink, but I suspect the entire crew would guzzle what they could. I'd send down a large barrel, if I were you. It would be hard to limit the number of mugs each crewman had. Rumor is they're a rough bunch. Do you have a poison that'll take, say, an hour to work?"

Zack looked down at the small balls sewn into the leather across the hem of his cloak. "I do believe I have."

Briggs's eyebrows jumped at that. "Well, in this situation, with the ship next to the rocks, I'd like to have a few archers ashore to provide cover."

"That would be the three of us. Ursel excels at hitting targets. Currat and I may be a little out of practice, but it'll come back; it always does."

"Well." Briggs rubbed his nose and drained his goblet. "I don't see any more rocks on the shoals to concern you. And yes, Bronson is ready to captain a ship, and my second mate is ready to be a first mate. Bronson may find it difficult to get a qualified first mate, but I can help him with that. A week, you say?"

"A week from today, with a day or two later as leeway. We'll have to start training our men tomorrow, and make a plan for more Men-in-Black with wagons. Do you have voyages scheduled?" Zack asked.

"No, the timing for me couldn't be better," Briggs answered.

"Can you and your men meet us at midmorning on the hill above your home?" Currat asked.

"How do you know where my home is located?" Briggs countered. "Oh, never mind. I forgot whom I'm dealing with. Yes, we'll be there. Be ready for some griping about riding horses—it's been years for some of my crew."

"Tomorrow, then!" Currat said.

They toasted their undertaking, and Briggs walked them off the ship.

They kept on walking along the wharf. "You do win arguments too, you know," Zack said after a while.

Currat chuckled. "By my later actions, not by my words."

"Isn't that better?" Zack reached out and momentarily brushed the inside of Currat's palm with his fingers.

Currat chuckled again.

They *did* finish the brandy in their room with lastmeal, along with another half-glass of wine.

* * *

THE moon shone brightly behind overcast skies, peeking out on occasion, which suited Zack fine. He and Currat had divided the gold to carry it easier. Spellbinder and Snowflake didn't seem to mind the heavy saddlepacks, but then, they were large warhorses.

Zack didn't envy the walk to the burial site he'd picked. They had looped back twice to ensure no one was following them. Arriving at the small stream flowing from a low mountain that went underground a short distance from the rather large pool it had made over the centuries, the spies inspected the area once more. Finding nothing out of the ordinary, they relaxed a little. The water, like all the streams and creeks in Hamptor and Arestead, produced undrinkable water, part of the hold Ozlid held over the kingdoms. One could bathe and wash clothes in it, but drinking it would make you sick and, in some cases, deaths had been reported.

Satisfied no one had followed them and no one loitered in the area, they unloaded rope and a thick, dark blue tarpaulin from their saddlepacks. Leaving the gold packed in small leather pouches procured in Hagan's End, they began filling the tarp, which had been made into a much larger pouch reinforced with binding rope on the outer edges. Once done, they tied it closed with ropes secured with slipknots.

Easing it into the water, Zack held the ropes while Currat squeezed the air from the tarp as it slowly descended into the nearly black water. After the last bubble escaped, Currat took one of the two ropes and they slowly let the gold sink. The pool, deeper than they thought, now contained a king's ransom at its bottom. Releasing the ropes and coiling them for the trip back, they waited until the moon made an appearance to look deep into the pool. Nothing seemed any different than before their arrival; its new treasure rested in unseen solitude.

The next day, they came again to look deep into the pool to see if the tarp stood out. It didn't; nor did the loops at its top they would use to pull it back up. Those ship's ropes, saturated in tar, would not weaken or rot.

Over lastmeal at the Blue Sail, they completely relaxed for the first time in two days. The fowl, served in spices and herbs, was delicious. The root vegetables added to the foods splendor and the bread tasted better than any Zack had had in a long time. The way Currat devoured his meal he must have felt the same.

"That was good," Currat finally said after his last bite, high praise, coming from him.

Yasho brought the bill for their stay. Zack noticed that the charges for food and drinks were missing. He looked at the innkeeper with a raised eyebrow, not overlooking the sparkle in his eye.

"I only do that for co-conspirators. I wish you could stay, but I know Ambassador Openhand will be glad that you're on your way. I sincerely hope he's not been taken to Ozlid. That would be tragic."

"Thank you for your generosity. You're really being generous to the Zenith Lord—he's where the gold comes from."

"Well, perhaps it'll help in the fight. I've heard wars are expensive."

Zack smiled. *He's not going to charge me even if I tell him the Zenith Lord's wealth is beyond his imagining, which it is.* "Thank you, Yasho. I'll mention it to the Zenith Lord. Will we see you at firstmeal?"

"Most likely. Sleep well."

"You, too. We'll be first for firstmeal," Currat said.

Zack watched Yasho perform his innkeeper's duties, greeting guests, ensuring all was well, and then he walked with Currat and him to their room. The first thing Zack did was to take both their cloaks to the bedroom area, and then return with two half-filled glasses of brandy.

Currat sat in front of the fireplace in a plush chair to the side of the table separating them. He raised his brandy in salute. "We *are* taking the rest of the spirits with us, aren't we?"

"Most definitely," Zack replied. "Unfortunately, I don't think the plush chairs will fit in our saddlepacks."

"Probably not."

* * *

ZACK rose early, before Currat, as usual. He finished his morning routine, and then started on packing the last of their belongings. Opening the door, he got their clean clothes, laundered the night before, and added those to the appropriate saddlepack. In his, he made sure the brandy bottle's wax seal was affixed properly and wrapped it in clean privateclothes. Laying out clothes for Currat, he nudged him hard, getting the response he wanted when his lover sat straight up, eyes wide. "If you hurry, we'll be the first for firstmeal as you promised."

"At the moment, if I hurry, I'll fall all over myself. Why is it that when we're on the road, I become alert and ready to fight so easily, but here, I'm as insensible to the world as a stone?"

"Here, you feel safe."

With an agreeable nod, Currat washed, shaved, and dressed in good time.

The dining area had just opened and the spies were indeed the first in the room. A serving maid Zack didn't recognize brought over ale and two heaping platters of steaming food. "Master Yasho left word you are leaving this morning for a long trip. I wish you safe journey, Master Stand, Master Duval." She hurried away before either man could answer.

Currat was about to take a large bite when Zack

stopped him. "Let's wait a few moments and see if the maid reappears.

Currat set his fork down. Several more guests came in, but two other maids took their orders. Zack waved one over. "Is there another serving maid working this morning?

The maid looked surprised. "No, sir, just Marianna and me. We arrived with the cook."

"Have you seen Yasho this morning?" Zack asked.

"No, sir, and that *is* strange. Sometimes he comes in later, but never when the inn is this full."

"Is Turlas or Cerrol here?"

"Yes, sir. They just arrived when I came out."

"Send them over, please." Zack tossed a silver in the air. The maid looked surprised, but caught the coin with ease.

The young men came out within a couple of moments with questioning looks.

"An unknown serving maid brought us this food and ale before the other maids arrived. Have you seen Yasho?" Zack asked.

They shook their heads.

"Start a search at once! Ask the cook if his stove was hot when he arrived."

A few moments later, Cerrol returned. "The stove was hot. The cook couldn't explain it."

They heard Turlas's shout. Zack and Currat hurried to the kitchen with Cerrol. Yasho, dazed and blinking in confusion, lay on the pantry floor with a cut across his forehead. A serving maid brought water, and he managed a few sips. A few moments later, Turlas helped him stand.

"What happened?" Currat said.

"I got here, and found a strange woman cooking on the stovetop. I asked her who she was and what she was doing here. She turned and smiled. Something hit me on the side of my head and that's all I remember until a few minutes ago."

"Turlas, are there rats near the town's midden trenches?"

"Oh yes," he answered.

"Is there one nearby?"

"A few streets over."

"Would you and Cerrol take the food on our table and feed it to the rats and wait to see what it does to them?"

Zack tended to Yasho and bandaged his forehead, as well as the wound over his right ear. "The cut isn't bad, and you won't need stitches. The blood is already dry. Yasho, look around and see if anything's out of place."

By the time the innkeeper finished a cursory look, Turlas and Cerrol returned.

"It didn't take long," Cerrol stammered. "I've never heard a rat scream before. It died before it could take a second bite."

"We might need to stay one more day," Zack said. "Yasho, please find out what you can. Turlas, would you and Cerrol talk to the townsfolk and see if anyone saw anything unusual earlier this morning or late last night?"

"It might take a while," Cerrol said.

"That's alright. Currat and I need to make sure that things are right before we leave. We'll be back by midmorning. Yasho, our saddlepacks are in our room. Please take them to your safe place."

"Of course," Yasho said. "This is terrible. Poison in the Blue Sail! If this becomes known, it could ruin the inn."

"I don't think your new partners in business will say a word, and no one else here at the inn knows," Currat said. "And we'll all keep it that way, yes?"

Turlas and Cerrol both nodded.

The spies left Yasho shaking his head, too, and headed to the stable.

The ride to the pool took nearly an hour. By the time they arrived, the early morning sun shimmered off crystals embedded in the nearby rocks, adding oranges, blues, and purples to the greys of stones and greens of treetops and grass touched by drops of water, reflecting an array of bright hues. The surface of the pool rippled from the breeze, causing strands of hair to flutter about Zack's ears. He pulled up the cloak's cowl, barely noticing the action. Currat kept his hair free.

From horseback and on foot, the pool's precious bounty remained no more than a slightly darker blue than its surroundings, giving the impression that the water went deeper. Satisfied, they rode back to the inn in a little better time with sunlight beaming on the trail, a firstmeal's appeal firmly painted in their minds.

Yasho served up two large platters of eggs, ham, and root vegetables with a little rabbit on the side at a big table with Turlas and Cerrol. Taking a seat, he sipped a mug of ale, not normal this early in the morning for the innkeeper. He again apologized for two guests being served poison at his inn, looking distraught and flustered.

Currat regarded him closely while he ate. "Yasho, I think that bump on your head has done more than you might think; you look tired. It's been over three hours since the incident; perhaps you should go upstairs and take a nap. There are more than enough people here to keep your guests happy. Turlas and Cerrol might be able to start learning about this side of a business.

"Yes," Turlas said. "We've watched you enough to know how to talk to guests and make sure they are enjoying the food. It'll be good for us…and we promise not to bother the serving maids!"

Cerrol smiled. "Leave it to Turlas to take away our fun. All right, I'll behave, if I have to."

"You do have to!" Yasho said. "And, I do feel fatigued. I'll take your suggestion, Currat. Perhaps when I feel better, some answers will present a solution."

"We did find something strange," Turlas said after the innkeeper left. "As we were asking around, we saw the healer rush to a home just outside town. He said he had a strange summons, so we followed. A young woman dressed like a serving maid and a young man dressed in work clothes sat on the floor, gazing into nothingness. The healer passed his hand in front of their eyes several times, and they took no notice. Their parents said they were that way when they came down for firstmeal. The man is strong, and the woman is comely. I think she may be the one you encountered. The man looked sufficiently strong to take down Yasho without an iron pan. It might be good to see if you can identify the woman—after you finish eating, of course." The last he said with a wide grin.

"Of course," Currat said.

Knowing they wouldn't be long at the Blue Sail, Zack and Currat had tied Spellbinder and Snowflake to hitching posts out front. The other two horses there belonged to Turlas and Cerrol. The ride would have been nice with the cool sea breeze, songbirds singing between the louder, raspy calls of sea birds, and the occasional greeting from passersby if their purpose were not so urgent. Unfortunately, Turlas and Cerrol didn't seem to appreciate their surroundings. Currat did, however, and smiled at the urgency of the two young men.

Soon, they arrived at the house. Turlas went in first to explain the purpose of the visit.

He didn't take long to return. "They don't believe the son or daughter could do such a thing. When I told them they might be under Ozlid's influence, they looked frightened, but agreed for you to come in."

They all followed him inside.

"Zack is here," Turlas said to the woman, and she immediately broke out of her trance. Leaping to her feet, she grabbed the knife she'd been sitting on and charged Zack with a wailing scream.

Before she could reach him, Cerrol's fist caught her under the chin, snapping her head back. Turlas caught her in his arms as she fell and carried her to a daybed, placing her gently down. Her mother covered her with a beautiful throw knitted in all the colors of a rainbow, and giving both Turlas and Cerrol a stern look.

"Yasho is here," Zack said. At his words, the young man rose, looking around the room. Not seeing Yasho, he collapsed back on the floor, assuming a sitting position and returning to a trancelike state again.

The young man's da started to speak. Zack put his finger to his lips and motioned them outside. When the woman started to come, too, he whispered, "Stay with your daughter." Looking relieved, she returned to a chair beside the daybed.

Outside, Zack turned to the man. "Do you know the name Wathdure?"

"He rules Ozlid," the man answered in a near snarl.

"Wathdure is very powerful. I believe he or one of his minions placed the directive in your son and daughter's mind to do what they have done. I know he has the ability to accomplish it." *Actually, it would be Shadure's handiwork, from what Gaz told us. But there's no need to open that unpleasantness now.* "I'm afraid I don't know how to free them from his control. I suspect it will disappear within a few hours to a day. The only thing I can suggest is to keep them warm and see if you can get them to rest."

The man agreed, thanked them for coming, and went back inside.

"That 'Thank you' didn't sound too sincere," Currat remarked.

Turlas nodded. "He probably thinks we're making things up."

"Possibly," Zack said. "But our presence here could be causing part of the problem. We're moving on today. The distance away from them may help."

"Will you be back?" Cerrol asked.

"Yes," Zack said. "But, it may be in weeks rather than days."

The men grasped forearms in farewell. Zack and

Currat rode toward the north road, cutting off on the smaller road leading to the back of Briggs's home.

They found the captain waiting for them there. It took another hour to reach the cliff overlooking the sea.

* * *

BRYAN cuddled close to Synithy, their lovemaking over, basking in contentment; he wrapped his arms over her shoulders and ran his fingers over her flat stomach. She giggled.

"What news from the taverns?" she asked.

"The tavern master at the Shimmering Oar received word that his brother was killed by Ozlidians. He took it badly, and he's not himself. But, I don't suppose I would be either."

"That's awful! I hadn't heard of it at the Blue Sail. Do you think Yasho will give you more work?"

"I think he might. Now, let's talk about better things."

"Like what?"

He leaned forward and kissed her on the neck at a special place. She moaned.

6

ZACK wondered if they'd have time to reach Ballrand's inn. It was the second inn on the road, and he'd pushed Spellbinder hard to reach it on his previous trip to Ozlid. He again set a ground-eating pace. The horses responded well, going from a gallop downward through a canter, trot, walk, and pace, and then back up again, allowing them enough rest in the slower gaits to keep going at the faster speeds. They didn't stop to eat midmeal, but they did stop long enough for the horses to drink a little water.

They reached the inn a half hour after sundown and entered the stable yard.

"Master Stand, Master Duval, you're back!" Tad, the stable boy, exclaimed.

"We are, indeed," Currat said.

"We are glad to see you too, Tad," Zack said.

The lad's eyes widened. "Master Duval, you can speak!"

During his escape from Ozlid, Currat's accent would have ensured his death. "I had to go to Jewel to find a healer who could cure me," he said in a perfect Hamptorian pronunciation.

"Oh, that's right, you and Master Stand are from there," Tad said.

"Master Stand is; I'm from here."

"Well," Tad said, looking deflated "I guess you really aren't brothers."

"No." Zack chuckled. "We're not."

"I'll take good care of your horses. They're wonderful."

Grabbing their saddlepacks, Zack and Currat left Tad

unsaddling Spellbinder as they entered the inn. Ballrand's expression showed surprise, and then a wide smile.

"Master Stand *and* Master Duval, it's good to see you both. How long will you be this time?"

"We may leave tomorrow, depending on what you can tell us," Zack said. "Oh, and Currat found an excellent healer in Jewel, and his speech problem is cured."

Ballrand swung his attention to Currat. "That's good news!"

"That it is, Master Innkeeper, that it is," Currat commented.

Ballrand basked in the compliment. "The inn is rather full. I have a large room, but it has only one bed, a big one."

"That'll do nicely," Zack said. "We are starving. Is lastmeal still being served?"

"If it wasn't, I'd reopen the kitchen for you two. Your killing of the bandits that plagued us innkeepers for so long rid us of an evil we couldn't overcome ourselves. Several of the innkeepers still talk about you. The common room has mostly cleared out. I'll get your lastmeals started and, if you like, join you when you've finished. My curiosity is certainly aroused."

The food tasted as good as they remembered. By the time they'd finished, only a few guests remained, and they sat several tables away. Ballrand joined them with a questioning look.

"Ballrand," Zack said. "We *are* jewel merchants, but we are more than that, too. What I tell you must remain between us. Talking about it could put you and your family in grave danger. Simply knowing will not, as long as you keep your silence. Do you wish me to continue?"

The innkeeper looked deep in thought for several moments, and then nodded.

"The land you call Jewel is where we live now. I was born there, and Currat has adopted it as his home. I think you know the real name of our lands is the Seven Realms.

It is ruled by High Lords, and overseen by our Zenith Lord."

Another nod followed.

"We work directly for a very high official who reports only to the Zenith Lord. We carry out, shall we say, certain duties for him. One of our assignments is to find out what happened to a high diplomat sent to Arestead's and your kings. He was not able to open full diplomatic relations between our countries, but he did get permission to open trade delegation offices. The efforts went well for a time, and then our ambassador disappeared, along with the men at his offices. We have been sent to find out what happened to Ambassador Openhand and his men, and to rescue him if we can. Oh, and by the way, would you like to buy any jewels?"

Ballrand chuckled and shook his head. "I doubt very seriously if I could afford your merchandise. Briggs has been able to supply us innkeepers with foods very hard for us to obtain. It increased business greatly, until it ran out. As to your ambassador, can you describe him?"

"He would come to about your chin, portly, with grey balding hair, average face with full lips. He was brought out of retirement for the assignment. I would guess he's reached seventy summers, but he's stronger than he looks. I never saw the men with him. I imagine he would be drugged and appear ill, with men helping him. Those men would be dressed all in black and probably riding large black stallions like Currat's."

"Men from Ozlid?" Ballrand asked.

"Probably," Currat answered.

"We, meaning innkeepers, know how to recognize Ozlid's men. They do wear all black, and ride horses like Currat's. Usually only one in the band will speak. The rest, evidently, have not mastered our accent, from the few words I've overheard. I haven't seen a group like what you describe, I'm afraid. However, I did hear from Delwick, the innkeeper at the first inn you reach from

Hagan's End, that a group similar to what you mentioned passed through with a wagon over a month ago. Delwick was told the man was too ill to be moved. Someone stayed with him at all times, bringing food and otherwise caring for him. Citing his health, the leader of the group placed the wagon away from the stable and asked that no one visit him. Delwick was suspicious of them, and wanted to intervene, but he had no one to help, and the Ozlidians her heavily armed. They only stayed one night, and left before firstmeal the next morning, paying with Ozlidian vouchers. We assumed they traveled north. No one saw them leave." Ballrand looked a little sheepish. "May I see one of your stones?"

"I'll show them to you when you take us to our room," Zack said.

Lastmeal's food lived up to Zack's memory. He wondered if Loyl, the girl Currat had mentioned as lovely and carefree still worked there. Upon escaping from Ozlid, they had an affair. He wondered how Currat would feel upon seeing her.

Ballrand came back when the ale was gone, bouncing a key in his hand. "Shall we?"

The room was large, with a fireplace and two large plush chairs. Smaller than the rooms at the Blue Sail, it was better than most inns provided. Ballrand's custom must have been good indeed; the bed and chairs all looked new. Zack and Currat threw their cloaks on the bed and turned to the innkeeper. Zack held out his hand for the key. Ballrand hesitated for an instant and handed it over, looking worried.

"Oh," Zack said. "The jewels."

Ballrand immediately looked more cheerful. Zack pulled the pouch from his saddlepack, opened it, and spread the jewels across the bed beside the cloaks.

"Great Stars!" Ballrand exclaimed. "Those could buy all of Hagan's End and every inn in Hamptor—maybe Arestead, too."

Zack handed him a large, brilliant diamond. "They wouldn't buy much of anything; they're fake." He went on to explain how they would return with the real stone if someone wanted to purchase one, and that the fake ones looked like the real ones.

Ballrand tossed the almost-diamond in the air, caught it, and handed it back to Zack. "What would these be worth if they were all real?"

"Around three thousand of our golds, maybe a little more."

"Nine thousand golds," Ballrand whispered. "I can see why you don't carry the real ones. How do you get them? What's your take?"

"We get a part of the sale, a small part, but enough for the two of us for a year if we sell just one. They belong to the Zenith Lord."

Ballrand looked at the gleaming stones spread out on the bed once more, and shook his head. "I bid you good sleep."

"Thank you, good innkeeper. We hope to see you at firstmeal."

Ballrand left, still shaking his head, while Zack replaced the "jewels" back into the pouch.

"Would you want that much wealth?" Currat asked.

"No. I wouldn't know what to do with it all. You have your golds Jarod gave you when you first went to Stonefire. They have been invested, as you know. The profits are quite good, and I have several investments that will more than supply a good retirement. We will live well, assuming we survive. Besides, the battles with the Dark may well cost all the gold and jewels in the Seven Realms. If we don't win, what difference does it make?"

"When do you think the real battles will start?"

"Jarod's son, the Darkslayer, must reach his age-of-man time and find his own Great Stone. He's barely three summers now. We have at least ten years, and probably more time after that, depending on how long his quest takes to find his providence. A few of the Stones are in play, but not all of them by far."

Currat answered the knock at the door before asking more questions. A serving maid offered them a small cask of wine. "Compliments of Master Ballrand." He reached into his purse and pulled out three coppers, taking the wine and handing her the coins.

"Thank you, Master Duval."

She turned to go, stopping at Currat's question. "Is Loyl still here?"

"No sir, I took her place. Her mother became stricken, and can hardly move without help. Loyl went to care for her in Hagan's End."

Currat nodded and the woman walked down the hall, bouncing the coins in her hand. Turning back, he caught Zack looking at him. "What?"

"Do you miss that life?"

"No."

* * *

THE next morning, Currat rose first, looking content when Zack had to wait to complete his morning ritual. When Zack had finished and dressed, he handed him his cloak. He smiled, and Currat returned the gesture. On their way out, the lock shot home with a comforting, solid sound. They found the common room half full.

When they were nearly done with their meal, three men came in, wearing the black of Ozlid. The leader looked around and sat so that his men had their backs to Currat before ordering firstmeal. Currat turned away, but thought he recognized the voice, and said so to Zack. They unhooked the guards on their swords and swung them into easy reach. Zack turned away too, watching the leader's reflection in his bronze ale mug. They waited, not wanting to show themselves by returning to their room.

The Ozlidians finished, paid, and left. Moments later, the leader returned and walked to Currat's side. Bending next to his ear, he whispered, "I don't think Wathdure can read my thoughts; at least, not yet. Why did you risk returning? Wathdure has implanted a likeness of you both in all his men with a directive to kill you on sight. My men didn't see you, I made sure of it. If possible, when you leave Hamptor, I'd like to go with you."

Currat looked up into his old friend's face. "Darr, can you abandon the army and hide in Hagan's End?"

"I wouldn't be able to hide long. Wathdure goes after deserters with a vengeance. He had the last one flayed alive, with his men pulling off chunks of muscle and feeding it to his dogs. He could only scream by the time one of the men hit a large blood vessel while digging out more muscle. He's as perverted as ever. I didn't know the man—a sergeant, I think. Over a thousand men watched the torture. The ones that got sick disappeared."

Currat nodded. "Do you know anything about an ambassador being captured?"

"Yes, he's being kept alive in a small village close to the border. I don't know why. If you want to rescue him, he could very well be a lure to capture you, if Wathdure knows you're here."

"Can he communicate directly with you?" Zack asked.

"No. I'm one of those he can't detect, one of the last ones," Darr replied. "I travel with only two men on assignments I make up. I get vouchers to pay the men, and operate by using a dead man's name. He also couldn't be detected, but he wasn't careful, and a messenger killed him. I killed the messenger, and threw both of them off a high cliff into a gorge. Wathdure had ordered him to roam Hamptor and Arestead, causing havoc without being seen. It's hard to miss someone wearing all black and riding Wathdure's stallions."

"Can you put away extra vouchers, change into regular work clothes, grow a beard, change horses, and then go to Hagan's End?"

"In one to two months."

"Do you know me?"

"Yes, you're Zack Stand. Wathdure wants you almost as much as he wants Currat."

"We have to at least try to rescue the ambassador."

"Frankly, Zack, I doubt he's still alive. The man watching him loves torture. If he is alive and you do manage to reach him, you might want to just end his suffering; he's probably near death."

Zack hit the table hard with his fist, causing Ballrand to look up and start over to the men. Nearly there, Zack stopped him in his tracks with an inconspicuous wave of his hand.

"If you can disguise yourself and wait at Hagan's End, we'll take you to safety. If you're not what you say you are, we'll kill you." Currat looked Darr in the eye. "I knew and liked you. We didn't serve much together, but I'd heard you're a good officer. We'll do what we can."

"Thank you!" The man in black looked relieved.

"Can you find out the ambassador's condition without endangering yourself?" Zack asked.

"I can try. I know a group that goes by there. I can make it look like I'm just curious."

"How is it that you and the other bands are able to roam Hamptor without interference?"

"Somehow, Wathdure installed one of his men as the head of the military here, and another in Arestead. Orders are that the military cannot approach us unless we are caught in the middle of a crime. Also, the military's men have been cut to the bare minimum that can still be called an army. Hamptor's patrols are cut so short we may not see one for a couple of months. When we do see them, they're so undermanned, they usually pay no attention to us, no matter what we do."

"We've heard there are more changes in the governments. Have you heard anything?" Currat asked.

"There's a rumor that Wathdure replaced two of each king's top advisors, and they have some kind of hold over them. He's virtually taken over the kingdoms without losing a man. There was another speculation that the kingdoms' water would be increased, but so far, that's proved false. I have to go, or my men will get restless. They think I'm going after one of the maidens."

Zack waved Ballrand over. "Ballrand, this is Darr. He's fighting Wathdure in his own way. His two men don't know. If he should come to you dressed in regular clothes, please let him hide here for no more than a few weeks. He'll have plenty of vouchers, and he'll be alone. Will you do that?"

The innkeeper looked at the enemy's uniform and nodded. "He's been here several times and always kept his men in check. He can stay. If he's fighting Wathdure, I'll be sorry to see him leave."

Currat looked up. "There's fighting and there's *fighting*. If he can also leave messages for us here, we'll get them from you."

Ballrand nodded with a slight smile and went to care for his other guests.

Darr said, "Thank you!" again, then turned and walked away.

* * *

BRYAN turned on his side, draping his arm over Synithy's bare waist. "What's new at the Blue Sail?"

She turned to face him. "The two jewel merchants have gone, but Yasho's keeping their rooms available, so I assume they're coming back. I know they come from Jewel. I would love to see their stones. I straighten up their rooms when they go down to lastmeal, but I've never seen anything that looks like it holds jewels. I want to see them."

"Oh, and what would you do if you found them?"

Her cross looks shattered when her smile destroyed it.

"Nothing! Silly. I just want to look like any woman would. You could buy me one." Her grin looked more serious.

"From what Yasho said the other night, I doubt if anyone in Hagan's End could afford even one of them."

"Oh, I know you have savings. You could get me one." Now she didn't smile.

"Those coins are for a house, not something frivolous like jewels."

She looked petulant. "A woman's jewels are not frivolous!"

It took longer than usual for Bryan to fall asleep that night.

7

THE weather didn't hold. Zack and Currat rode north. Late in the day, a violent storm swept down on them. Several times they sought the protection of forest trees to spare them and the horses from the rain blowing nearly horizontally in the fierce wind. It lasted two days. Tired, muddy, hungry, and wet, they arrived at the next inn. Paying extra for a tub filled with hot water for bathing and laundry to be done overnight, they began to relax in a spacious room with fireplace and comfortable chairs—not plush chairs, but adequate.

Two older boys rolled a tub in the room, barely fitting it through the wide doorway. Buckets of steaming water soon followed. When the boys returned on the last trip with a small bucket of soap and drying clothes, Zack and Currat had stripped and stood with blankets wrapped around them from the waist down. One of the boys noticed them both ready to bathe and looked like he would make a comment. He obviously looked at the guests' muscular upper bodies and stayed quiet. They left with the dirty clothing.

Currat and Zack climbed into the tall tub at the same time. The water that would normally come to their waist reached their chests. They took turns washing each other's backs. Once clean, they soaked until the water had cooled. They dressed and pulled on their boots, at which time the boys returned. The older boy looked longingly at the short swords and daggers lying on the bed, but said nothing.

Their leather cloaks, hanging on hooks next to the door, repelled water as well as oilcloth, and hid many more weapons. Zack remembered the boy staring at his short sword and dagger. He strapped on his weapons and donned his cloak.

Currat followed suit. "Do you think the boy would try to steal our weapons?"

"I don't want to take the chance. You remember how long it took to get perfectly balanced knives and swords for you? I haven't been here before, and it's not on Briggs's list of better inns. That list saved us a lot of grief on my first visit and your escape from Ozlid. It's best to leave at sunup and rest a day or two at the next inn. In fact, why don't we have lastmeal here?"

Currat nodded and hung his cloak back on the hook. He pulled the cord next to the door. Moments later, the older boy arrived. Looking somewhat disappointed, he hurried away to fetch lastmeals and a cast of wine.

"Am I being overly cautious, or is…"

"I think any of those boys would steal all we had if they had the chance. Frankly, after seeing the common room, I'd rather eat here with you."

Zack smiled. "Agreed."

When the food and cask of wine came, the boy placed platters of steaming food on the table just big enough for two and had to set the small cask on the floor. The mugs barely fit on the table. The server's attitude changed to a bright smile when Zack gave him four coppers. He gave a mock salute to his forehead and left.

The food wasn't the quality of Ballrand's inn or the others on Briggs's list, but it was prepared well enough, and filling. The wax seal on the cask hadn't been broken, which brought a smile to Zack's face.

Zack tapped his saddlepack. "A little brandy?"

"Before bed, and very little. That wine is strong!"

It was strong. The men went to bed satisfied and content.

* * *

LEAVING early the next morning after a fairly good

firstmeal, they found the younger boy at the stable. The spies smiled upon seeing Spellbinder and Snowflake. The horses' grooming was excellent. Their coats shined from extra brushing, and the tack had been thoroughly cleaned and the metal polished.

The boy looked into Zack's eyes. "I gave them extra oats. The black wouldn't take the sweetstones, but he sure gobbled down an apple. The bay liked the sweetstones."

Zack looked the boy in the eye. "You like working with horses, that's evident."

"It's better than dealing with the men who frequent here. My brother hates horses, even riding them. He fancies himself a warrior. I told him he better start liking horses. After I showed him how to treat them, he seems to like them a little better."

"A warrior?" Currat asked.

"I know," the boy answered. "He doesn't have the muscles to win a fight. He thinks he can. All he could talk about at lastmeal last night was how big you are. Da told him he needed to be that big to be a fighter. Is that true?"

"Mostly," Zack said. "There are smaller men who are excellent fighters, but they've trained for years, and they are quick. They survive by getting inside a bigger man's range and stabbing him, most of the time, and getting away with that is where the practice has its worth. Your brother would have a hard time."

"Oh, he's not really my brother; he's my cousin. My mom and da died years ago, killed by Ozlidians. My uncle took me in. I was little and after a while, I called him Da."

"You have a talent with horses. Snowflake, the big black, doesn't take kindly to strangers. He's caused problems before. Spellbinder, my horse, is a little more gentle, but if he thinks someone is going to mistreat him, he'll tear a barn down, and has done so more times than I like to remember."

"What's your name?" Currat asked.

"Simmon Cusor."

"Do you like it here?"

"The boy looked around before answering. "Not really. My uncle and aunt took me in, but it was clear they did it out of obligation. They work me harder than their son, but I guess that is to be expected. Neither likes horses, so I mostly get to do what I like. I don't show it off, but I'm stronger than my cousin and uncle. My aunt never wanted me and made that plain. She'd be glad if I left."

Currat knew what Zack wanted and decided to preempt him. "Simmon, we are from the Seven Realms, the land you call Jewel. The Zenith Lord rules it, and he has a very fine Guard with thousands of horses. Someone with your talent would be prized there. Do you think you'd like that—leaving family, friends, and the life you know here?"

Simmon became so excited Currat thought he might come out of his skin. "Yes, sir! That sounds like a dream!"

"Think hard on what we talked about this morning," Zack said. "We'll be back through here in a hurry. If you decide you want that life, you must be ready to go at a moment's notice. Do think hard over this. Sometimes, you don't know you'll miss a place until you're gone."

"Sir, my uncle takes me to Hagan's End once a month when he buys meats. He usually ends up drunk, and I drive the wagon home. Is there a place I could hide there? He takes most to the coins I get, but I have almost a silver's worth. I could pay my way."

Currat looked at Zack, "The timing might work. Yasho seems the fatherly type."

"Do you know where the Blue Sail Inn is located?" The boy nodded. "Ask for Yasho, and tell him Zack Stand sent you. If anyone tries to turn you away, tell them Currat Duval will be very upset, and Zack Stand will be furious. Once you reach Yasho, tell him I said to mention Zack and I would take care of the bill if he would take care of you. Tell him your uncle shouldn't be told where you are, and you'll be leaving on Captain Briggs's ship. Can you remember it all?"

"Zack Stand, Currat Duval, and Captain Briggs, yes, I can remember the names," Simmon said.

Zack threw him a silver. The spies mounted and left him standing there with a big grin and his mouth open.

A mile up the road, Currat made his reservations known. "We came here to rescue an ambassador, not recruit boys for the Zenith Lord's service. What are you planning?"

"I don't have all the details yet, but I'm working on it. Ursel will need manpower and men familiar with Hamptor. They could be valued members of his group or replacements later on. At this point, it's an idea, nothing more. Give it some thought; you always see the problems in what I decide. I wanted to talk to you about it. Now is just sooner than I planned, only because I don't have all of it put together yet."

"I'll give it some thought."

They slept under the stars until Zack got to the inn he wanted.

* * *

IT was late when two exhausted spies spotted the building.

"Currat, do you remember the story about Ursel and the twins?" Zack pointed and smiled at the old sign on the door about Black Stones after all this time. "Well, that's the inn. The signs are left over from my going north to reach Ozlid. Wathdure offered huge rewards for a Black Stone like the one Mountglen wore, as you know. That was before Mountglen lost his head, literally, and High Lord Kyle Byrne came into power and changed the realm's name to Stonecrest. This is one of the best inns on our trip besides the Blue Sail, and possibly Ballrand's place."

They rode their horses to the stable yard and turned them over to a new stable boy Zack hadn't met before. They made arrangements for their mounts' care and carried the usual belongings to the inn's front door.

Zack leaned his head in the front door and yelled, "I WANT TO KNOW ABOUT BLACK STONES!"

The aftermath came immediately: "There's no cursed stones of any kind here! Can't you read?!" Kerk came flying around the corner with a sword in his massive hand, his over-muscled body panting. I'll take your nuts, you id..i..ot... Master Stand! It's really you?"

Before he could answer, Zack found himself lifted off the ground, saddlepacks and all, in a massive bear hug.

"Derk, Da, come! It's Master Stand and someone who...Master Stand you didn't say you had a brother!"

There are times when I wished Currat and I didn't look so much alike. "We're not related by blood," Zack said after he caught his breath and got back on solid ground, his chest hurting. "And it's good to see you, too! I trust no one asks about Black Stones."

"Just you," Kell said, coming around the corner. "The word traveled rapidly. My business increased by half again. Most people gave up on finding the accursed stone, but I left the signs up. They seem to calm the crowd. We still get some no-goods who want to fight; they give the boys something to do."

"Kell, we need to rest a day or two. We'll need a room with a large bed. We share a room for safety. Your good food will be most welcome, too. When it's convenient, I'd like to speak with you and your sons...Oh, forgive me. This is Currat Duval. He's the officer who rescued me from Ozlid. He now works with me for the Zenith Lord of the Seven Realms. We're here for two reasons. I'll explain when we meet. Now, we need food, wine, and rest."

The common room had a few more tables squeezed in, the place clean as always, the fireplace still vented well, and reduced the smoke to a minimum. As usual, Zack picked a table in the corner of the far wall, sitting with his back to the wall. Currat joined him on his immediate left. Zack had taken his battle sword from its roll; he unhooked the pin holding it to his side and swung it athwart his lap. He also ensured that his short sword remained in easy reach.

I don't know why I felt the need for my bigger sword; it's a feeling. I learned long ago to trust those thoughts.

Currat didn't ask questions; he just added his own array of hidden weapons. Lying across their laps, the swords nearly touched.

Two mugs of wine, softly set on their table by a new serving maid Zack didn't remember, would satisfy a thirst that had been building since midday. "I'll have your lastmeal here, quickly." She nodded and hurried away.

Zack liked her voice. Wearing all white, the skirt flared out near her hips and the bodice tightly held voluptuous breasts. Her auburn hair fell close to her waist in loose curls down her front and back. Light blue eyes lit up her face over a small, perky nose and lips that stretched into a smile when she talked. The sway of her hips was pleasing but not out of place, leaving no doubt she would earn many coins over the period of the night.

"You find her appealing?" Currat asked.

"Once, much more than now," Zack answered.

Currat smiled.

Two full, steaming trenchers of food came to rest as lightly as the ale. Her genuine smile lasted until she turned away.

A small bowl of seasoned stew sat on one end of the trencher. Zack and Currat attacked it first.

"This is good," Currat said.

"I agree."

Not many more words came while the food disappeared. Derk approached. "I see you found our food pleasing."

"Probably as pleasing as Adel."

The big man actually blushed. Zack couldn't bring himself to call the twins "boys" any longer. The gentle giant before them faltered, "You know about Adel?"

Zack chuckled. "Ah, my big friend, you well know I'm discreet. This is the first time I mentioned her since I left here, years ago."

Derk nodded and walked toward the kitchen.

"Adel?" Currat asked.

"Ursel had a problem with the ladies; the twins took him to see her. He has no more difficulties."

"That big man had women problems? I find that hard to believe. He was so gentle and caring when he rescued me and took me to Briggs's ship. Women love that in a man. Besides that, he's handsome."

"I'll explain another time." Zack's grin left an even more questioning look on Currat's face.

Kell showed the spies to a large room with fireplace, plush chairs, and a wide bed. The room had the same color scheme of browns and golds as the room Zack had occupied before. Two windows allowed moonlight to spill into the dark room. A large tub sat in one corner. Kell lit the lamp by the door from the one he carried, and then did the same to the ones on each side of the fireplace and bed. The lamps were a luxury and rarely found. Zack looked around and turned back to Kell. "You outdid yourself."

This is my finest room. Most won't pay the cost, but those that do make up for the times it sits empty. I'm fairly particular in letting it—I don't want it torn up, after all. But, for friends, I offer a generous discount."

Zack smiled. "I'm glad I'm a friend."

"I'll bring the boys up around midnight if you think you'll still be awake."

"We will, but we may be very late for firstmeal."

Kell laughed. "I'll put something aside for you." He tossed Zack the key and left.

The spies placed battle swords on the outside edges of the bed and took their cloaks off, then sat and sharpened the many pointed weapons they kept hidden in their cloaks. Finished, Currat went to the saddlepacks and retrieved the brandy, still over half-full. He took two goblets from the tables beside the bed, poured them a quarter-full, and handed one to Zack. Easing back into the overstuffed chair, he again watched the fire through amber liquid.

A knock at the door shattered the quiet, making the crackling fire sound distant. They looked at each other and frowned. It was not even close to midnight.

Opening the door, Currat found smiling twins carrying large buckets of steaming water. Derk chuckled. "It comes with the room." They quickly filled the tub in two trips. Derk followed Kerk, stopping at the door. "See you at midnight," he said before leaving.

Currat relocked the door and began undressing, leaving his untouched brandy by the fireplace. Zack joined him and the two slid into the vaporing bath, enjoying the soothing relaxation until the water cooled. They emerged, and put on the drying clothes placed beside the tub, and took more from the stack at the end of the tub. Now dressed in privateclothes and trousers, they returned to the warmth of the fireplace and warmer wine.

"What are you planning?" Currat finally asked. "You have never kept me out of things before."

"I'm sorry. I'm trying to work it out in my head, and I'm in a quandary," Zack said with a grimace. "We're supposed to find Ambassador Openhand. All indications are that he's dead, or would not live through the move across Hamptor. I think we must still find him and see if he can be rescued and if so, that's what we'll do. The other plan is to establish a group in Hamptor to harass and kill the Men-in-Black. They're not really your people any longer; they're men Wathdure's turned into creatures of hate and death. If I can collect some men to go to the Seven Realms for training to come back to fight here, it'll cause havoc and kill some bad men terrorizing Hamptorians. But, what if all it does is initiate more reprisals from Ozlid? Can I live with that? Can you? Sure, some lives will be lost, as happens in all battles; so perhaps a better plan is to get men inside the kings' circles of influence. What would that do, and how could the person promote disruption to Ozlid's plans? The main overall goal is to slow the Dark's advance, if it's even possible."

"What are you going to discuss with Kell and the twins?"

"Two things. First, can they shed some light on the ambassador and his condition, and second, how would they feel about fighting the Men-in-Black? I wouldn't want to go further than my thinking of bringing it to Jarod's attention." Zack slumped in his chair and sighed. "I agree, I've held this from you for too long, and I *do* value your thoughts. You tell me many things I've not thought of in my plans. I'm sorry."

Currat thought deeply for several moments. "I'll want to think about your quandary, but I do have some comments. I know the ambassador's state worries you and I know you won't give up on him. You're laying groundwork here for something that may not come to pass, and that'll make you and the Seven Realms look weak. I agree the Men-in-Black need killing, but I think it would be better to arrange deadly accidents than to engage them in open combat. Wathdure might not become as suspicious as from an open attack, at least for a while. Getting someone in the king's inner circle would take a highly trained spy, and I think a woman would be better than a man. You've known Jarod for a long time; which of these do you think he'd be agreeable to doing?"

Even through his gloom, Zack smiled. "Yes, my dear Currat, I should have involved you long before now. I'll try not to make that mistake again. What do you propose for the ideas we present tonight?"

"Find and rescue Openhand, and form a group to harass and kill Men-in-Black, but with a strong emphasis on not doing anything without guidance."

"I like your ideas, and I like the idea of a little more brandy. Maybe a quarter glass; I want it to last."

"I'll get it."

Currat had no sooner sat back down, glass in hand, when another knock sounded on the door. "I'll get that, too."

Kell, Derk, and Kerk stood outside, staring at Currat's half-undressed state. "The common room emptied out earlier than expected. We can come back later if you wish."

"No, we're enjoying a drink before the fireplace. Come in and pull up some chairs."

They rearranged chairs, and Kerk sat on the floor so they formed a semicircle around the fireplace.

Derk spoke first. "I saw that you looked alike, but this is beyond belief. Even your feet are the same!"

Currat and Zack both chuckled, but said nothing. Zack started by inquiring about the ambassador, asking pertinent questions to gather any information they might have.

Derk looked at Kerk and nodded.

"We've heard of, but have not seen, a small, abandoned tavern close to the border," Kerk said. "It seems that a group of black wearers have taken it over and are just sitting there. They don't let anyone in, but they don't venture out, either. Their supplies come from over the border and, being so close, no one has tried to stop the deliveries—as if anyone would. It seems like a good place to hide someone, but why not just take him into Ozlid?"

"To set a trap, and they know we would know it's a trap, which means there's more to the tavern than meets the eye," Zack replied. "To attack it or try to get in clandestinely would be foolish. We need a way to get them out, all of them, including the ambassador if he's there."

"Fire?" Kell asked.

"The problem with fire is controlling it, and that's hard to do when you don't know who or what's inside. We might well burn the ambassador to death. I'm not ruling it out, but it takes a great deal more planning than simply shooting a fire arrow at the building."

"Well, that ends that!" Kerk said.

"Not necessarily," Zack replied. He appraised his guests. "You know we're spies. It doesn't take a lot to figure that out. My previous mission was to gather information on Ozlid, and as you all know, it almost got me killed. What you don't know is Currat was captured and tortured beyond belief. Our High Healers in the Seven Realms are far more advanced than the ones here. Getting him back to good health took a long time and a giant effort. His suffering was far worse than mine."

Currat sat very still, not looking up.

"He doesn't like me talking about it except in private. Now, he's probably very mad at me, but you need to know how deeply he feels concerning the defeat of Wathdure and the Men-in-Black. He *was* an Ozlidian officer, and his father was a high-ranking administrator at the palace. Currat's father and several of his friends were killed during our escape. He's been trained as a spy, and can speak with an accent from the three of your kingdoms, as can I.

"It is greatly important that you don't go off on your own without us, or someone like us, guiding you. You won't live long no matter how tempting it feels. Do you all understand?" Zack's words caused three nods and three grave miens. He liked that.

"We are bringing this up now for two reasons," Currat said, coming out of his gloom. "There's the idea that an effort *might* be started with the Zenith Lord's blessing, and that is the only way it would happen. The cost alone of mounting an effort that'll work is beyond the stars. Let me show you something." Currat got the bundle of fake stones and unwrapped it on the floor in front of the fireplace.

Kell, Kerk, and Derk all gasped.

"These stones are fake," Currat continued, handing a large brilliant stone to each Hamptorian. "Could any of you tell the difference?"

"I've seen a few small jewels in my life, but nothing with the color and purity of these," Kell said. "The ones I saw had flaws and discolorations in them."

"The Zenith Lord has many, many times these that are real," Zack said. "He also has a vast amount of gold. It will take those kinds of resources to pay for what I'm proposing. He may not send a hundred pounds of gold, but he might spend a huge amount on training and mounting such plans—yet, I don't know if he would *do* anything. We are not discussing this with anyone else in Hamptor or Arestead.

"I'm telling you to determine what we might expect from the men you know, and how good they are at keeping secrets. Their information would be quite valuable to Ozlid. The men in such a group must be highly dedicated and completely trustworthy. My question to you is: do you know men like I've described? I would suggest that, above the things I mentioned, the men must have lost a loved one to Ozlid. Do such men exist?"

Kell looked at his boys before answering. "We don't talk about it outside the family for the reason we are innkeepers, and it shouldn't be common knowledge. My daughter and the boys' true sister died at the hands of Ozlidians crossing the border. Her death was horrific. We *are* the kind of men you want."

Zack nodded. "We both know your feelings. As I said, Ozlid killed Currat's father, and friends, and bandits killed my wife and daughter."

"How can we kill them?" Derk asked.

8

A fine day to kill Men-in-Black, Zack thought early the next morning. *But will it work?* He nudged Currat awake. "It's time."

Once dressed, the two men looked over the message once more. "The message is written like a real one. The signature, which I copied from memory, will suffice," Currat said. "Who knows, perhaps it'll get a Master of the Gold very dead."

"It might, if the Men-in-Black are smart enough to save it. You still think false dawn is the best time, Master of the Blue Currat?"

"Yes, that part of the road is good, and Snowflake shouldn't have a problem."

"Then let's go see if our friends are ready."

Arriving at the stable, they found Kell and Derk ready to mount, and Snowflake and Spellbinder ready to go. Looking uncomfortable and anxious, Kerk sat on the seat of the small wagon the inn used to collect food from local farmers, bypassing Ozlid's embargo. They took the trip north slowly, looking for dangers to the horses, the main problem being the road's ruts. The full moon's light helped.

Derk rode up beside Zack. "The tavern is around the next bend."

"Stay here."

Currat slipped off Snowflake and changed into the messenger's black uniform Derk had found near the border, at the bottom of a ravine next to a dead horse; the body had dissolved, leaving an odor. Kell had said it took many kinds of washing to remove the smell. Currat and Zack had no uncertainty concerning the messenger's body; this one, like the others, was one of Wathdure's necromantic creatures, its nose and mouth covered over with flesh, like the one that had attacked Zack. The mask it wore covered the entire face, except for its eyes. Enhanced with Wathdure's directives, it had one sole purpose: to kill anyone who got in its way of delivering Wathdure's messages. Currat didn't like the messengers; none of Ozlidian's military did. The silent creatures possessed great strength, and could move faster than one would think. Zack and Currat had learned that the hard way on their escape to Hamptor. None, other than Wathdure and Spercine, seemed to know the creatures' true nature until Zack had killed one.

Snowflake shied away before Currat whispered soothing words to him. In his disguise, he mounted and guided the big animal, once a messenger's black stallion, into the woods, heading north.

"He won't take long. Be ready on my signal," Zack said. He too, slipped into the giant pines' cover and disappeared, headed toward Ozlid's border. As he headed out, he heard the others speak—the last words to reach his ears.

"What happens if they don't believe Currat is a messenger?" Kerk asked.

"We rescue him," Kell answered.

* * *

CURRAT didn't like being in the messenger's uniform. It brought back too many unpleasant memories of bodily corruption and Wathdure's evil. He positioned Snowflake a distance from the tavern, allowing him to ride in at a gallop without sweat on his coat, like when a true messenger rode one under Wathdure's magic, riding many hours, even days without harm.

Judging the time, Currat started his run. The lone, half-asleep sentry, sitting beside the tavern's door, started and sat up, looking wide-eyed at the galloping messenger. Likely, no messenger he had ever heard of went this far out of Ozlid. He called out, urgency commanding his yell.

As Currat finished the last ten yards, a tall Man-in-Back rushed out the door. Currat reined in, thrusting the message packet toward the door. The taller man took it without looking up. Currat reared Snowflake, and rode north at a gallop.

Zack watched from the trees as the man tore open the packet and pulled out the parchment. He seemed to read it twice, holding it up in near dawn light.

"ALL MEN MAKE READY TO RIDE!"

Men-in-Black tumbled out, some pulling on various parts of clothing or boots, hopping on one foot.

They have little or no training, Zack thought.

Confusion reigned as men saddled horses and one of them seemed to argue with the taller man, gesturing toward the tavern's door. He stopped when the tall man held up the message, and then hurried to his horse. Mounting it, he led another horse to the front of the tavern, and stopped at the front door. The leader got on his horse. Seated, feet in stirrups, he raised his arm and gave the signal for a gallop.

Well, at least they know some *military protocols.* Two men started out at a trot, and then rushed to catch up. *I take that back.*

Zack produced a perfect vocalization of a screech owl and led Spellbinder to the road. He waited impatiently while the others reined in before the tavern and dismounted and drew short swords. Currat came last, the mask off and brandishing his battle sword, as did Zack.

Kerk eased the wagon close to the front door, tethering the horse at a hitching rail.

Kell stood on one side of the door and the twins on the other. Zack tested the door and, finding it unlocked, he entered.

The room, gloomy from the morning hour, smelled of

dirty clothing, urine, and feces. Currat came beside him and pointed to a mound in a corner, slightly moving. He pulled back the covers, allowing more odors to escape. The ambassador's eyes fluttered open, trying to focus.

"Ambassador Openhand, do you think you can ride?" Zack asked.

The old man gasped, and Zack knew the answer. He pulled two more blankets from nearby pallets. *I hope there's no vermin in these.* Gently wrapping the ambassador in the covers, the twins picked him up as tenderly as they had Zack years before, and carried him to the wagon, laying him on its bed, already cushioned with a generous scattering of hay. The ambassador made no sounds other than a soft gurgle. The team started south well enough, riding slowly.

Zack raised his arm, signaling a stop. "Listen," he said. The sound of galloping horses moving toward them sent a chill up his back. His terse voice carried command. "Kell, you and your boys guard the ambassador; pull the wagon off the road if you can."

Zack and Currat's horses stood at the back of the wagon, facing north at an angle. The sun's rays, filtering through trees, brought birdsong alive, covering the possible doom coming toward them. Judging from the sounds, Zack figured, there were four, maybe five riders coming at them.

He relaxed when he saw only three men, until the other two raced to catch up, all in Ozlidian military uniforms. *Their being this far from the border doesn't bode well.* He and Currat readied battle swords at the same time in one smooth flow of sparkling steel. Placing arms across their horses' sides, they hid the weapons, but had them at the ready.

Currat started to put the messenger mask on, but stopped at a warning glance from Zack.

No, that would make them stop.

The soldiers passed, glancing at the wagon and the

mounted men. The Master of the Blue leading the party reined in and circled back to the front of the wagon. Zack sheathed his sword and rode beside the wagon, facing the officer. "What are Ozlidian military doing this far south of your border?"

"Where did he—" The master pointed his sword at Currat. "—get that horse?"

Currat rode up beside Zack, leaving room for free use of weapons. "I got him the same place you would, if you ever rise through the ranks," Currat said in an Ozlidian accent.

"TRAITOR!" the officer yelled. Raising his sword, he started riding forward, but stopped to stare down at the hilt of Zack's dagger sticking out of his chest, even as Currat's knife hit him in the throat. He slid off his horse, which promptly bolted.

Zack readied his sword for attack and Currat raised his. They rode into the four horsemen, slicing the first one down.

"Get the wagon clear!" Zack said in a loud enough voice to be heard.

A sergeant moved to intercept Kerk's departure. Currat charged him. The sergeant turned to face his advancing foe, raising his sword. Steel raked against steel. The Ozlidian horses seemed not to like the battle around them and fought their reins, leaving the men struggling to gain control. Spellbinder and Snowflake, trained warhorses, charged. Two men converged on Currat while the sergeant focused on Zack.

Zack rode toward his enemy, striking fast, ramming his sword hilt to hilt and pushing hard, unseating the man. Over raging curses, the sergeant thrust his sword at Spellbinder's throat. The warhorse reared, his hoof smashing against his attacker's hand. The sergeant dropped the sword with more violent curses. Zack wheeled Spellbinder around and took on one of the men attacking Currat.

After two sword thrusts, the Ozlidian lay dying on the ground, his horse scampering away, not looking back. *Smart horse,* Zack thought.

The sergeant's bellow alerted him. He swung off Spellbinder and turned, pointing his battle sword at his attacker's chest. Zack lunged and the sergeant parried, coming back around and slapping Zack on the shoulder with the flat of his blade, an act of desperation. Zack twisted and connected the hilt of his sword with the man's jaw; the sergeant fell to the ground.

Zack turned to assist Currat, and saw the last attacker looking bewildered at the sword sliding out of his abdomen. Currat's sword came down across the man's neck, fountaining blood across the road

The pair cleaned their swords with the fallen men's attire. Then, they bound and gagged the sergeant, throwing him over one of the horses that came when Currat whistled a specific call. Zack looked at him, and then the horse.

"It's a call they learn when being tamed. Most forget it soon enough, but he's still young," Currat explained.

They stripped off the men's uniforms and carried the bodies a few yards into the forest, dumping them into the first ravine they found. The uniforms and saddlepacks stayed with Zack.

Derk waited a short way down the road. He glanced at them with wide eyes as they approached, noticing the sergeant strapped over the horse. "What are you going to do with him?"

"Get what information we can from him, and when he can tell us no more, kill him," Zack said flatly to the young man.

The color drained from Derk's face.

"What did you expect? He saw our faces, and probably heard a name or two. If we let him go, he'll have a very large group of men, not in uniform, searching for you so they can torture you to death by flaying your skin off your body. I've watched it being done, and it looks like it hurts a great deal, especially when they get to your genitalia. Actually," Zack said in an instructive way, "I don't think it hurts that much more than, say, your arm. It's the idea that causes men to scream more."

White-faced, Derk spurred his horse forward to catch up with the wagon, moving at a slow pace to comfort the ambassador.

"What did you do that for?" Currat asked.

"I heard the twins talking, and I got the impression they thought encounters like this one followed certain rules. I needed him to know they don't. I'll have more to say later on to them, but for now it's time for them to learn how cruel and evil Ozlid can be. And not only Ozlid, but also bandits from everywhere they roam. I'll even it out. The twins and Kell need to understand who they're dealing with before taking on a viper's nest."

* * *

LOOKING down on the sergeant in Kell's cold room, hollowed out deep below the inn, where he kept barrels of ale and casks of wine alongside containers of cream and butter, Zack and Currat sat on low barrels with cloaks on. The sergeant began to move, a low moan becoming a curse.

"You do curse a lot, Sergeant," Zack said offhandedly. A fresh stream of expletives streamed forth. "Now, Sergeant, talking like that has reprisals." Zack's knife flashed in the dim light, cutting the sergeant's belt, pulling the shirt up and ripping it apart. He looked at the knife's blade, testing it with a hair jerked from the man's chest. Letting it slide down the blade, it fell back toward its recent home. "I'd lay very still if I were you." He leaned down and shaved the hair from around the man's nipple."

"What...what are you doing?" The sergeant's voice cracked mid way.

"Preparing your chest and nipple, of course."

"For what?"

"Sergeant, do you remember the crossbeams standing in the yard before the entrance to the fort at the border? I'm sure you must. They held men who said they knew about the Black Stone, but really didn't."

"I don't know what you're speaking about."

"Sure you do, you were there." Currat said. "You didn't participate in the cutting, but you cheered the ones who did to greater torture."

The sergeant looked closer at Currat in the dim light. He leaned down and turned up the lamp.

"I remember you. You were a Master of the Blue. You're a traitor." The sergeant's mouth twisted in disgust.

"A traitor to what? Wathdure's evil? Your cohorts who loved the torturing? Your loss of all decency, compassion, and service to the people of Ozlid? Yes, I am a traitor to all that. You, on the other side, are a degenerate deviate devoid of caring or kindness. Now, I think it's time for Zack to start."

"Start what?" The sergeant began to look concerned for the first time.

"Oh," Currat said, "the flaying of your body. Knowing Zack the way I do, he'll start with your nipples, slicing through them and then pulling the strips of skin and flesh toward your testicles. He'll go slowly. To hurry would put him in the class of your torturers. No, he's a master at taking his time, making sure you can feel every minor pull of tissue. Over a long time, it's the loss of blood that will kill you. I'm looking forward to him starting on your privates. It'll be a few hours before he gets there, but don't worry, he knows how to keep you conscious and alert to sense every nuance of his efforts."

Zack bent down and sliced a bit of skin below the nipple and pulled until about an inch of it oozed blood to pool a bit over muscle.

The man's scream filled the small room. "No, no more! Tell me what you want. I'll do anything you say!"

"I don't know," Currat said. He pointed to Zack with his chin. "He loves his work. He doesn't toil on innocents. Oh no, he goes after bandits like the ones that killed his wife and daughter, and other scum like you. He says watching them die takes away what was done to his family *and* him. Oh yes, his torture left scars that plagued him for years, until a Master Healer of the Seven Realms rebuilt the missing tissue and made his skin smooth once more. Unfortunately, I don't think you'd live long enough to reach the Seven Realms."

Zack bent toward the sergeant's chest.

"No, no, noooo!"

Currat reached out and stayed Zack's hand.

Zack stood, disgust showing in his face.

"Why were you so far from the border?" Currat asked.

"The Master of the Blue who led us wanted to impress Master of the Gold Duran by getting information on you. Word reached us that you had returned."

"Who brought you that word?"

"A man named Juston Dowell. That's all I know."

"Did Duran know of your disobedience?"

"No, no one knew."

"What messages have come from Wathdure and Spercine in the past several months?"

The sergeant began to relax. "Not many. It's been strangely quiet. I think most of the pouches contained our pay vouchers and words from families. I've told you all I know. What's going to happen to me?"

"We talked about death by torture, but since you cooperated—" Zack lunged forward, forcing a long, pointed, slender rod up the sergeant's left nostril. He died instantly, leaving a small trickle of blood coming from his nose.

Derk stepped into the light, followed by Kerk and Kell. "Did—did you have to kill him?" Derk asked.

"The sergeant didn't know me that well," Currat answered. "He was assigned guard duty on the walls for the most part. I saw him many times from my window urging the men carrying out the torture to more drastic and painful efforts. Once, one of the torturers tried to give the knife he used to him. He refused. They knew him for what he was, a coward. That didn't mean they stopped him from coming by to watch and cheer them on. They seemed to like him yelling instructions; some, they followed.

"So, to answer your question, what would we do with him? He saw our faces. He recognized me. It wouldn't take much to link Zack and me together. There would have been a hundred, maybe more, men sent to find us, and they would know exactly where to start. Your whole family would be killed, probably by fire when they burned the inn down for working with us. There would be nothing left to prove you had ever lived, except in the minds of your neighbors, who would resist acting, for fear of them reaching the same fate."

"There is one thing that is easy to forget," Zack said. "We are at war with the Dark's lords and minions. You've lived for years with Ozlid controlling your water to the point that you no longer see it as an act of aggression. Many Hamptorians look at Wathdure's machinations as a part of life they must live with for all time.

"If you do not do something, your life will never get any better! Wathdure will see to that. I wouldn't be surprised if he sees you as fodder to create more of his necromantic army. He'll need many combatants to fight the Light's Source. The Stones are growing in power, which means the Dark is doing the same."

Zack paused for a moment. "This is the war we're fighting. Some day, Wathdure will take a more active interest in Hamptor and Arestead. You, as a country, have two choices. You can drop to your knees and take what's coming, or you can fight to delay and help conquer the Dark. That's a decision you must make. The Seven Realms can help, but we can't do it for you."

"Do you think we have a chance to survive?" Kell asked.

"Your country, maybe not; your people, probably some, maybe all," Currat answered. "If you attack in complete rebellion, no. Wathdure could kill any or all Hamptorians on a whim, but that's not his goal. He needs your people!

"The Dark must conquer the Stones of Power and those who reside in the Seven Realms. Hamptor and Arestead are stepping-stones to my lands. Wathdure already controls the kings. He's virtually subjugated your lands without losing a man in a battle. I have word that men aligned with Ozlid have replaced top advisors to both kings. Wathdure can continue going the way he has for years. I suspect he'll start increasing your water supplies, and perhaps escalate the vouchers he pays for goods, all to allow you to build your population. Knowing you're nothing more than fodder for war cannot be something you want to live with." The Hamptorian's faces displayed the distress they must have felt. They shifted from foot to foot, looking disgusted and bewildered.

Zack added. "I don't know much about the Great War two millennia ago, but the Zenith Lord does, and I think that's why he'll help your country. Any limitations we devise, meaning both our lands, will help the war against the Dark, and keep your people alive. It's a decision that must be made sometime. Now is perhaps too early, but being prepared is not!"

Kell sat down, looking despondent, frowning. The twins looked to be almost in shock.

"How much training would it take to fight men like you did today?" Derk asked.

"Not much, but the men today, except for the Master of the Blue, didn't know how to fight very well. You wouldn't have a chance against trained soldiers."

A female voice carried through the door, "The healer

is here."

"Derk," Zack said. "You and Kerk strip the sergeant's body and burn his clothes. If he had a purse, it's yours. Let me have any papers you find. Carry the body far away from people and dump it where vultures, or the like, will easily feast. Keep in mind, this is a part of fighting, too."

"Why do we have to strip them?" Kerk asked.

"Scavengers will destroy the body beyond recognition," Zack replied. "The clothing would identify the remains as someone who belonged to Ozlid, and that would bring repercussions."

The twins didn't look too happy, but started ripping clothing off the corpse.

* * *

ZACK and Currat followed Kell to the ambassador's room. A serving maid sat next to the bed with a damp cloth and the healer stood, bent over the body buttressed up on pillows. They both looked around when the men entered the room, closing the door behind them.

"He is hot and needs water," the healer said. "Dianna here is giving him as much as he can take when he stirs. I got him to swallow Feverfew and some herbs to help his breathing. There's not much more I can do until he wakes—if he wakes."

"It's that serious?" Zack asked.

"It could be," the healer said. "His body will decide in a day or two. I can't tell you much more. I'll come back tonight. If there's a change, summon me."

The healer left; the serving maid stayed. Zack and Currat went to either side of the bed. Zack leaned close. "Ambassador Openhand, I'm Zack Stand."

The ambassador stirred, his eyes quivering until, after several heartbeats, they stayed open. The old man took a long time to focus on Zack's face. Finally, he spoke, "Zack, it...is you. You rescued...me."

"Several folks took part in the rescue. You'll meet

them all in time. Now you need to rest, drink plenty of water, and try to take some meat broth. Can you do that?"

"Now that I know I'm...I'm safe, I'll try hard to recover."

"Ambassador, do you know Juston Dowell?"

"Oh, did you catch him?"

"No, should we?"

"He is...a traitor. He...betrayed our delegation and... delivered me into Ozlid's hands. Find him if you can; he's...dangerous."

Zack left the patient, and the serving maid scurried to find meat broth. Heading downstairs, he approached Kell in the common room. The other man sat alone at a far table, with no one around him. "May I join you?"

"Of course. The midmeal crowd has left, and the common room won't begin to fill for another hour or two. Zack, I've been thinking about your earlier words. The twins and I aren't the type of men to sit and wait for our destruction to come, and I don't think most Hamptorians are, either. You are right. We've grown accustomed to Ozlid's treatment of us. When the water first became rationed, a big outcry ensued. Frustration followed from the lack of action taken by the kings. Rumors ran rampant, listing reasons why the kings didn't act. Chief among those centered on cost. Many said the treasury couldn't support a larger army. My opinion is that the kings became complacent, and wouldn't act until their options ran out, if indeed, they ever had any. The fact remains: we have no guidance in what to do. You laid out one opportunity. Are there more? Is there a better one?"

"Kell, I operate under the command of my Zenith Lord. The only thing I can do is contact him and get his reaction to the problem. I've sent a proposal outlining some of the actions we discussed. I may already have a reply waiting in Hagan's End. Briggs gave me a list of inns, and I've stayed at the same ones this trip with one exception. Briggs said if a reply came, he would send it on with his deliverymen. How long before you expect them?"

"It's been some time. They could arrive any time. But, isn't it dangerous to send something like that by such a method?"

"Not really; it's written in code, a very hard cypher to break."

"How's the ambassador?"

"I got him to speak. He said Juston Dowell had betrayed him, and that he's a traitor. Have you heard of him?"

"No, but I'll put the word out to find him, and not to alert him that I'm looking."

"I don't know, Kell. You would need to emphasize that the information is important, and give it only to those men you deeply trust and enjoin them in the same restrictions. The last thing we need is to alert him. It'll be imperative to capture him alive. He's from the Seven Realms, and we need to know who turned him into a traitor."

A man entered the common room in familiar robes to Zack, who raised his hand. The man hurried over.

"Zack Stand?"

"Yes, my good priest. What brings you so far from home?"

"You do. First, I must see the engraving on your battle sword."

Zack pulled the blade free, holding it in the light. The priest nodded, and Zack sheathed the weapon.

The priest looked relieved. "I am Priest Jasper Trunnet. The Zenith Lord sent me with a flock of birds and something else." He looked between Zack and Kell.

"It's fine. Kell here is the inn's owner, and he can be trusted."

The priest reached into his robes, pulled out a packet with Master Gaz's seal, and handed it over.

"Kell," Zack said. "Can you find a room for Priest Jasper and a place in the stable where he can care for his birds in a safe place?"

"I can do that. Let me get the key and introduce you to the stable boy. He's a good lad, and will be glad to help you."

When Kell left, Zack leaned toward Jasper. "Do you have enough coins?"

The priest looked relieved. "If I hadn't found you here, it would be hard making it back to Elizabethville. I learned our coins weigh more than Hamptor's do. An innkeeper named Ballrand exchanged mine for theirs. Briggs said I could trust him."

Zack chuckled. "He did the same for me on my previous trip here. And yes, he's trustworthy." He reached into his purse, withdrew several silvers, and passed them over to the priest. "I assume our Zenith Lord wants a way to communicate."

"Yes, he does."

Kell returned and the priest followed him upstairs.

Looking at the packet, Zack knew a long afternoon awaited him. He carried it to his room, saw that Currat was sleeping, and opened it by the fireplace, resting in a plush chair.

As the sun waned, he pulled the cord next to the door and when the serving maid answered the call, he ordered lastmeals and wine for Currat and he. A sleepy murmur came from the bed. "Who came?"

Zack went in to sit cross-legged on the bed and explained the events of the afternoon. "I've ordered lastmeals, and I'm about halfway through decoding Jarod's message."

Currat smiled. "I can help with decoding and thanks for not waking me. I needed the rest."

Zack's smile showed equally warm. "The message is in five parts, and I've done four of them. If you'll do the last one, I can start on the second pass to join the many portions of one part with the fragments of another part. You know how to decode, but you still need to learn how to put it all together. We may be up until late."

Zack and Currat took a leisurely break for lastmeal and half a goblet of wine. Zack needed the break from looking at the myriad of code numbers. They talked about mundane happenings and observations since arriving in Hamptor, as they hadn't had the time or inclination to do so before. The fields remained rough with little growth; the water lanes feeding the crops, if there had been any, lay dry and crusted. Currat had turned into an excellent spy and noticed events differently than Zack. His mind, as quick as the other man's, sought other aspects of an event. They usually came to the same conclusion, but through separate routes.

Deciding to return to the decoding, Zack rose as a knock sounded. "A long night," he said.

Priest Jasper entered the room, looking like he missed little. "Have I interrupted something important?"

"We have a few moments."

The priest pulled over and settled on a smaller chair, motioning Zack and Currat to the plush chairs. He looked at Currat, "You must be Currat Duval. I'm pleased to meet you."

"And I, you."

"I won't take much of your time." He glanced at the decoding parchments. "I assume you have a long night ahead of you, and interruptions become bothersome. The Zenith Lord visited the crater for the first time since his son arrived. Unfortunately, he didn't stay long. He wanted me to come here with my birds to facilitate communication between you and him. I implanted homing directives into the birds' minds, and let them out every morning to get their bearings. They should have no trouble reaching the Seven Realms and the garrison at Elizabethville. I have five birds, and the priest at the garrison should easily send them back here, which means

I need a place the birds can return to. I understand this inn is roughly halfway to Ozlid. Will it do?"

Zack said, "Let me think on this, and I'll have a decision by tomorrow."

"Thank you, and my room is quite nice."

Zack returned the priest's smile and let him out.

"That's one problem solved," Currat said.

"Perhaps."

They proceeded to match streams of numbers, and then decipher the numbers into letters and letters into words. They finished near midnight, and Zack read through the completed document, handing each page to Currat when he finished with it. When Currat handed back the pages, Zack took them to the fireplace and threw them in, watching as the parchment turned black and finally, to white ash, leaving not a scrap to read. He stirred the fire and added wood for the rest of the evening.

It took a long time to find sleep and they tossed and turned most of the night, occasionally waking.

9

FIRSTMEAL did wonders to make Zack and Currat feel whole again. The serving maid passed by, and stated the ambassador slept well and drank two mugs of broth over the night.

"You need rest," Zack said.

"I'm on my way to bed," she replied. "My sister will sit with him now."

Zack smiled and handed her a silver coin. She seemed about to object, but didn't, pocketing the coin and walking away.

"That's good news," Currat said.

The priest entered the common room, looked around, and then started toward them. "May I join you?" His voice expressed kindness.

"Of course, Priest Jasper. We're finished eating, but this will give us time to talk," Zack said.

"I think I will do well in Hamptor," Jasper said. "My robes are different than those of Hamptorian priests. Nonetheless, they do offer protection. Not many here want to harm a priest of the Light."

"I don't recall seeing any priests here," Currat said.

"They don't show themselves much, and the meetings they preside over are almost clandestine," Jasper replied. "I met with one upon arriving at Hagan's End. I didn't divulge my real purpose here. He seemed genuine in his beliefs. I still asked him to keep my visit to him secret. He said he would. I wore my robes on the off chance you might see me and approach. I plan on changing later today to normal Hamptorian clothing. I've asked Kell to say I'm a bird trainer if anyone asks. After all, that's not far from the truth."

Zack chuckled. "I'd say that *is* the truth. This close to Ozlid is not a good place to make fervent prayers to Light's Source. I don't know if Wathdure could sense you, but it's not worth the risk. And I think you're right to change clothing."

"Can the birds make it to the Spires without stopping?" Currat asked.

"No. I've directed them to rest overnight outside Hagan's End. I do have one that would make it there without stopping. It has the longest wingspread I've ever seen. The Holy One summoned it. I must let it fly every day. Sometimes, it's gone until sunset. It eats fish, and I suspect it flies back to the sea to feed and then returns. It rides high air currents, making it hard to see. I'm to use it only for emergencies, when time is of the essence."

"It seems our Zenith Lord expects trouble," Currat said.

"It's better to be prepared, but I think you're right," Zack replied. "Jasper, Kell and his sons are trustworthy, and will keep you and your birds safe. You needn't worry when speaking with him in private."

"That's good to know," the priest answered. "On the way here, I only spoke somewhat freely with Ballrand, and that was only because of Briggs's recommendation, and the need to leave word for you. He told me you'd continued north."

The serving maid came to their table and Zack raised his hand for quiet. Her beauty shone through her smile. Wearing white like the rest of the maids, her raven black hair, pulled tight into a bun at the back left a striking impression; not severe, but showing off her high cheekbones, deep green eyes, and long eyelashes.

"What would you like to drink with your firstmeal?" she asked Jasper.

"Water will do," he replied.

Distracting from her physical appearance, her voice

grated on Zack's ears, sounding unusually high and sharp; he began to wonder how many serving maids Kell had.

The rest of the priest's firstmeal covered the news from Stonefire and the crater.

"You have dark grey robes trimmed in black," Zack said as the priest started to leave. "I've not seen that before, and I do have a message for Master Gaz and the Zenith Lord."

Jasper leaned over him and whispered, "I'm a warrior priest, trained with sword, short sword, knife, and archery since my Age-of-Man time. There are few of us now, but I'd not be surprised to see more very soon. What is the message?"

"Ambassador alive, recovering from treatment by Ozlidians. Juston Dowell traitor."

He nodded, stood straight, and left.

"It seems the Holy One is not wasting time training some priests, and that's good," Currat said as the priest walked out of earshot.

Putting on their cloaks, Zack and Currat walked outside. The crisp morning air felt refreshing. The inn's vents eliminated a lot of the smoke, much better than most, but the smell stuck to their clothing, annoying both men. The breeze wouldn't take all the odor away, but eased it a bit, giving the spies time to walk about and observe the happenings around the inn. On this morning, this consisted of a man looking at them, hurrying to his horse, and riding north at a canter.

"Again?" Currat asked.

"I'm afraid so," Zack replied. "I think it's time to ride south."

Currat nodded.

They found Jasper feeding the birds; with one cage's gate open. Looking up, the priest said, "I fed a bird, implanted your message, and sent it off."

A moment later, he released the largest bird the spies had ever seen from its cage. It soared high, huge wings catching an air current and leveling out—floating, but at great speed, south.

"Jasper, I wanted to make this our outpost, but it seems we're too close to Ozlid. I would like you to return to Ballrand's inn after you've rested here for a day. We have a few Ozlidians to kill first, and perhaps a traitor, and then we'll be heading south later today. Drawing any attention to Kell's inn with the ambassador inside is too dangerous for both. Don't speak of this to Kell or the twins until I've briefed them on what's going to happen."

The priest nodded. "I rather liked it here, but Ballrand's inn is nice, too. I'll be on my way in a day."

The spies turned and motioned the stable boy to saddle Spellbinder and Snowflake, but he'd already started lifting a saddle almost bigger than himself over a horse. The men helped, and gave the boy three coppers when finished, one more than expected. The lad smiled his appreciation.

The road north gradually improved as they traveled. Two miles from the inn, Men-in-Black approached them at a trot, from a half-mile away. Instinctively, the spies unhooked their battle swords in unison. The weapons swung down at their sides, ready for use.

"I'm tired of being on the defensive," Zack said. "Let's charge."

Currat smiled and nodded.

Guiding their mounts with their knees, both men drew their battle swords and reached over their shoulder to pull a dagger from their cloaks. They waited until the on-coming riders stopped a quarter-mile away before urging their horses into a gallop. One man seemed to be issuing orders when he caught sight of them galloping forward, surprise registering on his face. He hesitated a moment before leading his men in their own charge.

The leader, to his credit, rode in front. In a flash, both of the spies' knives flew through the air and ended their flights buried deep in his chest. He fell forward and his horse continued. Rocked by the gait, the man fell to the ground on Zack's left side. The large black horse kept going, its mane flowing upward, its tail out straight, spreading hair wide in a beautiful sweep.

The enemies started to slow, but Currat and Zack swept through them; blood gushed over black shirts from sword cuts on gurgling throats. The last man turned his horse and tried to gallop away. Another of Zack's knives slammed deep into his back. He collected the men's purses.

Currat sounded the strange whistle, calling the big blacks. When they gathered around him, he reached into his saddlepack and withdrew sweetstones. The stallions, having never been treated well and or given treats, sniffed the sweets and backed away a step, whickering nervously. Currat smiled and gently stroked them, whispering soothing words. He called Snowflake and gave the big black an apple, offering the sweetstones to his brothers. One horse took it out of Currat's hand, chomped, and then chomped some more before nudging forward for another. Currat sidestepped him and gave the sweetstones to the other horses. Soon, he had to mount Snowflake to keep from being knocked down.

Zack chuckled. "Creating monsters of your own?" He stepped in and took up the petting and calming words. When he, too, began to receive nudges, he led the stallions to low hanging tree branches and tied them. They had enough lead to munch on the green grass near them.

"I'm getting tired of stripping corpses and lugging bodies," Currat said.

"Me too," Zack replied. We'll leave them where they fell. We have their saddlepacks, purses and horses, and I have a use for them. Let's head back and make ready to ride south."

Movement in the trees caught Currat's eye. He dismounted, walked north a few yards and silently entered the woods. Shortly, a loud moan drifted from the woods. Moments later, Currat emerged, lugging a body behind him. "Didn't I say I was tired of lugging?"

"This one we'll take with us. Leave the rest where they lie."

Currat popped the moaning man on the head and enjoyed the undisturbed songbirds nearby. They strapped the unconscious man to a horse and rode south, leading the blacks. A mile from the inn, Zack asked Currat to ride ahead and have Kell meet him on the road.

Currat handed over the reins of the horses he led and galloped south. Not long afterwards, Currat and the innkeeper returned at a canter. When they reined in, Zack asked Currat to show the unconscious man's face to Kell. He looked.

"Do you know him?" Zack asked.

"Yes, he lives in the village south of here. He's not well thought of there."

"He's the man who informed the Men-in-Black of us," Zack said. "I'll take care of him. Kell, please take the blacks to your stable and put the saddlepacks in my room. Notify the priest that Currat and I will leave this afternoon. I'll explain after I take care of him." He pointed with his chin to the unconscious man. "Give me a moment, and you can have his horse, too." Zack handed the leads to Kell and pulled the man to the ground with a thud.

Kell grimaced, but took the horses' reins and turned to lead them south. Currat dismounted and went to Zack's side.

"Just one more lugging, and I hope we'll be free of that chore. I have his purse; we'll leave him dressed," Zack said.

Currat nodded. "I like that idea, and I like 'leaving him dressed' more."

* * *

ZACK and Currat sat with Kell and the twins in the deserted common room.

"It's not safe for us to stay here, and not fair to you and the inn's business," Zack said. "The Ozlidians will think nothing of burning you out to make an example. You can't fight them when they send a hundred men. The one thing I *do* need is to get the ambassador to Briggs's ship at Hagan's End. However, he won't be able to ride. Is there someone nearby with a coach we could buy or hire and a maid to tend to him on the trip?"

"There's Adel," Kerk said. "I don't know if she has the horses."

Currat chuckled. "We have four black stallions in your stable. They could pull this inn to Hagen's End!"

"I could spare the boys for a week, but no longer," Kell said. "I have a man who helps out from time to time, but he won't work longer than a week without starting to drink all the wine he can find. I'm sure Adel would loan us the coach. She never uses it any more."

Derk and Kerk looked surprised.

"Oh, wipe those looks off your faces. You think you're the only ones who bedded Adel?"

Now the boys looked astonished. "Da, *you?*" they said in unison.

"No, not me! Your mother would make you the new owners shortly after my cremation if that happened! Do you actually think I'd let my boys of fifteen summers spend the night away without knowing whom they spent it with? Adel assured me she would take good care of you and keep you out of trouble...and she has. She's a good woman, and I respect her. I think if you were not twins...!"

The stable boy entered, and ran up to their table. "Master Kell, if those big blacks—not Master Duval's horse, the others—if they're going to be here long, we need to arrange for more food and someone to help me with the grooming. They're...rambunctious."

The men at the table laughed or smiled or both. "Don't worry, they'll be gone soon," Zack reassured him. The boy nodded and hurried away.

"Kell, if it's alright with you, have your sons take me to Adel's tonight with the blacks."

Kell looked at the sun shining through the front window. "It would be better if you go now. She's not that far away. It would be quite late if you wait." The twins nodded.

The spies also rose and headed to the stable.

The boy looked up cheerfully at Zack while saddling Snowflake and Spellbinder. "You don't waste time."

Zack smiled back. "Not when I can help it."

The four men, each leading a black, rode out moments later.

Adel's home, located on a hill just before the village, looked large. She stood on a balcony looking down at men and horses. "Kerk, what have you brought me today?" she called out.

Moments later, they sat around a circular table, drinking cool wine. The tethered horses munched on green grass in Adel's spacious fenced yard nearby.

Zack observed the woman. *She is certainly beautiful!* He cleared his throat and explained all he dared, mainly why they would like to let Adel's coach.

"You are from Jewel, and you wish to send your ambassador, who the Ozlidians nearly killed, back there. He's bedbound and needs tending," she told him and Currat.

Zack nodded.

"Perfect!" she said. The men at the table looked surprised. "My dear horses were old and sick. They had to be put down; I cried for a week, especially when you two didn't visit!" She glared at the twins. "Now, if your friends from Jewel had come by..." She studied Zack and Currat with appraising eyes for a moment. "Well, perhaps not."

"I've never told this to anyone, but with my relationship with Derk and Kerk, I don't mind them knowing. I love them, and I know they love me…well, to an extent. On a trip to the border to find furnishings for the addition to my home—" She looked at the twins. "—you remember that time when I sent word that I was ill, and couldn't see you for a while." They both nodded. "The Ozlidian soldiers at the border beat and raped me."

Derk and Kerk stood up, knocking their chairs behind them.

"Easy, my loves," she said. "I'll eventually get my revenge, and I think this is an excellent way to start. The only thing I worry about is Ozlidians recognizing the horses."

"I can help with that!" Currat said. "You won't have a problem."

She raised an eyebrow. "When do you want to leave?"

"Tomorrow," Zack said. "By then, or no longer than two days hence. I imagine a rather large band of Ozlidians will be searching for Currat and me. I would prefer being farther south when that begins…and we still have to make preparations."

"What sort?" Adel asked.

"When I was wounded, I rode in a large coach with the floor built up to seat level to make a bed over half the interior. The same arrangement would do well for the ambassador, and then I wouldn't worry so much about him making the trip. Once he's on Captain Briggs's ship, he'll be fine."

"Derk, do you and Kerk own any black clothes?" Currat asked.

"Yes," Kerk answered. "Shirts and trousers. When Da decided to make everyone wear the same colors at the inn, he decided on black first. But, when all the Men-in-Black started killing in the area, he switched to white. The men still wear back trousers, but with a white shirt."

"Good. Does anyone know where I can get gold

ribbing for them?"

"Yes," Adel said. "In my sewing room."

Currat went on, "The shirts need to have a small rib of gold at the end of the cuff and where the cuff attaches to the sleeve. The top of the shirt must be altered to a band of material going around the neck with a golden fastener in its front center. It, too, must have a golden rib at the top and bottom of the band. The shirts are what personal servants and guards to very high officers wear. One of these men is an Officer of the Black, Saunderson. He's known for being ruthless and having officers and men who displease him disappear. He initiated much of the tortures used on men, women, and children. The only fortunate thing about him is his signature—it's unique, and on every set of orders coming from the palace. Every sergeant and officer has looked at it many times…and I can forge it perfectly. You'll carry a signed pass that will look real. It'll be worded in such a way that should scare the Seven Hells out of any Ozlidians in the military reading it. It's an unusual title, Master of the Black—like my father had—and is in the country's administration. All other ranks in the military at the officer level start with Master of the…and whatever color his rank signifies. My rank was Master of the Blue; it's the third level up of officers. Saunderson reports directly to Wathdure and Spercine."

"If my two lovely loves can get their shirts to me before sunset, I'll have them ready by morning, "Adel said. "I'll have my stable man start cleaning and polishing the coach today. I'll have the kitchen make food that will last over the trip and soups and broths for the ambassador. I also have a brace of knives I once threw with great precision. I'll try to get a little practice in before we leave."

Zack looked at the twins. "Now *that's* the kind of woman one of you should marry," he said, and chuckled.

"Oh, my dear spy, the three of us are already married

in all but being officially sanctioned, and sadly, that'll never happen."

The twins looked at each other and then at Adel, back at each other, then Zack and Currat, then each other again, and finally back to Adel. Kerk took Derk's hand, put his arm on his shoulders, and said, "She's right, isn't she?" After a moment, Derk nodded.

Adel slipped between the two tall, young men, and they swallowed her up between them. After a moment, the trio burst out in muffled laughter.

When the men left shortly thereafter, the home had already become a nest of activity. Adel gave orders efficiently, but with a voice that ensured cooperation and respect.

The twins didn't talk much on the way home. Kerk said he would take the shirts to Adel. Derk said they both would. Zack and Currat exchanged smiles while riding in front of them.

* * *

THE next morning, a magnificent black coach, trimmed in gold with black wormcloth shades behind the windows, rolled into the stable yard behind four magnificent stallions, with a mare tethered behind it. Adel's stable man set the brake, jumped down, handed the reins to the stable boy, untied the mare, and rode back the way he came, leaving the boy staring after him with an open mouth. The boy anxiously tied the team to the hitching post and ran into the inn.

Soon, Zack, Currat, the twins, and Kell followed the boy into the stable yard.

"Seven Hells," Kell said. "I knew Adel had gold, but not enough to afford something like this."

"I guess it's good Kerk and I are married to her," Derk said.

Kell's mouth opened, and then snapped shut with a smile growing across his face. "You do know she's almost as old as your mother, don't you?"

Kerk looked at Derk, surprise showing on his face, then shrugged. "It doesn't matter."

Derk nodded.

Currat thought, *I hope I look that good at her age.*

Working all day and late into the night, Zack, Currat, and the stable boy upgraded the inside of the coach for the ambassador, matching its overall elegance.

The next day, Adel arrived in time for firstmeal wearing a beautiful black dress that could grace any ballroom, making every woman envious of not just it. Her jewels, understated and expensive, added more elegance to the already-exquisite woman. She went directly up to see the ambassador. Returning a half hour later, she joined Zack and Currat, sitting down at their usual out-of-the-way table.

Currat looked at Adel. "She is stunning!" he whispered to Zack.

"You and the coach are magnificent, and yes, I know you far exceed the coach in elegance and beauty," Zack said.

Looking at Currat, Adel asked, "Does he speak to you that way?"

Currat snickered. "Not nearly enough."

Adel gave Zack—who had the good sense to stay quiet—a withering stare.

Derk and Kerk arrived a little later, both, looking a little rumpled and sleepy.

Zack looked at Adel with a raised eyebrow. She shrugged and smiled, leaving no doubt the twins had had a good, but busy night.

Kell arrived soon after, looking smug. "I've prepared an exceptional firstmeal in honor of my new daughter-in-law." He gave Adel a warm smile that took any sarcasm away. "Seriously Adel, I'm happy that you make the boys happy, and as long as you're content too, I have no problem with them being with or living with you.

Although, as you know, they work long hours, but I'll see if I can alter that a bit."

"And how does your wife feel?"

Kell chuckled, and the twins paid rapt attention. "She nodded, smiled, and walked away. She'd come out, but you know how shy she is."

The twins heard their mother's call and hurried toward the kitchen.

Adel turned to Zack, giving him her undivided attention. "Zack, I brought a considerable amount of gold with me. I know the difference in the currency rates of our countries. I would like to take the ambassador to Stonefire. I've heard about the Spires, and I'd like to see them. Is that possible?"

"If that is your wish, I see no problem, since you've helped us so much. I'm sending a message to arrange a coach for the ambassador at Elizabethville. How did you get along with him?"

"He's definitely a charmer and, I would imagine, an outstanding diplomat."

"He is that," Currat replied. "Although, I doubt you'll need much gold."

"Oh, that's for shopping for me and my two men."

* * *

THE coach rolled out as the sun's first rays spread long shadows across the road. Zack had a weird feeling, remembering the same trip he took, badly hurt with Doris, the woman he'd rescued from murdering bandits, as well as her daughter Rachel. *I hope this trip will be as successful.*

He and Currat would shadow the coach and disappear if Men-in-Black arrived. Currat had worked long hours on the document, and knew it would pass inspection. He impressed on the twins and her not to speak to anyone unless there was no other choice. If accosted, the twins would stop the coach, jump down, and stand on each side of the coach's door, hands on the hilts of their swords. Adel would pull the black wormcloth aside and drop the window enough to hand the document to one of the twins, who would hand it to the leader of the men. They would see her face and little else inside the coach. She would give the men a contemptuous smile while they were looking at the document, which stated she and her party should not be disturbed in any way and alluded to dire consequences if these instructions were disregarded, worded exactly how Saunderson would write it, one of Currat's best forgeries, possibly. Zack smiled.

He and Currat would ride ahead and, if they didn't encounter any problems, make as grand arrangements as possible at the inns where the coach would stop. Zack thought the trip to Hagan's End wouldn't take more than a week unless they had to stop for the ambassador to rest. The old man seemed overjoyed at having a beautiful woman riding and tending to him. Indeed, Zack thought Adel's presence might be doing as much good as the healer had.

The twins drove the coach well, avoiding obstructions in the road. The large, thick wheels proved big enough to let the horses pull the coach out of the road ruts, and it also had an excellent metal spring system to smooth the ride further.

Zack stopped at the next inn, the Silver Bird, according to the neat sign swinging quietly above the door. Looking inside, he saw no one to concern him. The inn looked clean, and the common room well vented to clear smoke. Zack saw a man he thought might be the innkeeper behind the bar. He guessed right.

The man looked up when Currat and he approached. "Two ales for two thirsty men?" he asked.

Zack nodded.

"Do you need rooms?"

"We do," Currat answered. "But not for us. A very important lady is riding south, and she will need your best room. She is traveling with an ill man. Her guards will carry the man to the room, and they will sleep in the coach. You will need to take lastmeals and firstmeals to them. The lady and gentleman will eat in their room. Be sure they have the absolute best you can offer. They are not to be disturbed except for meals, arranging baths, and laundry. If their quarters have a connecting door to another room, that would be excellent. Coming and going from the inn, she'll have her two guards, but one will be carrying the gentleman. Four large horses pull her coach. They will leave immediately after firstmeal the next morning. If anyone approaches her or the gentleman, a guard will draw weapons. If whoever comes near doesn't back off, the guard will kill the assumed attacker. I repeat; no one is to speak or approach the lady and gentleman. They should arrive within the next hour or two. What will be your bill?"

The innkeeper looked shocked. "I...I'll...let me see," he stuttered. "The best room is twenty coppers and that includes the adjoining room; my best wine is the same, and I can assure the small cast is the best in Hamptor. I have special venison in my cold room for lastmeal and pork for firstmeal and for eight meals the price is twenty coppers with a discount. The baths and laundry for two is ten coppers. The fee for the horses is ten coppers, assuming you want extra oats and grains." Zack nodded. "All together, the bill is eighty coppers."

Zack laid a silver coin on the counter.

"One moment and I'll return with your twenty coppers."

"No need," Zack said. "Our demands are unusual, and we want to ensure you do everything possible to accomplish them. If you can improve on them, we'll pay the difference. The lady and gentleman's privacy *must* be provided."

"I can do better than that. If you wish, I can have a guard at the rooms' doors?"

"That won't be necessary. The lady is a master swordswoman and as deadly with knives; she carries six," Currat answered.

The innkeeper blanched. "I'll see the lady and gentlemen have the best care. Only my best serving maid or myself will wait on them. Will you be nearby, or need meals or a room?"

"Yes, we'll be close and no, we won't need anything except care for our horses, and they should have the same as the coach horses." Currat added ten coppers to the coin on the bar.

"My name is Jermone. May I have the lady and gentleman's name?"

"No, you may not, Jermone. As I said, they *will* have complete privacy. And, the lady is very beautiful. Upon seeing her, some men may act on an urge to approach, especially if they've had too much ale. I repeat: such a circumstance could be deadly."

As Zack and Currat left the common room, Jermone hurriedly gave orders to his staff, and sent for the stable boy. They walked around to the back of the inn. A boy of about fifteen summers ran to the back door. "I'll be back, soon!" he said.

The spies found the best stalls for the six horses, three on each side in the middle of a line of nine facing nine more. The spies moved Spellbinder and Snowflake into the middle of the ones they picked. Currat had trained Snowflake, but the other four blacks knew little more than normal movement of reins, and now a craving for sweetstones. They took the saddles off and placed them on stands at the back of the stalls, with saddlepacks over their shoulders. Zack looked up to the large loft filled with hay, and pointed at it. Currat nodded.

The stable boy returned as they started grooming the horses. "Sirs, I'll be glad to do the brushing."

Zack stepped out of the stall. "We picked the stalls on either side of our horses for the coach's stallions. They are as big as ours and are feisty. It would be unwise to put a mare in heat anywhere near them; I'd suggest another inn. They are more than strong enough to pull this structure down. If you talk quietly to them and scratch them, they will be fine. The black here likes apples. The others like sweetstones. Where will you put the coach?"

"Sirs, there is a barn behind the paddock, but I imagine it could fit here," the boy said, looking around.

"It will be tight, but here would be best. Two guards will sleep here. I wouldn't disturb them. You won't see us, but we'll be close. Do you have any questions?"

The boy shook his head.

The spies left to scout the area. They walked a few yards into the woods and circled around to where the trees thinned and the village began. They decided to visit the inn two blocks away. Its sign squeaked loudly—not a good sign. Surprisingly, the inside had clean floors with fresh straw, and the fireplace only emitted a small amount of smoke into the room. They took a table in their preferred place facing the door with their backs to the wall, battle swords athwart their laps. Soon, a serving maid came over and took orders for lastmeal and ale.

They watched the few tables with guests—an elderly couple, two men who looked like shopkeepers, and a young man that seemed to be drowning his sorrows with two mugs on his table. No weapons could be seen on any of the guests.

The innkeeper came over. "Welcome, gentlemen, I'm Dosset, the innkeeper. I don't allow weapons in my inn."

Zack and Currat stood, letting magnificent battle swords swing down to once more grace their sides. Zack pulled the sword's hilt up two inches showing exquisite emeralds across and below the guard. "Dosset, we are precious gem merchants from the lands you call Jewel. We wish to have lastmeals with no more than two ales each. Then, we'll move on. We will *not* give up our arms." Zack laid a silver on the table.

Dosset looked up to the spies' faces, both a head taller than he, and took the coin. "In your circumstances, I'll be glad to make an exception. The young man yonder is having troubles. He can get mean when he drinks. He's had his limit, and I'm not serving him any more. If he should give you any trouble—" The innkeeper re-examined the spies' physique. "—try not to hurt him too badly."

Zack smiled and nodded as the innkeeper moved on to his other guests.

The lastmeal proved to be good and plentiful, the ale full-bodied. With the food and drink settling in their full stomachs, Currat paid the serving maid, and they rose to leave. The young man got up, too, and moved unsteadily between the spies and the door. The innkeeper blanched, and came around the bar carrying thick wood in the rough shape of a sword.

The young man looked at Zack and Currat's stature and swords, then the innkeeper's stick, and stumbled back to his table.

When they reached the Silver Bird, they saw the coach's rear disappearing into the stable. They watched from the shadows as Derk carried Darius into the inn. Adel stepped out of the coach, taking Kerk's hand. On the ground, she kissed him lightly on the lips as he briefly hugged her. She stood there for a moment, smoothing the skirts of her long dress. While adjusting her bodice, Kerk tried to help, a mischievous grin on his face, and she pushed his hands away with a pleased smile. She fluffed her hair, and looked in the coach's window glass to check her face, which was still perfect, even at this late hour. Looking satisfied, she took Kerk's arm and let him lead to the back door.

Hearing shouts and commotion, the spies hurried to the door. Looking inside, Zack noticed not one, but two tables with four Men-in-Black each. One man in partic-ular whistled and yelled vulgar remarks at Adel. A door crashed open upstairs, and Derk half-ran, half-jumped down the stairs, sword drawn. Adel stood behind Kerk, a knife in her hand.

The drunk started forward. Adel's hand blurred, and the dagger blade sunk deep into the man's thigh. "You miserable bitch!" he yelled.

Adel looked at him with cold eyes while another knife popped into her hand from her sleeve.

"STOP!" A tall, lean man clad all in black started down the stairs.

"The whore knifed me!" the drunk yelled, struggling to pull the dagger free from tight muscles. His hand shot upward, blood dripping from the knife and spurting from his leg.

Zack recognized a major vessel had been cut, and shook his head. The spies had quietly drawn short swords in one hand and a knife in the other as they stepped a few feet inside the common room.

The raging man flipped the knife and threw it directly at Adel. Kerk's sword flashed, swinging upward. The knife sailed off into the rafters. Jermone hurried from the kitchen, looking horrified and raising a chopping knife.

The man on the stairs yelled once more, "STOP! I ORDER IT!"

The drunk labored beyond reason and limped toward Adel. Derk's sword rammed into the man's stomach and out his back. He put his foot up to the man's chest, pushed and watched as he sank to the floor, releasing his muscles hold on the bloody weapon.

The other seven Men-in-Black advanced with drawn swords. Their leader raised his hand and stepped toward Adel, unarmed. "You and your man killed one of my men. I think it's time you and your party died!"

Adel smiled.

The leader looked startled at her reaction.

Reaching into one of her dress' hidden pockets, Adel withdrew the parchment with ribbons shaking loose and flowing downward from its leather case. She handed it to the shocked man. He took out the scroll and unrolled it. Taking note of the seals first, he blanched, looking faint. He read the parchment twice then looked up with barely-concealed panic.

"My lady, please forgive my men. They've had too much to drink."

"If my dear Officer of the Black is away reviewing troops, I can relate this amusing incident to Spercine over tea as she parades her latest conquests in front of me," Adel said in a perfect Ozlidian accent. "My, how she loves those young men. My guards served her well for four years. You have no idea how many ways they can kill you. Our dearest Wathdure may even be present, but probably not. He's away so much, I think monitoring his men."

"My lady, please don't do this. It could mean our deaths. We've served well."

Two more black-clad men, obviously not hearing the conversation, rushed forward with swords drawn. They both fell dead at the same time with two identical daggers lodged deep in the back of their necks.

"You and your men grow tiresome," Adel said. Her knife lashed outward at the man standing before her, slashing his neck.

Two men advanced on the spies. They fell as two more daggers sank into muscled chests. One looked down at the hilt of the knife before he fell. The other fell before he could see what had killed him. The usual surprised expression cast on both their faces stayed with them in death.

Kerk took the parchment from the dead man's hand, rolled it, placed it in its case, and handed it back to Adel. The remaining three men made the mistake of drawing their swords, proving no match for the flashing silvery steel coming at them. They died quickly, after which Zack and Currat cleaned their swords on the black uniforms.

Adel and the twins casually walked toward the stairs, passing the astonished innkeeper. "Would you be so kind to take us to our rooms?" she asked, reverting to pure Hamptorian accent, which left Jermone looking more dismayed.

Zack stopped the innkeeper before he could escort Adel and the twins. "I told you, you would have trouble if someone came close to the lady. She has skills that surprise me at times. Have the bodies burned. Bring their saddlepacks to me unopened. Keep the scums' purses for your trouble. The leader's probably contains gold. Tell no one what happened tonight, and close the inn until we leave after firstmeal. I can tell the lady is upset, and that's not good."

Jermone hurried to catch up with Adel and the twins.

After checking on the ambassador, Adel joined Zack and Currat in her room. They could hear Darius laughing. She closed the adjoining door.

Zack looked toward the ambassador's room with a raised eyebrow.

Adel chuckled. "He wanted to know what generated all the noise. I only said, 'killing Ozlidians and he seemed to appreciate our efforts."

"I didn't know you could speak with their accent."

Adel looked at the twins. "My loves, you go on to the coach. I probably won't sleep until late. If you visit me, have the stable boy stay with the coach. It's a favorite of mine."

Kerk smiled. "What do you mean, *if?*"

She laughed and pushed them out the door.

Zack and Currat sat in the room's two chairs. The one lamp, turned low, cast the room in deep shades of browns and greys.

"You should have told us you could speak with different accents," Zack said.

"I see now that I should have done so earlier. I told you about my rape. What I didn't divulge is Saunderson was the man who captured and kept me for three years, using me as he liked. Spercine watched at times, while some of her 'boys' bedded me, two and three at a time. I enjoyed them, but I couldn't let Saunderson know. I think that's where I developed a taste for muscular twins. Spercine had a penchant for them."

"I know. Did some of the gold rings go where I thought?"

Adel laughed. "You *were* there. Yes, the ones in their crotch went where you guessed. Luckily, they took them off. Not the nipple rings. They loved having them played with by gently twisting and pulling. But you don't want to know Spercine's perversions. It's enough to say she has many.

"Saunderson liked the idea when I proposed that he train me how to fight. He took on the proposition with gusto, and nearly killed me in doing so. Three years later, I'd gained enough expertise that I could easily kill the average soldier. Saunderson thought I loved him, which amused me. He thought all the women he took loved him. The ones I talked to didn't, and there were several.

"The woman from his bed is how I escaped. Like Spercine, he'd let one who had greatly pleased him go with a pension. The one he released from service—a real tyrant to the rest of us—I killed and took her place." Adel spoke as if her actions were an everyday occurrence. "We had the option to take all our coins at one time, or spread the earnings out yearly. I told the goldkeeper I wanted it all at once, and followed him into the vault. I killed the letch and took several times the favorite's pension. The guards heard and saw nothing. I'd hid the gold in my dress's many pockets that I'd fashioned for that purpose. It's a wonder I didn't clink with every step." Adel's beautiful smile spread across her face.

"I knew I couldn't stay in Ozlid, nor did I want to. I befriended a Master of the Blue and we went to have lastmeal by the river away from the western fortress. He was a nice man, and hated the things Wathdure did. I didn't kill him, but I did drug him. I waited until the patrol passed out of earshot before taking his horse and weapons, packing some of the gold in the saddlepacks, and rode into Hamptor. I left him a note saying, *I could have killed you*. I don't think he ever mentioned me. No patrols sped south into Hamptor." She shrugged, as if it wouldn't have mattered if they came after me or not.

"My village is hard to find. It can't be seen from the main road. I settled there and built my house using all local people and helping many with healing and learning. The townspeople think me strange, to say the least, and I'm sure they've seen the twins visiting me. They aren't overly friendly, but they appreciate what I've done for them and leave me alone. I don't think they'll change their minds when the boys move in. I *do* love them deeply. They love only each other and me. Oh, I don't think they make love, but they do kiss." The smile reappeared.

"I'm telling you all this because I want you to understand, and possibly help me with them. I want to go to Stonefire and see the Spires. I also want to buy clothes for them and me...some jewelry, too. The things you can get in Hamptor are of low quality, and that's Ozlid's doing. I would love to take my boys, but it would put a hardship on Kell. He's a proud man, and he'd never take coin from me to hire men to take his sons' place while they're gone. I doubt the twins will be pleased, and I'd like you to help make them understand."

"I must say Adel, when you want to share a tale, you certainly know how," Zack said. The spies smiled and soon she did, too. "I don't think there'll be a problem with any of this. We often have visitors to the Seven Realms. The difference in currency usually drives them back, however. I can speak with my superior. We may be able to find a way to save you some money, but I can't promise anything."

"And yes," Currat said. "We'll help the twins understand. I'm sure they won't be happy, and neither would I if my lover went away for a month or two. There is a place in Hagan's End where your coach and horses will be safe and well cared for as long as you're away."

"You mean the stable behind the Tarnished Anchor?" Adel asked.

Zack laughed. "Are you sure you're not a spy?"

"We'll see what we can do for you," Currat said. "I imagine you'll want to see Darius before retiring, and we need some rest. We'll meet you at firstmeal."

As they left, Adel stopped Zack after Currat had gone down the hall. "I'd hate to hear that Currat is distressed over something."

Zack smiled. "So would I."

He joined Currat downstairs to observe the activity. The bodies had been removed and blood disappeared under soapy water and hard scrubbing. The wood would have to be sanded to get all the blood out and from the expression on Jermone's face, he knew it, too.

They found the twins in the back of the coach wrapped in each other's arms, snoring gently, the sound barely more than heavy breathing. The stable boy slept on a horse blanket stretched across some hay. None of them woke when they climbed to the loft.

* * *

BRYAN, while on an errand for Yasho, saw Synithy leave Zack and Currat's reserved room. He frowned. *Why is she there?*

10

ZACK And Currat woke early. After climbing down from the loft and knocking on the coach's door to wake the twins, they went into the inn to find a bath and shave. The room, located where Jermone had said, had everything they needed except hot water. They had bathed in too many streams and rivers for it to matter. The water didn't help much with shaving, but they knew that would happen.

Settling in the common room, they watched a serving maid taking steaming firstmeals out the back, returning with the stable boy and disappearing into the kitchen. Moments later, she returned, loaded down with two full trenchers of hot food and two mugs of ale. She set everything in its proper place. "I'm glad you killed those men. Four of them raped my best friend a few days ago," she whispered before hurrying away.

"Hamptor needs men to eliminate the bastards," Zack said. "I don't see a way to do that without the Zenith Lord's help. We have the gold to start and train many men."

"I think he'll listen and approve *something*."

"I do too, but when, and will it be enough? Does Ursel have the skills to train men here? Does he still want to?"

Jermone interrupted their thoughts, coming close to the table. "May I sit?"

Zack nodded.

He kept his voice low in the empty room. "You and the lady and her men helped Hamptor last night. The Men-in-Black run wild, doing whatever they want, and no one can stop them, or even tries. We don't have the weapons, nor do we know how to use them."

"How would you like to see that change?" Currat asked.

The innkeeper dropped his head and spoke softly, "I would like it a lot, but my friends and I don't know how. We don't have the gold to buy weapons, and we'd be outmatched anyway."

Currat gave him an understanding nod. "Sometimes change is already happening when you least expect it. We are returning to the Seven Realms, but there're many here who think as you. Find out who can be trusted. Test them carefully, to make sure they don't run to the Men-in-Black to sell your plans. You have the weapons from last night. Hide them away. Don't let anyone know you have them. Do many people come through here from Arestead?"

"Great Creator, no. Arestead is poorer than we are. To be honest, I'm surprised they still exist. The land is rockier there than here. They once traded their leathers with us for wheat and other foodstuffs. Now, what they have, they must keep. It's sad. Seven Hells, it's sad here, too."

"Remember our words," Zack said. "Don't take action, but be prepared to do so."

Jermone nodded and returned to the kitchen.

Derk entered and waved on his way upstairs. Moments later, he brought Darius down, one step at a time, gently holding him in his arms like a newborn.

A picture played in Zack's mind of the massive twins lying on either side of Adel. Glad he and Currat shared a strong, muscular build, but not the exaggerated physique of the twins, he smiled at his lover and sipped his ale.

Moments later, Adel floated down the stairs and swept through the room, giving the spies a brilliant smile and blowing them a kiss.

Zack and Currat clicked their mugs together and left after a last sip of ale.

* * *

THE next two days went well until an hour before sunset, when seven Men-in-Black stopped the coach.

The twins set the brake and jumped down to stand by the door, hands on the hilts of their swords. One man drew his sword and started riding forward. Zack and Currat hid within hearing range, their swords drawn.

The leader ordered him to stop and sheathe his sword. The man looked surprised, but complied. Riding forward, the man dismounted near the coach door. He looked closely at the twins' shirts. "You are the elite guard. May I ask who you carry?"

"You may not." Adel said in Ozlidian as she pulled the wormcloth back, showing her whole face. "You may, however, read this." She passed the message case through the window to him.

He took and opened the case. Unrolling the scroll, he looked first at the seals and lost the color in his face. He read the missive twice, just as the other had done. He rolled the scroll, slipped it back in its case, and handed it to Kerk, who passed it back to Adel.

"My lady, we would be pleased to form an escort to honor you."

"Thank you, but it's not necessary. I'll not bother you further."

With that, the twins climbed to their seats, released the brake, and guided the horses back onto the road.

As the coach moved away, the man who had drawn his sword rode to his leader's side as he mounted. "Why did you let them go? That coach would bring an excellent price. We could have taken the guards."

The leader sadly shook his head. "Did you see the gold ribbing on the guards' shirt?" The man nodded. "Do you know what it means?" The man shook his head. "Those men are members of Wathdure's elite guard, and are charged with protecting the most important people in

Ozlid. They know ways of killing you in a heartbeat that you would never even dream of. Would you like to know who signed her pass?" The man looked a little hesitant, then nodded. "It was a signature I know well, Officer of the Black Saunderson. I assume you know who he is."

The underling shook his head.

"Seven Hells, I command a group of idiots," the leader said. "He is the highest-ranking officer in the military, and reports directly to Wathdure and Spercine. I assume you know who *they* are."

The man's understanding dawned as his face paled and he sat open-mouthed staring at his leader, who slowly moved onto the road headed north. His men followed with a lot of talking.

The spies had heard and watched the entire encounter, hidden only a few yards away; their cloaks turned to the side that matched the brush around them, swords at the ready.

When the last man disappeared around the bend, they rose and Currat sounded a low whistle. Spellbinder and Snowflake moved toward them from the woods. Both nudged their owners for attention. They got it.

*　*　*

THE spies sighed with relief at seeing Ballrand's inn. The place should have been mostly empty during the midafternoon. They found the innkeeper wiping down the bar with a small tub of wax sitting nearby. He looked up and smiled.

Zack and Currat sat at their preferred table. A serving maid rushed over. "I can still serve midmeal, if you wish."

"We do." Currat watched the maid return to the kitchen. *She's not Loyl, but do I want to see her?*

Ballrand headed over, and Zack motioned him to sit. "It's good to see you, both of you, again. What's the news from the north?"

"More Men-in-Black filtering down, causing havoc,

killing and robbing. We took down several, but that is for your ears alone," Zack said. He went on to describe his needs for the ambassador and Adel. "They'll leave early at false dawn. I want to reach the Blue Sail by evening. The ambassador's health improves, but he's still weak. Ozlid's Men-in-Black nearly starved him to death."

"By the way, I assume you're looking for a strange man with a lot of birds?" Ballrand asked.

"He's here?" Currat asked.

"Arrived last night. Nice man. There's something calming about him."

"There should be. He's a priest of the Light," Zack said. "He'll probably change back into his robes tomorrow. Please ask a serving maid to fetch him."

As if on cue, the serving maid brought the spies' midmeals and ale. Ballrand sent her running upstairs.

"Have you seen more Men-in-Black this far south?" Currat asked.

"Yes, just in the past week. They don't cause trouble, and they behave. Two groups stayed a night and paid with vouchers. One man had dried blood on his shirt. He didn't seem to think much of it when I asked if he wanted it laundered, but the only man who spoke whispered to the man. The man shrugged and took his shirt off and handed it to me. As I carried it into the back, I saw the man speaking again. When I came back, a clean one had replaced the shirt. The man looked perturbed. The only man that spoke to me paid their bill the next morning after firstmeal and they left."

"The man who speaks is trained in your accent," Zack said. "The others are not; theirs is thick Ozlidian. They seem to have infiltrated much of the land we've traveled. They do rob and kill. I'm beginning to wonder if that is to replenish funds. Some seem to have vouchers while others don't, Kell told me."

"Kell! I haven't talked with him in a long while."

"His sons, dressed like Wathdure's elite guard, are

driving the lady's coach I told you about," Zack said.

Ballrand chuckled. "The last time I saw *them*, they came to about my knee. Kell has reason to visit Hagan's End every year or so, but not in the last three years. I have no reason to go north and I don't want to."

"The twins have grown a little," Currat said.

"Which reminds me, we've collected swords and black clothing throughout our trip south. They're hidden in the bottom of the coach. Warn your stable boy to stay away from there."

Ballrand nodded.

The priest walked toward the spy's table in his theological robes.

"Jasper," Zack said, "Please join us. Have you had midmeal?"

The priest sat in the one remaining chair, smiling. "Yes, in my room, thank you for asking. The birds are well. I let the big one out this morning. It flew straight toward the sea. I think it was hungry."

"The ambassador will be here later today. How did you get ahead of us?"

"I had my best bird scouting from above. It found a lesser-traveled road cutting across land and rejoining the main road a few miles north of here."

"*You talk with birds?*" Ballrand asked in disbelief.

"You've heard about our healers using a graystone to help in the healing arts. Some priests have the ability to place messages into a bird's head or retrieve one," Zack explained. "In rare cases, a priest can see through a bird's eyes. I've talked about the Stones growing in power. The priest's ability is new, *and* one he hadn't mentioned." Zack looked pointedly at the priest.

Jasper blushed. "Priests shouldn't brag!"

"There's a difference between bragging and saving lives," Zack said quietly. "We'll talk later."

"I hadn't looked at it that way. I suppose I could be of further use, but it requires a great deal of effort and I need to rest afterwards," Jasper said apologetically.

"We'll talk later," Zack reiterated.

The coach's gold trim caught Zack's eye through the window across the room. "Ballrand, we'll need some meat broth for the ambassador soon, and possibly a midmeal for the twins and a very beautiful lady."

Ballrand looked astonished. "Don't tell me you have a stone that can see into the future!"

"No," Zack said. "I just saw the coach go by the window."

Ballrand looked perplexed, and then laughed. The others smiled, and then laughed, too.

The back door to the stable yard opened, and Ballrand turned to look at Derk carrying Darius. He rushed forward to show him to his rooms, stopping suddenly when he saw Kerk and Adel. Catching himself, he rushed on, grabbing some keys behind the bar and starting upstairs. Derk followed close behind.

Kerk and Adel came over to the spies' table. Kerk pulled an adjoining table over and held the chair. She sat, giving him a knee-withering smile. Sitting on one side or her, she left a place for Derk on the other side.

Adel turned to the priest. "I hope to receive your blessing, Priest Jasper."

"You *and* your party already have it, my lady." Jasper looked pleased.

Zack reasoned he found that pleasure in priestly duties.

"How's your trip been?"

"The ambassador still improves and he walked a bit last night. I've heard sea air is good for recovering patients; I hope that's true."

Derk joined them, with Ballrand in tow. The innkeeper looked in awe of the twins until he saw Adel. Stumbling, he caught himself and sat. "My lady, tidings of your beauty preceded you, but I had no idea. I think you're the most beautiful woman to ever grace my inn, if I'm not being too bold in saying so."

Adel's laughter brought the pure tone of silver chimes to Currat's mind.

"How could such a charming compliment cause annoyance? Thank you," she said, looking at one twin and then the other. "My husbands to be, Kerk and Derk, I believe you know."

"The last time I saw them, they were skinny and barely came to my knee. Wait! You're marrying *both* of them?"

"Well, not legally. We love each other completely. There's no jealousy among any of us. Tell me, Priest Jasper, would Light's Source frown on our union?"

"That, dear lady, is a question for the Holy One, not a lowly priest. Our teachings tell us that the love you describe should never be discounted or discouraged, be it between a man and woman, or two of the same gender. Love is love, and in its unsullied form it is prized above all else. I've never heard of a case such as yours, however; hence, I suggest you look to your Holy One."

"Ah," Zack said. "Such heady matters before midmeal. Speaking of which, have you seen the man Darr and I introduced you to?"

"I thought you knew. He's upstairs, got here two days ago."

"Would you let him know I'll visit him in his room in an hour or so? Now, Master Innkeeper, I think Currat and I could use another mug of ale while I watch these tiny boys eat half the inn."

Ballrand left and Currat grinned. "Adel, it's good you have coins put away, or your *husbands* could make you a pauper by feeding them."

"Ha!" she answered. "We could always visit the inn. I don't eat much, and Kell is used to feeding my men."

"You needn't talk as if we're not here. We know how to earn money for food," Derk said.

"I know you do, my love. You both do. If it ever comes to that, I know I'll be well taken care of for as long as I live." She leaned over and kissed him. He seemed mollified.

Mmm, still a little young in his thoughts, Zack mused.

The conversation stayed light while Adel and the twins ate. As they finished, Zack said, "Boys, let's take a look at the coach."

Outside, the twins looked surprised when he opened the door and motioned at them to enter. They filled the coach, even with Zack sitting on the bed for Darius.

He looked them both in the eyes. "I know you both think you know a lot about women, but making love and knowing women are two different things. I firmly believe Adel loves you both, equally and very much. I think she's sincere when she says she wants to be with you the rest of her life.

"That said, women have needs few men understand, and that includes me. Adel wants to visit Stonefire, the capital of the Seven Realms. She will be gone for five to six weeks."

Both of the twins started to speak. Zack held his hand up for silence. To his astonishment, the gesture worked. He continued, "Her actions are no more than they seem to be. She'll buy some things she feels she needs, and probably something for you two, see the Spires, and return. She can buy things there she won't find here."

"But...but..." Kerk started.

"Don't try to understand her desire. They often make no sense to us men. Remember, she thinks you're going to take vows with each other, and I'm sure you will, and that each of you will mean them in your heart. Such a day is more important to a woman, and you know how emotional they can get."

The way the twins nodded, Zack realized they had discovered a woman's whims and desires made no sense to them.

"I think you'll be very pleasantly amazed when she returns. Let her have her way with the trip, and you'll probably have a night you'll long remember until she returns, then you might have another!"

Zack watched the twins for a long moment.

They both nodded, and Kerk said, "It will be as you suggest. Should we show our sorrow at her departure away from us?"

"Most definitely!" Zack said.

The twins followed him back inside. They went straight to Adel; each picked her up under one arm and moved away from the others. They brought her face to theirs, first one, then the other. The kisses lasted long, and passion reigned.

Finally setting her down, they both said, *"We'll miss you!"*

"Try not to stay too long," Derk added.

Adel nodded, her eyes moist. "My dear loves, I will hurry. Now, I must take care of the ambassador." She smiled coyly. "I'll take care of the two of you tonight."

Standing between the tables, Zack sensed the sincerity from each of them. He asked Ballrand for the room number Darr had taken. Currat headed for the stable while he went upstairs.

The Ozlidian immediately answered his knock on the door. "Zack, I was getting worried that you'd fallen on hard times."

Zack stepped back and looked Darr up and down. "You *do* look different. If I didn't know you were going to change your appearance, I might have not known you. The beard helps, and I don't remember seeing the style in Ozlid. But then, I didn't see many beards there at all."

"They're not restricted, just out of favor at this time. I'm glad you're impressed."

"We, you included, leave for Hagan's End very early tomorrow morning. You'll ride in the coach. I think the ambassador will be able to sit up for the trip. If not, he can stretch out on the seat and you can sit across from Adel. She's very beautiful, but leave her be in a romantic sense. The mountains of muscle driving the coach would become quite upset. Also, I wouldn't ask about her experiences with Ozlidians. But, you can tell her you stand against Wathdure's practices, and you want to free Ozlid of both him and Spercine. Heed my words well, and you'll be fine. She *is* very nice."

"I'll heed your advice. Is there anything else I should know?"

"If Captain Briggs's ship isn't at anchor, we'll stay at an inn. The innkeeper is a friend, and if he knows you want to fight against Wathdure, you won't have a problem. The ship's company is Hamptorian. Briggs will explain. You'll be fine; those men hate Wathdure."

Darr nodded. "I'm actually enjoying this. I know it's immature to call it an adventure, but I do feel like I'm starting a better life. I can no longer stomach what so many in the Army have become. They're evil, and you know that first hand."

Zack told him what had happened to Currat at the hands of the Ozlidians. "He doesn't like to talk about it, and I wouldn't bring it up. For future reference, he's a good man, and you could learn a lot from him. Being from Ozlid, you'll have things in common to discuss. I'd take it slow, and let him open up first."

The other man nodded. "I'm sure I could learn much from both of you."

On that note, Zack said his goodbyes and left to find the ambassador.

When he knocked on their door, he heard laughter inside. Adel opened the door with a smile. She waited until he entered and she shut the door before saying, "You wonderful spy. What did you tell my twins to make them understand so quickly?"

"Something you wouldn't understand, like I wouldn't understand what you ladies discuss about men. We would each think the other not sound of mind. Changing the subject, which I think is wise, will the ambassador be able to sit up tomorrow?"

"I believe so," Darius answered. "I did so today for a good while. Why?"

"There's an Ozlidian officer who believes the same as Currat. He's going to the Seven Realms to learn how to fight Wathdure. I believe he's sincere. Nonetheless, I *am* a spy. You needn't try to draw him out; in fact, that would be bad, but if he doesn't sound right in talking with you, I need to know."

Adel laughed. "Do you trust anyone?"

Zack smiled. "Currat; my superior, who you might meet and who the ambassador knows well; the Zenith Lord and High Lord Kyle Byrne; the Holy One; and a few others. Neither the ambassador nor I will discuss my superior or any of the others in any detail. I'm sorry, my dear Adel, but spies are spies. Perhaps my spymaster will turn you into one as well."

Adel laughed once more. "Now, I think that would be fun, but perhaps too deadly near my men."

"I think, with a little training, your men could be quite deadly themselves. That's something you might want to undertake. A couple of hours a day in weapons instruction might have many benefits and draw you closer together, if that's possible. I'm not sure it is; your love is plain to see."

Adel looked into Zack's eyes. "True love is easy to see, no matter the gender," she whispered.

A knock sounded behind him and made him start. Adel smiled before answering the door.

The twins rushed in. "Five Men-in-Black are downstairs!"

"Derk, tell the man in room four to stay in there." Zack went to where he could see and waited. The obvious leader seemed to have control over his men. They sat at an out-of-the-way table, talking. Once, the leader spoke for a long time, stopping only when the serving maid came near. After she left, he continued as if explaining something of import. His men all listened, saying little.

Derk appeared at Zack's side. "The man in room four wants to know if he can take a quick sighting of who's here."

He might know them. "Tell him to stay behind me until the timing is right," Zack said.

Moments later, Darr stood at his elbow. When the leader showed his profile, Zack nodded.

Darr stood beside him for a moment. "ZACK STAND. UP HERE!" he yelled.

Zack felt the beginning of a stab from Darr's knife before the Ozlidian's body rose into the air and sailed across the room to crash onto a table near the bottom of the stairs. The double agent's body landed face up, his neck at a strange angle and eyes wide in death.

As Zack drew his battle sword and short sword, wishing he'd worn his cloak, he looked to his side; Derk looked pleased at saving his hide.

The leader and his four men drew swords and advanced. Kerk appeared, seemingly out of the wall, sword in hand. He gave Derk his blade.

Adel materialized at the top of the stairs, also sword in hand.

Currat came in at a run, sword and short sword drawn.

"Derk, you two stay back and protect Adel." Zack saw the question on her face and winked where the twins couldn't see.

He took the steps two at a time and reached the floor as the leader lunged. Zack pulled away, catching the man's sword with his short sword. The clash of steel on steel echoed across the room.

Pushing up and around, the leader stumbled to the side, slightly off balance. He recovered and lunged again with his knife, keeping his sword free. Zack parried the smaller weapon and came around with his sword, connecting with the man's blade and sliding them to the hilts. The enemy pushed away, but not before Zack sliced into the leader's knee, feeling bone. The leader screamed, but didn't go down. One of his men, who reeked of sweat, pulled him back while a third man slashed his sword wildly at Zack.

Twisting around, Zack's short sword connected as he thrust back, sending the man's blade over his head. The smelly man helping the leader rushed forward and met Zack's sword cut across his chest. He parried and slinked underneath Zack's short sword thrust. Off balance, he fell toward the stairs as Zack came around, cutting across his dirty neck with his battle sword dividing bone. Smelly fell dead.

The leader tried to rise and thrust again with his sword. His knee couldn't hold the weight and he collapsed, shoving his sword into the calf of his other leg.

The third man, sword recovered, ran forward and stopped, looking down at the knife sticking out his gut; blood gushed forth. He fell forward, his body going into shock.

Zack looked up the stairs and caught a satisfied smile curling Adel's lips. He sought out Currat in time to see him nearly decapitate a Man-in-Black while his cohort lay bleeding on the floor, alive and moaning.

Zack covered the space between them and took Currat by the shoulder. "Are you hurt?"

Currat smiled and looked down. "No, but you are."

Zack hardly remembered Darr's cut. Now, he felt it. "It's not bad."

"Anytime you're hurt, it's bad," Currat said gravely.

Zack smiled.

Ballrand came forward with a basin and strips of cloth, Adel on his heels. She sat Zack down on a tabletop and took his shirt off in a fast, no-nonsense way. The cut, slightly below his bottom rib, didn't look too bad, and the blood had already lessened to a dribble. She folded a cloth from Ballrand and put pressure on the wound in a practiced manner. Waiting a moment, she took the cloth away. The bleeding had stopped. Taking a clean small strip, she folded it into a square and placed it over the wound. Then, wrapping his body with a longer strip and holding the square in place, she tied the ends. Two more strips fastened around him, and she looked satisfied.

"You are lucky," she said.

"No. Derk was there."

Adel looked pleased.

Ballrand sent his young son, Tad, away through the back door with his mother. "I'll pull a wagon around to the back. I assume you want to have the bodies cremated."

"No, I was stripping the bodies and leaving them in the wood for scavengers, but I left some by the road still dressed. We always take the horses and give them away or sell them. Now, I'm concerned. The horses are not common here and those having them might come under attack from the Men-in-Black."

"I wonder how many horses Briggs can get on his ship," Currat said. "I've been asked many times to sell Snowflake at ridiculous prices. If we could load them at night without being seen, they might bring a pretty, round gold coin.

"Ballrand, can you keep them here for two days?" Currat asked. "No, wait. Yasho has that warehouse he's not using, and it's near the quayside. The Men-in-Black are not as many in Hagan's End. Besides, if we leave them here, it could put your family at risk. This is too big a strategy to start now. It's going to take some planning. I suggest we take the tack and saddlepacks and set them free. That alone should cause some consternation."

Zack looked at his lover. "I knew I kept you around for a reason." He smiled and slapped him on his back. "Yes, I think we make a good team."

Currat smiled from ear to ear. "That might work if I could find a way to stop your snoring!"

"I don't snore, and you know it."

Adel chuckled. "You men are definitely men!"

"Ballrand," Zack said. "If you can bring that wagon around, we'll get it loaded. Look after Tad and your wife. They don't need to see this."

The twins already had pieces of broken furniture in their hands. "Sir, where do you want this?"

Ballrand shook his head and grinned. "If you'd stack them by the fireplace, it's the only use I see for them."

"Boys," Zack said. "When you load the wagon, take the purses and give them to Master Ballrand. If there are vouchers in the saddlepacks, give those to him, too. Any parchments you find, give to me."

"Ballrand, can you get your serving maids to straighten up the common room? You'll have guests soon."

"We'll do it," a female voice said from the stairwell. In moments, three maidens worked to make things right as the twins lifted two bodies at a time and carried them out the back. It didn't take long after the bodies were hauled away.

By the time Ballrand returned, the twins had given Zack a large purse full of coins and a large stack of vouchers. Zack gave them all to Ballrand when he came back into the room. His eyes widened. "Perhaps," he said, "we should do this more often."

Currat and Zack laughed. "I don't think so," Zack said. "All the bodies going out the back could dwindle your guests."

"There is that," Ballrand agreed.

An hour later, the twins and Currat returned from dumping the corpses. Walking in, nothing looked amiss and guests sat at tables, eating and drinking.

"Come to think of it, I'm hungry, too," Currat said. "I think it would be wise if we all ate in our rooms, however, or together in the ambassador's room. It's big enough."

"I like that idea," Adel said from the bottom of the stairs.

The ambassador looked pleased for the company and ordered a fine wine. Catching himself, he asked, "Can we afford it?"

"Surely," Zack said. "We have all these." He opened the saddlepack he'd brought with him and laid a large stack of vouchers on the bed. "Ballrand said he could use them."

Adel frowned. "We don't like them, but we're stuck with them. How is Ballrand going to use them?"

"Let's ask him," Currat said.

Moments later, Ballrand came with the serving maids to deliver six lastmeals of steaming stew. "I can sell them at a discounted rate to anyone going to the border to get whatever they can't get here. The Men-in-Black throw them around, and overpay as often as not. I have quite a collection. It helps me, and if I need anything, I can usually find someone to bring it to me. I haven't been to that accursed border in years. It's a long trip from here, and most people go in groups of ten or more for protection. About a month ago, a group of thirty made the journey with four wagons. I sold them a lot of vouchers, and they brought me the linens I needed. It works out."

"Well, it seems you'll have a lot more," Zack said. "We'd like your best cask of wine, and we have all these to pay you. Will it be enough?"

"Enough?" Ballrand laughed. "That would buy the whole inn!"

The lastmeal satisfied their hunger, and the wine started them talking about pleasant things. Zack and Currat listened as the ambassador kept everyone laughing with stories about things he'd negotiated; in some instances, leaving out the names of the parties involved. Nearby, the twins played a game with cards Ballrand had loaned them.

Adel patted Zack on the shoulder and nodded for him and Currat to join her in the adjoining room. Darius played with his wine goblet as if nothing had happened.

"How many fighters do you think can be raised in a year?" Adel whispered once they were alone.

"It's hard to say," Zack replied. "Once word gets out, there'll be a lot of volunteers and a lot to weed out. Some men say they can fight, yet faint at the sight of blood. Others could be spies wanting to sell information to the Ozlidians. We've already seen that on this trip. We have to be careful."

"At some point, I'd like to take a more active role," Adel said. "Some of the things I want to buy in Stonefire are weapons. My men need training. I'm constantly surprised at their speed for men so big, but they need to maintain their skills and learn new ones. A slow sword is a slow sword, no matter how big the man wielding it, but I think we should return before they come looking."

The three rejoined the others in the main room. The twins continued playing their game, and Darius had more wine in his goblet. He started a new anecdote that soon had Adel's clear, tonal laughter gracing the room.

Zack retreated into his thoughts. *Could Adel effectively run an operation? She might, if given the tools and training. Perhaps Gaz would be best to answer that question. I have a long night of report writing ahead.*

Currat helped, but Zack's thought became true, as he had said. Looking at the stars, he determined it was well after midnight, and he still had several pages to go. He had undressed and lay on the bed with a light blanket over him. Zack joined him, letting Currat's light snoring lull him to sleep.

* * *

CURRAT finished washing in predawn quietness before waking Zack. Ballrand delivered an early firstmeal of steaming porridge, eggs, a thick slice of ham, and fried bread as Zack dressed. "The others?"

"Serving maids are taking firstmeals to them now,"

Ballrand answered.

Currat nodded. Zack stepped forward and held his fist out to Ballrand, dropping a gold coin into his outstretched palm. The innkeeper began to object when he cut him off. "We've put you, your family, and your inn in jeopardy, asking you to engage in dangerous actions you wouldn't normally do. This will help you and your inn. It's given with our deep appreciation."

Ballrand started to speak, stopped, and started once more. "Zack, you, Currat, and any friends of yours are welcome here any time. I'm glad I could help." That said, he headed for the door, gently closing it behind him.

The twins stood aside the coach, waiting. Darius sat up in his lounging position. The stable boy had washed and rubbed the coach to a high gloss. He stood by, smiling. The spies mounted as Adel swept through the door. Derk helped her into the coach and got a kiss for his effort.

Zack placed a silver coin into the stable boy's hand, generating a startled expression. Before Tad could say anything, Zack motioned the coach forward and rode onto the road, heading south. The coach followed in predawn light. A hundred yards back, Jasper rode on the seat of his cart, his birds quiet. He kept Currat's pace without trouble.

Currat took the front and maintained a ground-eating gait. Zack took a position behind the coach. Due to Darr's timely demise, his absence left the coach bed available, without crowding, to Darius if he wanted it.

A mile down road, Zack noticed four big, black horses grazing on fresh grass. He smiled. *Can we start shipping them to the Seven Realms to generate funds for Hamptor and Arestead's benefit? Perhaps the Zenith Lord would want them for his top officers in the Guard?*

As the sun rose, they stopped to water the horses in a stream near the road. Jasper caught up and led his mare to drink. He turned as Zack approached, watching him closely. "A message?"

"Yes," Zack handed the priest a parchment with three lines of coded letters. "For the large bird. Time is important. Can you have it return to Hagan's End?"

"It can go there. The Blue Sail Inn is part of its memories."

"The crossing must take it a day, at least. Will it need water?"

"It drinks seawater."

Jasper turned to his cages and opened the bottom one. The bird waddled out on its duck-like feet, looking up at the priest, who knelt before it and gazed into its eyes. After a few moments of Jasper reading the message and relaying parts to the bird, it spread its ten-foot-long wings and, with a few flaps, rose gracefully upward. The magnificent bird circled once, gaining height, and then flew south. "It'll reach Stonefire in three days, rest a day, and return. I'll have to wait in Hagan's End for his return. I assume there's more to this trip than what we've accomplished."

"Yes, a good bit more. Are you ready to return to the crater this early?"

"Not in the least! I've been there for the last ten years, studying, learning to fight, sharpening my skills, and lately, teaching warrior priests. I love the tower, but I love seeing the world, too."

The journey continued at its fast pace, with Zack and Currat rotating gaits to save the horses and eating midmeal while riding. The non-appearance of the Men-in-Black gave Zack hope, not much, but some. Late in the day, as the sun disappeared, Hagan's End sprawled afore them.

Pulling up in front of the Blue Sail's massive doors made mostly of thick glass, Derk set the coach's brake. Darius had reclined the last few hours of the trip; but he still looked fine and said so.

A few moments later, Yasho rushed out. Seeing Zack and Currat mounted, he sighed deeply. "The last time you arrived with a coach, your wounds nearly killed you. I'm glad to see that's not the case on this trip."

Zack chuckled. "Me, too."

Kerk helped Adel from the coach, and Yasho beamed. "Lady Adel, how wonderful to see you. You look as beautiful as ever."

Kerk mumbled something under his breath.

"Yasho, it's good to see you, too," Adel offered. "It's been a long time. These are my men, Derk and Kerk. We'll need a large room with a large bed."

Yasho didn't blink, "Of course, my lady. And, I assume these are Kell's boys?"

Adel nodded, her eyes sparkling.

"If you boys will take Ambassador Openhand to his rooms and return, we'll take care of the coach and horses while Yasho whips up his wonderful lastmeals for us," Zack said.

The innkeeper gave a flourishing bow and rushed back inside. Kerk held Darius, and Derk preceded them to open doors. It didn't take long for them to return.

"Yasho is settling Adel in our rooms," Kerk said. "Darius has a connecting room. The inn is unbelievable. How long will we be here?"

"It depends on Captain Briggs," Currat said. "Yasho can tell us his destination and when he left. He should return in no more than four days."

As if summoned, Yasho burst through the doors. "Zack, the ambassador looks terrible. What happened to him?"

"Over lastmeal or later," Zack answered.

Yasho nodded, and returned to being an innkeeper. "One thing can't wait! Simmon Cusor! He's been here a week. Do you know the name?"

"I trust you've seen to his care as you would any guest," Zack asked.

"I hardly ever buy clothing for my guests. I couldn't have him running around like a street urchin!"

"Has he given you trouble?" Zack asked. "Has he wrecked your room? Has he behaved badly?"

"Well, no," the innkeeper admitted.

"Don't worry, my friend, he'll leave on Briggs's ship for Elizabethville," Currat said. "He's been treated poorly. He has fifteen summers, and he wants to go."

"Well, he has been well-behaved, and stayed in his room most of the time. And, if truth be known, I like him, and caring for him made me happy. I'll be sorry to see him leave."

Zack smiled. "We liked him, too. I'll visit him in a while."

Jasper's cart swung around the corner, and he set the brake behind the coach. "A fast trip. I enjoyed it," he said as he reached them. He turned to the twins. "Will you help me take the birds to the roof?"

The twins started unloading the cart, one birdcage at a time. Jasper led the way to the stairs behind the inn.

Returning, Zack led Kerk, who drove the coach, and Derk, who drove the cart. He sat on Spellbinder, also leading Snowflake to the stables behind the Tarnished Anchor. After settling the arrangements, the men walked the short blocks to the Blue Sail.

"Master Stand, do you think we'll have to fight to protect Adel?" Derk asked.

Zack looked the young man in the eye. "I think at some point in time, all of Hamptor will fight to protect their loved ones. Sooner or later, Wathdure will start capturing men and women to feed his necromantic army. Hamptor and Arestead will have to fight, or be devoured."

"What kind of army?" Kerk asked.

"Wathdure animates the dead and places simple commands in their heads, like kill Hamptorian soldiers," Zack said.

"What?" Derk wore a stunned expression.

"Currat and I saw many and killed one. It was one of

the messengers Wathdure sends to the forts at the border. Hope you never see one, and hope even more that you don't become one."

"But...but how?" Kerk asked.

"Through the use of the Dark's Source. It's gruesome; I wouldn't mention it at lastmeal. You might not want to eat. This could be a long conversation and I'm tired...perhaps another time. All I want to do now is eat and sleep."

The men joined Adel, Jasper, and Darius at a table for eight.

Adel said before anyone could ask. "Darius came down with the help of one of Yasho's men. He managed the stairs mostly by himself. I'm so proud of him."

Zack's attention was drawn to her pleased smile. *Her beauty would make anyone proud. I wonder if the twins know what a treasure they have.*

Yasho joined them then. "Do you know when Briggs is due back?" Zack asked.

"Well, I was right; I thought that would be your first question. He left yesterday for Elizabethville with a cargo of cotton Wathdure's men didn't find."

"Who looked?" Currat asked.

"The grower has plants in the flatlands fifty miles northeast of here. Men raid his crops twice a year. He harvested half his yield and dug the plants under. When the men came, all they got was half the pickings."

"Are the men dressed all in black?" Zack asked.

"From what I understand, yes," Yasho answered. "Their clothing fits a little loose from those monsters you killed here if what I heard is true, but yes, all in black."

Currat nodded. "The Men-in-Black are moving south. In the Seven Realms, we would call them bandits working under a central command. They travel in small groups from four to seven with one man as a leader who speaks in a Hamptorian accent; the men under him don't. They arrived at Ballrand's inn. We had to kill them, and a spy trying to go to Stonefire. That's only a hard day's ride from here. If they make it here, you'll need more guards, and you can't leave one alive if they make trouble."

"It's that bad?" Yasho said, shaking his head.

"I think you have about a year before they have enough men to do real damage. Wathdure has to train men in your accent, and that takes time. The men we've encountered under the leader are low-quality soldiers. One didn't know the commanding officer of Wathdure's military." Zack smiled. "The leader is a trained soldier, but the men below him hardly know which end of a sword to grab. *I wonder how long that will last? Wathdure is no fool. He'll eventually come after Ursel's groups, but when, or does he really care?*

Becoming more serious, Zack said, "At first we stripped them, burned their clothing, and put the bodies in wooded areas for scavengers. The last few times, we left them on the road and freed the horses, the same big blacks like Snowflake, which brings me to a question I'll discuss when Briggs arrives, but it'll involve men here, perhaps the ones that helped on my previous trip.

"At any rate, things are going to get much worse in Hamptor over the next few years. Wathdure wants to attack the Seven Realms whenever the first opportunity presents itself. Currat and I are not the only spies the Zenith Lord employs. Information comes from several sources." *Some only the Zenith Lord knows!*

Yasho lowered his voice, "I've spoken to those men. They want to fight!"

"Can you arrange a meeting for tomorrow night?" Zack asked.

"Yes."

"We need to set our proposed actions quickly," Currat interjected. "We must leave shortly after Briggs returns. We have a proposition we think he'll like, and you, too. But, one thing at a time."

Serving maids brought steaming platters of food and a

cask of wine. While eating, the conversation centered on much more pleasant subjects.

* * *

YASHO, Zack, Currat and the twins waited for the men to arrive. Adel sat in a corner of the room, having told Zack she had no plans to take part nor pledge her or the twins' involvement until they were fully trained.

A knock came, and the door opened to allow serving maids to bring mugs and pitchers of ale to the large table in a private dining room. One maiden carried a large goblet of wine to Adel, placing it on the small table next to her chair. The other maidens poured ale and they all left.

Moments later, the door opened again, and Sonkek Rus, Eckert Oldsi, and Bryan Daven walked in. Zack and Currat rose and grasped thick forearms with the men.

"Currat, you live!" Sonkek said.

"With you and the others' help, I did."

"And Zack, you look more fit than when I last saw you," Bryan added.

Zack laughed. "All I have now is a small knife wound that's healing nicely on its own. Now, there is a lady sitting in the corner. These two over-muscled lads protect her, although she can throw a knife very well. She and the twins will remain unnamed while we talk. There is a very good reason for it."

"I'm not sure what all this is about, so Zack and Currat, if you'd please explain..." Yasho said.

Zack nodded. "You have probably heard of the growing trouble with the Men-in-Black. They travel in small groups." He described the actions their enemies had taken, and how he and Currat dealt with them, giving details about the men's lack of fighting skills and inability to switch accents, except for the leaders. "We've killed several, but I believe many more will come and eventually reach here. They stay in small villages, and don't seem to go against men where they might lose a scuffle. They misjudged us completely. We're going to make a proposal to Captain Briggs. If he accepts, it might slightly change our plans.

"When these Men-in-Black are encountered, they must be killed to the last man, and their bodies stripped and dumped where scavengers will find them and their clothing burned. If you see a gold-trimmed black coach with the twins driving, both wearing a black shirt with gold ribbing at neck and cuff, don't approach unless they signal you. The lady will be away for several weeks, but you may see more of her and the twins when she returns.

"To reiterate, do not allow a single one to escape. We won't put plans in place for some time, at least a month or two, but I wanted you to have this information and find if you want to kill Ozlidians…"

Eckert looked at his cohorts, and they all nodded. "We do," he said.

"From our experiences when you helped save Currat, we felt you would. You men here, and possibly a few more, will become the foundation of what we do. We must be very careful. I could have died, except for the aid of one of the twins at Ballrand's inn. A spy attacked me, one I didn't expect. He had a perfect Hamptorian accent. I don't know if he lived here and sold information to Ozlid, or if he came from there. One Hamptorian man, selling facts to Ozlidians, warned them we would attack to rescue someone. You noticed I haven't used names for the twins or the lady, and I won't. That is something you need to copy. Outside this circle, if the men you encounter don't know your names, don't tell them, or if you must give a name, don't use yours. Once things start happening, you'll receive more instructions on how to stay alive. If you act now, there's a good chance you'll be dead when we return.

"One last point—as I remember, you men are excellent in fist fights, but not very good with a sword or knife. Is there is a sword master in the area? Can you get some training in weapons?"

Sonkek looked at Eckert. "Your uncle trained me in our military. Do you think he'd help us? I don't know how we'd pay him, but we'll find a way."

"I'm the way," Yasho said. "Zack and Currat have given me funds for this purpose. Don't tell the man where the payments come from, but it won't be a problem."

"Now, I have something hard for you to do," Currat said. "I remember being told you men like your ale. You can't get drunk in common rooms. When men drink, they talk, and at times raise their voices. Think back to the men saying something they would never do publicly, admitting to things that could get them in trouble if the wrong person heard them, including wives. It's going to be tough, but easier if you help one another."

Eckert looked at the others, "Can we manage it?" All three men nodded.

"Start your training. I think you'll find you like it more than you think. Currat and I may be gone for a while, but we will return." *If Gaz doesn't have other plans for us.*

* * *

LEAVING *again*, Bryan thought. *I wonder if Synithy will search their rooms. I don't like the idea, but should I say anything to Yasho?*

11

ZACK sat with Currat, watching Briggs's seamen reefing the sails. It looked like the captain had kept his word concerning the ship; it seemed new. Even from the inn across the seawall the decks shined, the sails gleamed bright white, and the brass sparkled in the sun. The crew wore matching clothing and looked smart. Briggs's captain's coat, the same color the seamen wore, had appropriate gold ribbing. His three-pointed captain's hat sported a long, black feather. Bronson, his first mate, was dressed in a more subdued version of the captain's garb, with a billed cap and no feather.

"Shall we make ourselves known?" Currat asked.

"We shall," Zack answered.

Soft breezes heralded the coming of spring during the walk along the quay, bright waves lapping at pilings creating a counterpoint to squawking sea birds. Crewmen swung to the wharf on ropes, and then caught the lines, securing the ship. The gangplank emerged, resting on broad boards.

"Permission to come aboard, Captain?" Zack yelled, catching Briggs's attention.

Briggs yelled back before completing his turn to see who called. "Zack Stand, you're always welcome on this ship, Currat also!"

In a few moments, Zack stood before the captain. "I know you're busy now, but I need a private discussion with you when you're done. We're at the Blue Sail."

"That would be most convenient. I'm starving for one of Yasho's midmeals, anything but fish. I can be there in less than an hour."

"We'll have a private room waiting with an excellent wine."

"Excellent wine? I'm in trouble now." Briggs laughed.

"When do you ship out?" Currat asked.

Briggs pointed toward the seawall, where seven loaded wagons began proceeding toward the ship. "Those will be loaded this afternoon. I'll leave on the morning tide."

* * *

YASHO opened one of his secluded rooms featuring a table for six and a fireplace with four plush chairs in front of it. Serving maids brought in two casks of wine, one red and one white, and placed goblets at each chair, next to well-rubbed platters.

"Yasho, can you join us? Is this your busy time?"

"I have my second running the kitchen and pleasing the guests. I had hoped you would include me."

"Yasho! No midmeal in a private room would be complete without you." Briggs beamed from the door. He moved into the room, grasping forearms with the others.

"Gentlemen, would you like to discuss our purpose before, during, after we eat, or all three?" Zack asked.

Briggs tapped a wine cask. "Perhaps before would be better."

Zack and Currat took turns describing their actions with the Men-in-Black. They left off on the subject of the horses. "What we want to know is," Zack said, "could you establish a trade between Yasho's men and buyers in the Seven Realms for the big blacks?"

"I've been offered a gold for Snowflake," Currat added. "I think you could find a market; probably less than a gold a horse, but close. In fact, the Zenith Lord may purchase all of them."

Briggs sat thinking for a moment. "The *Silver Dolphin* could handle ten mounts on a trip. How would we get them aboard without causing notice?"

"About five hours before dawn should be a good time

for that." Currat answered. "How long would it take to get them on board?"

"About ten minutes each, but I think I have a better idea. There is a spot, an hour up the coast, where the water is very deep next to a cliff wall. It's hard to get to by land unless one knows the pass between the huge boulders along the coast. I happen to know the way. We must wait for calm seas, but we would have the same wait at the wharf. I can buffer my ship from the coastal rocks with fenders. I've done it before. When do you think we could start?"

"As I see it," Yasho said, "you need to find your customers and I need to get my men in place. I know of a natural box canyon with grass and water where we can lead the horses. It's up the coast, too. We could easily build a herd and take them to the seaside as needed."

Zack nodded at Briggs. "It seems you and Yasho need to do some planning and see if this venture is possible. Now, let's eat; I'm starving!"

"There are several things still to consider, and I'm famished, too," Briggs said.

"Oh," Zack said. "You'll have another passenger as well. A young man of fifteen summers named Simmon Cusor. As usual, he'll go to the garrison."

Briggs stared at Zack for a moment, turned to Currat, and then slowly shook his head, a resigned smile on his face.

Yasho rang a bell and shortly, serving maids brought platters of delectable goodness—venison in a spicy mint sauce, leafy greens with small onions in a cream sauce, and a large root vegetable with butter. A sweet cake dripping with honey brought smiles all around.

After the serving maids cleared the table of empty salvers, with the sated men sipping wine nearby, Briggs sighed. "The more I think of this venture, the more I like it. I doubt we'll make a dent in Wathdure's herds, but it will give us an opportunity to make coin to be used in more decisive ways. Now, I must return to my ship and give Bronson and the crew time to rest—after the cargo is loaded, of course. Zack, do I need to see the garrison commander other than to present the lad?"

Zack smiled. Walking to his cloak, he pulled out the packaged, sealed accounts since the last report and tossed it to Briggs.

The captain weighed the bundle in his hand, his eyebrows rising in surprise. "Mmm, a lot's happened."

* * *

WITH Simmon Cusor's passage confirmed, Zack and Currat knocked on the young man's door. The lad grinned when he saw his guests. He ushered them in and sat cross-legged on the bed, giving his visitors the plush chairs.

"Are you still determined to go to the Seven Realms?" Currat asked.

Zack didn't think the youth's smile could get any wider, but it did.

"Yes, I've given it a lot of thought over this past week, and long before I arrived. A few things happened that make this choice best for me. My uncle got drunk and tried to beat me. He got in one good punch before I pounded him pretty well. Neither my uncle nor aunt said anything about it the next day. They doubled my duties, though, making me late for lastmeal, when nothing remained but scraps. Also, my aunt cursed me every day. My cousin stayed away; at least, something good came out of it besides my pleasure from watching my uncle bleeding on the floor. My aunt stopped washing my laundry, adding another chore. It became clear they both wanted me gone, and they got their wish. My uncle ordered me to go with him to Hagan's End to purchase supplies, as usual. When he went inside the warehouse, I went down the street and hid behind barrels where I could watch him. He cursed a lot when he realized I'd left. It took him twice as long to load the wagon as when I did it. Afterward, he took the wagon to the stables behind the Tarnished Anchor for safekeeping and stayed at the tavern. The next morning, I asked the tavern man what had happened to him. He'd slept off his stupor on the floor, and left straight away at daybreak; evidently without giving me a second thought. I'm glad."

"We are, too," Zack said. "I've asked my superior to put in a word for you with the Zenith Lord. I suspect he'll see to your education and training in a place that's good for you. You leave at first tide tomorrow morning on the *Silver Dolphin*; she's the big ship at the wharf. Captain Briggs is expecting you, and we'll walk you over in the morning. All your bills here are paid, and you should call for a serving maid to take your laundry out for cleaning tonight. Once you arrive at Elizabethville, you'll have a horse or ride in a coach traveling with the Zenith Lord's guardsmen to Stonefire. There, a man named Michael Gaz will take care of you and get you settled. Do you have any questions?"

"How can I repay you?"

"Study hard, mind your trainers, and stay out of trouble," Currat answered.

"I will, I promise. Will I see you again?"

"We get to Stonefire at times, but we usually don't have a lot of time. If you're nearby, yes," Zack replied. Simmon's smile became infectious. "You'll need to wake early. The first tide is before sunrise tomorrow and you have to pack your fresh laundry. I'll send a saddlepack for you to keep. Do you need anything?"

The boy shook his head.

Zack and Currat both offered their forearms. They got hugs and slaps on the back instead.

*   *   *

ZACK paced in his room while Currat watched from a plush chair. "You've done that long enough. What's eating at you?"

"Our original mission is over, and we haven't received new orders from Gaz. He should know what's happening from our last report, yet we haven't received a packet or message by bird. Going to Arestead is pointless. Do we stay here and continue organizing a resistance force, or do we return tomorrow? What do you think?"

"I think you're too captivated with fighting Wathdure at this juncture," Currat replied. "Besides, what exactly can we do? Yasho, Turlas, Cerrol, and the rest of Yasho's men have their own plans to accomplish, taking time and leaving us not much to do. *They* need to do this, not us."

Zack grimaced. "Why can't I see things the way you do?"

Currat smiled. "You want to get revenge on Wathdure and Spercine. I do too, but now's not the time, and possibly not the place. We don't know what new information Jarod might have, or Gaz for that matter. I think your desires are governing what you want to do rather than what is needed, and I've never known you to do this before."

"Why didn't you mention it earlier?"

"I would've later today. I wanted to see if you would work it out before now."

"My dear Currat, I just did with your guidance. I'll send word we're leaving tomorrow. I just hope Briggs has room for our horses. My head seems clearer, much stronger."

"Do you think an outside influence affected you?"

"Now that's a thought I'd prefer not to ponder on too much. I'll go make arrangements for all of us."

"I'll start packing saddlepacks."

* * *

IT took Synithy longer than anticipated to find Bryan's hiding place. The search proved worth the effort. He had saved much more than she thought possible. *Perhaps I should consider staying. No! He's good in bed but wants to spend money on things other than me.*

The door bar shook. WHO'S IN THERE?

Synithy recognized the barkeep's voice. Her mind snapped. *Nosy bastard!* She leaned out the upper window and looked for an escape. The sharp pounding on the door startled her, causing her to trip forwards farther through the smaller window, hitting her head and falling even more. She struggled, dazed, dropped the box containing the coins and sought to pull her way back into the room. The sharp pounding on the door confused her and she recoiled. Her scream cut off abruptly when her neck snapped on the hard ground at the back of the inn.

PART II

12

ZACK looked out over Elizabethville two hours before sunset, with Currat and Simmon beside him as they approached the coast. The sails billowed bright with the sun behind them. Sea birds made a racket low in the sky. The voyage, smooth and fast, gave him time to think. He shared his ideas with Currat and appreciated his perspective.

No message had come before they'd left. Neither of them liked not knowing what their next assignment would be, or where they might be posted. Briggs did have room for the horses, but not birds. Jasper would return in a few days, on Briggs's next round trip. The ambassador took the second guest cabin, with a daybed for Adel, and the spies took the first, both of ample size. Simmon bunked in a second cabin boy's cubby that was not in use.

As the ship approached the dock, Zack saw a coach standing by. *That's unusual. If it were for us, normally we'd find it at the garrison.* His curiosity aroused, he sought out the captain on the poop deck.

Briggs noticed him as he climbed up the steps to the captain's level, and came over.

"Are you expecting a coach?" Zack asked.

"No," Briggs answered.

Bringing the ship into port was a busy time for the captain. Zack left him to his duties and returned to the bow.

Currat had to hold up his hand to stop the onslaught of Simmon's questions and turn to Zack's side. "I take it the captain is not expecting a coach."

"No, and you read me so well, as usual. I suppose it's for the ambassador and Adel."

"I should, after all this time and what we've been through. Let's bring our gear up?"

"I don't know if it'll save any time, but we would be out of the way at the bow."

Currat signaled for Simmon's attention. The boy looked up at him with wonderment in his eyes. "Bring your saddlepacks up and wait for us here." The lad scurried below ships without causing a problem with the bustling crew.

Zack and Currat followed him down, swung on their cloaks, and carried saddlepacks—theirs and others'—back to the bow.

As they headed across the deck, Bronson stopped by. "Do those cloaks have an armory hidden away?"

Zack laughed. "Would you like to find out?"

"No," the first mate said, walking toward the main mast.

The ambassador came off in a carry chair supported by two large crewmen, with Lady Adel walking beside him, wearing a white skirt with a blue top that matched the sky. Briggs unloaded the horses next. The spies soothed them with an apple and sweetstones while yelling thanks to Briggs. Zack mounted, pulled Simmon up behind him, and followed the ambassador and Adel toward the coach. A few yards before they reached the coach, its door opened and Michael Gaz stepped out. Zack didn't like a surprise like this, and he knew Currat didn't either. The spymaster waved the crewmen forward, and they helped the ambassador into the coach.

Currat introduced Lady Adel to Gaz, who said a few welcoming words before offering his arm to steady her as she climbed inside. Gaz turned to Simmon and introduced himself. "You may ride in the coach, but if the ambassador becomes ill or needs to lie down, I'd want you to ride with the driver. Will you do that for us?"

"Of course, sir. May I ride a way with him now, sir?"

Gaz watched as the lad scampered up beside the driver before turning to the spies. "I know you don't like surprises, and neither do I. The Zenith Lord read your dispatches with interest. We agree with your assessments and conclusions, and he wants to discuss some alternatives with you. He's at the Silver Tankard."

"*What?!*" Zack and Currat exclaimed at the same time.

Gaz chuckled. "He's inspecting the garrisons in Stonecrest with Kyle. I think Franc Horn nearly pissed himself."

Zack whistled. "Seven Hells, Gaz, I nearly did! You shouldn't spring things like this on us. We have delicate hearts."

"Perhaps," Gaz replied. "But, for now, we'd better make haste to the inn." As the coach pulled away, revealing a guardsman holding Gaz's horse, he mounted and the three rode north.

Zack didn't notice the clamor of the open market as they passed. He glanced over at Currat who seemed deep in thought, letting Snowflake follow Gaz.

The inn looked different, somewhat smaller, but perhaps that was due to the ninety guardsmen surrounding it. *He doesn't like traveling with a large escort. Is this a small one?* Men stepped forward to take their horses to the stable yard. Snowflake reared, and Spellbinder followed, probably thinking it was a good idea. The guardsmen backed away. Calming their mounts, Zack and Currat dismounted and handed the reins to the startled soldiers. They took them, reluctantly, and led the now-docile stallions away.

A Lieutenant of the Guard stepped forward. "The inn is closed."

Gaz looked at the young officer. "Son, I'm Michael Gaz. Do you know what position I hold for the Zenith Lord who is waiting for me and these gentlemen?"

"No, sir." The officer looked unperturbed. Two

guardsmen behind him tried to hide their smiles, but not well enough. "I have my orders; no one may enter."

"I'll try one more time. Do you know the names and reputation of Zack Stand and Currat Duval, and have you heard of their famous cloaks?"

"Uh, yes, sir." The blood drained from the officer's face.

"Well, son, this is Zack and Currat. I designed those cloaks they're wearing. Now, we are going in, and if I have to, I'll call Jarod Greatstone out here and have you demoted to below private, if there is such a rank."

The door opened. "Did I hear my name?" Jarod stood there, in full battle dress.

"POSITION ON THE ZENITH LORD!" the officer screamed.

"Who sent you here, lieutenant?" Jarod asked.

"The...the garrison commander, Zenith Lord," the officer's voice quivered.

Jarod looked around. "You have ninety men here?"

"Yes, sir!"

"Well, lieutenant, Master Michael Gaz reports directly to me. Zack Stand and Currat Duval report directly to Master Gaz. These three men could kill or maim every single one of your men and probably not have a scratch on them. On my orders, Lieutenant, return your men to the garrison and thank the commander for her thoughtfulness. You're dismissed to duties."

"Yes, sir!"

Jarod sighed. "Gaz, one of these days you're going to give one of my officers a death attack."

"I know, my lord, but I seldom have time for fun," Gaz replied.

Jarod chuckled. "Well, after all the pranks I put you through, I suppose I can't scold you too much." The Zenith Lord's gaze settled on Zack. "Does my spymaster play jokes on my spies as well?"

"No, sir. I don't think he believes we have a sense of

humor," Zack replied.

"Is he right?"

"For the most part, sir."

"Well, come inside, and let's go over your reports. I'm very interested in some of your ideas," Jarod said as he led them into the main room. "I read your conversations with Darius before you arrived. His first-hand experience from the Men-in-Black greatly disturbed me. Are the underlings really that stupid?"

"It seems so, the *leaders* of these small groups are army officers," Zack answered. "From the age and demeanor of the men under them, I suspect they have no training except in bar room brawls. None I have seen showed much education. I got the impression a few might have been farmers.

"Sir, on my previous trip, I found many men convicted of crimes that were put outside the cities and society of Ozlid in a large area between the border and the other side of the mountains. Their families were sent with them. Wathdure allows them to return to society for actions performed on his behalf. I suspect that is where these subordinates are gathered. Some of the men are sent there on nothing more than the word of an officer and without a trial. You have families who have done nothing illegal living next to murderers and thieves."

"That does sound plausible, and almost a certainty. It's too bad you didn't catch one to confirm your hypothesis," Gaz said.

"We were able to interrogate two," Currat said. "Both seemed the kind to have committed major crimes. The spy who wanted to come here had an education, and held the rank of Master of the Blue, which was my rank. It's third up the ladder. I believe he worked by Wathdure's orders rather than coercion."

"I like the idea of forming a resistance to Wathdure throughout Hamptor..." Jarod began as the door opened and Ursel stuck his head inside.

"Come in!" Jarod continued. "I was about to mention your name."

"My Zenith Lord, Master Gaz, I'm honored to see you." Without a pause, he went to Zack and Currat, hugged them both. Upon releasing them, he said, "My friends, I hoped to see you when the Zenith Lord summoned me here." Turning to Jarod, he said, "How may I serve you, my lord?"

"It's my desire for you to serve me by serving Hamptor."

"I'd like that, sir."

"The reports of your training in both weapons and spy craft are excellent. I would have liked you to have another year of military practices, but Gaz tells me you're ready for what we have in mind."

Zack glanced at his Zenith Lord with a raised eyebrow.

Jarod chuckled. "Zack and Currat have just returned from Hamptor, rescuing an old friend and ambassador I sent there. They can tell you what happened. In their duties, they found other problems plaguing your homeland, ones that need our attention. They'll explain what they found, after which, I need to know if what they propose interests you. But all that can wait for a while." Jarod motioned for Franc, who sat nervously across the room at the bar. "Good innkeeper, may we have lastmeal and some wine?"

Franc nearly fell off his stool. "Of course, my Zenith Lord." Looking even more nervous, he rushed to the kitchen,.

Gaz chuckled.

"Ursel, how do you feel about Adel?" Zack asked.

"Fondly," he answered.

"Would you like to continue your relationship with her?"

"As friends, yes. I think anything other than that would bring down two very large twins on my head."

Currat smiled. "You'd be right about that. She's going

to marry both boys—well, so to speak. The three of them are quite committed to each other."

Gaz raised an eyebrow. Jarod smiled.

"Adel is here, upstairs, taking care of the ambassador. I think she'll be glad to see you," Currat went on.

"The night I spent with her changed my life so much for the better. I have Zack and the twins to thank for that experience. I have no intention of being more than good friends to all of them."

"Good," Zack said. "Why don't you go up and invite the ambassador and her to lastmeal?"

Ursel put on his *little boy* smile—one that somehow didn't look ridiculous on the huge muscle-bulging man as he went upstairs after getting the nod from Jarod.

"I never thought I'd see a larger version than you two, my best spies," Gaz said.

"He's a big man, yes," Zack agreed. "Nonetheless, he has a bigger heart, or did when I knew him a few years ago. Has he learned to put it aside when needed?"

Gaz nodded. "Indeed he has."

A quick squeak, followed by a generous laugh, sounded from upstairs. Shortly, Ursel appeared on the stairs, holding Darius in his arms like a babe. Adel followed, her face radiant and happy. Zack looked on with satisfaction. *This should be a pleasant evening.*

* * *

ZACK sat, sipping wine in his and Currat's room, catching up with Ursel's adventures since coming to the Seven Realms. The previous hours, mainly spent telling the big man what had happened in Hamptor, left him visibly depressed. Zack hoped speaking about his time in the Seven Realms would bring back his usual good demeanor. It seemed to have worked.

"Do you think the central men we have, Yasho with his men and the twins, will be enough to start your plans?" Zack asked.

"Don't forget Ballrand and some of the other inn-keepers," Currat pointed out. "They would be very good at supplying information. The problem is going to be monitoring the men and weeding out those who would betray us for any reason. Given the right inducement, good men will do many things they wouldn't normally consider. Wathdure and his men are very good at prying out weaknesses. There'll have to be a constant surveil-lance on those we choose.

"You must have a group of men you absolutely trust. As you form other small units to carry out missions, they should not know your names, or anyone else's unless they need to in order to finish their assignment. You'll need to disguise your intentions and way of life to exclude any suspicion falling on you or your inner circle."

"That could be hard," Ursel said.

"It needn't be," Currat said. "If I know Gaz, we'll be there to help you, at least for a while. I know you've had some training, but not nearly enough for this kind of operation."

Zack sat up in his chair. "I'll be back," he said, and then rushed out the door.

Ursel glanced curiously at Currat, who rolled his eyes. "Yes, he still disappears with no mention of what he's up to."

"The time I knew him, he was pretty unwell. I still don't know how he accomplished the things he did in his condition. And that goes for you, too."

Before Currat could answer, Zack returned. "Well, that's put in place now."

Both men's questioning looks focused on him.

"Oh," he said, "I asked Gaz if Jasper could remain in Hamptor. When he agreed, I sent a message for Briggs to tell him when he returns to Hagan's End. It seems we'll be here for a few more days. I think the ambassador and Adel will leave for Stonefire early tomorrow. Gaz has something in mind, but he wouldn't discuss it when I spoke to him earlier, downstairs. He infuriates me when he does that!"

"I know what you mean," Currat said, "I don't know *anyone* who would do that to me!"

"What?"

Ursel and Currat chuckled at Zack's puzzled expression. They continued visiting a while longer, until the last drop of wine dripped into Ursel's goblet, and the men went to their respective beds.

* * *

THE next morning, Zack and Currat listened to Gaz's information and plans an hour after firstmeal in his rooms at the garrison. Dressed in his unassuming way, in medium to dark browns, he would pass for a midrange merchant. Short, thin, average looking with wiry hair— few would suspect he could kill quickly and silently in many ways. Zack knew.

He appreciated Gaz's additions to his overall plan that he and Currat summarized with Ursel. They would have time on the ship to go over it all with the new spy on the voyage to Hagan's End. Ursel's excitement, infectious and troubling, concerned him.

"Currat, remember your enthusiasm and eagerness when you started your spy training?" Zack asked. The other man nodded. "It took a while for you to calm down and look more normal, as normal as we can with our horses and weapons. We must quickly ingrain those precepts in Ursel's consciousness; he already stands out as it is. We can't do anything about his physical attributes, but we need to tone down his demeanor, especially when working with prospective fighters. Otherwise he'll be hard to disguise when recruiting men."

Zack paused a moment, then continued, "I thought about his interviews being in a darkened room with lamps behind him, seated and possibly a murky wormcloth in front of him. He should sit and try to alter his voice, and it takes practice to develop consistency. Also, he should have an alternate way of leaving unseen. Can you think of other protocols he needs to establish his *net*?"

"He should arrive before the appointed time and leave after his recruit is gone. An armed man needs to be hidden in the room with him and another two or three outside to see the comings and goings. The horses or anything else that could identify the men must be out of sight."

"That's all good," Zack said. "And once he's accepted, his trainers must do what they can to mask their identity, and that will be hard."

"Do you think it wise to allow the recruits to form their own groups?"

"I think the only way is to keep their anonymity for this to work. Also, once a man is established, he needs testing on a regular basis by men he doesn't know over ales or other diversions. There's a lot to teach Ursel and our central group."

"That's a lot to learn in a short time," Currat said.

"Well, we have time to do it well, and we can always conduct some missions to test how things are going. I would like to find a place for the horses, and see Briggs's plan in action." Zack thought for a few moments before continuing. "Jarod knows about the gold from our reports. I talked about weapons for our men. He said he would send a few at a time, and, as usual, he's right. A large shipment could draw attention, and storing them would be a problem, along with possible theft."

"Let's go find Ursel and see if we can pound some dullness into him," Currat added.

Zack chuckled. "And, we need to find the Zenith; he's leaving for the garrison northeast of here. It'll probably be a while before we again see him. I understand Gaz will be here another day and then return to the Spires. I don't know how much time we'll have with him. I suspect he'll be closeted with Calbris for a while."

That drew a laugh from Currat. "I hope that closet has a big window in it. Poor Gaz might suffocate from the stench!"

13

BRIGGS shouted orders from the stern. Crewmen handled ropes and sails, easing the big ship into the current; the overcast sky seemed to give the sailors additional urgency. Nonetheless, the westward wind promised a quick crossing.

Three hours later, however, gale-force winds threatened to destroy the sails, and Briggs ordered them reefed. Still, the storm pushed them westward. A nearly horizontal rain made the men miserable and the deck dangerous.

Zack and Currat joined Ursel in his cabin. The young spy looked a little green.

"The seas getting to you?" Zack asked.

"Some, but I'll manage," the big man replied. "I'm a little uncomfortable, but I don't feel ill. I brought a bucket in…just in case…the crossing to Elizabethville would give me any distress."

"Smart!" Currat said. "Do you have any thoughts on the events we discussed?"

"I would like you or Zack in the room on my first few meetings with possible fighters. I'll have to teach others the characteristics of selecting fighters, and I want to feel proficient in what I'm doing."

"I don't think that'll be a problem, and it's a good idea," Zack said. "Anything else?"

"I thought I'd sit in a low chair or kneel before a table to make me look shorter. Six feet, six inches does stick out some."

"Some!" Currat guffawed. "We draw attention wherever we go, and we're four inches shorter. The average height of five feet, seven inches doesn't help. Many of the Ozlidian officers are taller. I think Wathdure uses his mind control to influence marriages, tall with tall. It's just an observation, but I wouldn't put it past him. Also, I believe he encourages certain men to join the army. I saw many who are not suited for the military, but wouldn't think of leaving. But that's another subject for another time."

The three continued talking until they began repeating topics, which signaled Zack to suggest lastmeal. Currat and he rose to go.

"I don't want to chance it. I should go lie down," Ursel said.

* * *

THE new, big spy shuffled toward his cot. *Am I really ready for this?*

* * *

ZACK and Currat met Bronson in the passageway. "I just came from your cabin. The captain would like you to join him for lastmeal. You may visit him now, if you wish."

"We wish," Zack said. "We'll see you there."

"How did you know I'd been invited?"

"It makes sense," Currat answered. "We've discussed some ideas that involve the ship and crew. I suspect he'd want your opinion."

Bronson only smiled and walked toward the upper deck ladder.

After a gentle knock, Briggs boomed, "Enter!" Seeing his guests, he went on, "Ah, I'm glad you can join me. I asked Bronson to dine with us as well."

"We know," Zack said.

"He told you?"

"No, we told him."

Briggs's puzzled look faded, and he pointed them to plush chairs with strange tables having high edges before them. The spies looked at them with mystified expressions. "These are bad weather tables. They lock to the floor, and the insets are for platters and mugs. The insets have water bases that allow them to stay level as the ship rolls. They work well, and you won't end up with your lastmeal in your lap."

Bronson arrived and took the last chair facing his captain, his pleasure showing.

Briggs had finished pouring wine when two crewmen brought in platters to join the mugs. Bright red lobsters stared up at those who would eat them. Carrots and peas filled out the rest of the crowded platter. The conversation remained on ships and previous crossings throughout the meal.

When sated, Briggs refilled the mugs and motioned them toward his desk, then pulled a cord. Moments later, while discussing how long he determined the storm would last, crewmen arrived, stacked the empty platters on the deck, unhooked the tables, and carried everything out. He smiled and pointed with his chin back to the plush chairs.

"Let's discuss horses," he said. "I spoke to Franc Horn and to the garrison commander about buyers for animals like Zack rides. I wanted to ask the Zenith Lord, but that proved impossible. The commander wouldn't let me near him. She sent me a message stating her ability to buy all that I could deliver at ten percent below the usual rate, and justified it by my not having to stable or feed the stallions until I found a buyer or hire a merchant to sell them and pay a commission. Naturally, I sent a message back agreeing to her conditions. I expect to have a contract waiting for me on my next trip."

"So, how many horses can we start loading and when?"

Zack smiled at the gold coins that must have been swimming in the captain's mind. "Crawford, I think we can round up ten or twelve fairly quickly. That's not my concern. We have to establish a highly-hidden holding pasture for them with water, see if the way to the sea is near and wide enough for them through the boulders, and try loading the first ones on the *Silver Dolphin*."

Currat nodded. "Timing is important. We need to know the tides' schedule and when to have them there. These steeds haven't been mistreated, but they haven't had a lot of care by their riders. They've never had apples or sweetstones or a lot of attention paid to them. Once they're assigned to guardsmen, their care will change for the better, *as well as* their attitude. Until then, they'll be skittish. A few days of good treatment will make your crossing better for them and you. Also, the ship should be tied up and ready to take them aboard when we get there. On the first few trips, unforeseen troubles must be worked out, and the procedures altered to accommodate the changes. It's a little more complicated than a normal cargo."

"Plus," Zack added, "the clandestine nature of this will benefit all of us. It's important that any members of your crew who talk too much in taverns be excluded. What we're doing is not illegal; the stallions are abandoned, albeit by dead riders, but prying eyes and loose tongues will cause repercussions we don't want, and could scuttle the whole venture. How do you plan on handling your crew?"

Crawford looked at Bronson and back to the spies. "I was afraid this wouldn't be simple. Bronson, I don't go drinking with my crew. What say you?"

"There are two I'd leave out of this. They are good seamen on a voyage, but one wouldn't be able to keep his mouth shut, and the other wouldn't stay sober. As for the rest of the crew, it's not easy to tell."

"Would extra coins make a difference?" the captain asked.

"To some," the first mate said. "But those are the men you wouldn't have to worry about speaking out in the first place. We've made the trip short-handed before. Determining the men to go is a guess."

"How much do you stand to make, and how much do you have to play with before the venture becomes not possible?" Zack asked.

"What have you in mind?" Crawford answered.

"Two crews," Zack replied. "The Aresteadian port is not that far away. Could you and the men you absolutely trust make it there and hire on additional crew. My understanding is vouchers are hard to come by, and more people are near going hungry. You should be able to find good men for a crossing. Would it take extra coins, and how would your regular crew react?"

"Most of the crew would like shore time," Bronson replied. "We've make trips to Arestead before, and the men didn't like it. When they went ashore, there was trouble, and not started by us. We would have a problem knowing whom to trust."

"A bad crew can wreck a ship, and I'll not stomach a bad crew on my ship!" the captain nearly yelled.

Bronson went on, "There is that fishing village two hours north of there. Some of the men there have worked on ships before—not big ones nor new ones, but ships. They rarely come down to Hagan's End, and if they are well paid and know talking will end the trips, they would probably work out. Captain, I think we'll have to talk to them first and determine the risk. You, the second mate, and me could make the trip without too much trouble using only top sails."

Crawford sighed. "I agree that is a better option than Arestead. Zack, whatever happened to just loading on some horses and transporting them to Elizabethville?"

Zack laughed. "I never said it would be easy. We can handle loading the stallions to the ship; you need to handle getting them to Elizabethville. We'll help as much as we can, but we know little of the men in Hagan's End or sailors."

"What would happen if you hired a crew at Eliza-bethville?" Currat said.

Bronson considered the suggestion. "That will work! With you, the second mate, and me, I know two men I'd trust. The seamen from Elizabethville will cost more. How will that affect the venture?"

Crawford became more excited. "With a smaller crew during good weather, not much. We'd have to make the extra crossing, that'll add two extra days. We could do it with two extra seamen rather than four if we take on extra duties. We will still make a profitable run...Zack, do you know anyone in Elizabethville who would know trustworthy seamen?"

Zack laughed. "I do have a certain reputation in some quarters. I think Franc Horn would know who to ask, and telling them I'm involved would provide some additional impetus for secrecy."

"We have a plan!" Crawford said. "We need more wine!"

"Will it help us sleep in this storm?" Zack asked.

"Most definitely," Crawford said. "I can't guess how you'd feel in the morning, though."

"I think we should take our chances with sleeping reasonably sober," Zack said. "A bad head on a rolling ship is not something I'd care to experience."

"Then my first mate and I bid you a good night," Crawford said.

With that, the spies returned to their cabin. "I hope the bird made it to Jasper before the storm," Currat said.

"Me, too. It'll be a nice surprise for Ursel."

* * *

THE sun shone brightly, and a comfortable wind filled the sails when Zack and Currat reached the main deck the next morning.

Walking to the bow, they saw Ursel looking out at sea. He pointed outward when they arrived. "Is that Hagan's

End?"

Currat directed his gaze at the hills behind a smudge on the horizon. "I believe it is," he said.

"It feels...strange," Ursel said as he studied the distant land. "I know I should think of Hamptor as my home, but I don't. I love my old country and people, but the Seven Realms is my home. I've learned more, done more and found better friends than I ever would have in my village. If I have the opportunity, I'd like to see my da and ma, but I don't think I'd want to spend much time there. We have much less in common now, and they would never understand what I'm doing."

"Ursel," Zack said. "We'll meet with Yasho, probably at midmeal. I want you to take charge of the conversation, explaining how you want things to go and what you need. I believe you won't have any problems, based on the long conversations Currat and I have had with you."

"Are...are you sure?"

"Very! The reports from your trainers indicate your competence for this assignment. We are here to help you when you need it. You'll eventually be the leader of this little war, one that may evolve into a large conflict. You should defer to us due to our experience, but it would be good to set the precedent that you'll take the lead in most matters. We'll counsel you as needs be, and do it in private. If you see one of us rub our lips, give yourself a way out of what you're currently talking about, and we'll advise you somewhere far from listening ears. We don't think it'll happen often. The main thing is that we don't want to contradict you in front of others."

Ursel heaved a nervous sigh and nodded.

Currat glanced at Zack, who smiled. "I'll return in a moment. See if we can have firstmeal on the deck. If we spill anything, Crawford would probably have us clean it, but that's okay."

Ursel grinned and set off to find the cook.

Currat also disappeared below decks, and as Ursel came back balancing three trenchers of food, he returned with a large bundle he set down behind him, sat with the others, and started eating without comment.

"Ursel, if you'll take the platters back, I'll give you this bundle when you return," Currat said after the last morsel of food vanished.

"Don't bother, I'm going that way," a passing crewman said. Reaching down, he took the trenchers with him.

Currat thanked him and passed the top part of the bundle to Ursel. He opened it, excitement spreading across his face. He stood abruptly.

"No, it can't be!" As he shook out the cloak, one knife slid free. With a grin, Zack caught it before it hit the deck. "It can't be!" the young spy repeated, swinging the voluminous garment over his shoulders. It came to an inch from the deck. He spread it wide, and then wrapped it close to him.

"It has many features I'll explain later," Zack said. "But now, you might want this." He proffered the lower part of the bundle to the startled young man.

Ursel unrolled the cloth, his face showing disbelief. He pulled free a magnificent battle sword with a plain scabbard to hide its cost, and gasped at the line of perfect rubies running across its ricasso. The sturdy stirrup hilt further disguised the sword's worth and also provided a brass guard, perfect for smashing a man's jaw.

"The sword is from the Zenith Lord," Zack said.

"The cloak is from Gaz. He said to wear it to keep you healthy," Currat added. "Oh, and be careful if you sleep in it at a cold camp; the knives are sharp!" He quickly showed Ursel all its hidden sheaths for some of the deadlier weapons, and pouches for equally lethal items and other things of value.

Ursel reverently fastened the sword to his belt, letting it fall inside the cloak. He looked almost dazed. Saying nothing, he pulled both spies to their feet and hugged them hard before starting to go below decks.

"That went well," Currat said. "I wonder what he'll do when he receives his next surprise."

"I don't want to guess," Zack said, wincing at his sore ribs.

By midmorning, the *Silver Dolphin* eased into her berth without a scratch, as usual. Sailors made her ready for disembarking and rolled out the gangplank. Spellbinder and Snowflake came off first, nudging their masters for treats. They calmed when Zack and Currat saddled them. The captain came over and observed Ursel standing next to them.

"Well," he said. "Have you two taken on a new jewel merchant?"

"That we have, Captain, that we have," Zack answered.

Crawford grasped forearms with the three men. "I'll send word when I have things in order for a stallion run." He returned to the ship and started issuing orders to unload a cargo of cloth.

Walking down the gangplank, Zack nudged Ursel to look toward the seawall. A stable boy led a large black stallion towards them.

"And this," Zack said, "is from Currat and me."

The boy neared and asked for Master Ursel. Handing the reins to a stunned new spy, Zack gave the boy three coppers and he rushed off.

"Go have a ride," Currat said. "Afterwards, take him to the stables behind the Tarnished Anchor and meet us at the Blue Sail for midmeal."

"The saddle, it's beautiful," Ursel said. He mounted. "I...I—"

"Go!" Zack said. "We have Evil to fight."

14

YASHO smiled as the spies entered through the glass doors to find a table set for midmeal. His eyes sparkled when he spotted Ursel following them, wearing a cloak of death, his posture full of confidence. He showed them to a table for six against the back wall, where all the spies could sit facing outward. While doing so, he grasped Ursel's forearm. "It's good to see you. I see you've advanced in the world."

Ursel smiled. "I had good training. The Zenith Lord greatly helped me. I'll remain after Zack and Currat leave, whenever that might be—probably not for some time. I understand we have plans to make. When can we start?"

"I think we're going to have our hands full!"

"No," Ursel replied. "We must move slowly, especially at first, but that planning process should start when you can arrange our central group to meet, preferably tonight in a private room or a large area we'll use as a meeting place and war room."

"War room?" Yasho nearly choked on the words.

"That's what this is, a war, albeit a small one at present," Ursel said. "Nonetheless, I understand these actions take on a life of their own, and we must be ready for it to happen."

Zack enjoyed the range of emotions showing across Yasho's face and body. "Ursel has indeed gone through much training. You'll find him more decisive than before." Currat seemed to agree with his sentiments, too, nodding firmly.

"I can see that, and I'm glad," Yasho said. "I may not be able to get all you asked for until tomorrow night, but

I'll try for tonight. Now, let's get some food ordered and I'll see to your rooms. I have two large ones with a connecting door."

Ursel nodded, and the innkeeper headed off to see to their accommodations.

"How did I do?" the young spy asked.

"Like you were born to do this, and I think you are," Currat said. "You know some of the men you'll meet with soon, but remember what we told you about them. The last time you met them, you were busy saving my life."

"I still have bad dreams about what they did to you," Ursel said in a hushed voice.

"So do we," Zack said. "They lessen in time."

* * *

YASHO proved his talent in facilitating occurrences in a short time. After the last lastmeal platters disappeared into the kitchen, he led men through a back staircase and knocked on Ursel's door. They entered as Zack and Currat came in from the open connecting door.

"I remember you, except two." Ursel approached the slightly taller of the men and grasped his forearm. "You are Turlas, I suspect." Stepping to the side, he clasped an outstretched arm. "And, you must be Cerrol. I'm glad to meet you."

Turlas and Cerrol looked up into Ursel's face, a bit of shock showing at his serious mien and obvious strength.

Very good! Zack thought.

The spies had brought the four plush chairs from Zack and Currat's room to add to the four in Ursel's room. Ursel motioned the men to sit, and he remained standing. He looked the newcomers in the eye and then began. "We must have a set of guidelines that may not be broken. The first is secrecy. If one of you talks to the wrong person about our affairs and is killed because of it, I'll be upset. But, if anyone's blabbering gets any of the rest of us killed, I'll care a lot and the one doing the talking, if he's alive, may not remain so for long. Each of you holds the lives of the rest of us in his hands and, more importantly, on your tongue.

"One of the first things to do is to find an obscure meeting place, one we can get to without discovery and one that is convenient on short notice. We need a short list of codes to use with each other, such as 'Did you see the sunset?' meaning, there's a meeting at sunset, or something along those lines. I'll ask Zack and Currat to work with me on establishing such a list.

"I want each of you to name three men who might like to kill some bad Ozlidians when we next meet. Remember, there are also good Ozlidians. Currat is one. His father and friends died while saving Zack. Unfortunately, you won't find many of the good ones here.

"Yasho, you know the city and surrounding area best. Would you please locate a viable meeting place, and devise a journal to keep records of our expenses?"

The innkeeper nodded.

Ursel reached into one of the secret pouches of his cloak and withdrew the gold coins Zack had given him earlier. "Here are five gold pieces to get us started." The newcomers showed their surprise as the gold clinked into Yasho's waiting palm.

"There is much to do. We'll meet again in two days to discuss our findings. Are there any questions?"

"Just one," Sonkek asked. "Who put you in charge?"

Ursel replied in a polite, unruffled voice. "Zack and Currat put me in charge because I'm a Hamptorian, and I'll be here after they leave for the Seven Realms. I have the training and know what must be done for success. Do you know anyone besides me that can devote full time to our efforts and who is qualified to lead you? Do any of you know anyone else with the experience to set up a spy and killing group besides Zack, Currat, and me?

"Uh…no," Sonkek replied as the others shook their

heads.

"There are other reasons. Who do you think will supply us with weapons to start? The Seven Realms. Who do you think is supplying gold for us to implement our plans? The Seven Realms. Who do you think will allow men or families in grave danger to survive across the sea? The Seven Realms. Do you think Zack and Currat are easy to replace? I can assure you, it's impossible at this point. Who took these valuable men from duties needed at home and sent them here to assist us? It was the Zenith Lord of the Seven Realms. Need I say more?"

Yes, he has matured, and learned much over the last few years, Zack thought.

Yasho stepped forward. "I think we should plan on meeting here in two days, as Ursel asked. I might not have found a suitable meeting place by then, and if not, we'll meet here. It should be at about the same time, and I'll bring you up through the inn the same way."

As the men filed out, Sonkek approached Ursel. "I didn't mean to upset you."

Ursel shook his head. "You voiced a valid question. I took no offense." They grasped arms, and Sonkek left.

When the door to the hallway closed, Currat smiled. "You did very well. How did you feel?"

"Nervous. I basically put into words the things we discussed. I didn't want to cover too much for them and *me*."

* * *

THE spies entered the common room, and Yasho rushed over to them. "You're a little early for midmeal, but I can have a mug of ale with you."

The three spies sat at the same table that Zack had begun to think of as his. After the serving maid delivered their ales and moved out of earshot, he explained the plans discussed with Briggs, ending with, "We need to see the area and plan the best assault. Do you know any archers that would meet our requirements for secrecy?"

"I can't go tomorrow, and I don't think I would add much if I did. Turlas and Cerrol should go, and I'll notify them when and where to meet you. The Arms Master I mentioned and his two sons are the best archers around here. An officer raped his wife and daughter at the border. They killed the wife, but the daughter escaped. She's never been right in the head since it happened. Will three be enough?"

"No," Ursel said, "but six will be. The three of us are good enough."

"I don't doubt it," Yasho mumbled. "The Arms Master's name is Cartel Yowell. We can ride out this afternoon. Don't expect the sons to say much."

The spies enjoyed their midmeal and waited until Yasho signaled them. Collecting their horses from behind the Tarnished Anchor, they rode northwest on a little-traveled road, more like a trail in the deep woods. They had to go around fallen trees that blocked the way at times.

After an hour of taking multiple animal trails, a large cleared area with three cabins, practice fields, an archery range and a paddock holding five horses came into view.

Yasho stopped them at the clearing's edge. "Cartel, it's Yasho with friends!" he shouted. "Don't kill us!"

A man of fifty-odd summers rode toward them. "I'm alone today. I have to be careful. Yes, Yasho, I recognize you."

"Nonsense!" Zack called. "Your taller son is about ten yards to my left and back a ways, and your other son is to my right at about the same distance. They would both have excellent targets if they could stay hidden."

The older man looked shocked, then angry, then smiled. "Come along then. You boys get back to the house!" he yelled over his shoulder.

Currat tried hard not to laugh, managing with difficulty. Yasho just shook his head, and Ursel smiled.

The ride down showed off the layout and development of land *and* a few traps Yasho must have missed.

They settled on a small porch. The sons entered the middle cabin without speaking. "So, who are your *friends?* Cartel asked.

Yasho spoke at length about the spies, what had happened to them, where they were from and their needs.

"All the Seven Hells," Cartel said. "*Yes,* we'll help you kill the Ozlidian scum." He glanced at Currat. "No offense."

"None taken; the men who do this are scum," Currat answered.

"Well, let's see if your *friends* are any good. I have to know whom I'm dealing with when it comes to fighting. Boys, bring bows and shafts."

The sons nearly sprang from their cabin and covered the distance at a near run.

"Who wants to go first?" the old man asked.

Ursel held out his hand and the taller son handed him his bow and three arrows. He looked around and spotted a man-shaped target some fifty yards away. Putting his cloak over one shoulder, he took aim. The arrow went through the dummy's upper left chest, and hit the tree behind it with a solid thud.

Neither the father nor the sons said anything.

Zack took the bow from Ursel. "I'm a little rusty." He took aim and let go. The arrow hit two inches to the left of Ursel's arrow."

Currat took the bow and his arrow hit between the two. He said nothing as he handed the bow back to the taller brother, who smiled. "You're all good."

"Boys, should we help them kill some Ozlidian scum?"

The sons looked at each other and smiled, their desire showing in their eyes before they returned to the cabin.

"Then it's settled," Cartel said. "Tell me when and where, and we'll be there." He started walking toward his guests' horses.

Yasho mounted. "I'll come back in a few days with a map and information on what we can expect."

"Good! The boys and I will take a ride up, and see the lay of the land."

"Actually," Zack said, "we're going up tomorrow to look for ourselves, meeting on the hill overlooking the town about midmorning. Captain Briggs and a few of his men will be with us."

Cartel thought for a long moment. "We'll be there."

The ride back went with little talk, although Ursel did address Yasho at one point. "When will you discuss training our men with them? If he and his sons are as good as you say, we need them as trainers more than fighters. Will they like that role more than killing scum, as they say?"

"I've known Cartel all my life. As children, we went to school together. He loved the army, and when they kicked him out and Ozlidians murdered his wife, he nearly died. His sons took care of him, and he recovered a little at a time. You'd never know it now, but he and the boys had a great gusto for life. Perhaps our venture will bring some of it back."

The four of them, more than ready for food and wine, took lastmeal in the spies' room with Turlas and Cerrol. They outlined the plan for the next day, as well as the objectives.

The men looked a little too excited to Zack. "We still have to be careful," he said. "Ozlid may already have men waiting there. Unless you want an arrow or knife in you, I'd be observant and quiet."

Turlas and Cerrol left in a much more somber mood.

* * *

COOL, crisp air blew in from the sea, lightly stirring the hill's yellow and blue wildflowers. The spies, Jasper, Turlas, and Cerrol, arrived first. Moments later, Briggs and Bronson reined their horses in from a canter. Zack

turned at the sound of horses riding hard and spotted
Cartel and his sons galloping toward them on stallions
matching Snowflake. *Ozlidian horses! We didn't see those
yesterday.*

The newcomers' longbows, loosely strung across their
backs, looked even longer than those he used in
Stonefire; the shafts, in quivers at their sides, the same.
Zack's own bow, made more for shooting from a horse,
hung with a full quiver behind the right stirrup. When
they stopped alongside him, he could see the horses had
not perspired. *The gallop was for show. Interesting…*

"Short bows, good on a horse if you know how to use
them," Cartel said. He didn't mention the hawk riding on
Jasper's shoulder without a hood, although he couldn't
hide his surprise at the battle sword showing beneath his
priestly robes.

"Currat's and mine are warhorses," Zack replied.
"Ursel's is in training. We can fire well from horseback,
although, Ursel will have a more difficult time, and he'll
shoot from the ground if the need arises. The bows are
thick, and the range is long. Our arrows have steel heads
and fly true. We like them, probably as much as you like
your longbows."

Cartel laughed. "I keep forgetting I'm with *real*
warriors. It's a pleasure to ride with you."

Turlas paced his horse next to Zack's. "Master Stand,
Cerrol said we would probably be outnumbered. He and I
aren't that good with weapons. How will we win?"

"Probably by ambushing them from concealment,"
Zack replied.

Trouble spread across the young man's face.

"Is that the way the Light's Source would want us to
kill?"

Cartel chuckled, earning a stern look from Turlas.

"The Light's Source wants us to defeat the Dark,"
Zack said. "There are *no* rules of war. Those are stories of
fancy men who've never lifted a sword in combat. You've

seen and heard the atrocities Wathdure and some of his minions did and are doing to your people. You know what happened to Currat; ask Ursel to explain his torture in detail, and try not to throw up your last meal. These men are evil. They do those deeds, or see them done without acting against them.

"The gold and weapons will give us a toehold of resistance to save Hamptorian lives. What we do in the next few days, if we're successful, *will* allow us to continue defeating Evil. Otherwise, some of your people will die, and many will suffer from the men we leave alive." Zack watched to see if his words had the desired effect; they did.

"We *will* be outnumbered. We must do what the situation requires to defeat the enemy. If you're that concerned, you and Cerrol should talk to *Warrior* Priest Jasper. He marches with our Holy One's blessing and guidance."

"As is our pleasure, Arms Master," Jasper said. Zack wheeled Spellbinder around and led the riders, using his knees to guide the big bay forward. He set the same ground-eating pace he used on long trips.

They skirted the forest for the most part, traveling through woods for short ways. Finally, they reached a point on the map he had memorized; a ridgeline, with the road passing between higher grounds the height of a horse. He stopped the column and nodded at the priest.

The hawk stared into Jasper's eyes for a long moment, and then took to the air. Zack used hand signals to instruct Cartel to dismount and water his horses at a nearby stream, the first one they'd seen in a while. To the rest of the party, he put his index finger over his lips. The rest of the men quietly followed Cartel's actions.

A quarter hour later, the hawk returned to Jasper's outstretched arm. Once more, bird and man looked deeply into each other's eyes. When the trance broke, Zack motioned the men close and nodded to Jasper.

The priest spoke in a low tone. Twelve Men-in-Black are in the next valley, in the open. One wagon, with a two-horse team and mounts for eight men, are tied along a tree line. The wagon is unhitched. There are no sentries, and there is a smoldering, unbanked cook fire in the middle of the camp. Six tents made from black cloth are set up in a line across the camp from the horses. The men aren't wearing arms. Behind the few trees is a rock face with large boulders, leaving few ways to retreat. The bird circled twice from a reasonable height for its eyes." He scratched the hawk's head feathers while talking and, as he ended the report, pulled a piece of chicken from an inside pocket and placed it in his palm. The bird snatched it without leaving a mark.

Cartel, his sons, Turlas, and Cerrol looked astonished, while Zack drew a representation of the camp on the ground.

"Cartel, I'd like you and one of your sons to cover the camp from the right, Ursel and the other son on the left. Currat and I will be in the middle. Priest Jasper and Briggs will guard the road with swords. Turlas, you and Cerrol will watch from behind the copse of trees at the top of the valley. You're to observe and when this is over, you'll write reports describing what happened, what you thought of the operation, and what you'd have done differently."

"But...but we want to fight!" Turlas said.

"And you will, when you know how to use those swords you're wearing. Right now, though, I need you whole and alive," Zack replied.

"Briggs, you, Bronson, and Priest Jasper will form a rear guard. Don't worry about protecting Jasper; he's a well-trained warrior priest, and can protect you if the need arises. Use the weapons you're best with in a fight. I know Bronson is good with knives, and Briggs, you're good with a sword. Keep it simple."

Cartel moved close to Zack and leaned close to his ear.

"A warrior priest who can see what a hawk sees; men wearing cloaks loaded with weapons—yes, I saw a few of the sheaths, probably not all—that someone not trained would never see, and colored to match their surroundings. Impressive," he whispered. "I think I want to visit the Seven Realms."

Zack chuckled. "Perhaps you will, one day," he said, then addressed the group, "Move to your positions and when you hear a hawk's cry, attack. I would like this ambush to go quietly."

Zack and Currat moved to the top of the hill and looked down into the valley—more of a dell—before each found a hiding spot on the road's opposite sides.

Once Zack had ensured everyone was in place, he turned back to Jasper and nodded. The priest concentrated on the bird for an instant before it screeched a startling cry.

Arrows flew.

Men-in-Black fell.

Blood soaked the ground.

Horses pulled at their leads.

A thirteenth man bounded out of a tent, a bugle to his lips. The horn's cry ended abruptly when Cartel's arrow cut through the man's throat. In less than a minute, the dell lay quietly in deadly disarray.

Zack signaled the men to reform on him. It took only a few moments. "Mount! Don't get caught on this narrow roadway. Turlas, you and Cerrol protect each other and stay out of the way. I suspect the men coming will be real soldiers. Bronson, how good are you with a sword?"

The first mate shook his head.

"Find a place where you can use your knives when we can determine their line of attack. We'll charge if they look like they'll come up the road. Keep close and wait for my orders. Jasper, can you connect?"

"I'll have to move off. The trance for that is deep." He urged his horse into the thickest foliage above the road, dismounted, and sat cross-legged. The hawk flew within a few heartbeats. It soared high and circled the dell twice, returning at full speed and slowing at the last minute to land heavily on Jasper's arm. He rode out of the trees to Zack, looking dazed. "Another twelve Men-in-Black are behind the boulders in a clearing. The passageway to the dell is narrow. A few of them argued and pointed this way. On the second pass, they mounted horses and started coming here."

Currat rode to the top of the hill, letting his head peek over into the dell.

Zack didn't need his partner's hand signal; he felt the pounding of charging stallions racing toward him. "CHARGE!"

He galloped toward Currat, who waited until they were side-by-side, and then spurred Snowflake into a gallop. They drew short bows and bolts, stringing the bows while guiding their horses with their knees. The first two Men-in-Black fell from galloping horses, one dragging against the ground, foot in the stirrup, blood spurting upward.

Ursel suddenly rode beside them, battle sword drawn. Zack and Currat barely had time to replace their bows and draw swords before the foe tried to surround them. Arrows from the hill took three more black-dressed riders down.

Zack caught a glimpse of Cerrol and Turlas riding toward the melee. *Young fools!* He turned back to block a downward flash of steel, then countered as Currat's sword stabbed through the man's stomach.

Briggs engaged a rider at the rear of the column and blocked a slashing down stroke, twisting about and burying his sword into the man's side, slicing through organs and sinew. Gore poured into the rider's hand, and a dazed look preceded a scream. Briggs twisted back, the movement blocking another rider, but not the flat of the man's sword slamming aside his head. He went down.

The rider turned about to finish the captain when an

arrow erupted through his left breast, the arrowhead clean, and the shaft running with blood. Dead before he hit the ground, he had voiced no sound.

Ursel parried a thrust; swinging in his saddle, he sliced through the man's neck. As he fell, Cerrol engaged another Man-in-Black not far away, his sword in an awkward position. Ursel moved to intercept the attack and glimpsed shiny metal coming at his head, a little too late. Ducking and rearing his horse, he forced it to come down on the attacker's stallion, his mount's hooves sliding off the other one's neck. The horse collapsed onto its rider's legs with the sound of crushing bones. His screams were cut short by an arrow buried into his right eye. Viscous, clear fluid streaked from the wound, with blood oozing down his cheek as he twitched, then laid still.

Cerrol lay motionless on the ground.

Turlas fought off an attack, but poorly. Ursel urged his mount forward, hacking his sword into the back of the man's head. As he slid off his horse, Ursel glared at Turlas and yelled, "Look after Cerrol!"

Two arrows from different directions pierced the rider closest to Currat.

Ursel and Currat rode toward a Man-in-Black, who dropped his sword, dismounted and lay on the ground. The dull edge of Ursel's sword rendered him unconscious.

Zack chased after the remaining two Men-in-Black. His knife struck home, deep in the back of one of the soldiers, causing him to slide off his stallion and fall. He did not rise.

Briggs, a line of blood across his face, rushed in from the left, barely controlling his mare, yet managed to shove his sword through the last retreating rider.

Zack and Currat rode to where Turlas knelt beside Cerrol's body. The young man looked up, horror filling his face. "He's dead."

Making the announcement seemed to change him. His body went stiff; his face masked his true feelings. Rising, he bent to pick up Cerrol's body, draping it over his dead friend's horse. Without speaking, he mounted and tugged the lead, guiding them onto the narrow road. Jasper joined him, talking quietly, their horses nearly touching.

They rode to the top of the hill, Turlas riding slowly toward Hagan's End, and Jasper returning to Zack's side. "I couldn't get him to talk. I gave them my blessing."

Zack nodded.

Ursel stood in front of the now conscious Man-in-Black. "Who are you?"

"Dannus."

"What are your orders?"

"To guard the wagons on the return trip to Ozlid. Are you going to kill me?"

"Your answers will determine if you have a quick, painless death or a long, agonizing one like other of your ilk performed at the border on crossed timbers, stripping skin and muscle off helpless men."

"I...I didn't do that!"

"You saw it!"

The prisoner hung his head. "Yes," he whispered.

"Are there more of you waiting for the ship?"

"You...you know about the ship! Ugh, no. My commander thought twenty-four men would be enough."

"Who would unload the weapons?"

"There is a hoist in our camp. The crew would fasten a chest at a time and we were to haul them onto the rocks. Wait...you know about the weapons, too?"

"What about the gold?" Ursel said—a question of his own.

Dannus looked thoroughly defeated. "It's arriving tonight. Is there anything you don't know? The first shipment disappeared, and another was hurriedly dispatched."

"How many will guard it?"

"I don't know. I assume twelve. I heard a Master of the Blue say that's the most men Saunderson wants to travel here at one time. The guards for the weapons were to ride a mile ahead and the guards for the gold a mile behind."

"Are there more men coming farther than a few miles north of Hagan's End?"

"No. We are to stay to the north, at least fifty miles."

"How many groups of you are there?" Currat asked from behind Dannus.

"No more than ten at—" Eyes wild, the man twisted around, yelling, "Currat!" He lunged up with near inhuman strength, reaching for Currat's throat.

Ursel grabbed Dannus' hair, reached under his chin, and sliced through sinew and bone, blood arcing to the side. He let go of the hair, letting the dying body fall.

"Well," he said, "that was quick and I assume relatively painless."

Currat smiled and slapped Zack on the back.

* * *

JASPER wrapped a bandage around Briggs's head wound, in case it bled. He raised his hands, palms up, silently mouthing a blessing.

Zack watched while eating bread and hard cheese, then rode around to the front of the captain. "Are you up for more fighting?"

Briggs looked up, life returning to his face. "Seven Hells, yes! I thought I heard the word 'gold.'"

Currat stepped up alongside Zack. "The gold, if we're able to hold on to it, is for funding our fight against Ozlid. Although, I suspect you'll be handsomely paid for voyages to and from Elizabethville, in addition to your commissions from the horse trade. I think now would be a good time for you to return to Hagan's End and bring your fighters back. We're about to have company, and I suspect the ship will be here within a few days, and we'll need supplies to augment whatever is here."

"Greed doesn't drive me. I know I'll make a great deal of coins helping you. I'll try to get back before nightfall. I'll leave Bronson here. If the gold arrives early, you'll need him."

Ursel came up beside them. "They have a good amount of supplies, but some of their cheese is moldy through and through, as is much of the bread. The ale doesn't smell right, either."

Briggs sighed. "I'll bring a wagon back."

"It's only an hour past midday…an hour there, two hours loading, and two hours back. Zack said. "Do you think you can return by sunset?"

"I think so. I can get stores from Yasho quickly. Do you want me to bring his three men with me?"

Zack thought a moment before slowly shaking his head. "I don't know how they would react in a serious fight with weapons they're not familiar with. Also, that much gold might be a problem for them. While I know you're not greedy, I'm not so sure about them, yet. They did help rescuing Currat, but they didn't do much more than they normally do in a brawl. I think we should hold off until they've proven themselves."

"You may be right," Briggs answered. "How do you plan to subdue the men with the gold?"

Zack smiled. "With open arms, of course."

Briggs shook his head, and spurred his horse into a canter up the hill.

Zack signaled for the men to join him. They gathered around. "Cartel, I know you want to retrieve your arrows. Let me know how you stand with them." The arms master nodded, and took his sons with him.

"Jasper, do you know how far the sea is from us?"

"Perhaps two hundred yards past the boulders the Men-in-Black came through."

"Not enough to do what you're thinking, unless we can find rope in the supplies here," Currat said.

"Bronson, will you and Ursel please see what's here, and what might be useful?" The men nodded and headed off.

Currat placed his arm around Zack's shoulder. "One more fight done, another coming. Do you think we can take a few days to relax after this?"

"Do you really know what Zack thought about doing?" Bronson asked, drawing a chuckle from Zack.

"He wants to tie rocks around the dead and throw them into the sea," Currat answered. "It would take a lot of rope to properly secure the rocks, and we'd have to strip the dead beforehand. If they floated up wearing black while the transfer is happening, it might cause a problem we couldn't explain."

Ursel waved at Bronson to join him, and the two walked toward the tents.

"How do they do that?" Bronson asked as they strode away.

Ursel's booming laugh was all Zack and Currat heard.

Cartel approached, smiling. "We lost three arrows. We had four extra in our saddlepacks, which leaves full quivers between us. Here are yours."

Zack took the proffered shafts and passed them to Currat, who walked toward Spellbinder and Snowflake munching grass away from the dead.

"I assume this wagon you're waiting on will come up the same road," Cartel continued. "If it's dark and we're wearing black, we should be able to ambush them from the back once it crests the hill. Will the wagon be heavily loaded, or is it more maneuverable?"

"It'll probably be heavy, depending on how many supplies and gold it's carrying."

"Gold! Will we get some of that?"

"When you train Hamptorians to fight, you'll be handsomely paid."

"Good. I like training men and getting paid. The army didn't pay all that well."

"How would a gold coin please you for training five

men over three months, and another gold coin each time you repeat the cycle?"

Cartel chuckled. "I think I would smile a great deal."

"As soon as this is over, I want you to start training Turlas."

"Send him to me two mornings after we finish here. I'll expect him an hour after sunrise for firstmeal."

"Good!" Zack said.

Bronson and Ursel returned carrying three large coils of rope. "There's more," Ursel said. "A lot more. It must have been allocated for transferring the weapons and gold. They had only one wagon; space would be a large consideration. I don't know if it's wise to use it for the bodies."

"We don't have the time or the energy to bury them. Does anyone know the direction of the current from here?"

"The sea birds followed the coast south," Jasper said.

"Good!" Zack said. "The ship will come from the north. We'll throw the bodies into the sea, and let it decide what to do with them. These men were evil; they have no redemption coming to them."

* * *

THE sun caressed the sea when Briggs's wagon crested the hill leading to the dell. Ursel waved him forward, calling Zack and Currat as he did.

Briggs circled the wagon, stopping beside them. "I brought a half wheel of cheese, ten loaves of bread, cured venison, and a barrel of ale. I didn't know how long we'd be here, and I don't want to make this trip every few days."

Zack smiled. "I don't think we'll be here that long. If the gold comes on schedule tonight, the ship might arrive in the next few days. They hurried to get the second wagon here tonight. The ship could arrive tomorrow."

Two men jumped from the wagon. Briggs introduced

them. "This is Cursong, my second mate, and Massion, a crewmember. Cursong is fast, and good with a short sword. Massion uses a knife and his muscles. Both men have ample reason to hate Ozlid. They also know that what we do tonight will become very profitable for them in the future." The two seamen smiled. "What did you do with the bodies?"

"Stripped and in the sea," Currat answered.

Briggs nodded. "There's a southern current this close to shore, but I wouldn't be surprised if a few of them wash up in or near Hagan's End."

Zack assigned sentries on a rotating basis, while Currat and Ursel banked the fire pit and started a cook fire. Strips of venison soon floated on stout sticks over an open blaze. It didn't take long to heat them. Ursel took bread, cheese, venison, and mugs of ale to one of Cartel's sons and Massion in the trees at the crest of the hill.

Once everyone had eaten, Zack called Cartel, Briggs, Ursel, and Currat to him around the fire. "Briggs, I want you to scout the docking site from above. We need to know what will be needed to use the hoist, and the best positions for men to attack. Cartel, I doubt if all the crew will be on deck when they start bringing up the cargo for unloading. I'd like you and your sons ready to put arrows in the men climbing up from below decks. Currat, Ursel, and I will target the men already on deck. Briggs, you need to advise us as the attack happens; we'll need to know how to change our plans in midstream." Currat, Ursel, and Briggs groaned at the pun, while Cartel looked perplexed. Zack chuckled before continuing, "Our main goals are to take the weapons, keep the gold, and take the ship. It doesn't matter if we lower the gold first. If they want that, we'll bargain to lower half first, and the rest when the weapons are on land. I saw nothing in the parchments that stated the protocols for the transfer.

"We found torches in one of the tents. Briggs assures me the ship wouldn't dock at night so close to unknown rocks. Nonetheless, I wouldn't be surprised if she's sitting off shore, waiting for sunrise to come in. We'll need to get everything ready as quickly as possible at sunrise tomorrow.

"Tonight, I don't want to fight in the dark. I'd prefer to ambush the murdering bastards as they ride in. If we place the torches around the camp from the road when they make an appearance, they'll be in light enough to target. That prisoner said not more than twelve would be with the wagon. They lost one wagon. I wouldn't be surprised if many more accompany the second shipment. If we're that outnumbered, we need to shoot from the dark and not be lured into a swordfight until it's unavoidable. If the fight starts going in their favor, shoot the horses. The horses pulling the wagon should be killed as we start the attack. Hopefully, we can spare them, as they'll make up Briggs's first shipments to Elizabethville."

Briggs nodded.

"Cartel, did you ever use hay for fires in a battle?" Currat asked.

"No, but I always wanted to!" he answered.

"Let's bundle some hay and roll them into the torches as they get in the circle. That should drive the horses crazy. They'll spook and hopefully charge outward, setting up good targets. If the wagon catches on fire, it doesn't matter. We have more wagons, and gold doesn't burn."

"I hate losing the horses. Not because I'll lose cargo, but because they're such beautiful animals," Briggs said. "Can we try and save them?"

"Not at the cost of our lives," Zack said. "If we shoot fast and true, there'll be no need to harm them."

Briggs nodded, but the worried look didn't leave his face.

The call of a nightingale floated through the air. Ursel looked at Cartel. "The hay!" They rushed to the back of the camp near the picket line.

Massion ran down the hill, stopping in front of Zack. "Torches about a mile away, moving slow."

Cartel signaled to his son. They and Ursel ran to the hill with bows and arrows. Zack set up a blind at the back of the camp, with his cloak turned to the dark side. Currat did the same with his and climbed a tree, finding a limb to brace him when he let arrows fly. Tying a rope to the limb allowed a quick way down. Jasper pulled knives from his robes, sticking them in the ground behind a tree, and readied his battle sword, letting it hang freely against his leg.

The sliver of a moon disappeared behind black clouds, plunging the camp into near total darkness. The torches hurt Zack's eyes as he searched the camp for flaws, knowing they seldom became clear before the fighting starts. He wanted to join Ursel on the hilltop, but too few men covered the camp. A thought occurred to him. He ran forward, grabbed an unused torch, lit it, and stood at the back of the circle facing the hill.

Before long, the tips of torches slowly rose over the hillcrest. As a horse reached the top, Zack waved his torch three times. The horseman waved his in return. He slammed the torch into the ground, returning to darkness, and watched the wagon coming over the hill. *Seven Hells, there's twelve in front; at least twelve more will be behind it.* He was correct. Sounding a screech owl's cry, he loosed his first arrow into the leading man before the column. Men yelled, some screamed as they dropped, others made no sound as they fell from horseback.

A bolt from Currat centered on the chest of one of the two stallions pulling the wagon; he went down, adding an animal scream to the cacophony reigning over the camp. The traces pulled loose, throwing the driver over the wagon. The second horse, landing on the driver before recovering and bolting, left the wagon completely, blocking the remaining men and mounts.

The men on the hilltop brought down six men in rapid succession. The remaining six charged between the torches. Three dismounted, two, sliced through the fell dead. The four able men at the front of the wagon did the same, drawing swords and searching for their attackers.

Jasper sidestepped a slashing sword, leaving a small cut on his right arm. He swung around, blocking another killing assault. Recovering from a roundhouse swing, his block left his sword pointing down. He added force, driving the blade through the Man-in-Black's right foot; jerking it free, he slashed upward, deep into the man's crotch as his short sword sliced neck vessels open. He backed away, looking for another foe.

Currat slid down the rope and, laying his bow and quiver behind the tree, drew his battle and short swords, charging a black-dressed figure five yards away. Halfway there, the man turned, raising his sword. Currat's blade danced before him, crisscrossing the air. His opponent moved in, blocking an upward stab to the stomach and hitting Currat near the temple with the hilt of a short blade. He stumbled back, his foot catching in a shallow hole and sending him to the ground. His enemy lunged forward, sword aimed for his chest. Currat deflected the stab, rolled to his right and dropped his short sword. While his attacker repositioned for another thrust, his hand flashed to the shoulder flap on his cloak, pulling a knife from its scabbard and sending it into the man's chest in one smooth motion.

Zack moved in on the last two aggressors with his battle sword ready. Too late, he couldn't keep Massion from taking a sword in his side, felling the big man. Zack yelled, and the two turned on him.

He dodged a sword slash from the first as the second man circled around behind him. Pulling away, he left the two facing each other three yards apart and charged, first to the man on his right and then, twisting half around, he plunged his sword into the second man's chest. Holding his sword to the side, he tumbled and rolled to his feet as a sword thrust through the air where he had just stood. Zack slashed across the man's chest, then stepped back and sank his steel deep, pushing through stomach and bone. The Ozlidian fell backward, his legs jerking wildly until death stilled them.

Briggs simply walked up behind a Man-in-Black and stabbed him in the back. As the dying man fell forward, he jerked his sword free and drove it through the back of the man's neck. Looking around, he stepped toward another darkly dressed man facing away from him. Before the captain could reach him, an arrow sliced through the Ozlidian's tissue and bone of his neck, gore dripping from the arrowhead's point.

The last Man-in-Black ran toward a horse. As he mounted it, Cartel's arrow ripped into the man's chest, making him fall to the ground.

Jasper rushed to Zack. "Massion is hurt worse than I thought. He needs to return to Hagan's End tonight. We have two wagons. Send him in one. The driver won't have trouble keeping the wheels in the ruts. I've impressed on him the importance of lying still. He should be fine if we make a bed of hay for him to ride on."

Briggs had trotted to the two men and overheard the conversation. "Seven Hells!"

Moments later, Ursel, Zack, and Currat eased Massion onto a thick pillow of hay. Cursong finished putting a stallion in the traces and climbed into the driver's seat.

"It's a nasty cut, but the sword missed the major vessels," Zack told him. "Keep the horse at a walk and he'll bleed less. If he starts bleeding a lot, tighten the bandage over the wound, and see it that helps. Get him straight to the healer."

Cursong nodded, and eased the wagon onto the road.

Briggs stood watching the men disappear over the hill's crest. He walked to Jasper, who offered prayers to the Light's Source.

Zack joined them. "I've seen men come through worse," he whispered. Briggs nodded and walked away.

* * *

"**I** don't like stripping dead men!" Briggs complained to no one in particular.

"None of us do," Currat replied.

Ursel bandaged Jasper's cut bicep, finding the wound more serious than he first thought. The priest had said prayers to the Light's Source while the big man stitched his arm, not acknowledging the pain.

Ursel finished his wrapping, and tied a clean cloth in place. "You won't be able to use this arm well, and try not to use it at all until the muscle can heal."

Jasper sighed and nodded.

With the priest unable to help, the other six men made the eight trips required to throw the dead into the sea. Jasper didn't say any prayers over the corpses, knowing they were part of the Dark, and beyond the Light's reach. He collected saddlepacks, stacking them near the fire pit before leading the surviving horses to the picket line and securing them. Afterwards, Zack asked everyone to find black shirts and trousers to fit them in case they became needed. Ursel and he couldn't locate any in their size.

Zack approached Briggs. "Well, Captain, the picket line holds your first three cargos of horses for the garrison."

The captain grinned. "Perhaps I should have sailed here instead."

"When this is over, return with the *Silver Dolphin*, and we'll see them loaded aboard," Zack said.

"That will be a pretty sight."

"As pretty as the gold dropping into your hand?"

"No, not that pretty!" Briggs glanced up at the sky, where the moon peeked out of the clouds. "Do you think the ship will arrive today?"

"Yes, or tomorrow. Ozlid rushed to get the gold here.

We'll have to be ready. Now we need rest; it's not that long before morning."

Zack passed his hand through his hair. "How many leaders will be aboard?"

"At a minimum, you need four men at the wheel. They're usually four hours on duty and off thirteen. On the *Silver Dolphin*, it's Bronson, two boatswain mates, and me, but our trips are short, so it's not a problem. She's probably a three-masted ship. With a crew of twenty, more likely thirty, she'll have at least four men reefing the sails per mast, and another four on the anchor. A ship like her will take constant rigging to tack into the wind. One crewman will be watching the orlop deck to make sure she's not taking on water. My point is, the crew will be very tired after a two- to three-week cruise. Storms and docking take all crewmen on duty, and it's a very busy time, as you know. When the crewmen start dropping with arrows sticking out of them, it should be easy for pandemonium to set in, especially if those arrows are in their leaders."

"Let's hope for twenty and not thirty," Zack said.

"Or more!" Briggs added.

15

ZACK roused Currat as the sun forged a false dawn. They cleaned themselves up as best they could in the stream, taking the time to shave. Jasper spread hay for the horses. Briggs and Cartel's oldest son collected arrows and washed them downstream, near where the water disappeared below the surface. The arms master and his youngest son walked down the hill carrying four large hares. Seeing them, Ursel built up the fire and prepared skewers for cooking.

When sunlight glanced off dewy, shimmering tree leaves, Briggs hiked to the rocks above the sea, smiling when he realized the horses would fit between them. Upon returning, he reported to Zack and Currat. "I used my spyglass and searched the horizon north and northwestwardly down to a due westerly direction. I saw nothing to report except an absence of nude men floating in the water, which delighted me. I'll look again every hour." He turned and looked longingly at the meat dripping its fat into the flames as Ursel turned the spits.

Before the hour was through, only bones remained of the four hares, along with a few crumbs of bread, and a small piece of rind from the cheese. Cartel had already buried the skins and viscera before butchering them for cooking. Ursel smothered the fire.

The men climbed the passage between boulders to the sea, bringing bows and quivers. Reaching the coast, they found the hoist, and set it up with its ropes hanging toward the sea. Zack, Currat, and Ursel labored to load a large rock into the hoist's net and lowered it to the sea and back up. Satisfied it would hold chests of weapons and gold, Zack voiced the realization it would hold three

or four men as well. Winding the ropes for use, the men
watched as Briggs searched the sea.

He swept his glass north and then slowly to a
northwestwardly direction. He stopped, adjusted the
spyglass, and peered at the same place for several
moments. "She's a big ship, as I expected," he finally said.
"She's under full sail and, if the wind holds, will be here
shortly after midday. I suspect a ship that large will have a
company of thirty men, probably more. She has three
masts, and I suspect she's wide for cargo; it's hard to tell
from here."

"Is there an order we should follow in taking her?"
Zack asked.

"Yes," Briggs answered. "You need to wait until the
anchor is lowered and made fast. The men reefing the
sails probably won't have weapons; they'll be sitting
targets, and Cartel's sons should be able to kill them in
short order. The captain and his mates will be on deck.
Those are the first ones you should kill. Anyone taking
command must die first. When the men start yelling,
others with weapons will come up from below decks. I
would have most of your bowmen shooting at those men
as they clear the ladder to the upper deck. It's narrow, and
you'll see them advance one by one. You must look for
more than one way to the decks. There'll be at least three.
While that is going on, make sure no one goes near the
anchor. Hopefully, there are no archers aboard. I
wouldn't expect more than one or two on a cargo ship,
but there's no way of telling. I know nothing about how
these ships are manned or their protocols.

"The ship is coming from the north, but that doesn't
mean she'll tie up with the bow facing south. Normally,
they want the anchor on the seaward side. She may swing
around and come in from the south. It shouldn't make
much difference."

"How are you with a bow?" Currat asked.

"Ha!" Briggs answered. "I shot one about twenty years

ago. There are eight of us. I suggest using me as a spotter, then place four men to aim at the commanders and those coming from below decks, and three for the riggers and anchor crewmen.

"If the captain is smart, he'll have his fighters, if there are any, stay below decks and make us go after them, putting us at much more risk. That's another reason to kill the command crew first. Without leaders, crewmen do strange things at times. I wouldn't be surprised to see some jump overboard and swim up or down the coast. My problem in advising you is that I've never been on one of their ships, or even seen one up close. They never dock at Elizabethville."

"Are there other dangers we might expect?" Currat asked.

"If someone should think of it after seeing they have no chance of survival, one or more may try to scuttle her. I doubt that will happen if the captain and mates are dead; it means almost certain death to the remaining crewmen," Briggs answered. "Once the fighting starts, I don't know what will transpire."

Zack chuckled. "Nor do I. After the first arrow is shot, the best-laid plans are just that—plans. Anything and everything can go wrong, and usually does. All I can ask is for you to help us stay aware of changes and what they mean."

"That, I can do."

Zack, Currat, and Ursel began piling up rocks if needed—small enough to throw, and large enough to do some damage. Cartel and his sons found places to shoot from, giving them full range, but also providing excellent cover.

Cartel signaled for quiet. Zack heard the sound of a horse coming up the trail. Cursong came around the trail with four arrows pointed at his chest. He stopped.

"Massion?" Zack called out.

Cursong's shoulders slumped. "He died ten feet from

the healer's home." He looked out at sea. "Is that the ship?"

Zack nodded.

"Good!" Cursong said. "I want us to get the weapons and kill Men-in-Black! Massion and I grew up together. We were like brothers."

Briggs and Jasper went over to talk with him.

At midmorning, Zack called the men together. "I doubt if any of the men on the ship have ever heard an Ozlidian accent. Nonetheless, Currat should do the talking, if any is required. Their pronunciation differs a great deal from ours. It may be as hard for them to understand us, as it is the other way around. It may work to our advantage, requiring them to bring all their leaders on deck to understand us, if it gets to that. I think they'll know what we mean when the arrows fly. Listen closely to the orders given. Knowing what they say may help."

He turned to Cursong. "Are you good with a bow?"

"No," the big man replied. "But I grew up using a sling, and I have one with me."

Zack filled him in on the plan, and he found a place where he could sling rocks, and built a pile of egg-sized stones.

Knowing that waiting for a battle, especially when men could see the enemy advancing, had negative effects, Zack kept them busy preparing to transfer the weapons to the horses. He sent several of the men to bring up the horses and establish a picket line out of sight of the sea. Cartel went over the shooting positions of his sons and seemed pleased. Briggs found the best spot to watch and still have cover. Cursong needed a spot where his sling wouldn't hit other men. He finally stood atop a boulder and loosed a few stones to get his range. He smiled.

The ship, three hundred yards out, outsized Briggs's estimate. He searched the deck and rigging before handing the spyglass to Zack who, when finished looking, gave it to Currat. When Currat handed it back to Briggs, he said, "She's big!"

"She'll have at least forty crewmen," Briggs said. "I'm counting five men on each mast and five making ready the anchor's windlass. There are four men wearing sailor's caps, three blue and one red. I suspect they're the captain and mates. Remember to wait until the anchor is set before killing them."

Zack asked each group if they'd heard Briggs's pronouncement. They had.

She came in from the north; her bow pointing south. One man operated the windlass and three watched the anchor's chain. At last, the chain went slightly slack. It took all five to set the anchor. When they raised their arms toward the man wearing the red cap, Briggs shouted, "Shoot!"

Two arrows knocked the man in the red cap off his feet. The remaining men who wore blue caps went down right after, two with arrows and one with a cracked skull from a perfectly aimed stone. At the same time, Cartel's sons shot arrows in rapid succession, taking out the men reefing the sails. One dove from the top spar of the center mast toward the sea. An arrow went through his thigh, forcing blood to fan out in the wind toward lapping waves.

Men in uniforms carrying bows raced from below deck. Zack, Currat, and Cartel shot arrows at the two ladders they used to come on deck. Jasper kept the quivers supplied. Two sailors got arrows off, striking rock and falling into the sea. Only one stood until a stone knocked him off his feet, his head cracked open. A few moaned until quieting shafts slammed into them.

Zack threw the ropes down. Currat, Ursel, and he descended hand over hand toward the deck. Cartel and his sons covered them while Cursong stood with a stone in his sling ready to fling.

Reaching the side of the ship, they pushed off the rocks and landed on the deck. Two men with swords charged from the nearby ladder leading down. Before Zack could completely draw his battle sword, shafts pierced both attackers, driving them backward to the deck.

One man came on deck, hands raised, and knelt down. Zack walked toward him. The man bent to put his head to the deck, his body shaking. Zack stopped beside him, his sword's point slightly above his neck. "How many more are on board?"

The man looked up with a puzzled expression. Zack pointed back down the ladder and counted the fingers off his free hand, bending each one. The man nodded and held up eight fingers; he also understood the motions for the others to come up.

One by one, the men came on deck and knelt like the first, their faces frozen in fear.

"Which of you can understand me?" Zack asked.

One man sat upright, his accent strong but understandable. "I'm Dackamo. I understand you. The only man left below is the cook. I think he passed out."

"Whom did the soldiers report to?"

"The Supreme Dynast of Sis'on."

"Do you serve him as well?"

"We hate him. He kills the families of those he conquers if they don't do as his officers dictate, and his soldiers think nothing of killing us if we don't do exactly as they say. They're never punished. Sometimes they humiliate and beat us for no reason, and they seem to enjoy it. There were twenty of us when we sailed. They used one man for amusement, and he killed himself before they came again for him. Most of us are weak; we were only fed leftovers of food and water, which sometimes was nothing. If you wish, we will fight against the Dynast."

"Why did they bring you?" Zack asked.

"Punishment for speaking out against our treatment while working for the Dynast."

All but Cartel and his sons had descended to the ship by now. Zack explained about the eight survivors, and why they shouldn't be killed. He asked Briggs and Cursong to search the ship and bring the cook on deck without frightening him to death.

Zack and Currat searched the soldiers, taking purses and looking for orders. The other men on deck threw the dead overboard. The eight from Sis'on seemed to thoroughly enjoy disposing of them. In their weakened condition, it took three of them to toss one soldier into the sea. They didn't complain, however.

Briggs and Cursong returned topside with a shaking man in tow. It took a while for the man to calm down. Once he did, Zack and Dackamo made him understand their instruction to cook food for all of them. Smiling now that he wasn't about to die, he disappeared below.

"Dackamo, are any of you sailors?" Zack asked.

"Myself and two others. We sailed to Jewel a few times. That's how I can understand you better then most. Once, one of your sailors filled in our company after we lost a man in a storm. He made a round trip and left the ship, but I spoke with him during the voyage, and we got to grasp each other's words."

Zack motioned Briggs aside out of earshot, "Would you and Cursong be able to sail her to Hagan's End with the ones here? It would be easier to unload her and transport the weapons from dockside than hoisting them here."

"It would be a short voyage, if you can call it that. We could make it in a couple of hours using just the upper and lower topsails."

"You'd arrive before Currat, Ursel, and me. I'll send everyone else with you. We need to secure the gold. But now, we need to get the horses down. We have twenty-four with the one Cursong brought back; how many will she hold?"

"She'll hold them all. This ship is huge. Unfortunately,

I don't think I'll be able to use her. You remember what Wathdure did to my old ship. I don't know if he can destroy her, but I wouldn't put it past him to try. I could sail her to Deepwells and change all her markings and decoration on the sails. I'm hoping Wathdure and this Dynast ass will think she was lost at sea. From looking the ship over, she did suffer a storm coming here. It's plausible she went down. If we're going to sail her to Hagan's End, we need to rearrange the cargo hold and make room for the horses. I think we can make two picket lines facing each other. The weapons are in plain crates. I'll have them brought on deck. We'll have them ready for you when you arrive. Then, I'll sail to Elizabethville to unload the horses before leaving for Deepwells. I should have plenty of coins from selling the horses to make over this ship. I'll follow the coastline. I don't think Wathdure can use his magic that close to the Seven Realms."

"I agree, but he will in time. Will the *Silver Dolphin* be safe while you're gone?"

"I'm thinking I'll have Bronson sail her beside me. I should be able to round up a crew of good men in Hagan's End and if these eight want to sign on, well, we'll see."

Zack and the others spent the rest of the day and the next morning loading horses onto the *Striking Wind*. At midday, Zack, Currat, Ursel, and Jasper watched as she navigated south, with only upper and lower topgallant sails billowing outward.

The process of loading the gold and transporting it to the pool in several saddlepacks took half a day. They reached Hagan's End by nightfall, glad to see the *Striking Wind* anchored behind the *Silver Dolphin*.

Zack's group found Briggs and Bronson chatting with Yasho at a large table in the feasting room, sipping ale. When they sat with them, a serving maid brought a pitcher of ale and mugs for the newcomers. The innkeeper smiled. "I've ordered lastmeal for us all."

"How did you know when we'd arrive?" Ursel asked.

"I had a boy watching from the hilltop when the good captain told me you'd come."

While the others chatted, Zack leaned over to Jasper. "Send a bird with a message saying a report will arrive at the garrison in Elizabethville for Stonefire by fast messenger."

The priest excused himself, saying he would return shortly, as serving maids set lastmeal platters on the table.

* * *

"I'M concerned," Zack said while sliding under the bed-covers. "Wathdure will be able to attack Elizabethville at some point. Let's hope we have adequate defenses prepared by then."

Currat nodded and turned down the lamp. "Now I'm concerned with saving the Hamptorians and us—but not in that order." He sighed as their bodies spooned together.

16

ZACK and Currat looked out the window as the *Striking Wind* left port, settling in the tide's forces. The big ship smoothly rode the waves, her sails billowing outward. The *Silver Dolphin* followed in her wake; smaller and faster, she soon came alongside her bigger sister.

"I can only imagine the smile on Briggs's face," Zack said.

"Briggs?" Currat replied, "Do you think the smile on Bronson's face will ever fade? Making captain at his age is no small matter."

"Neither is killing Men-in-Black. Let's go do some planning over firstmeal."

Arriving at their usual table, they smiled at the small card on it that read RESERVED. Zack and Currat took their regular seats. Zack raised an eyebrow when the serving maid set a full pitcher of ale and six mugs in front of them.

"Just wait," she said. "There's more coming, like every other day you're here."

Currat's lips curved into a broad smile.

"I think she favors you," Zack said.

Currat chuckled and then frowned, pointing his chin toward the kitchen door. He quickly smiled and waved Turlas over. The young man looked as if he hadn't slept in two days. He sat next to Zack, and Currat poured him a mug of ale.

"Turlas, talk to me," Zack said quietly.

"I...I can't, not now."

Currat caught Turlas's eye. "You must. If you don't, your feelings will fester. How long had you known

Cerrol?"

"Since as far back as I can remember. We were close, like brothers; we did everything together. We even shared women once in a while. I...I loved him. He was my family."

"I suspect you've heard what happened to Zack and me. I lost my father and friends escaping from Ozlid, and bandits killed Zack's wife and daughter. You'll go through many emotions before it all falls into perspective, but you must deal with those feelings, and you can't let them eat at you."

"I'll try."

"Do you still want to kill Men-in-Black?"

"More than ever."

Zack nodded. "You'll be one of Cartel's first men to train. He'll be expecting you tomorrow for firstmeal an hour after sunrise. I wouldn't be late. Take your dark thoughts and put them to use learning the skills you'll need to avenge Cerrol's death!"

Turlas frowned, but a few moments later, he offered a tentative smile. "Thank you."

Jasper came from the entrance and Yasho from the kitchen, both arriving at the same time. Yasho squeezed Turlas's shoulder before sitting next to Zack. Jasper took the seat next to Turlas.

Zack slid a ten-pound bar of gold wrapped in cloth over to Yasho. "Add it to your coins for our efforts in fighting the Men-in-Black."

After testing the weight, the innkeeper let out a low whistle. "This should give us enough to last several years."

"Don't be too sure," Currat said. "Bribes can be expensive, which brings up another point. If someone ever tries to expose you unless you pay them, do what it takes to get whatever they're holding over you, and then kill them."

"Where are the weapons?" Zack asked Yasho.

"Under lock in my strong room at my warehouse. I'm glad it's a big room. There were more chests than I expected. I opened one; it contained swords in scabbards. I can take the two I brought back to your room."

Ursel appeared next. Smiling, he walked over and sat next to Yasho. His nod to Turlas seemed to send a silent message. The man gave a weak smile back.

Sitting tall and stretching his shoulders, Ursel grunted. "What's for firstmeal? I'm starving. Where are the weapons?"

Yasho laughed. "What difference does it make? You've never left anything on a platter yet." He went on to describe their earlier discussion.

Moments later, two serving maids brought in five steaming trenchers of eggs with cheese, ham, and fired bread.

They all started at once.

Jasper finished last.

As he looked around the room, Zack started, his face turning serious. The others looked toward the door as Cartel sauntered to the table. He sat in the last seat and Ursel poured him a glass of ale.

"I have bad news," the Arms Master said after drinking. "My cousin came down from the north. He told of several groups of Men-in-Black, numbering ten each. They robbed two inns. One was Ballrand's. The bastards killed several guests. They brutalized the innkeepers, and didn't seem to care if anyone heard their accents. I think our war has progressed."

"Cartel," Zack replied, "Turlas will arrive at your home tomorrow as you requested. Are your sons available to fight?"

"They are, and I can, too."

"You are far too important to risk in a skirmish. Losing your training skills would set us back a long while," Currat said. "There are few men who can teach others how to kill and stay alive. We need you preparing men. Bryan, Eckert, and Sonkek will soon join your efforts."

"Gentlemen, we need recruits who know how to fight. Suggestions?" Ursel asked.

"Do you remember the army captain from your last visit?" Yasho said.

"Vaguely."

"The army retired him without a pension, as the crown did many others, stating they didn't have the coins. He's done a lot of work around town doing repairs, and he knows many folks and their dispositions. He doesn't talk much, and I don't know how he feels towards Ozlid, but I think he would be a good place to start. I can set up a lastmeal meeting tonight in one of the private rooms. He's always eager for work prospects."

"Do you trust him?" Ursel asked.

"I think I would if I get some right answers to my questions. I'll go slow, and see how our conversation progresses."

"What you're doing is dangerous," Ursel added. "A quiet man often has deep convictions. If he's that guarded, you may not learn much. Hamptor cheated him; he may have mixed feelings concerning Ozlid. I suggest we follow our original plan, and test him without him seeing our faces."

Yasho looked at Zack with a questioning expression.

"Yasho, Ursel has received much training in the last two years, very intense training. From what I read in his reports, he soaked it up like a sea sponge. He's very knowledgeable. Currat and I are here to advise and lend support when needed. I don't disagree with what he's said. I do think you're taking a chance. Nonetheless, you know the man better than we do. I do have a concern that you're breaking a protocol before it's put in place."

"Perhaps you're right," Yasho said. "If I send for him, I know which way he'll come. There is a place where he could be captured, and it's near a location where you could interrogate him. I'll have time to show you after midmeal today."

* * *

ZACK stood in the shadows, waiting with Currat and Ursel across the way behind trees, their swords ready. A man walked briskly toward them with a military gait. He passed Zack and stopped. "There are three of you. Do you plan to kill me?"

In answer, Zack stepped forward and placed the tip of his sword on the back of the captain's neck. Ursel and Currat walked forward and put a hood over their prisoner's face, tied his hands behind his back, and walked him to a deserted barn. A room at the back of the barn had a stool facing a tabletop on two sawhorses covered with a dark wormcloth to the floor. Zack sat behind the table with bright lamps glowing behind him. Ursel and Currat stayed back in the shadows, their weapons ready.

"Your army cheated you out of your pension. What do you think of Ozlid?" Zack said in a perfect Ozlidian accent.

"I suspect you're going to kill me, so why not say the truth? I hate you murdering bastards!"

"Hate can be channeled into actions that could make you wealthy while your country continues to fall under our influence. We will win eventually; join us and reap the rewards. We don't care if you hate us or not. We want your services, and we'll pay well for them."

The captain struggled with his bindings. "If I get loose, I'll kill you with my bare hands!" He yelled.

Currat and Ursel, grabbing him on either side, pushed him back in his seat.

"That's all we wanted to know," Zack said, switching to Hamptorian.

Currat pulled the hood off. The captain squinted at them while his eyes adjusted to the light. Ursel and Currat stood back in the shadows, but he didn't try to move. Turning forward, he locked his gaze on an undistinguishable Ursel.

"Captain," Zack said. "I apologize for the deception, but we had to be sure of your motives. We are establishing a force to combat the Ozlidians we call the Men-in-Black. Our efforts will *not* be in open rebellion. We will kill them and take their purses, vouchers, and horses. The coins, and whatever else of value will go to the families of those they harmed or killed. The horses will disappear, and be sold where Ozlid won't find them. The coins from those sales, after commissions, will go to fund our efforts.

"We would like you to join our clandestine enterprise. Is this something that would interest you, killing Ozlidians? Before you answer, you should know that several teams of Men-in-Black have come farther south than ever before and are killing guests at inns and beating innkeepers. My information states they attacked Ballrand's inn in the last two days.

"Also, with your training and knowledge of the men and women in Hagan's End, we'd want you to take a leadership position in putting together teams for fighting the enemy there. What say you?"

Ursel moved forward and untied the captain's hands, and then returned to the shadows without being seen. The captain ran his hands through his hair.

"I understand your need for secrecy. As you must know, I'm Captain Derkson Tomwell. You must be very sure of those you enlist to your cause. And yes, I would like to be one of your men. My brother, his wife, and their son lost their lives to those cowards during one of their waves of attacks against small homesteads and farms. Yes, I *need* to kill them, if for no other reason than to restore a modicum of honor back to my country."

Zack rose. He moved to the back as Ursel took his seat.

Ursel placed the lamps on the table and introduced himself. "I have extensive training in what we want to accomplish. I'm in charge of our groups. You'll be given information as it's needed. You'll also be given coins as needed to use in establishing your group. You'll not know the members' names in other groups unless a joint venture is required, and perhaps not even then. You'll be required to vouch for each man before you recruit him. You and we must investigate them first. Ultimately, we'll have groups throughout Hamptor."

He pushed ten silver coins across the tabletop toward Derkson. You may use the coins to buy what you and your group will need. We do require an accounting on a monthly basis. We have a few men now, and some are being trained in basic weapons use.

"In the beginning, we need to send a group north to attack the Men-in-Black. We don't want Ozlid to think we're based here. That plan is dangerous. We'll leave the Ozlidian bodies where they fall, and you'll take the horses with you... That is the most dangerous part, because it identifies you. The Ozlidians will attack you on sight if they see the horses. You may want to wear black clothing to give you an advantage. If your men are wounded or killed, they must be returned to Hagan's End. Our main attack protocol will always be by ambush. If there's a wagon, we'll take it and we'll want all the saddlepacks."

Ursel went on to describe how the spoils would be distributed. "Their men have always stayed quiet. That has recently changed. In these latest attacks, men spoke using their normal accents. They don't seem to mind us knowing who attacked them at this point. I suggest you recruit men who have lost loved ones to the Ozlidians."

The captain again ran his fingers through his hair. "How many do I need in a group?"

"Enough to kill ten men without injuries to you and yours," Ursel said. "You'll strike from cover. If your men are archers, it'd be a great advantage. Many hunters could fill that need. Until your men are used to what they need to do, I'd suggest you have at least five in your group, including you. I've never seen one of the Ozlidian groups with archers. They fight with swords and all, but the leaders are mostly poorly trained. You'll be given a place to take the horses to graze, and I suggest that be done at night. Moving slowly, those big horses shouldn't have a problem with holes. They seem to have excellent night vision. Do you have men in mind?"

"Yes, I do, enough for two groups. They are mostly hunters with arrows and knives. Most are young, and all have lost family to the Ozlidians. None drink to excess. Three served with me in the army, and are well trained. It wouldn't take much to train the others in the ways of an ambush. I think I could have them ready in two weeks. They have work to do supporting their families, and the coins from this would help."

"You'll be contacted tomorrow, and told how to communicate with us. That knowledge is for you alone! Secrecy is still our best friend. Wait five minutes to leave, take the coins, and turn off the lamps. Until we again meet."

"I'm eager to start. I haven't felt this good since long before leaving the army."

Without another word, Ursel stood and left unseen with Zack and Currat. They waited until Derkson left, and checked to see if the lamps were out.

"Do you think we should buy that barn?" Ursel asked on the way to the Blue Sail.

"Let's see what Yasho thinks," Zack answered.

* * *

ZACK ordered lastmeal in the spies' rooms, and left word for Yasho to join them when he could. Ursel left the adjoining door open and the men stripped out of their cloaks and boots, leaving weapons within easy reach. Currat brought in a half-full wine cask and mugs. They sat around the fireplace in plush chairs, sipping wine.

Lastmeal came. The venison, root vegetables, bread, and honey cakes disappeared in quick fashion. Ursel spent the time talking about his training under Gaz and others. Zack and Currat thought it was about what they expected. They were both pleased that the spymaster and the Zenith Lord had taken an interest in him, and liked the maturity he'd gained.

Yasho arrived in a rush. "It's been one of those nights, but it ended well. I trust your night made you happy. Oh, speaking of happy, here's some rather nice brandy I thought we could enjoy."

"I don't think we should get *too* happy," Zack said. He detailed the meeting with Derkson, the possibility of buying the barn, and asked how communication between the groups might work."

"I think I need that drink now," Yasho said. He poured them each a portion before continuing, "For the time being, I'll use street boys to deliver messages to hiding places several hours before they should be retrieved. It was the only thing I could come up with on short notice. I didn't know about Derkson's family members being killed, but he's so close mouthed about everything, it doesn't surprise me. I suspect he'll have some quality men assembled in a short time. I also don't think we need worry too much about the men he chooses."

"I still want to interview them as we did him," Ursel said. "I can tell a lot about a man by the way he moves and answers questions. I am also anxious to see if any of them recognizes me on the street or in a tavern. Yasho, you're coordinating a lot. I don't like the idea of you using street boys for messengers. One of them might figure out that the man picking up the message would pay him again to find out who sent it. I don't want anyone coming near this place to get a message, but that doesn't mean another inn like the Tarnished Anchor could be used, or even markings in certain places, done at night and checked to make sure no one is nearby. I know a code that might be useful. It's not difficult, and would be easy to break by someone who knows cyphers, but it would suit our purpose for the most part. I told Derkson someone would tell him how to communicate with us tomorrow. We need to address this tonight. It would be bad if we fell down on the first objective, leaving Derkson thinking we are children playing games."

Yasho looked up. "He goes for a ride along the seawall every morning at sunrise. No one is there at that time. A message tied on a string dangling from the upstairs window of an abandoned warehouse would work. One building has a secret door leading to the warehouse next to it. The person dangling the note could go out the other way, or just stay there for a while. Any of us could lower it as he draws near. That would give us time to plan a proper way. What do you want the note to say?"

"Need I ask how you know about secret passages?" Zack asked.

Yasho smiled wryly. "I own them."

Zack returned the smile. "Tell him to wear a white shirt on his ride when he has a man for interviewing, and to bring him to the barn the next night at midnight. Have him tear the message up and throw it in the sea. We'll need to watch and see what he does. If Briggs is in port, that'll be easy. If not, I have a spyglass and can watch from far away on the seawall."

Zack raised his hand for quiet. He padded to the door and jerked it open, looking both ways in the hall. He saw no one, but heard light feet going down the stairs.

When he got downstairs, knife in hand, he saw no one around.

* * *

SUNLIGHT slowly inched across the warehouse floor through cracks in the large door for raising and lowering cargo, facing the sea. Ursel crouched by the largest crack, waiting. Strong sunlight changed the warehouse's floor's color to a lighter oak while dancing sea caps sparkled. A pebble hit its roof.

He lowered the string, measured to end at a rider's height. A moment later, the string pulled taut, and then slackened. A hundred heartbeats passed before the horse moved away. Ursel quietly drew his battle sword and pulled a dagger from its sheath.

The back upstairs door slammed open. Six Men-in-Black charged in, looked around and then faced Ursel. The man, slightly in front, fell while he stared down at Ursel's knife's hilt in his midsection. Zack's knife hit the man behind him in the throat, sending blood spurting onto the man's face next to him as the secret door pounded open.

Currat and Jasper rushed in. The Men-in-Black bolted toward the warehouse's seaward end, brandishing weapons.

Ursel's sword blocked a downward slash. Moving in with his short sword, he stuck the blade between ribs and into a beating heart. It took effort to pull free, gore dripping from the blade.

Swords crashing against swords broke the morning quiet; the lapping waves were no longer heard amid the commotion. Starting to retreat toward the back door, the Men-in-Black must have realized how much their opponents overmatched them.

Jasper thrust his sword through his attacker's midsection, and the man fell with a moan, eyes glazing over. Zack and Currat's daggers took down the last two Men-in-Black just before they reached the back door.

The spies moved through the men, finishing them with sword thrusts. Then, they rolled out a heavy cargo net while the priest opened the large seaward door and swung out the hoist. Ropes attached, Zack and Ursel raised the bodies off the floor, winching them down into

Turlas's waiting wagon. Later, they set off to take the fallen enemy's black stallions to a pasture by the sea.

* * *

YASHO looked relieved when the spies, the priest, and Turlas walked briskly to their usual table. He rushed over with a pitcher of ale and mugs. As he placed and poured, he asked, "Well?"

"Six attacked," Ursel said. "We killed them, stripped them, dumped them in the sea, found their horses, and worked up one great appetite. Cartel's oldest is leading the horses to the area below the boulders for grazing. He's meeting his brother there, and they're going to rope off the area and put a gate where the road starts."

Zack waved at a serving maid to get her attention. Upon seeing him, she dropped the platters she was carrying and ran toward the kitchen. He raised an eyebrow at Yasho.

"Sonkek is in the alley. He'll catch Carroll, and take her to the barn. I told him to watch for such behavior and what to do. She's been serving here for about six months. I never saw her do anything out of the ordinary before, but perhaps I didn't know what to look for. Now, let me order food for you. I don't think you'll want to question her on an empty stomach!" With a satisfied look, he turned and sauntered toward the kitchen as serving maids rushed to clean up the dropped platters.

"I'm not looking forward to you interrogating her," Turlas said to no one in particular.

"One of two things will happen," Currat replied. "Either she'll become emotional, or she'll try to kill us. There doesn't seem to be a middle ground for women. I doubt she'll try to use poison to kill herself, but it's a women's method. I didn't notice a trace of Ozlidian accent, but most think I was born in Hagan's End when I use your accent; the rest think northern Hamptor. She could be well trained. Sending spies into Hamptor might be new, or it could have been going on for some time. I think I know how to find out."

Yasho returned, carrying a full pitcher of ale with serving maids hoisting full, steaming platters of cheese, eggs, venison, and bread.

Seating himself, he asked, "Do you think there could be more here? The rest of my maidens have been here for at least two years."

"I think we'll find out tonight, Yasho," Currat answered.

* * *

ZACK Eased into the barn. Sonkek walked quietly to him. He started to speak until he saw Zack raise a finger to his lips and motioned him toward the door. He glanced back at the woman; she seemed asleep.

Zack spoke in a whisper from outside as Sonkek stood half in, half out of the barn. "In a few minutes, act like you're dozing. Don't make snoring sounds, just let your head fall against your chest a few times, and then let it remain there. Currat will speak to her in undertones. Act as if you hear nothing."

Sonkek nodded and returned to his spot, sitting on the floor with his back to a post. He eyed Carroll sitting in the chair, her hands and feet bound with rope. He tried to see if she'd loosened any of the knots, but he sat too far away to tell for sure. A few minutes later, he started to nod. After a short while, he feigned sleep. He let some time pass before he roused and scratched his nose, letting his head fall afterward.

Currat eased close to the split in the wall where Carroll sat. Speaking in a cultured Ozlidian accent, he asked, "Who are you?"

Her head jerked toward the wall, and then whipped back before again trying to see out. She answered in an Ozlidian accent—not as cultured as Currat's, but genuine. "I'm Josset. Who are you?"

"All you need to know is that I'm an Ozlidian officer. I saw them take you to the barn, and recognized the streak in your hair from your description. What have you to report?"

She looked around again before answering. "I'm sure Currat Duval and Zack Stand are at the Blue Sail. I heard them talking about selling some of our horses, but I don't know to whom. I've tried to get Yasho, the innkeeper, to talk about guests in the inn, but he's a tightlipped bastard. There's a large Hamptorian named Ursel who arrived recently. He wears the same kind of cloak as Currat does, and has an adjoining room from Currat and Zack's.

"I heard them planning a way to deliver a note to a man on horseback, but that's all. I nearly got caught. One of them stopped the conversation, and I ran. A moment later, a man followed me downstairs, but he didn't find where I hid. I passed the information on to my user. Will you get me out of here?"

"I'm one of the new detachments with nine men. I'll do what I can."

"I heard you were coming. I hope you kill a lot of the Hamptorian scum."

"Who told you we had gotten this far?"

"Daphine at the Tarnished Anchor. I'm glad I wasn't assigned... Wait, you should know that. Who are you?"

"I'm who I said I was. We have put two more women in place over the past two months. They were told not to contact anyone but me. I was simply making sure they had followed their orders."

"That's good! Who are they?"

"You won't be told now, especially since you're caught. They may try to torture you."

"That'll never work; I have my poison, and I *will* take it if I have to. I don't fear death nearly as much as I'm frightened of Wathdure."

"Be careful what you say. You never know when he's listening. I've been here too long. Try to last until late tonight, and we'll rescue you." Currat moved away before she could answer.

He walked back to the Blue Sail while telling Zack and Ursel what he'd learned. He turned, holding the door for them, and then letting it close. Withdrawing the small spyglass from his cloak's hidden pocket, he adjusted it and looked out at sea. Smiling, he followed his companions to their regular table for midmeal.

"The *Silver Dolphin* is coming in," he said as he sat down.

"I wonder what she's bringing us," Zack said.

17

AS they waited for the kitchen to open, Yasho joined them. Currat went through the events once more as the innkeeper listened, nodding when appropriate.

"Do you know this Daphine at the Tarnished Anchor?" he asked at the end.

Yasho scratched his cheek. "I've heard of her. She's supposedly an excellent prostitute, but likes giving and receiving it very rough. One man left with blood seeping through the back of his shirt. He returned the next week asking for her, however. I learned long ago not to be surprised at what people do and enjoy."

Turlas looked disgusted.

"Yasho," Zack said. "I need you to hire messengers to go as far as Kell's inn, stopping at all the inns on this list and telling the innkeepers we want no trouble and a great deal of privacy. Also, inform them that we are not part of the Men-in-Black who have troubled them, and will pay handsomely for our needs. I've put down the approximate days of arrival, but it could vary. I know you'll send only men you trust, and pay them well, as you always do."

"I know just the man and he can take two horses, making his time much faster." Yasho looked up, his smile widening as he stood. Lady Adel, perfectly groomed in a beautiful pink and white gown flowing to the floor, swept into the room on Priest Jasper's arm,. The men stood, Ursel holding a chair for her. Turlas's mouth hung open far too long.

Adel kissed Ursel on the cheek and sat on the proffered chair. Yasho bowed and rushed to the kitchen to fetch food.

"Don't just sit there; tell us everything!" Currat said.

Adel's laughter, light with sparkling tones, captivated Currat as it had before. *I wonder if the twins know what they have.*

"I met the Zenith Lord! Great Lights, that man is handsome! Through him, I got weapons for my darlings at no cost! He said something about them being captured in bandit raids. It was breathtaking. Master Gaz introduced me to a dressmaker who fashioned five gorgeous gowns for me, and three suits each for the twins at very reasonable prices. They're going to look so striking. I did find some jewels and I had rings made, and of course, a few baubles for me. The trip was a splendid success. Captain Briggs, and later Captain Bronson—" Currat and Zack looked at each other and grinned. "Were both most cordial and treated me well. Both trips had calm seas and cool breezes. Except for terribly missing my boys, I had a wonderful time. Captain Bronson said he'd find you once the ship is properly moored." Looking at Turlas, who had since closed his mouth, she added, "*And* who is this addition to your group?"

"Forgive me, Adel," Zack said. "This is Turlas. He's helping in our efforts."

Adel nodded to the young man. Currat wondered if Turlas's blushing cheeks came from the attention, or from the obvious undressing he did with his eyes. Adel seemed not to notice.

Yasho returned with serving maids in tow. Platters in place, the maidens left, leaving Yasho to pour Adel a goblet of wine from a small cask. Zack looked at his platter consisting of a large portion of sea bass over rice—both difficult to obtain—glazed carrots, peas with onions, and light, puffy rolls.

"Yasho! With this midmeal, we all need excellent wine."

The innkeeper looked a little chagrined and waved a

maiden over. Soon, another small cask and several wine goblets appeared. Jasper beseeched the Light's Source for guidance and help against the Dark.

The midmeal lasted through leisurely bites and sips of wine. Adel stopped eating halfway through her platter and entertained the rest with tales from her trip; plays, concerts, staying in the Spires, and a great deal of purchasing items for her and her men.

At the end of the meal she turned serious and shifted her attention to Zack. "What do you suggest I do for my trip home?"

"I still think the coach is the best way." He went on to tell of the latest trouble from the Men-in-Black and their increase in numbers. "Zack, Ursel, and I need to travel north to see Kell and establish groups on the way back. If Yasho can do without Turlas, he may come with us."

Yasho nodded, while Turlas's eyes grew round.

Zack added, "Ursel is not known, and he can speak with an Ozlidian accent as well as I can. I'm hoping we can make better time without the need to care for the ambassador. I trust you have the document Currat forged for you."

"I do," Adel replied. "Looking as fresh as the day he wrote it."

"We may have others with us, but I must talk with someone first. When do you wish to leave?"

Adel laughed. "Surely you jest. If the horses could manage at night, I'd be leaving in a few hours. Tomorrow morning at the latest."

"I'm sorry, Adel, but if we can't get everything done this afternoon and tonight, you may have to wait a day. The delay would be necessary—regrettable, but required."

"What can I do to help?" she asked.

"I'll let you know shortly. I need to speak with Yasho for a moment, and then he can get you settled. Yasho, if you would, please." Motioning for Ursel and Currat to join him, Zack walked a few steps away, with the others following.

"We'll need a seamstress to make black shirts for the men going on this trip, like the ones the twins wore," Currat whispered, and Zack nodded. "The one made for Ursel should have double gold ribbing woven into a pattern on it. I would like to have Turlas with us, as well as Cartel's sons, which would mean someone would have to look after the horses. Send Sonkek to find the sons and send them here, and then stay until whoever is going to check on the horses daily is found, if it's not him. It'll require time. This is where coins must be spent for everyday services. Pay the men well. Send a message to Cartel explaining why we need them for a few weeks in the broadest of terms."

Yasho nodded. "Actually, I can go after I get Adel settled and be back before lastmeal. I'll personally explain the need for his sons in more detail. I can have the seamstress here, too."

"Perfect!" Zack said. "Tell Cartel they'll be killing Men-in-Black. There are other things that need handling as well. The coach must be made ready, and I suspect Adel has quite a few trunks to load on it at daybreak. We'll need to hide the weapons and her jewelry well. Then we must coordinate with Bronson. We need also take care of the spy at the barn. Currat, Ursel, or I can do that onerous task, but help in the disposing of the body would be good. I'm sure more items will be needed as the day goes on."

"I'd better get started," Yasho said. "I have a room for Adel next to yours." He headed back to Adel, and soon they both disappeared up the stairs.

Zack motioned for Turlas. "Please send a boy to the stable behind the Tarnished Anchor with a message that the coach and its horses must be ready at sunrise, as well as our horses."

Bryan Daven rushed in from the kitchen, looked around, and hurried on to Zack. "Master Yasho said to help any way I can. He said to tell you Sonkek is on his way."

"Bryan," Ursel said. "How difficult would it be for you to be away from Hagan's End for a few weeks?"

"Not very," he answered. "I mostly work as a guard for various innkeepers. They send for me when I'm needed. If I'm not here, they'll send for someone else."

"We'll talk more about that later tonight. Please take a message to Captain Bronson on the *Silver Dolphin* asking him to have Lady Adel's cargo ready for loading onto her coach at sunrise and to join me here for lastmeal. Stay available nearby in case you're needed…and, thank you."

Bryan smiled broadly and made his way out.

Jasper joined them. "Can I help?"

"Yes," Zack said. "Someone has to kill Wathdure's evil prostitute. I don't like killing women. After that, we have much to do, and you'll be needed."

* * *

URSEL entered the Tarnished Anchor and asked for Daphine. Sitting in a dark corner wearing a black cloak with the cowl pulled over his forehead, Zack kept his face in shadow. A surprisingly beautiful woman approached Ursel with a smile in an otherwise hard-set face. Her eyes narrowed as she looked up at his height.

"You asked for me?" Her voice sounded like her face—beautiful, but hard.

"How much for two, and you'll need time to recover. You'll have no broken bones and only minor blood loss. You will be bruised, including your face."

Her smile widened. "That'll put me out of action for at least a month. I'll need six silvers for that much time."

"Agreed."

Zack stood, still in shadow, and followed the two upstairs to a room completely different than the downstairs. It contained a large bed, plush chairs, a fireplace, and was as clean as the downstairs was filthy.

Ursel spoke in high Ozlidian. "I'm Master of the Gold Dawson. Report!"

"Who's he?" she asked, pointing to Zack, who stood in front of the window, looking out.

"My superior," Ursel answered. "Now report, or do you wish to meet our lord Wathdure before you ought? He doesn't take kindly to failure."

Daphine's face whitened. "I heard from Dyman, a worker at the Blue Sail, that Josset disappeared after a commotion in the main feasting room. The *Silver Dolphin* returned captained by the former first mate, Bronson. Captain Briggs shipped out on a huge ship I've never seen before. He hasn't returned. Nothing else is new. Are you going to use me like you said? I'd enjoy that from you."

Ursel made to take off his short sword, but instead, he drew it and rammed the point into the startled woman's throat. As the light in her eyes began to fade, he answered, "No."

Zack turned with a raised eyebrow as Ursel cleaned his sword on the dead woman's dress.

"You don't like killing women. If they're part of Wathdure's evil, I don't mind," Ursel said.

* * *

"I'M Zack Stand, and you're Josset. I don't like killing women. What information do you have that will save your life?"

"I don't mind dying. I have served Wathdure faithfully, and he'll reward me."

"You mean like the ones he puts in the necromantic army?

Josset jerked at that, but recovered quickly. "I served him faithfully, and I *will* be rewarded."

"Mmm, Wathdure reports to Shadure, who reports to the Dark One, who receives the evil spirits of the deceased. Somehow, I don't think the Dark Source's ruler much cares what Wathdure said to you. I seriously doubt

Wathdure cares."

"I have nothing to say! You can't frighten me."

Zack reached to his shoulder scabbard for a dagger. Taking aim, he made to throw, but Josset slumped suddenly, frothy white foam oozing from her mouth. Walking forward, he realized he needn't feel for a pulse. Her dead eyes stared into nothingness. He cut her bonds, and she fell off the chair on the right side. Walking to the other end of the barn, he eased the door open. Jasper walked to him.

"She took poison; must have had a small vial in her mouth when she was captured. Wathdure is telling his followers they'll be rewarded in death. I suspect he doesn't say anything about failure. I can't imagine the Dark One rewarding anyone."

"It doesn't," Jasper said. "The Holy One taught us the Dark gains its power from the spirits' suffering it collects. That power is passed on to a select few to implement the Dark's goals. He discovered that in a passage from an ancient scroll written during the Great War two millennia ago."

"I don't like killing a woman; I don't mind killing a minion of the Dark. Still, I'll tell the person who discards her to the sea to leave her clothes on. Wathdure's creatures dissolved in seawater. It'll be interesting to see what happens to her. I don't remember the bodies we threw in the sea coming back to the surface. A few of the ones from the Eastern Kingdoms did float—at least, for a while. It may provide insight to Wathdure's methods, but now, we are needed back at the inn."

He paused, and then continued, "There is one other matter. I'd like you to send a bird with Lady Adel, allowing her to send us a message and one back to her. Do you have such?"

"Yes. She showed an interest in the birds, and I explained about their care and uses. I could send a cage and bird with her in the coach. The cage has receptacles for seed and water. I'll advise her on how to send a message."

"Good. I'll give her a simple code to use."

Jasper nodded as Zack pulled the door shut.

* * *

ZACK pulled Yasho aside. "Do you have a man named Dyman working for you?"

"Yes, he does maintenance on the inn. Why?"

"He's a traitor. What do you know about him?"

"He came to work about six months ago. He works hard, and doesn't cause trouble. I believe he said he came from northern Hamptor, and his village had been nearly destroyed by Men-in-Black, but he didn't call them that; he said 'raiders.'"

"Is he working today?"

"Yes, I called him in for a problem in the kitchen."

"Send him to Ursel in a half-hour."

Three quarters of an hour later, the man lay dead with a broken neck in Ursel's room. Zack came through the connecting door. "Did you learn anything?"

"Only curse words in an Ozlidian accent."

Zack nodded.

* * *

ZACK learned more about the Blue Sail. Workrooms for craftsmen occupied the back of the bottom floor. The spacious room for clothing had four workstations with many bolts of cloth, ribbons, trim, and accessories in many colors. The men had been measured and directions given for each shirt. Two seamstresses had promised the work would be done by an hour before sunrise. He ordered the men back at that time for a last fitting.

He had requested a purple bar across Ursel's shirt on the chest and a cloak with the same woven gold trim along the edges. He'd heard of the position, Master of the Purple, only one time while at Wathdure's palace on his previous visit. The lower echelons had probably never heard of the rank's degree. Cartel's sons arrived last, and Zack finally learned the reclusive men's names—Dartel and Eartel. They had returned home, and brought an impressive array of weapons with them.

Zack's lastmeal with Bronson was enjoyable, with the new captain displaying more depth than he expected. *Briggs made a wise choice.* He wasn't sure when his former captain would return from Deepwells.

As Bronson left for his ship, Yasho walked over to his table. "The messenger is on his way."

Zack, Ursel, Currat, Yasho, Bryan, Dartel, Eartel, and Adel arrived one after the other in the fitting area of the clothing room. It didn't take long; the clothing didn't require but one alteration. Adel had previously looked at the garments and given her approval. She waited to see how the fit would be on the men. Yasho had ordered three black leather cloaks with cowls for Dartel and Eartel, who would be driving the coach, and Bryan, who would ride at the back of the coach. All three would openly bristle with weapons.

Zack pulled Adel aside, handing her a parchment. "This is the code. I assume Jasper told you about it."

"Yes, he did. I like the birds, and I'll enjoy caring for one."

Zack smiled. "You might like the code, too." He left her with a wondering expression. A few moments later, her laughter rang through the room.

The men changed into their clothing and rushed to the inn's entrance after Adel's final endorsement. The spies and Adel entered the waiting coach while the drivers and Bryan climbed on board. The first rays of sunlight kissed the sea as the coach pulled to a stop aside the *Silver Dolphin*. Bronson had everything prepared as Zack and he had discussed the night before. Seamen hoisted four large trunks to the top of the coach, and two more stowed below Bryan's bench across the coach's top, along the back edge.

The spies stayed behind as the coach's four black stallions pulled her around.

"Again, *Captain* Bronson, I wish you the best for safe trips and fair winds with calm seas," Zack said. "When you see Captain Briggs, tell him there should be more horses ready to try out their sea legs."

Bronson grasped forearms with them. "Stay safe. I never want to see any of you in the same condition as when you returned from your first visit to Ozlid, and I sincerely hope it was your last visit to that horror. Ursel, I enjoyed seeing you again, and the conversations we've had. Stay well. I look forward to seeing all of you in good health again."

Currat smiled. "Keep those rough seas at bay, Captain."

The spies mounted and rode toward the coach on the main road north, with the four blacks trailing behind on long leads. Ursel joined Adel in the coach, with Zack and Currat hanging back, allowing space to maneuver out of sight if needed. The sons set the fast pace Zack had ordered, rotating the gaits.

They reached the Running Bull Inn as the last bit of sunlight flickered through the nearby tree branches. Adel and the men, cloaks pulled tight around them, climbed the stairs when Zack and Currat entered from the stable entrance. Ballrand had planned well. Adel had a large private room, as did Zack and Currat. Ursel had his own. The sons and Bryan would share another room, from which he had taken the large bed out and moved three smaller ones in. Lastmeals were served in their rooms.

Satisfied, Zack hoped the rest of the inns reacted in kind to the messenger's orders. He had requested Ballrand join him when the common room had cleared.

He and Currat were enjoying a goblet of wine when the knock came at the door.

"Men-in-Black are here!" a serving maid hissed.

She was out of sight when they rushed to Ursel's room. He answered the door at once.

"It's time to test your accent," Zack said.

They collected Adel on the way. She and Ursel walked leisurely down the stairs and into the common room where two from a table of nine Men-in-Black harassed two merchants.

"STOP!" Ursel said in a tone that carried through the room. His high Ozlidian accent brought instant stillness to every person there. "Who's in charge of you?"

A man rose, wearing a bewildered expression, and approached Ursel and Adel. "I am, and who are you?"

Ursel pushed his cloak apart, showing the purple stripe on the uniform and the gold braid on his collar. Then he moved his hand to his battle sword showing the same braid woven at the cuffs. "What is your rank?" he said in a deadly voice.

"Master of the Blue, and I still want to know who you are," the Ozlidian officer replied in an arrogant tone.

Ursel sighed. "I loathe dealing with idiots! Have you never heard of a Master of the Purple?"

The officer hesitantly shook his head.

"Perhaps this will help inform you." Ursel opened the leather case holding the forged document. He casually handed it to the officer.

The man looked at the seals and ribbons first. When he saw the signature, *Officer of the Black Saunderson*, his face paled. He read the orders twice with shaking hands before handing it back. "How may I be of service?"

"First of all," Ursel said, "there are only three Masters of the Purple. We report directly to Saunderson. When he's not around, we report to Mistress Spercine, or our lord Wathdure. Now tell me your name, or should I kill you?" Ursel eased his battle sword up, allowing the officer to see the precious jewels. "This sword is *not* for show. The blade is exceedingly sharp, and it'll cleanly take your head. For the last time, what is your name?"

"Officer of the Blue Eric Bosweel." The man's voice shook.

Ursel nodded as if taking a mental note, "I'll remember you, but I have a terrible memory for names. Pray I forget it by the time I write my report to Saunderson. Keep your men in line and quiet, and leave this innkeeper alone. He has value to us. Tell no one you saw us, including your superiors, but pass the word around about the inn. If I hear one word about our men bothering anyone here, I'll have the distinct pleasure of presenting your head to our Mistress Spercine. She likes misplaced heads, in case you haven't heard."

Ursel tried not to chuckle as the man pissed himself. Adel had no such constraints of rank; her laugh, with its shimmering tones, filled the room. They turned and made their way up the stairs in the same casual way they'd descended. As they paused where the stairway turned, Bosweel and his men made a hasty departure.

Currat met them at the top of the stairwell. "Well done! Your accent and tone nearly destroyed him."

"Well," Ursel said. "He did piss his pants. I thought that a good implication of success."

Currat chuckled. "Now I know what caused the laughter." They walked down the hall to their rooms.

* * *

THE next morning, not wanting the inconvenience of keeping cloaks wrapped tightly around them to hide the black uniforms, they had firstmeals in their rooms. Afterwards, Ballrand had the coach and horses ready. He tried to wave off the silver coins Zack proffered to him.

"You are in business," Zack said. "We will be back and forth. You provide excellent service, and have taken significant risk and harm. Please, take the coins." His smile warmed his words.

The jingle of silver dropping in Ballrand's hand produced a smile on his face as well.

Zack and Currat watched the coach moving north for a hundred yards before following.

The coach was stopped three times before reaching Kell's inn. The Men-in-Black numbered nine to ten in each case. The leaders had similar responses to those at Ballrand's Inn, and let the coach go without incident. Zack and Currat watched from cover each time, ready to engage if required.

Halfway to Kell's Inn, they passed the messenger on his way back to Hagan's End. Zack held his hand up and the man reined in.

"Any trouble?" he asked.

"A Men-in-Black squad tried to rob me. Those big blacks can't maneuver in tight places, however, and the woods offered an escape route. They soon gave up. I passed two other groups, but they didn't bother me. My horses are deceptive; they are better than they look."

"What did you discover at the inns you visited?" Currat asked.

"I told them about the coach and your disguises. Only one didn't smile. He'd been robbed the week before, and two of his guests died. His name is Ober and the inn is the Running Rabbit."

"We saw three Men-in-Black groups stop the coach," Zack added. "They all headed south. If you happen to hear them at night, make a note of where they camp. I suspect it'll be a cold camp or one with well-banked fires and a good way off the road. Don't approach them. We don't want those good horses rider-less."

The messenger chuckled, waved, and started south.

"We need to concentrate on the groups moving south and work our way north, Zack said. "Of course, it would be nice if we can establish a few groups as we go, but it takes time to train the leaders, and it's time we don't have. Perhaps Ober's inn will be a good place to start planting seeds." Currat nodded as they started north again at a canter.

The coach could be seen in the stable area at the Running Rabbit, and the only black stallions there was theirs. When they entered, the man behind the bar took one look at them and frowned. Zack held up two fingers and Currat and he picked the type of table they liked. Moments later, the barman delivered two mugs of ale, still frowning.

"I assume you're Ober," Zack said.

The man nodded, looking edgy.

"We're not going to rob you or molest your patrons. I believe our messenger had mentioned us, and I can only assume the lady and her escort have rooms. They probably asked for lastmeals to be delivered there. We would like to discuss what the Men-in-Black did to your custom at a better time, and quietly. Perhaps you can come to our room after the common room closes."

Ober's shoulders loosened a bit. "Yes, I can do that, and yes, the lady and her escort are having lastmeals upstairs, except for the man staying with the coach. What do you want to discuss with me?"

"Killing Men-in-Black," Zack answered.

Ober smiled for the first time since they arrived.

The large room assigned to Zack and Currat didn't have the fine furniture like the Blue Sail, but everything was clean, and the bed had no vermin. It did have a fireplace and two straight chairs. The colors remained the same as most inns—browns, tans, golds, and a bit of blue for accent. The white window curtains filtered the night breeze. A tub and hot water cost five coppers, and they ordered one sent up. Laundry cost another five, and they ordered that service for everyone in their group.

The serving maid brought in their lastmeal. "Your tub may be late. We have only two, and all those in your company ordered one sent to their rooms. Your coachman is using the one off the common room."

Zack nodded and passed three coppers to her. She smiled, showing too many black-rimmed teeth.

The tub came as late as the maiden had indicated and the men delivering the steaming water looked tired. After bathing, they'd just put on fresh privatecloths and trousers when Currat answered the knock on the door. Ober took one look around and came in, saying, "The boys will be up later to take the tub. What do you want to talk about?"

"First," Currat said, "we need to know why you want to kill Men-in-Black."

The innkeeper looked back and forth between them and finally sighed. "It's true what I told your messenger about those bastards killing two of my custom. What I didn't tell him is they held me and made me watch all ten of them rape my wife. She hasn't talked since, and won't let me touch her, not even a kiss. I'm not sure she'll ever recover. The last thing they said when they left was that they'd be back."

"I'm sorry," Currat said. "If you'd like, perhaps the Lady Adel will talk to her. It *might* help."

Ober thought a moment before nodding. The boys came for the tub, and Zack sent a note for Adel and Ursel to join them. She arrived as the boys took the last of the bath water out in large buckets and rolled the tub out. Ober seemed somewhat awed by her presence. She still wore a fine dress and a beautifully jeweled necklace with opals encased in gold wire frames.

Currat explained the problem.

Adel said, "Oh, the poor woman. Of course I'll talk to her."

Ober called for one of his boys to take her to his wife. "As you can see, I'm not a robust man for an innkeeper. What can I do?" he asked when they left.

Before Zack could answer, Ursel arrived and sat on the bed beside Currat. "I'm sorry for the delay. I had just gotten out of the tub when your note came."

Zack nodded and explained where they were in the conversation. "Ober wants to know what he can do."

"I think his best efforts would be in coordinating the actions of others," Currat said.

Ursel explained their mission. "Do you know men who feel as you do, and would be willing to put their lives at risk to kill the bastards?"

Ober answered immediately, his voice strong and filled with conviction. "Yes, over the last year, several men and women have been killed or raped. Some of the ones raped, like my wife, might have been better off dead."

Ursel told of the requirement for secrecy, which Ober seemed to understand. "Most importantly, I can't impress enough the need for testing the men you choose and waiting until plans are worked out. You need to find men who are good with archery and throwing knives or laying deadly traps. Our main goal is to kill without being killed, and that is best done by ambush."

"One of us will remain in the area to intensely train someone you may know," Ursel said. "I won't share my real name, and I use many names. The man sent to you can be identified by the question, 'I've never liked the color blue; do you have a room without it?' and as I said, he may be someone you know. You and the men you select will be killed if what you're doing becomes known to the wrong people."

"We found folks selling information to Men-in-Black," Currat added. "They're dead now. We urge you not to start a mission without guidance. There are actions that must take place afterwards, things that, if done wrong, could still get you killed."

"I understand completely," Ober answered.

I'm not sure I like the way he said that, Zack thought. *Something is not right.* He considered Currat and Ursel's concerned expressions. "Well, I think we've covered all we can tonight. You will be contacted soon."

Ober left, smiling.

The spies, alone and after checking the door, took a moment to mull the meeting over.

"Who wants the watch?" Zack finally asked.

"I'll take it," Ursel said. "But, I don't think anything will happen until an hour or two before daybreak. We shouldn't kill him if he does something, until we know what he's done."

"I've noticed Bryan snores," Zack said. "I'll take his place on the coach and send him to your room. There are some trees a little to the south that gives a view of the road both ways. If Ober is up to something, I don't think he'll check the horses, and he might not know how many we have. If he leaves, I'll follow with Ursel. Currat will stay on guard with the sons."

* * *

THE night turned cold and Zack shivered, pulling his cloak around him. The stable yard door eased open. Ober quietly walked to the stalls, looking over his shoulder at the coach four times before leading his horse out to the road, heading north.

Zack and Ursel gave him room and followed out of sight. When they came around a bend, they spotted Ober's horse and went deeper into the shade of the trees. A few moments later, Ober rode past them, going south. They led their horses to where Ober had stopped.

Zack pointed to a flat rock, different than those around it in color and mass. "Are they that stupid?" he whispered to Ursel, who smiled and nodded.

They couldn't read the note in the dark. Ursel took it with him and rode towards the inn. Zack hid.

The sunlight's first rays filtered through some of the trees when a lone Man-in-Black rode directly to the side of the rock. He dismounted, checked under it, got back on his horse, and rode back north. When he was out of sight, Zack returned to the Running Rabbit and joined his companions at the table. Ursel passed him the note under the table after he read it.

Have important information concerning those you look for and those in their party going north. It's worth many vouchers.

"The wife?" Zack asked Adel.

"Too many contradictions, especially when she's tired. She's lying. I asked a serving maid if Men-in-Black often stopped here. She said they did. When I asked if they caused trouble, she said no. I acted pleased and she looked relieved."

Ursel shook his head. "Handling this will take some thought, but we should act soon."

"We're two days from Kell's Inn," Zack said. "Four days to go and come back is too long. We need to put a plan in action today. I think we should let the Men-in-Black handle it for us. I suspect we'll see a group today. The one looking for the note had not ridden far." He explained the plan.

"I can do that," Ursel said.

* * *

TAKING their leave from the inn, they rode three hundred yards north of the rock Ober used, and saw what looked like a abandoned farm house sitting two hundred yards back at the end of a wide trail. As the coach pulled to a stop alongside the way to the structure, a Man-in-Black looked toward the road and rushed back inside. Moments later, nine Men-in-Black rode toward the coach.

Ursel stood with his cloak thrown over his shoulder, revealing his shirt. The sons—Dartel and Eartel—rose from their seats, notching arrows, but not putting tension on the strings.

Zack and Currat listened from the other side of the coach. Snowflake and Spellbinder's leads were fastened to the back.

The leader dismounted and approached Ursel while paying attention to the coach. His eyes widened when

Adel opened the door and, taking Ursel's hand, stepped to the ground. She handed the leather case to Ursel.

Ursel looked at the man before him. "Stand to position when you address a Master of the Purple!" The man looked confused, but snapped to. Ursel eyed him from head to boots. "You are in charge?"

The Master of the Blue nodded. "Yes, sir."

Ursel regarded him with amusement. "You've never seen one of my rank, have you?"

"No…no, sir."

Ursel took out the document and handed it to the officer. He did the same as the others and nearly collapsed before handing the parchment back.

It's amazing what those seals do to a man, Zack thought.

"You are gathering information from the Running Rabbit and sending it to the palace?"

The officer seemed to find some strength. "Yes, sir!"

"Have you paid him much?"

"Yes sir, a good bit. He has a lot of information."

"Some of the information has proven false. Officer of the Black Saunderson is not pleased. He hadn't reported your name to Spercine when I left the palace. Nonetheless, Wathdure paid me a visit last night. It seems our lord found the information untrue on his own. I suggest you remedy the situation today. Our lord wants nothing standing, and no one left alive. Do you think you can do that?"

"Sir, yes, sir!"

Rolling the parchment and placing it back in its case, Ursel gave his hand to Adel and she climbed back into the coach, clutching the case. Fifty yards north, Bryan reported Men-in-Black galloping south.

18

ZACK Rode beside Currat. "We should reach Kell's Inn by midday. Adel is probably jumping out of her skin."

"What do you think the twins are doing?"

"I don't want to guess." Zack chuckled.

As they neared the inn, the two men rode forward, outpacing the coach. They had barely given the reins to the stable boy when the twins half-ran, half-tumbled into the yard. Zack held up his hand before they could speak. "She's about a half-hour behind us. Go get cleaned up, and I think you should count on not sleeping here tonight."

Zack and Currat laughed when they blushed before nearly colliding with each other going through the door into the inn.

A moment later, Kell appeared, shaking his head. "I keep trying to remember having that much energy, and those memories seem to slip away. What is the news?"

"There's a lot," Zack said. "Ursel is with us. He's changed for the better—more mature and very well trained. We can talk whenever you have the time. It's been an eventful trip at times, and we are tired. We'll need two large rooms, one for us and one for Ursel, with a connecting door if possible. Three more are traveling with us. If you have the rooms, give them each one; if not, they can share. Are Men-in-Black here?"

"I do have the room and no Men-in-Black. Two groups came through a week ago, but none since then. I expect some to arrive any time. Several groups looked like they wanted trouble, but once they saw my boys and the sword I put over the bar, they have all backed off so far.

I'm wondering what would happen if I told them I didn't mind them staying here if they left my custom and family alone. I thought I might learn some of their plans."

"Mmm," Currat said. "Let's discuss it with Ursel. The idea might have merit. We must keep in mind that these groups coming down seem to operate under loosely defined orders. One may be reasonable and another cause trouble."

"I can see that happening," Kell said. "Come, I think I can find some cool ale for you."

The common room's coolness and dim light pleased the spies. They found a table next to the back stairs on the darker side of the room and against a wall, giving them a full view of the space and a quick escape if needed. As they sat down, Zack looked around and shook his head.

"What?" Currat said.

"I wonder if we could disguise ourselves?"

"I don't think so, unless we chop off some of our legs. We're seven inches higher than the average man here. I guess we could be made up like old, ill men, and have the sons take us in push chairs and hide all the weapons under our blankets."

Zack shook his head. "We must be tired!"

Kell came over with a pitcher of ale and six mugs. Setting them down, he pulled a table and chairs over. "Do you think Adel will want wine?"

Zack and Currat nodded.

"Derk is on the roof watching for the coach. Kerk is washing his face and cleaning his mouth. I've never seen them this excited!"

Kerk, followed by Derk, took three steps at a time and jumped the last six before running out the entrance.

Kell looked hopeless. "I think the coach is here!"

Laughter, talking, and giggles drifted into the inn, followed by two booming voices. "URSEL!"

Zack and Currat stepped out into the stable yard as the

sons brought the coach in. They and Bryan jumped down, also looking tired. He motioned for the stable boy. "Take the horses out of the traces, but leave the tack on them. I don't think the coach will be here that long. Give them some oats and water, and then let them loose in the paddock." He turned his attention to the sons and Bryan. "We'll be here a couple of days to rest. The innkeeper has rooms for each of you. I suggest you get your baths this afternoon. I don't think the twins will be here overnight."

Bryan laughed. "From what I saw, they might not make it until nightfall. But then, if I had a lady like Adel, I'd still be in the coach with the wormcloth pulled over the windows."

"And," Currat said, "that's why you *don't* have a *lady* like Adel. I think if we looked ahead, we might have planned on arriving later in the day."

Entering the common room, all ten of them met at the tables Kell had put together. Kell took the sons up to put away some of their weapons they'd refused to leave in the coach. Bryan went up to wash off the dust he'd collected from sitting on the back of the coach. By the time they all returned, Adel was telling the twins they'd have to wait until nighttime to hear all the tales of her trip.

Zack knew the tales wouldn't be on anyone's mind that night. Currat looked at him and winked.

"I know it's a little early, but I already have midmeal going, and it should be ready in a few moments," Kell said.

"Kell," Adel said. "I never knew riding in a coach that long would work up such a huge appetite. An early meal is fine."

The nods of agreement around the table left no doubt. Kell smiled and rushed off to the kitchen, reluctantly followed by the twins.

"I need to rest this afternoon," Adel said. The men at the table laughed, and Adel blushed when she realized what her thought implied. Then, she laughed, too.

The midmeal was good. Kell sent his fire-pit boy to Adel's home and soon, her stable man arrived. To the twins' dismay, she went home after telling them a lady has things to do before entertaining gentlemen. Kerk and Derk took it with grace, but Currat could tell they were about to jump out of their skin with anticipation. They were kept busy delivering and removing tubs and water during the afternoon. Zack, Currat, and Ursel bathed first and sprawled out with trousers and loose shirts on and a small cask of wine in Zack and Currat's room, the connecting door to Ursel's room open.

"I think we're getting old, Currat," Zack said. "Ursel doesn't look nearly as tired as I feel."

Ursel chuckled. "Riding in a coach for six days is a lot easier than on horseback. Even now, I'd still not want to face either one of you in a fight."

Currat smiled at Zack. "He certainly knows the right things to say. I wonder who Gaz found to teach him that charm."

"I bet it was a woman."

Ursel chuckled and shook his head. When they started their second goblet of wine, the conversation came around to more pressing matters. "I was disappointed with the happenings at the Running Rabbit," he admitted. "Thinking back, when the maiden said the Men-in-Black didn't cause trouble, she had a deceiving look. At the time, I thought it was my imagination."

"No, you were right in suspecting her," Zack replied. "An inn is a closed place to work. Not much goes on without the other workers knowing what's happening. The Man-in-Black said they'd paid Ober a lot of vouchers. When that much comes in, it's hard to hide from everyone and if one sees what's happening, they'll all know in a few days. Maidens like to talk."

"Are we going farther north?" Ursel asked.

"Would you like to see your family?" Currat asked.

"For no more than two hours, if at all. My father

wouldn't understand my not wanting to stay and take over his work at some point. My mother would be calculating what woman she could put me with for marriage. I don't want either. Zack, you remember my problems there. I don't want to revisit them. My battle sword and weapons are part of me, as is Arrowsmith. That's the name I've decided on for my horse." Pride could be heard in Ursel's voice. "He's getting used to me, and I made sure I paid attention to him whenever we stopped. He seems to like the training I'm giving him to become a warhorse."

He rose from his chair and paced the room. "I don't know what my family would think and when they see the jewels on my battle sword, it will raise a lot of questions. Seven Hells, just seeing the sword would raise questions I don't want to answer. I'd like to keep everything about what we're doing or my time in the Seven Realms private. My mother wouldn't be able to keep quiet about it, and my Da would suspect my loyalties to the family. I'm content just sending a message stating I'm well and prosperous, and perhaps a gold coin with it."

"If I remember," Zack said, "your village is about a two-hour ride from here. I think we should be able to send a messenger, maybe Bryan, to them. Men-in-Black wouldn't go after one man if he went into the woods or across fields; at least, I don't think so. They must be used to people avoiding them by now."

"Then, it's settled," Currat said. "I'll ask Bryan if he will go. I wouldn't want to trust anyone we don't know with a gold coin. We'll wrap it and the message, but unfamiliar messengers sometimes don't come back."

Ursel answered the knock on the door and admitted Kell. The innkeeper pulled another plush chair from Ursel's room. "I have a bit of time before lastmeal, and if I'm needed one of the boys will find me."

The spies took turns telling the plans they'd made and considered for forming the groups to attack the Men-in-

Black.

"I know one man," Kell said, "who probably wouldn't need scrutinizing. He continually rants about the murderous Ozlidians."

Zack looked at Ursel. "Should I tell him or you?" The spy smiled and nodded back. Zack continued, "Those type of men are the ones you should investigate the most. Many times their ravings are a ruse. Untrained men often make serious mistakes; ranting and raving is one of them. I would seek him out first and clear his name, or if the situation demands it, kill him. Killing men you've known for a long time is hard, much harder than taking down a Man-in-Black you've never seen before he rides at you with a raised sword. Kell, what we're proposing takes dedication to our cause and the will to make it work, no matter what the personal expenditure might be. One unpredictable man or woman can cause the death of your entire group. I've known men who, at the haranguing from their wives over where they went without telling them, have ultimately caused the death of both. It's best if married couples work together, and in many cases like yours, the children, too.

"As you know, Adel is already with us. The twins would never do anything to put her at risk and neither would you. But how about your inn's staff? Running your group from the inn would put everything at risk, including workers and patrons. The same would be true if Adel tried to have her members' meeting at her home. The village folk would eventually notice and gossip would flow. Those kinds of places are dangerous." He went on to describe the problems at the Running Rabbit.

"What would you suggest?" Kell asked.

"You have an advantage," Ursel answered. "Adel and the twins will never expose you, leaving you with people you can completely trust. If you meet someone while on a hunting excursion, you have someone to keep the watch and ensure you're not being overheard. I have men who have fought and killed with me. Yet I trust them only so far. I'll still observe them for any signs of discontent or hard feelings. Causing someone's feelings of being slighted or not having what they consider their due can have disastrous effects."

"I must say," Kell said, "some of these are things I'd never considered. What else is there?"

"A great many subjects," Currat said. "One of the most important is finding a way to verify your peoples' reports and actions without them knowing, and that is another reason to keep your identity secret from all but your principal group. They are your sons and Adel; I'd not consider adding anyone to them until they've completely proven themselves."

Zack frowned in thought as Currat went on.

"You must find a way of communicating without discovery. That can be hard. One of the best ways is to have a place to leave a mark, such as a broken stick, or rocks placed a certain way, that would alert the spy to go to another place known only to him for a message... perhaps a hollow in a tree, or an abandoned animal's hole. In these cases, you need someone to make certain you're not discovered setting up the alert.

"These two, I feel, are the most important things to consider. Next comes the need to plan attacks where your men are not discovered executing them. It's not good to kill nine or ten Men-in-Black a hundred feet from where schoolchildren are on a trip to learn nature's ways. You always need to ensure complete control over your men's actions and their surroundings."

"Do you know back roads to Hagan's End?" Zack asked.

Kell ran his fingers through thinning hair. "There are some that intersect with the main road for short differences, and then return into the countryside."

"One of the efforts we'd like to put forth is taking the Men-in-Black's horses to a grazing pasture an hour northwest of Hagan's End. It would be something to think about in the future. From this distance, it could be quite dangerous, time-consuming, and would require several men to scout front and rear for unwanted eyes. It may not be worth the time or possible violence to the men. But, if groups worked together so each went a relatively short distance, it might work."

"I'm afraid you're right; it would be too long a trip for one group," Kell said. "But I'll keep it in mind for multiple groups."

"Have you ever heard of barge traffic on the river having problems?" Currat asked.

Kell became excited. "No! There are roads going to the river from many villages west of the north-south road, and its delta is two miles south of Hagan's End. I've heard there are barges for sale due to the decrease in goods traveling on the river these days. Some are large, capable of holding eighteen to twenty horses. The river flows fast, but without rapids. Men-in-Black would have trouble keeping up with the barge while trying to navigate through trees and villages; they wouldn't get a mile. Some of the roads to the river skirt the villages. It's possible to lead the stallions through without being seen."

"That would be a whole other effort, needing coordination and additional men," Zack said.

"It's a good idea," Ursel said. It would offer less risk than shooting Men-in-Black. From what Briggs said, we'd have enough coins to pay the men well. *Still*, there's the secrecy problem. I wonder if Ozlid would care if we took the stallions."

"Wathdure may not care," Currat said. "Space is a cardinal consideration. Ozlid doesn't have the vast lands of the Seven Realms to keep huge herds of stallions. There are few pastures for them, and not many have horses other than the military and Wathdure's messengers. I suggest we buy a barge and test the scheme. It could be used for many things, including moving men out of danger."

"I agree," Ursel said. "Perhaps Yasho would know what's available."

* * *

BRYAN volunteered to take the message to Ursel's parents. The big spy briefed him on what to expect and where to find their cottage. He explained the village didn't have an inn, but it had a tavern with good food and ale in case there would be an answer to come back. Bryan rode out an hour after daybreak.

* * *

URSEL watched him go with mixed emotions; he wanted to see them, but not what would follow during his visit. His thoughts turned to Marcella and their clandestine meetings at the Blue Sail. He wondered if she would grow to love him as Adel loved the twins.

* * *

THE twins arrived in time to help with firstmeal, looking more rested than Zack anticipated, with abundant smiles and blushes throughout. When they brought ale behind the serving maidens carrying firstmeal, Derk said the weapons she gave them nearly matched the quality of Zack's blades. Adel wouldn't let them see their new clothes, however, until a special occasion arose.

"Seeing her after so long a time classified as an exceptional moment, but she wouldn't budge," Kerk said. "Da agreed to let us practice weaponry for an hour at sunrise before coming to the inn. He said those skills are more important than serving firstmeals. Derk and I are excited about improving what we can do to fight, but we both feel Da needs more help with us away after lastmeal and not returning until morning. He can't and shouldn't handle the tubs and water, even if he had the time."

"Do you know men that need the work?" Zack asked.

"What about—" Derk started.

"No, his wife is about to give birth," Kerk said.

"There are the—"

"They fight too much."

"I know. So what about—"

"Yes, they're strong enough and need the coins. When Ozlid killed their uncle, they swore revenge."

Derk looked at Zack with a lopsided smile. "See, that was easy."

Ursel laughed. "They sound just like you two." He said to Zack and Currat.

"It's a learned process," Currat said.

*   *   *

THE spies and the twins set up a target and practiced archery in the afternoon. Dartel and Eartel opened up and discussed their training. The former did most of the talking, but the latter interjected with a comment from time to time.

As they walked from the trees, Bryan rode toward them, bent over his horse's neck, tightly holding the leads of three black stallions. His left arm was soaked with blood.

They stopped his horse and took the leads.

"I'm so glad to see you!" he said. "I don't think my arm is as bad as it seems. The two that came at me couldn't fight very well. I got one with my short sword and the other with my long sword. But the leader cut me as the second one fell off his horse. The one falling still had his sword in his hand and he grazed the leader's horse in the right gaskin. He reared, throwing the man. My long sword slashed his throat."

They walked his horse to the stable. Zack and Currat helped him down as the sons took care of the horses. When Kell saw them enter, he sent a boy for the healer and brought water and cloths to Bryan's room by the time Ursel eased him down on his bed. Currat had slit the shirtsleeve open, exposing a shallow cut across the triceps. He cleaned the wound and put pressure on it when the water made it bleed. The blood had already stopped flowing when the healer arrived.

The healer gave Zack a pointed look. "Whenever you're here, my services are needed more than normal. Should I get an assistant until you leave?"

Zack laughed. "I don't think it'll be necessary."

"He won't need stitches, and you had the wound properly wrapped. I'll leave him in your care. Send for me if it becomes infected." He pulled a poultice from his bag and ordered it soaked in warm water before applying it.

Zack handed the man the ten coppers he requested for his services and walked him to the door. Kell followed him downstairs.

Bryan sat up to reach for a clean shirt that Currat passed to him.

"You did well," Zack said.

Bryan's expression was sheepish. "It was all luck, only three men—two who couldn't fight and a frightened stallion. Calming him took some time. He wanted to run, but I whistled like Currat showed me, and he came right over. The other two grazed alongside the road, and didn't protest when I took their leads...Oh, Ursel, I nearly forgot, I have messages from your parents in my saddlepack. Your ma insisted on feeding me midmeal while we waited for your da. I told them I'd met you in Hagan's End. Your ma asked a lot of questions I couldn't answer, and your da, only a few I could answer, mostly about your health.

"Your ma waited until her husband arrived to open your message. When the gold coin fell out of the box, she nearly fainted. Your da had to get her water. They read your message, and then wrote their reply. I implied I'd give it to you when I returned to Hagan's End. I think whatever you said in your message mollified them about your absence."

Kell returned with bread, cheese, and ale. Bryan smiled and began devouring his meal. Ursel thanked Bryan and left to find his messages.

* * *

ZACK found Ursel leaning against a tree behind the stable, folding the messages and shoving them in his pocket. "Is everything good?"

"Better than I thought. My da thanked me for the gold, and stated the coins he'd get from selling the charcoal forges and the forest he owns would allow them to have an excellent retirement when the time came. My ma went on about my health and prosperity, and also said they're enjoying good health and the business remained profitable. Ma did say she wanted me to come back and settle there…"

The big man paused briefly before continuing, "Do you remember the woman who caused me so much trouble?"

Zack nodded.

"Her name is Naydene. Her mother killed her da after a brutal beating. The village elders knew of her mistreatment and didn't charge her. Fran, the girl who was with her the day of the *incident*, told Bryan what happened; Naydene has never gotten a marriage proposal. Fran married the tavern owner's son and has two boys. Naydene got what she deserved. She was evil-minded. Fran was always sweet, and I'm glad she found happiness.

Ursel looked thoughtful. "I'm pleased at how this all turned out. Letting my parents know where I am and what I'm doing would put them in danger if I ever got caught. I'm sorry about Bryan."

Zack chuckled. "I wouldn't be too regretful. He'll have a small scar he can brag about, and a good learning experience. If he'd faced ten instead of three, you probably wouldn't have your messages, and we'd always be wondering what had happened to him."

19

THE last day at Kell's inn, the spies came together at Adel's home for lastmeal. They perused the weapons she had bought in Stonefire, giving their approval. When it became time to eat, Zack and Currat enjoyed the venison, root vegetables, a mixed berry crumble for dessert and an excellent wine. Currat looked on as Ursel beamed at the twins' happiness and snuck a gaze at Adel. She caught him, but didn't acknowledge it in any way Currat could see. Meanwhile, the spies worked out a simple code, identifying Ursel's messages. While there, they retrieved their short bows and bolts for the trip to Hagan's End from the coach. The bittersweet valedictions lasted only a few moments, and the ride back to the inn was quiet.

Kell brought the traveling group trail food as the twins returned to the inn an hour after sunrise. The farewells, said in words and waves, left Currat wondering when he might see them again, if ever.

Many things needed accomplishing before their return to the Seven Realms. He wondered if Zack wished for Stonefire the way he did. He shook his head; they couldn't leave until Ursel had his operation firmly set up, and that could take months.

* * *

WHEN Zack passed the burned timbers of the Running Rabbit, he caught Bryan and the arms master's sons smiling and nodding to one another. He wondered how many more such sights they'd see before the smiles stopped. Currat rode close and touched Zack's shoulder, his smile full of sadness. Zack nodded, and they rode farther south.

The rest of the trip to Ballrand's inn over the next few days went without incident. Zack supposed it to be due to them going the same direction as most of the Men-in-Black. He looked forward to seeing the tall, thin innkeeper, wondering what mischief his young son Tad had embroiled his young mind in recently. The wanderlust he'd first expressed years ago had vanished, but Zack and Currat thought his sense of adventure endured.

The lad, now fourteen summers old, took the horses as they dismounted in the stable yard, his smile as infectious as ever. He proficiently handled the leads, talking to and calming the big blacks. As he passed, he said, "Master Ursel's comments to the Men-in-Black must have worked. We've not seen any of them since you left. It's nice to see you dressed in something besides black. Will wearing regular clothing put you in more danger?"

Zack watched Tad with interest. "It could, if Men-in-Black are looking for Currat and me. We are tall, and Wathdure has described us to his men. They don't know Ursel; at least, I don't think they do. Wathdure has many powers, however and I wouldn't discount anything concerning him. Tad, you've heard and seen a great deal of the Men-in-Black and us. You must keep all of this to yourself. Talking about it, even with those you trust, could cause grave problems for all of us, including you and your family."

The boy nodded. "My da said the same thing. I have a few friends I see once or twice a week, and it was hard not to say anything, but when da said what he did, it made things a lot easier. Both of my friends I see the most have asked if we are troubled by Men-in-Black. I just reply 'some,' and let it go. They work on their da's farms and don't know what the Men-in-Black do. I tell them to stay clear of them."

"That's wise," Zack said. "How far is the river from here?"

Tad threw him a questioning look. "About five miles west."

Zack nodded, and the boy continued settling the stallions.

Ballrand chatted while showing the spies to their rooms. "I hear Briggs is back in a huge, red ship with bright yellow sails named *Sunbright Seas*. I thought the man was joking about the name, until another traveler said the same. I know he's done quirky things in the past, but this?"

Zack laughed. "I know—the first time I saw his old ship with those different-colored sails, I thought it must be a carnival on the water. I knew he wouldn't do such things to the *Silver Dolphin*, but I didn't expect something so colorful. I've seen his new ship, and it is *big*! One thing's for sure; no one will miss it."

Returning to a serious mien, he said, "Tad told me the river is about five miles west of here. Is there a back road going into Hagan's End from the river that would be mostly unseen by anyone?"

"Let me think…there might be. I seem to recall something from long ago. There's an abandoned village on the river. I know there's a road from there to here, about a half-mile south. It continued across the north-south road for a mile and reached the forests, following them to the outskirts of Hagan's End. It's not been used in years since the new road north was built, and I have no guess if it's still passable."

"Who?" Currat asked after the innkeeper left.

"Bryan, I think."

Currat nodded.

* * *

THE ship stood out and was hard to miss. She would have drawn attention from just her size, but the bright, true reds and yellows drew both the eye and a smile. Crewmen scrambled to unload cargo before sunset.

Zack chuckled. "The old Briggs is back." Currat just shook his head.

Reaching the Blue Sail Inn from the Tarnished Anchor stables, Zack sent a message to Captain Briggs asking him to join them for lastmeal. Yasho greeted them warmly, and had them settled in time to eat. The sons had veered off for home, leaving Bryan to join them. An answer arrived from Briggs, saying he would be available. Zack requested a private room. Within the hour, Yasho sent a serving maid to announce Captain Briggs's arrival. When Currat and he reached the room, Bryan and the captain sipped wine with Yasho.

"Really, Crawford, red and yellow?" Zack said.

The captain's laughter boomed across the room. "I figured if Wathdure looked for me, he'd find me, so why not have some fun? The colors aside, you should see the fittings. She's beautiful! I fully intend to keep her in the condition she deserves, like the *Silver Dolphin*."

"Well," Currat said, "*Sunbright Seas* fits her well."

"Ah, you noticed!" the captain said, smiling wider. "I appreciated the name's romance. On your next trip to Elizabethville, you must sail on her. The way she handles rough seas is phenomenal. She's also quite spectacular below decks, with three large guest cabins."

"We'll look forward to the voyage. It sounds like you spent much on her at Deepwells," Zack said while looking at Currat with a smile.

"That, I did. It all came out of my commission, and I think Yasho is happy with the profit. I understand it goes to those who lost family to the Men-in-Black. I'm even more glad about your use of the funds, but not by much!" Crawford smiled from ear-to-ear.

"Speaking of commissions, we might have found a way to transport horses to the grazing pasture, but I need your insight. I understand there's an abandoned village near Ballrand's inn, five miles west on the river and back roads, coming out along the forest north of here. What do you think of using barges?"

Yasho looked at Briggs, and they both started to answer at once. Briggs signed with his hand for the innkeeper to go first. Yasho took a breath. "The *road* from the village is not much more than a trail at this point. I heard a guest describing it last year when he hunted the area. The way from the north-south road has always been little more of a trail, but it should be passable with not too much effort. I've heard there are three barges for sale near the delta. They dock at the pier aside the short road to Hagan's End that also leads to the channel back up river. One is fairly new and it's large and covered. There shouldn't be a problem buying draft horses to pull them upstream." Yasho used the same hand signal back to Briggs.

"I too, have heard there are barges for sale. The delta is shallow, and not a place I can bring the *Sunbright Seas* to; nonetheless, a barge can follow the shallows to a drop off a mile south of the delta. I could anchor her there the same way I did when we took her. I had the same kind of hoist installed on her that's on the *Silver Dolphin*, but with a larger reach she can easily handle. We could try it to use in emergencies. I've not tried to anchor there, and I don't know what damage the area might cause to my ship. It must be a real crisis for us to attempt it. I can sail there, and send a diver down to look at what we face. It may not be bad."

"I think we should buy the barge now," Ursel said. "If we don't use it for horses, there're more uses for it, such as for disposing of bodies at sea and getting supplies to our groups. The Men-in-Black don't bother with the barges, and I can see them leaving the river traffic alone to allow Hamptor to get some things done. If they attacked everything, Hamptorians might raise a response Wathdure doesn't want.

"We also need to establish the groups to take the horses from holding areas that also have to be found.

Lady Adel may have one, and that would be a good place to start. Mapping the area from the river to our pasture needs doing. Yasho, do you know someone who can accomplish it?"

The innkeeper thought for a moment, rubbing his chin before answering. "Yes, and I have an excuse for having it done. We've talked about opening an inn or cheese factory. That property is on the way to the pasture. There's a surveyor in town that was thrown out of the army for assaulting another officer. He drinks a bit, but not when he's working. I'll tell him I need to know the possibility of using the river to take cheese north. Come to think of it, why not have him explore the landings and way to the north-south road? He could do it faster than establishing new men to accomplish the same thing."

Zack gave Ursel a discreet nod.

"Let's get him started," Ursel said. Pay him the going rate, and perhaps promise a bonus for completing the maps faster than normal. We had thought about using Bryan for the exploring. This will keep him available. I like that."

Bryan looked disappointed, but didn't speak.

"I saw that look," Ursel said. "You need the arms practice more than riding all over the wilds of Hamptor."

"I'll see the surveyor later today," Yasho said. "I also talked to Turlas. He's in favor of our venture to start a cheese factory rather than an inn. After a bit more thought, I agree with him. I should have the building process begun by next week. It'll take several months to complete, and I may have to order some materials from the Seven Realms."

Currat smiled. "Yasho, you do like getting things done."

"Well, I do try while trying not to be too trying."

The others groaned.

* * *

ZACK sat with Currat, Ursel, Yasho, and Bryan in the feasting room the next day after the firstmeal guests had left and the staff had brought the room back to its usual pristine cleanness. "Yasho, what do you need from us?"

The innkeeper answered at once, as if he'd given the subject much thought. "Captain Bronson is leaving on the evening tide. If possible, I'd like to have as much information as possible from the Seven Realms on building and running a cheese factory. I know some of what is needed, and I have set a meeting with three dairy farmers to discuss what they know. I'm sure they'll be most happy to help in order to sell more milk. Still, your country is more advanced than ours, and any help will be greatly appreciated."

"I'll have a note for the garrison commander, and another for an innkeeper to send with Bronson. They should be able to help. Is there anything else I can do for you?"

"Not that I can think of right now," the innkeeper replied. "What are you planning?"

"Currat, Bryan, and I are going to Ballrand's inn to see how many black stallions we can round up. I want to use the back roads, and see what we're up against in getting to the pasture with a small herd—no more than twenty horses, if we can find that many. That is, if you can spare Bryan."

Yasho smiled at the young man. "Bryan, you're fired."

Bryan's shock showed on his face. "But—but—"

Yasho held up a hand. "You'll still be paid as if you're here full time. You're needed working with Ursel more than here, and that's why we have the coins to run our groups. If Ursel has no objection, I'll leave you to him for whatever he requires."

"I'm pleased, Yasho," Ursel said. "I was going to mention his involvement with us to you. We need to start on several activities, and he'll be an asset. He'll ride north at sunrise tomorrow. I have set a meeting with Captain

Derkson for tomorrow night. I could be very busy this next week. I'm hoping that is the case. Also, I'll see to his weapons training."

20

THE ride north went without incident. That wasn't the situation at Ballrand's inn, however. When entering the stable yard, Zack saw nine black stallions in stalls. Tad came out with a bruise under his right eye. Bryan looked as if he wanted to kill someone. Zack bristled with anger.

"Are they staying overnight?" Currat asked.

Tad nodded. "They hit Da when he didn't have enough separate rooms for all of them. They refused to double up, and killed a guest to get the room for their last man. Da ordered the women away when the trouble started. That angered them more. I think they would have hurt Da more if they didn't need him to serve them."

"Which one hit you?" Currat asked.

Tad lowered his head. "The leader. He spoke with our accent. The others sounded like Ozlidians."

"I want you to get your da to come here when he can, and then I want you to hide in the loft over the stalls. If it looks like you're in danger, just motion for him," Zack instructed.

As Tad scampered for the inn, the spies took their horses to the back of the stable and tethered them out of sight.

Ballrand found them there. He looked haggard, his normally clean apron smudged with grease from cooking. "Kill them!" he cried. His voice rocked with emotion.

"I plan on it," Zack said. "What room is the leader in, and are the others still in the common room?"

"They got here for midmeal, and most of them have been drinking ale since then. Four have gone up to their rooms. The leader didn't drink much, and he's in the common room finishing his lastmeal. Two have their heads on the table, and the other two are not far from falling over."

"Can we get to the leader without him seeing us?" Currat asked.

"If you come through the kitchen, none of them will see you."

"Ballrand, I've never seen your kitchen. Why don't you show it to us?" Zack asked.

The innkeeper smiled. "It would be my pleasure."

Zack took his short bow and quiver of arrows before following Ballrand around the side of the inn.

The kitchen lay in disarray from lack of staff. Zack eased the door open and peered into the common room. Pulling the door toward him, he nocked an arrow, handing four others to Currat. With the first shaft, he shot the leader in the neck. Currat had the second shaft ready and within two heartbeats it flew into the skull of one who now lay on the table beside the dead leader. The third man started to rise. The next shaft struck him in the left eye.

"Nice shot," Currat said.

"Not really," Zack replied. "I aimed for the right eye. He moved."

The next two shafts powered into skulls, knocking the men over their chairs.

"Let's get the bodies out of sight," Zack said.

Moving the dead, Zack was glad to see his placement of the arrows had produced a minimum of blood. They took them, one at a time, out the back door to the stables. Tad didn't look at all shocked at seeing the bodies. Zack felt a pang of wistfulness at the thought of this young boy, who wasn't the least bit moved by the sight of death. *They grow up too fast!*

The spies followed Ballrand upstairs. "Take me to the farthest room where they are and we'll work back toward the stairs. I assume you have your master key," Zack whispered.

Ballrand nodded and stopped at the last room on the floor.

"Watch what I do," Currat whispered to Bryan. He nodded to the innkeeper.

Ballrand opened the door and stepped back. The Man-in-Black lay on his side facing the door. Currat silently slipped in to stand behind the sleeping man, pulled his head back by the hair, and slit his throat in one quick motion. Zack slammed a pillow across the man's neck as the knife cleared the body, with a trickle of gore staining the bedclothes. Blood soaked the pillow and not much else. Ballrand looked pleased.

Two rooms down, Zack indicated for Bryan to use the pillow. The Man-in-Black faced away from the door. Bryan was a little late with the pillow, and some blood splattered on the wall. He looked contritely at Ballrand.

"Don't worry. That wall needed plastering anyway," Ballrand said, smiling.

In the next room, Bryan had the pillow over the Man-in-Black's head nearly before the knife had finished its purpose. At the room next to the stairs, Zack motioned for Bryan to use the knife. The door swung open to reveal a Man-in-Black facing away, slashing the air with his sword. Bryan rushed in and caught the Ozlidian from behind, reaching around for his chin. The man jerked his sword arm backward into Bryan's inside thigh. Ignoring the cut, he stabbed his knife into the swordsman's throat, crushing small bones. Gurgling sounds stopped when the Man-in-Black hit the floor.

Zack looked down at the small trickle of blood seeping from Bryan's inner thigh. "What is it with you and thigh wounds? Now the women will definitely swoon."

"I did quite nicely with just the old scar. I didn't need this one."

"That's good," Zack said, while pulling the embarrassed young man's trousers down and looking at the cut. "Ballrand, can you get some water and cloths to wrap this young man's claim to disaster in?"

"Right away." The innkeeper chuckled. "And I'm sure my wife can mend the trousers."

Bryan blushed, again. After the innkeeper left, he frowned.

"What ails you beside your leg?" Currat asked the young man.

"I…I guess I still have a problem with the way we kill them. It just…doesn't seem right."

Currat placed his hand on Bryan's shoulder. "You know what these men do without compulsion. They kill women and children and torture to death men on the filmiest of excuses or for no reason at all. They killed a man here just to get his room. I think many of the Men-in-Black may be under Wathdure's influence, but that means they won't change. We have little choice. Many innocent lives will be lost if we don't act. We don't have the men or training to face them in open combat. Should we let them continue their crimes while we do nothing?"

Bryan still looked troubled, but said nothing.

* * *

AFTER carting the bodies outside, Zack ordered them placed in Ballrand's wagon, and the purses and all of their saddlepacks put in what would be his room. Zack asked the innkeeper if he knew a place where he might leave the black stallions until they could be herded to the sea. Ballrand indicated a location where a nearby farmer slaughtered his goats that had an adjacent field not in use. Bryan, in still ripped trousers, and Currat drove toward the site. Once the wagon was out of sight, Ballrand rang a bell beside the stable. Women's heads peeked from around a haystack on the other side of the paddock. The innkeeper nodded, and they started for the inn.

An hour later, Zack had finished going through the

Men-in-Black's saddlepacks, finding the usual orders and vouchers. He'd transferred the coins from the purses to the leader's large one. Not as much as some he'd found, there were still three gold coins and a handful of silvers. He placed the rolled vouchers in a pouch the leader used to give to Ballrand. The coins would go for the continued relief of Hamptorians, leaving an impression of where they came from and how they got to them without jeopardizing the spies.

Ballrand's wife opened the kitchen again, and made lastmeal for the men from Hagan's End. The innkeeper had closed the inn for the night. He sat with the spies while they ate. Halfway through the meal, Zack slid the voucher pouch to the innkeeper. He looked inside at the voucher's denominations and whistled.

Zack shrugged. "It takes vouchers to have blood sanded out of floors, plaster walls, and replace bed-clothes. I want to leave at sunrise with the horses. Do you know of any other stallions in the area we can take?"

"There's a farmer whose land is northwest of here. He complains of ten stallions grazing on his land."

"Do you know the surveyor, Jax Topin?"

"Yes, he was here five nights ago, and again two nights ago. He said something about searching out the old trails from the river to someplace above Hagan's End. He seemed happy on his return trip, so I assume he found what he wanted."

"Is the farmer you're talking about near the old trail?"

"About a half-mile east of where the trail turns west. It'll be a few days' ride. Do you want me to have travel food made up for you? I think the vouchers will more than cover the cost."

Zack nodded. Ballrand smiled again.

* * *

THE spies crested a hill, and Zack could see the stallions grazing in a dell below. It took little time to round them up, place leads on those that had lost theirs, and add them to the nine they already had in tow. They regained the trail without seeing the farmer.

The second night it rained, but not before they had time to build a shelter with an oilskin tarp in a stand of cottonwoods. The welcome downpour allowed them to refill their water bags and sang them to sleep.

The morning brought clear skies and a hot firstmeal. At midmorning, the trees along the trail lessened and, an hour later, they ventured out to see Hagan's End below them.

Eartel waved from the pasture. The spies returned the salute, and Zack was surprised to see three additional stallions standing near the trees at the back of the dell. They trotted forward to meet the newcomers as they passed through the gate.

"It's good to see you," Eartel said. "I can do only so much target practice."

"It's good to see you as well," Zack said. "Has there been any trouble?"

"No. Yasho or Turlas bring in supplies every three days, and they should arrive later today. He told me about the *Sunbright Seas*. I'm looking forward to seeing her. Dartel should be here in three more days to relieve me. I'm running low on food and ale, but if the supplies come, we should have a decent lastmeal.

"I rode out yesterday to get some exercise for me and a horse. I found the three blacks grazing just past the woods on the seaside of the road. They still had leads, and came to me easily."

He must miss his brother, Zack thought. *That's the most I've heard him say at one time.* "We have a few supplies left. It should be good either way. The ale will be appreciated."

Currat and Bryan finished taking off the stallion's leads, letting them roam the enclosure. Zack dismounted, and Currat took Spellbinder's reins while going to the picket line and unloading saddlepacks. The men sat around the fire pit as Eartel broke out mugs and poured ale from a large cask.

Zack stretched his legs out and leaned back on his elbows. *It's good to relax. I wonder if Briggs is in port.*

Currat looked lost in thought, while Bryan still wore a troubled mien.

"What?" Zack asked the two men.

"He's still unsettled over the way we kill the Men-in-Black," Currat said.

"Bryan, you have a sister, I think?" Eartel asked.

The young spy nodded.

"What would you do if ten Men-in-Black raped her, cut off her nipples and nose, and branded 'WHORE' across her forehead?"

"I'd kill every last one of them."

"You remember old Master Jerome who lived half way to Ballrand's inn?"

Bryan nodded. "He traded with my da."

"I guess you know his son and wife died of the flux. The only family left was his granddaughter. Men-in-Black did that to her. She hung herself, and he drank himself to death. Now, are you still upset about killing the bastards?"

Bryan slumped in thought. No one spoke for a quarter hour. He let out a groan and re-crossed his legs. "Not as much, but I still don't like it."

"Bryan," Zack snapped. "None of us like or want it done. We all despise killing that way. Not every man is meant to do what we accomplish. If you're not one of them, there's no shame in finding other ways to help our efforts. You must find at least some peace with what we do, or it'll eat your insides out, and you'll be no good to anyone, least of all yourself."

The young man nodded and took a long draught of ale.

After a few moments, Eartel broke the silence. "Bryan,

come practice archery with me. It's a lot more fun in a competition."

Bryan seemed to come out of his thoughts. "Shooting with me is no contest for you! Alright, let's do it."

As the two men moved away, Zack and Currat took a sigh of relief. Zack threw his partner a meaningful look. "Perhaps."

Currat nodded.

An hour later, the crack of a whip brought the men alert.

"That's Yasho's signal," Eartel called out.

Zack and Currat sheathed their swords.

Coming down the hill, Yasho beamed at Zack and Currat. His energetic wave nearly made him drop the wagon's reins. The draft horse turned his head back to Yasho and snorted. He halted the wagon near the picket line as Eartel and Bryan came over. The young men started unloading supplies while Yasho walked to the fire pit, smiling. "I see you found a few strays."

"Nine were not strays," Zack said. "Their owners had terrorized Ballrand's inn."

Yasho's smile faded. "Well," he said. "Briggs will be glad. His ship is in port, and I don't think he has a cargo for her."

"We'll ride back with you. We need to sleep in a real bed!" Currat said.

Yasho's smile returned.

When the last of the supplies sat neatly stacked, Zack motioned Eartel away from the others. The young man came close. "Eartel, how would you feel about talking out Bryan's feelings with him?" Zack asked.

"I wouldn't mind at all. I felt the same way at one time."

Zack nodded and walked with Eartel back toward the horses and Bryan. "Would you mind staying overnight here?" he asked them both. "We'll be back tomorrow about midday."

"That would be great. We can shoot more," Eartel said.

Bryan shrugged, smiled, and nodded.

Zack and Currat rode ahead of the wagon to the Tarnished Anchor's stables. On the walk to the Blue Sail, Yasho kept the spies amused with tales of goings on at the inn.

The *Sunbright Seas* seemed to fill the water's vista when they turned seaward. Zack sighed with contentment at the sight.

It looked large from the hilltop, but not this big. It amazes me every time I see it.

Yasho sent a message to Briggs and Bronson, asking them to meet for lastmeal. He next settled the spies in their rooms. The agreeing reply to his message came swiftly.

* * *

ZACK and Currat sat drinking wine from a goblet when Yasho ushered the captains into the private room. Smiles, grasping arms, and slaps on the back done, everyone settled around the table for eight in stuffed leather chairs, while Yasho poured the wine.

A few moments later, a serving maid interrupted the conversation by opening the door. Yasho nodded, and she hurried away as Jasper entered and closed the door behind him. The talk continued, with Yasho grinning from time to time. He listened intently to the account of happenings during Zack's trip, but said nothing.

Three serving maids returned with platters of steaming food and two small casks of wine, followed by three musicians with string instruments, one with a big-bellied base supported by a narrow leg and a lady pushing in a harp. Yasho looked as if he'd found a chest of gold. He busied himself getting the instruments placed and helping the harpist set up before sitting back at the table. He seemed quite proud. "I suggest we continue our present conversation later over brandy." No one objected.

The venison, seared on hot coals, and then basted with butter, herbs, and spices smelled mouthwatering. A salad with hard-to-find produce, leafy and root pods dressed with a flavored oil and vinegar caused a few smiles while the vegetables cooked in butter and spices caused Briggs to shake his head.

"What is the occasion?" the robust captain asked.

"Two things," Yasho answered. The estimate for our venture came in under what was originally quoted…and …today is the anniversary of the inn's twenty-fifth year in business."

Zack stood. "To the Blue Sail; may she ride high for another twenty-five!"

The others rose and clinked goblets, to Yasho's obvious enjoyment.

The lastmeal done, the musicians dismissed, the platters cleared away, and the goblets refilled, the men settled in plush chairs set in a semicircle before the fireplace. Zack told everyone what had happened on the spies' trip, leaving out his concerns about Bryan. On his part, Briggs told of Bronson's two successful voyages to Elizabethville. Smiling, he recounted sailing with a huge cotton shipment on the *Sunbright Seas*. "It would have taken two trips on the *Silver Dolphin*," he said. "Now, I have twenty-two lovely horses to crap all over my beautiful deck." The men all laughed. "But my commissions make it all worth it."

Zack sat up straighter. "We know the way from the dock west of the north-south road to the pasture is clear. What's happening on the subject of a barge?"

"On Briggs's recommendation after seeing what's available, I bought a large one that we think will carry up to twenty horses," Yasho said.

"Twenty!" Briggs said. "She'll likely carry twenty-five, with room for hay and supplies. She has a sleek bottom that'll help the draft horses and a curved bow to glide through the current."

"Be that as it may," Yasho continued. "It will require two draft horses to pull her upstream to the dock near Ballrand, and two weeks to the one near Lady Adel. The channel is on the far side of the river, which helps, and the way should be clear, from what I heard bargemen say."

"Jasper," Zack said. "I think it's time to send a message to Lady Adel, letting her know the barge is available. She has a few blacks there, and a run is in order, if only to see its feasibility."

"She's communicated once indicating she has twelve horses," Jasper replied.

Zack looked at Yasho. "We have a barge. Do we have bargemen?"

"I think so." Briggs said. "We need to validate their feelings toward the Men-in-Black, but I don't think there'll be a problem."

"I assume Yasho has the men's names and how to reach them?" Zack asked.

Briggs nodded.

"Let me discuss it with him tomorrow. Currat and I are tired. We need some rest before contemplating heavy matters, especially after the wine and brandy."

"Me, too!" Yasho mock-slurred.

After jovial farewells, Zack and Currat headed for their room. Closing, locking, and bolting the door, Zack threw his cloak on a chair in the anteroom and began to strip. Currat, following suit, then brought out the last of their brandy with two goblets. The men sat in their privatecloths in their comfortable chairs, looking at the dancing flames coloring the bricks of the fireplace in deep oranges and yellows.

Zack took a cloth off the table, soaked it in the basin of water, wiped his face, and wrung the excess into the fire. Bright orbs of color reflecting the various hues of the room—browns, reds, yellows, and blues—shot into the air and fell into the fire with a hiss.

* * *

AS Zack and Currat finished their firstmeal in the feasting room the next morning, Yasho came over with two steaming mugs. "Something special," he said. "It's a tea Bronson brought over from Elizabethville. I added sweetstones and a little cream."

Blowing across the top, Zack tasted the hot liquid. "It's good," he said. Currat also nodded his approval.

"Yasho," Zack continued. "What can you tell me about the bargemen Briggs found?"

"Not much besides their names and where to find them."

Ursel came over and sat down. "Sorry I'm late. I met with Briggs before he left port on a rush shipment. His crew had worked most of the night, but he'll sail directly to the shore by the pasture to get the stallions on his return and sail back to Elizabethville without returning to Hagan's End. He filled in more information about the bargemen than we discussed."

"Your timing couldn't be better. I'd just asked Yasho about them," Zack said.

"There's four, and it would take them all to handle a barge that big—three on the barge and one on the towpath going upriver, and all four to handle the poles and cargo going downstream. I would suggest having two more for emergencies when a regular bargeman isn't available or for special shipments. As Briggs said, the barge is covered. It has flaps over windows that can be tied back. If needed, we could transport fighters with a cargo.

"Three live here, but one lives close to the delta. I'll send messages to them about working on a large barge. I want to interrogate them one at a time over the course of a day. We'll need set it up like we did for Captain Tomwell, but with the added precaution of seeing if they talk about it to strangers, perhaps with Turlas."

Zack moved his fingers across his lips. Ursel continued, "It's something I need to further think about. I should have it worked out by tomorrow morning in time to send the messages after firstmeal."

"Let's plan on meeting here in the morning," Zack said. There were nods all around.

Yasho left to see to his other guests, and Ursel looked at Zack with a raised eyebrow.

"It might be best if you could have different men talk to the bargemen to see if they disclose our plans," Zack said.

Yasho returned and sat quietly, listening to the conversation.

"It'll take some investigation to see where they go for ale," Ursel said. "Also, I received a message from Captain Tomwell; his men are ready for interviewing. He says he has five men who are all excellent with archery and knives. He used the message criteria I sent him, and no one saw me pick up his reply. Perhaps we can have all the men validated in two days. I'd like to send Tomwell's group out on a mission north toward Ballrand's inn, or even farther, soon."

"I agree," Zack said. "The sooner the better. Like all of us, I'm anxious to get our groups organized and working, but we must consider the problems in moving too fast. One of our goals must be establishing groups north of here. Tomwell knows a lot of men, some of whom may live north of Ballrand's inn." A short pause, then he added, "When do you next meet with him?"

"I told him in my message I'd contact him within two days. He'll check for another message at midmorning. I can set up an appointment for tonight at the barn."

Yasho asked, "Don't you think we should send the barge to Lady Adel's area?" Yasho asked.

"I'm in favor of that," Ursel replied. "Jasper could send a bird announcing the time of arrival. On the first run, someone they know should be aboard the barge."

"I can't be away from the inn for that long, but Turlas could go," Yasho said. "It would be good experience for him."

"The first trip," Zack said, "could be dangerous. We don't know these men, and it would be good to see how they react with each other. Currat and I can go. We're good at hiding our battle swords, and the bargemen would only outnumber us two to one. We can handle them."

"You'll be gone a little less than four weeks," Ursel said. "I'll ask Jasper to send a bird letting Adel know you're coming. I think you can use the bird on the trip back. Let me know when you're three days out from the landing near Ballrand's inn; I'll send Tomwell out in time to meet you there, hopefully, with horses, vouchers, and purses. Which brings up another point—we need to establish a way of distributing the coins to families harmed by the Men-in-Black."

"Yasho," Zack said. "You're in a position to hear about the bastards' atrocities. Could you set up a way of receiving messages from trusted innkeepers naming those who lost family members or were assaulted by them? We could then send coins out. We have to be careful how that's handled. It wouldn't be good to add a message, just the coins."

"Why is that?" Yasho asked.

"Sooner or later, the Men-in-Black will find out what we're doing," Currat explained. "If they find the recipeents, they won't know any information to give up. We don't want a trail back to us. When they do find out, we'll have to change the way we distribute the coins. Also, we don't want the innkeepers hassled with requests for coins. Secrecy must be kept in all we do, and we must make the innkeepers aware of what could happen if they're discovered. It's a risk to them, and to us if they talk to others. I have no problem with Ballrand and Kell; they know what's at stake."

"I *understand* that!" Yasho said. "I certainly don't want a line of people asking for coins to offset what the Men-in-Black did to them. The inn would greatly suffer, and I probably wouldn't live long!"

"I'll interview the new men with the necessary precautions," Ursel said. "We should have the barge ready to travel in three days if there are no problems with the men. I'll set up seeing Tomwell's men tomorrow and the bargemen the next day. We need to get messages to the barge folks. Yasho, can you take care of getting them ready for us?"

"I will," Yasho replied. "Also, since Ursel might be meeting them during the day, I have a screen he can use to hide his features."

"That would simplify things, but it's not possible," Ursel said. "There will be at least three men involved, and we need to hide their faces as best we can. I see no way of protecting our men if we meet in the daytime."

"There might be," Yasho said. "I'm sure you remember the Sailor's Quest inn, where Currat was tortured. We might be able to use one of his rooms with screens in place to hide three men. The bargeman would receive a message to meet the barge's owner there. Jadel, the innkeeper, has never talked about what happened, except to me. He's extremely grateful Ursel saved his wife, Surelle, and his daughter, Risa. I don't believe any of them would ever say anything about the bargemen's visit. Ursel, I'm sure Jadel would welcome a visit from you."

"That could solve problems with the men Tomwell recommends, too." Ursel said. "We won't often need a room. I doubt he'd receive a visit from the Men-in-Black, but if he did, he can plead ignorance. Many innkeepers don't remember guests for long, usually only the ones that give them trouble. I'll pay Jadel a visit this afternoon. For now, we can interview Tomwell's men at the barn. I'll set that up for tomorrow night and, if Jadel agrees, we can interview the bargemen the next day."

"I suggest we meet back here for lastmeal," Zack said.

* * *

THE feasting room contained only a few guests when Zack and Currat settled at their usual table while waiting for Yasho and the others. Jasper arrived first, with a small white feather on his shirt. He looked happy. "It seems," he said, "that the big bird is a female, and had some fun on her last flight over the sea. She laid the biggest egg I've ever seen this morning, and is quite protective of it. I hope you don't want a message sent to the Spires anytime soon."

Jasper's smile was infectious, and Zack and Currat both laughed at that.

"I got your message," the warrior-priest continued, "and yes, the same bird we send to Lady Adel will find its way back from the landing near Ballrand's inn, or anywhere along the route it traveled north. I suggest sending the hawk. I wouldn't want the bargemen thinking a pigeon would be good for dinner. They'll think twice about approaching an un-hooded hawk."

"I might think twice!" Zack said.

"Nonsense," Jasper replied. "I'll introduce you to him before the flight. He'll be fine when you take him from Lady Adel's home or the nearby landing. Don't get upset if he goes on a hunting trip once in a while. In my experience, he's never gone long, and always returns with a full stomach. If anyone he doesn't know approaches, such as the bargemen, they won't do it again. His beak and claws are razor-sharp, and he knows how to use them."

Ursel pushed through the swinging doors and headed for their table, all smiles. A serving maid followed him, bearing a pitcher of ale and mugs. She set them down as Ursel sat. "I'll tell Yasho you're here," she said.

Zack eyed Ursel. "Well?"

"Jadel and his family didn't want me to leave. I explained our needs, and they are glad to help and understood the need for secrecy. I don't think there'll be a problem. He had screens, also. We tried them, and they worked fine. We can see through to the other side, but can't be seen. I sent a message for Tomwell to bring his men tomorrow starting at midmorning, and every two hours afterward. I suggested he bring them here tomorrow for lastmeal. Yasho can seat them a few tables away, and you can observe them from a distance."

"I could do what?" Yasho asked as he came up behind Ursel.

Ursel explained and the innkeeper nodded. "Seating them near you won't be a problem. Also, I've arranged for a closed pasture near the trail to our place by the sea. Tomwell should be able to find it on the back trails. Turlas knows where it is, and he can take any horses on to the seacoast."

Zack said, "If the interviews go well, Currat and I could start for Lady Adel's three days from now. We'll need supplies for the bargemen and us. I want the men well paid, as we discussed. The food should also be better than average. We want them to like working the barge for more reasons than good pay. We'll need to stop any bad behavior, and periodically keep an eye on them in the taverns, especially right after we take them on, and after the first trip."

Ursel nodded his agreement. "We can use Sonkek, Eckert, and Bryan for the taverns. Men are used to seeing them working at the various inns anyway. We also can have them listen for gossip and news. I imagine they hear a lot from the patrons. Yasho, do you see any reason not to use them for information gathering?"

"No, it's an excellent idea. All three have approached me separately asking for more involvement in our operations. They are already bringing me tidbits of news from the taverns. So far, none has risen to the level to speak of it with you, but I've encouraged them to keep listening."

"That's good," Ursel said.

"I'll be seeing Briggs next," Zack said. "I'll impress on him the need for our communications to go smoothly. Jasper, can one of your birds be linked to a ship?"

The priest thought for a moment. "If the ship is in dock, yes. On the open sea, I doubt it. The bird would fly itself to death trying to find Briggs out there. The big one would have the capacity to search, but finding a ship on open seas is a large task. In an emergency, I think I could direct it back here after a day of looking, but not the smaller birds. I've asked the Spires for more birds, and some should arrive soon. We can have one for each of our outposts. Because we priests can link with the birds' minds, people seem to forget they can carry written messages."

Zack said, "I'll leave in the morning to meet Briggs. Ursel, how do you see this going?"

The big man stroked his chin as he thought. "If Jasper can figure out the best use of the birds for the messages, and Yasho could school our men on how to get information out of drunks, Currat could come with me on the interviews. I'm sure we'll see each other beforehand, but let's plan on meeting here for lastmeal three days hence."

The men nodded and began to talk about eating.

21

ZACK bid Currat goodbye, and rode out to the pasture near the trail to the seacoast north of Hagan's End. He found it without trouble, and was surprised to see two black stallions nibbling on dew-drenched grass. Both still had saddles strapped on them, and immediately came to him when he whistled. He tied leads from his saddlepacks on them and rejoined the trail.

Arriving at the pasture, he smiled when seeing Bryan shooting with Eartel. They saw him, and rushed to open the gate at the bottom of the road. The men removed saddles and tack, getting rewarding nudges from the new arrivals. They added the saddles to a growing pile, and Zack put the saddlepacks on Spellbinder for later inspection. The small herd now numbered twenty-four.

Zack looked at the close grouping of arrows on the target a hundred yards away, then back to Bryan. "You're doing well. How often are you practicing?"

"I come out every morning and wake Eartel. We have firstmeal together and start shooting. We usually practice for a couple of hours."

"I appreciate the company," Eartel said. It can get lonely out here, although the horses have become almost docile. I don't know why, but they are easy to control, and several will play at a time. Nothing rough and no fights, but they do seem to enjoy the day."

"I imagine it's because they're farther from Ozlid's influence, and they're getting better treatment than they've ever had," Zack said. "I'm going to go to the coast and see if I can spot Briggs's ship."

He followed the trail up through the rocks and

boulders, hearing the sound of arrows hitting the target below. Reaching the sea, he pulled his spyglass from his cloak and searched the far horizon. Bracing himself against the strong wind on the cliff edge, he eventually found a dot if color above the sea. While walking back to camp for firstmeal, he'd decided to check again in an hour.

Yasho had supplied the camp well. There were even some honey cakes. The men worked together cooking two rabbits and frying flatbread. Zack caught Bryan's eye. "You'll need to see Yasho later today. He'll talk with Sonkek, Eckert, and you. We'll need you in the taverns for the next few days. Currat will show you where to observe men coming from the Sailor's Quest. It's important. Yasho will explain."

"I don't get any fun!" Eartel said begrudgingly.

"You will very soon," Zack replied. "You may be riding out in a few days, and not to see the scenery. Your archery skills will have a good target, I assure you. And now that I have you excited about things I shouldn't say any more about, I'll go check the horizon again." Both men grumbled, but laughed as Zack walked away.

The ship seemed like much more than a dot in the short time he'd been away. Still hard to make out the vessel, the sails left no doubt. Zack hoped it would arrive by midday. He loped back down the trail.

Rejoining the men, he shot arrows for a while, impressing the bystanders. After a while, they each pulled curry brushes out of the supplies and started working on the stallions. The big blacks liked the attention, and some of their grateful nudges nearly knocked them over.

As the sun reached its zenith, Zack went back to the coast. Briggs's ship was now three hundred yards out, and carefully approaching the cliff. At a hundred yards away, Briggs returned Zack's wave, and his crew set about hanging fenders over the side to protect the hull. The crew's efficiency heightened Zack's impression of Briggs's ability to shape his men into the finest sailors.

Trotting halfway back to camp, Zack let out a shrill, loud whistle. A few moments later, Eartel led three stallions through the boulders.

Zack jumped from his vantage point atop a boulder and returned to the coast in time to see the huge ship gently rocking in the calm waves. Swinging the hoist out, he lowered the ropes. Briggs attached a captain's chair, and Zack pulled him up.

"Zack, it's good to see you, and I'll like seeing twenty-two stallions, too."

"Well, you'll like the count of twenty-four more, I suspect. I added two this morning. Did you have any difficulties with the last shipment?"

"None whatsoever. They calmed more and more the farther away we sailed from this accursed land. By the time we came into Elizabethville's port, they didn't fight the hoist, but they did seem happy to be on the ground." Briggs chuckled. "I don't understand that. They are fairly intelligent for horses. Before I forget..." Briggs reached around and pulled a packet from the back of his coat. "I hope it's important."

Zack placed it in his cloak's large pocket. "It's probably more of the same, but then, I never know what Gaz has come up with to torment me." His laugh took any perceived sting out of his words. "By the way, I've been meaning to ask you if there is a market for used saddles?"

Briggs laughed. "There's a market for everything. All you need do is find the right buyer."

"Well, we have a growing pile of saddlepacks and saddles."

Briggs smiled, "Send them down. I'll have room, even with twenty-four horses aboard."

The first horse arrived and looked out at the vast sea. It didn't seem to like what it saw, planting its legs and snorting noisily. After a few calming discourses, it didn't fight the straps as Briggs removed the captain's chair. The black panicked a little when the hoist swung out over the ship and on the trip into the hole. The second stallion seemed not to mind at all.

Eartel and Bryan took turns leading the mounts one at a time to the cliff, and brought up the leather goods last. Late afternoon approached when Briggs reattached the captain's chair, returned to the ship, and waved at the men on the rocks from the *Sunbright Sea's* deck. Zack returned the wave and then they went back to a nearly deserted camp.

Since the enclosure would be empty, Eartel decided to return home for a few days. "I think it's time for Dartel to stay here a while. It's too much time to think."

"You might be away from here longer than you expect," Zack responded. "You and your brother just might be on a mission to end up with more stallions. I won't know for a few days, but it's a possibility. Remember well, you don't discuss what I've told you with anyone but our principal group."

Bryan and Eartel nodded with a stern look. Then, Eartel took the trail home.

"Bryan, meet me tonight for an early lastmeal," Zack said.

The young man smiled and hurried toward the Blue Sail as Zack headed to the stables aside the Tarnished Anchor before walking the short distance to join the youth.

* * *

YASHO was already seated at *their* table, looking excited as Zack approached. "I got the messages out to the bargemen per Ursel's instructions. They've all replied, stating they would meet us on time at the Sailor's Quest. Jadel has agreed, and is setting up the room. He didn't want to charge me for it, but I insisted."

"Good," Zack said. "We need to always pay our way.

We will need someone other than the Yowell brothers to watch the stallions' enclosure soon. Those young men are too important to our missions to post them there for days at a time, or longer. I had originally thought to use Bryan for that, but he needs some experience with the Men-in-Black and their methods. Would Sonkek or Eckert be better suited for staying alone for a week or more at a time?"

"Sonkek blusters and he can be rowdy, but I've always thought it's more of a front. There are times when he's quiet for long periods. He's more of a loner than he likes to show."

"Is there someone other than those three? I want them to start weapons training as soon as Cartel can get them practicing. Bryan may have trouble on this mission I'm sending him on, but one of the brothers will be there to look after him. He won't know that, but he'll be protected. He needs to see some of the slaughter the Men-in-Black commit on Hamptorians."

"One of the inns near the delta closed," Yasho said. "They had a lad of about fifteen summers working as a stable boy. He's a little old to continue that role. I believe I remember someone saying he also has reason to dislike Ozlidians, like so many of us nowadays. He's staying at his aunt's home here. I'll investigate—discreetly, of course. Perhaps you'll have five to interview tomorrow. If he looks promising, I'll send a message to meet Ursel at the Sailor's Quest."

* * *

URSEL made his way to the usual table after two days of selecting men and a lad, joining Zack, Currat, Jasper, and Yasho. The men ordered firstmeal, and some of the tea Bronson had brought from Elizabethville.

"Are you still unsure about the last man you saw yesterday?" Zack asked.

"You mean Naz. He was quite close-mouthed, and

didn't express much after I gave him several tries. Bryan said he was as non-vocal in the tavern and would hardly acknowledge him. Later, someone said something about men from Ozlid killing a friend last year. Naz just said, 'bastards,' and stormed out. I'm not so unsure of him after that. Still, after our first run, I'd like to keep a close watch on him for a few days. I was surprised at the hatred coming from the stable lad. He told of his twin going north of Ballrand's to work at a farm last summer. Ozlidians caught him in the open with the farmer's son. The son got away, but the twin was killed. When I told him what our mission entailed, he became excited. If Yasho will have him, he agreed to work at taking horses to and from the stables and watching them until Briggs arrives."

"Then I'll have him," Yasho said. "I can keep an eye on him."

"Good. I'll send a message to report to you tomorrow morning." Ursel looked over at Jasper, who sat smiling and about to burst. "Why are you so happy?"

"Bronson arrived last evening, and brought me five more birds! I heard you say you're riding north tomorrow to meet the barge at the landing near Ballrand's inn. I'd like to go with you, and take him a bird. I'll train him and Tad on how to care for it, and how to send messages while you're at the landing. I'll also tell him to release the bird with no message if there's real trouble at the inn."

"What if it just gets out?" Yasho asked.

"Without being tossed in the air, they'll fly around the area and come back before long," Jasper replied. "When I stamp a location on them, they develop a longing for it. They seem happy when they're *home*."

Ursel smiled. "I'll be glad for the company. Be ready to leave at sunrise."

"I'll have a firstmeal and traveling supplies for you an hour before first light," Yasho said.

"For Currat and me, too, please. We're to meet the

bargemen an hour after sunrise and it's a good hour away."

Yasho grinned and nodded.

"Now," Zack said, "we need introductions to a hawk."

* * *

ZACK finished packing their supplies that would augment the ones Yasho had ordered delivered to the barge. He secured a wide leather strip on his left shoulder and a rough leather glove that Jasper had given him on his right hand. As he completed his preparations, Jasper arrived with a sharp-taloned bird. It unceremoniously hopped onto Zack's leather strip as if it'd known him all its life. It danced a bit when he mounted, but folded its slightly raised wings back and settled down quickly once Zack found his seat. He reached back over the bird's head with his left hand and scratched its head feathers, as Jasper had shown him. When Spellbinder moved out, the hawk's body rode easily with his movements. After a few moments, the bird jumped to the coarse leather covering Zack's cloak over his left shoulder and settled down again.

When they arrived, the bargemen had already spread straw in an area for the horses. Zack and Currat eased their stallions aboard without a problem, and the men poled the flatboat across the delta to the waiting draft horses. Zack told Franzt to pass the word to the men not to try to pet the hawk as he held him next to a round stake jutting from the roof of the boat at the bow. The bird hopped up and started pruning its feathers. The man looked as if the caution wasn't necessary, but nodded.

Zack and Currat stowed their provisions in the bow away from the rest of the supplies. They kept their cloaks over their battle swords. The draft horses munched on grass and drank river water when the barge stopped for meals. Horance stayed with the large draft horses on the towpath, and ate from the supplies in his saddlepack draped over the larger draft horse's rump.

They timed their midmeal for later than usual the next afternoon, to coincide with their arrival at the landing near Ballrand's inn. Pulling in north of the landing, they let the ropes out and poled back across the river to the pier, or what was left of it. They tied up as Ursel and Jasper emerged from woods along the trail, once a road before the trees had begun encroaching on it.

Noticing Jasper's robes, Cerrit waved the other bargemen forward. "Are you a priest of the Light?" he called. Jasper nodded, and the men came ashore and knelt before him. Franzt did the same across the river.

"May we have your blessing?" Cerrit asked.

The priest raised his hands, palms upward, and intoned, "May the Light's Source bless and protect you. May you find strength and fortitude in the fight against the Dark. Help those you find in need, and always keep the Light's teachings."

The men rose and bowed their heads to Jasper before returning to the barge to prepare the men's midmeal.

"I didn't expect that," Zack said.

"Neither did I," Ursel replied. "But, I'm glad for it."

Jasper merely smiled. "I'll go aboard to bless their food and let them know Ursel and I have already eaten."

"The trail?" Zack asked Ursel.

"It's narrow in places, but the stallions won't have a problem. Someone has been digging up the saplings, and I assume replanting them where needed."

"Then we should return in three weeks with black stallions. I wonder if Adel will have more than twelve by then. Briggs was right. The barge should accommodate twenty-two stallions plus ours, and the draft horses underneath the roof. I don't foresee any problems at this point." Zack looked at Currat, who nodded.

The hawk flew over and landed on Jasper's outstretched arm. The priest scratched his head feathers before he flapped to his perch to prune himself. "Has he hunted?"

"He flew out last evening an hour before sunset and returned afterward, still nibbling on meat stuck on its beak," Currat said. "I removed it and held it in my hand. It gently took the meat without touching my palm and flew to its perch. I didn't know birds pruned their feathers so much."

Jasper laughed. "Hawks and the larger carrion eaters do more so than pigeons. The big bird smells of the sea, but never of the fish it eats. Remember, when you're two days out of here, send the hawk home as I showed you, and there'll be someone here to take the horses."

Both spies nodded.

"We'll head out now. Safe journey," Ursel said.

"To you, too," Zack and Currat said in unison.

* * *

THE barge tied up to the lnading on the midday they'd targeted. Leading his mount, Adel's horseman moved from the shadows of the trees and approached the landing. Spotting Zack, he said, "Lady Adel will be here in a few hours. We have fourteen stallions. I hope you have room for that many."

Zack smiled at the reclusive man. "We have room for them and eight more."

Nodding, the horseman mounted and cantered eastward without further comment.

As the bargemen poled to the far shore to load the draft horses, Currat observed the scene with Zack. "I wouldn't mind a night at Adel's, but I don't think it wise," he whispered.

"Neither do I," Zack replied.

In less time than he thought possible, the barge returned with horses and men, refusing Zack and Currat's help while tying her up and cleaning the deck. The hawk took a look around and then flew higher, gaining blue skies and navigated in wider and wider circles until, on the fourth, it dove into the forest on silent wings.

Zack watched as Horance approached him and said, "I have some ale, if you and the others would like some."

The bargeman shook his head. "If one of us asks for ale or you ever see any of us drinking it, it's a sign of a major problem. It's a silent code most bargemen use and an unwritten rule; we never drink ale or wine out of port. It's also something only those on the river know. We'll definitely take you up on it in Hagan's End, however."

"It would be best if we're not seen together, but I'll make arrangements for all of you to have a round or two."

Horance nodded and gave a mock salute.

The spies spent the next hours cleaning Spellbinder and Snowflake and their equipment before taking them off the barge. They rode the two steeds bareback along the trail, but never out of the barge's sight. Coming back from land and after getting them reestablished on the barge, Adel led a string of stallions toward them. Her horseman followed at the rear.

Zack and Currat helped her from her saddle and lightly set her aground. Her smile was as breathtaking as always. "How are my handsome spies?" she whispered.

"We are fine, beautiful lady," Currat said. "And, how are your handsome twins?"

"As vivacious as ever. They wanted to see you, and begged me to ask you to stay overnight. I told them I didn't think it possible, but I'd ask."

"You were right," Currat said. "We can't leave the barge unprotected, especially on this first voyage. The bargemen seem to be working out, but I don't want them left alone."

Adel sighed in disappointment. "I understand, and I'm sure the twins will as well. At least I brought some fresh fruit and honey cakes for you and your men. I would have brought some ale, but bargemen don't drink it while on the river."

"Adel," Zack said. "Is there anything you don't know?"

She laughed and winked at him. "I've made it a point to always study the men around me."

The bargemen approached, giving Adel an appreciative eye, and took the lead horses onto the barge. Spellbinder and Snowflake stood tied near the bow. Horance noticed their look. "We thought you'd want them last on. It's easier to jump from the stern if the need arises."

Zack nodded. "Good thinking."

"We understand the difficulties that could arise," the bargeman continued. "And we know we may not always have men of your caliber to protect us, but we acknowledge the need. We're aware of where these horses came from, and we hope their previous riders are dead!" Without waiting for an answer, he led the next three horses toward the river.

"You chose your men well," Adel said.

"Actually, it was Briggs's doing," Currat said.

"Will you come back this way on horseback?" she asked.

"It's possible," Zack said. "But I don't know when or how many of us. One of us should always be in Hagan's End, and I doubt if you'll see Ursel up here for some time. There is a great deal to put in place, and we're only getting started."

"I understand; I'm disappointed, but I realize the need. The twins are doing nicely with their arms practice, and their archery has improved remarkably. They are itching to take down some Men-in-Black, but they are also needed at the inn. I suspect if the bastards make any trouble there, there'll be more horses to go downriver. Kell had hired a man he trusts, and plans on getting another, so the boys will be free for other activities."

Zack fished in his pouch and handed Adel two gold coins. "Give him one to offset his costs. It comes from our budget for such use. Adel, the other is for you. Keep us informed on his needs, and we'll see you both are reimbursed for your costs incurred in killing Men-in-Black."

She reluctantly took the coins, but then smiled. "I know a prostitute who was tortured by the Ozlidian military; after they used her, she escaped. She's at my home and I'm teaching her our accent. She's about healed, learns fast, and is quite beautiful. I'm thinking of opening a small inn north of here and letting it be known that she likes Ozlidian officers. She says she wants to slit their throats before they can enter her. With a little instruction, she could acquire the skills to get them drunk and acquire information from them before she takes to the knife. I haven't said anything to her about it yet, as I wanted to talk to you first."

Currat rubbed his chin. "If you're sure of her, send a bird when you think she's ready to undertake such a venture. One of us will come up and see her."

Naz approached. "Forgive me for interrupting, but we have over an hour of light left, and we wanted to know if you wished to start downriver."

"Would it make that much difference?" Zack asked.

"It would allow us to dock in the wild, and not where men are likely to find us."

"We'll be aboard in a few moments," Zack said.

Naz nodded and walked back toward the river. When Zack turned back, Adel was mounted and ready to leave. She blew the spies kisses and wheeled her stallion around, cantering back toward home.

As they boarded the barge, Naz came forward. "I feel rain in my bones."

"I suppose we'll move faster downriver. If that's so, bring on the rain," Currat said.

Naz laughed. "Not too much, mind you. This ole river doesn't have rapids, but it often feels that way after a heavy downpour."

Zack nodded and watched as the bargemen pushed

the flatboat into the current, and then to the river's center. As they moved faster, the hawk ruffled its feathers. When the sun set behind tall trees, the bargemen pushed hard to the shore and tied up again. The crew was tired and soon fell asleep. Zack and Currat rotated the watch, as always. Near midnight, the rains came and Currat moved inside the enclosure, keeping watch out the stern.

* * *

AS morning broke, the current pulled harder at the lines securing the flatboat. Naz approached Zack. "We may get to your landing faster than you thought. The rain looks like it'll be here a while."

"You can travel in it?"

"Oh, yes. If we stopped for rain, the river would become loaded down with barges, or it once would have done so. The traffic now is a fifth of what it once carried. We have oilskins to keep us mostly dry. After firstmeal, we'll push off. As I said, there are no rapids on the river, but you'll think there are if this keeps up for more than a couple of days."

"Do you need our help?"

"Perhaps. If so, wear gloves. We're used to the poles. They can quickly gouge a hand if the inside fingers and palms aren't thickly calloused."

"I'll keep that in mind—thanks."

Rivulets of rainwater streamed through narrow gullies carved in the deck to larger ones at the sides of the barge, and then emptied out from the stern. Zack hadn't noticed the slight, outward incline from the barge's center until he watched the rainwater disappear. Cerrit came aft and uncovered a rain barrel. Horance tied back the canvas flaps from over the one-foot square *windows*, allowing light to flood into the boat's interior. Franzt locked a hood above the brazier, located in the middle of the stern deck, venting the smoke off to the side. Shortly, he had full firstmeals of hotcakes and strips of dried venison ready with honey on the side.

Currat looked at the large meal with a surprised expression.

"In weather like this, it's best to eat well," Franzt said.

The draft horses seemed calm, munching on hay spread before them. A few of the blacks didn't eat, and seemed on edge. Zack and Currat made the rounds, soothing them with calming whispers and scratches in all the right places. Naz pulled back the canvas cover blocking the view of the bow, allowing fresh air to flow through to the stern. After some of the stallions began to eat, the others followed suit. Zack and Currat passed buckets of water to the herd.

Men and animals cared for, Naz uprooted the stakes and pulled in the lines, jumping back onto the flatboat while the bargemen held it in place, or tried to, allowing sufficient time for the operation. All four men pushed hard, and soon reached the river's center.

"The water comes higher on the poles now, and I noticed it came close to overflowing the banks," Zack said to Currat.

The river, no longer a slow-moving waterway, had more than doubled its speed. The churning flow carried them downstream at the speed of a horse's canter. Two on a side, the crew poled hard, sometimes rising up off their feet to keep the craft in the best location on the river. Zack observed them in awe. *That looks hard, and I bet it's even harder than it looks!*

Currat walked to his side. "I bet that's harder than it looks," he said, and looked askance at Zack's laughter.

The rains ended on the evening of the second day. At sunrise, Zack scratched the hawk's head feathers and then tossed it upward. It circled once, gaining height, and flew south. At midday, the bargemen poled the craft as far as possible toward the river's swollen banks at the landing near Ballrand's inn, and tied her up to nearby trees. The spies offloaded the stallions during the afternoon, settling them and securing them on long leads to trees. Several looked back at the river and snorted. Zack wondered what they would do upon seeing the ocean. The saddles and tack came next.

He waved Currat over to his side. "I need to go to Ballrand's and discover what's going on there. I can make it by nightfall. There's a full moon, and I can walk Spellbinder back here."

"I'll find a tree and rest in the limbs with a full quiver of arrows, and get a good view of the river and trail. Trouble usually happens when you don't expect it."

Zack chuckled and picked up Spellbinder's saddle. Currat called the bargemen together and explained what they planned.

"Do you expect difficulties?" Naz asked.

"No, but it's good to be prepared. We won't leave you unguarded."

The crew seemed to relax as they returned to the barge to bring the draft horses onshore. Currat had climbed fifteen feet up a mature oak when Zack started west, answering his wave.

22

THE trail's condition surprised Zack. There were few holes in it, and several had recently been filled. The normal underbrush encroaching on it had also been cut back. It made Zack uneasy. *If someone's using the trail on a regular basis, it could be a problem. I don't think the Men-in-Black would go to the river, but if they did, why?*

He reached the main north-south road a few minutes before sunset. Checking both ways for riders, he traveled north the hundred yards to Ballrand's inn and turned into the stable yard. Tad looked up from dropping a bale of hay down from the loft and smiled. The stalls hosted no black stallions. *The lad has grown.* "I'm not staying long; keep him saddled."

Tad frowned.

Leaving Spellbinder munching oats, he crossed to the inn's back door. The innkeeper saw him as he entered and pointed to a back table. Before he had settled in, Ballrand set a mug of ale on front of him.

"Lastmeal?" he asked. Zack nodded and watched as he headed toward the kitchen door. Moments later, the innkeeper returned with a steaming trencher of food that smelled wonderful to Zack after the days of traveling and the fare on the barge. The seared pork with herbs and spices tasted as good as it looked, and the vegetables had been done in a butter sauce with more seasonings.

Zack finished as Ballrand drew close again, and the spy motioned his host to a chair. "If you have time." He pushed a chair out with his foot, and Ballrand heaved a sigh before sitting.

"The lastmeal was excellent; my compliments to your

wife."

"She saw you come through the door and did a little extra. I'll tell her you enjoyed it. Are you staying overnight?"

"No, I'm going back to the river when the moon makes an appearance. We'll bring stallions through tomorrow about midmorning."

Ballrand nodded. "If there's trouble or Men-in-Black here, I'll send Tad a way down the trail. You told me about Ursel posing as a high Ozlidian officer and telling the Men-in-Black to pass the word the inn was not to be disturbed. It must have worked. I've seen very few of them, and the ones stopping here for a meal were most polite and left after eating. That's not the case for the inns north and south of here. They're harassed, but the killings have stopped, at least, inside the inns. A few reports of merchants found on the side of the road without purses, their horses close by, came in a week ago. I sent men to have the bodies cremated and notify their families, if known."

Zack nodded. "You're a good man."

"All of us have to do what we can. This is a war! Even the more reluctant innkeepers are beginning to acknowledge it."

"Let me have a list of the innkeepers that are the most ardent in their understanding of the current dangers and want to take action. A group will come through here in a week or so on a *hunting* trip. The leader can talk with the innkeepers and perhaps gain their involvement at a future time. We are being very careful on who we bring in to join our efforts."

"I think that's wise," Ballrand replied. "The one innkeeper south of here seems noncommittal when the subject comes up. He came through going to the border and wanted to buy vouchers. I casually talked to him and he avoided the subject, becoming uneasy. His wife scowled at him, too. I think she wanted to say something, but chose not to do so. I didn't get a chance to talk to her alone. He recently bought the inn, and renamed it Tankard's Delight. I thought it was a stupid name, but of course, I said nothing. His name is Torrance Spotfish and his wife's name is Milfred. I'd never heard the surname before now. His accent is more northern Hamptorian."

"We'll see what we can find out about him."

They talked for another hour. Zack left when moonlight shown through the front window. Tad had readied Spellbinder. Zack noticed he had filled out, and looked like he would be more muscular than his father. He wondered if he would make a good fighter. *I'm getting cynical...*

The trail proved easy, even at night, and he made good time back. Currat came down from his perch when he spotted Spellbinder. He kept a bolt notched until he could make out Zack's features. Zack told him the important information Ballrand and he had discussed. "We need to discover what information we can about the Spotfish's background. Bryan might be the one for digging that mine."

The bargemen sat around a small fire in the brazier on the flatboat. Zack approached them and acknowledged their greeting.

"You've all done well on this trip, as best I can tell. Remember, we'll still pay you for the days you don't work. That, and future trips will not happen if you ever talk about our activities. I'm pleased to have you as a crew, and my comments are no more than a reminder."

Naz spoke up. "We've talked amongst ourselves, and we know what a good contract we have with you. Also, we hate Ozlidians, Currat being the exception, of course. We're glad to take part in bringing the bastards down. I wish we could kill every one of them coming into Hamptor, except we'd get ourselves killed in the process. None of us are good with swords or arrows."

"That may be," Currat said, coming up beside Zack.

"But you are performing a vital function for us, and you'll help in the overall effort to fight your invaders. We'll not be going on but a few trips. The men traveling with you are excellent fighters. Zack and I will brief them on what we learned on this trip. We didn't know very much about being on a barge until now, and they won't, either. It'll be up to you to train them as you did us. Tomorrow, you'll return the barge to the delta. How can we be sure no one will steal it?"

Horance laughed. "We'll take the draft horses with us, and the men on the delta know and like us for the most part. A few are not so sociable, but they don't have anything against us that we know about. Anyway, one of us will always be onboard, or not far away. We're a closely-knit group on the river, and if anyone tried to mess with the barge, an alarm would go up."

"I'm glad you worked it out. It's one thing we don't have to worry about, and that helps more than you can know," Currat said.

"We understand your wanting to take the stallions across land and not down the delta where Briggs could be seen taking them on board. Someday, I would like to see how he gets that much horseflesh on that monster of a ship. That *would* be a sight to describe to younglings. That is, if there're younglings to tell them to!"

"We're not sure what Wathdure has planned for Hamptor and Arestead. Whatever it is, it won't be good and it'll help the Dark," Zack said.

Zack and Currat chatted with the men on less important subjects for a while, and then Zack took the first watch as the others wrapped up in sleeping blankets.

* * *

THE air smelled fresh, with the land giving signs of renewed growth when Currat gently shook Zack awake.

After firstmeal, the spies waved farewell to the men on the barge as it eased toward the river's center. They watered the stallions, and got them ready to travel.

Approaching the north-south road without incident, Zack stood watch while Currat led the stallions across to the trail. A hundred yards up the path, the troublesome underbrush thinned out. Zack brought up the rear. Looking back, he could no longer see the road, and breathed a sigh of relief.

The sun shone brightly in a nearly cloudless sky, with only a few puffs of white clouds scudding to the north. The air, clean and crisp, still smelled fresh with new growth of the surrounding flora.

The spies approached the farmer's dell when Currat stopped the column. Zack rode along the side of the stallions to Currat, who had dismounted and unpacked his short bow and a quiver of arrows. Zack quickly tied the front horse to a low hanging, sturdy limb. He followed Currat's actions and soon stood beside him. Yelling could be heard coming from farther up the trail. Reversing their cloaks to the multicolored side and easing forward, they knelt just inside the tree line, giving them a full view of the dell.

Fifty yards into the clearing, four Men-in-Black surrounded a man in work clothes who was down on his knees, with his hands tied behind his back. Zack and Currat each strung their bows and nocked a bolt.

A Man-in-Black strutted toward the swaying man with a bare sword in hand. He raised his arm to strike. Zack's bolt pierced the Man-in-Black's back; he fell forward, dropping his sword and screaming in agony. Currat's shot took the only mounted Man-in-Black to the ground; his stallion sprinted away.

The remaining Ozlidians turned to look at the trees, groping for their swords. Two more arrows, shot at the same time, found their targets, leaving no one standing.

Zack approached the only living man left, cut his bonds, and caught him before he fell to the ground. The nearly unconscious farmer looked up into Zack's eyes and whispered, "There's…there's more…of them."

Zack eased the farmer down, and then flashed hand signals to Currat to fetch their mounts. The man pointed to a trail on the other side of the stream running through the dell before he lost awareness. A minute later, Currat rode forward, leading Spellbinder to his master. Zack mounted and placed his crossbow in its holder in one smooth motion.

They raced toward the trail at full gallop, leaping the three-foot stream onto the path before slowing to a canter, and then, as they saw smoke rising a hundred yards away, to a trot. More raised voices came from around a bend. Zack and Currat controlled their stallions with knee signals, restringing the bow and moving the quivers into close reach.

Moving slowly, the spies rounded the bend to see six Men-in-Black, three mounted and the others circling an older woman. A younger man lay on the ground with frank blood seeping into the soil. The one closest to a straight-backed woman backhanded her to the ground. He pulled his right leg back to complete what would have been a vicious kick to the woman's midsection when Currat's steel-tipped arrow passed through his neck. Before the shock of seeing a comrade fall dead wore off, Zack's shot took down the closest rider, and Currat's took the next nearest. While the last rider spurred his stallion toward the spies, they shot two more bolts at the remaining horseless men. Zack rode out to meet the last Man-in-Black, battle sword drawn and forming an aggressive display of slashes and counter cuts in the air— but Currat's bolt slammed into the Ozlidian's skull first, missing Zack by mere inches.

Zack raised his sword in salute to Currat and they rode to the woman, who was trying to rise. Currat dismounted and went to her aid, lifting her to her feet. She surveyed the area around her and gave a curt nod to no one in particular. Zack helped her toward the bleeding man

Currat knelt beside, surveying the damage.

"Are you steady enough to fetch water and clean cloths?" Currat asked.

The woman nodded and started toward the farmhouse ten yards away. Currat popped open the heel of his right boot and withdrew a poultice of herbs. After snapping his boot back together, he applied pressure on the cut. The woman returned with a bowl of water and strips of cloth, suspiciously looking like they might have once been a dress sleeve. Currat cleaned the wound below the man's right clavicle while Zack soaked the poultice in water. The spies applied the pouch together, wrapping the strips of cloth around his opposite shoulder and underneath his arm, holding the herbs in place. They dribbled water in the young man's mouth, and patted his forehead with a wet cloth.

The agrarian ran into the yard, out of breath and red-faced. He looked at the young man. "All praise to Light's Source!" The patient blinked his eyes and, after a few tries, he seemed to focus. "This is my grandson, Rozbert," the farmer said. "I'm Collan, and this is my wife, Pennison. Are you the ones taking the black stallions?"

"Yes, we are," Zack said. "It's best if you don't know our names. We also take the Men-in-Black's purses and use the coins and vouchers for the good of Hamptor. I keep the saddlepacks to find information on their activities. None of this should be public knowledge. If you happen to be in the dell when our men come to collect the stallions, please ignore them and do not approach. The least you know, the better. As far as you're aware, we don't exist."

The farmer looked at his wife and they nodded. "We understand."

"Do you know how they found you?" Currat asked.

"The one who beat me said a stallion led them here," Pennison replied. Collan seemed to notice her reddened face for the first time and cursed.

"I don't know if I believe him," the wife continued. "There wasn't a stallion at the dell, and not one here either."

Rozbert looked at his grandparents and hung his head. "I told someone at the Tankard's Delight that we'd found them grazing on our farm. Black-dressed men were there, and I think these are the same ones."

His grandfather regarded him kindly. "Don't worry, they won't be telling anyone else. If you see the man you spoke to in the first place, you might ask him not to say anything."

"No," Zack said. "Tell him they moved on, and no others have been here. You can even lament the fact, saying you would have liked to keep one to use on the farm, but decided against it because they look too difficult to handle. You want to leave the impression that you're no longer interested in them, and they're more trouble than they're worth. Say it any way that's natural for you."

The young man nodded.

"There's a path west of where the stream comes in from the north," Collan said. "It's overgrown but passable, and leads to another area nearly as big as the dell. The stream loops around and intersects it. We don't plant either of the dells, because it's not enough area for a good crop. If any stallions come here, we can take them there. If it helps us and our neighbors, you can use the hidden dell to pasture the horses until you come for them."

While they talked, Currat had collected the purses and saddlepacks. He combined the coins into one bag and handed it to Zack, who fished around and handed the farmer a gold coin. "This is for your farm, and to ease the treatment you received from the Ozlidians. If you know of your neighbors that are in need of coins from the damages caused by the Men-in-Black, put a note in a saddlepack and leave it just inside the second dell. But you must be careful. Don't let on that something good may befall them and if it does, looked surprised and ask questions about how their good fortune arrived. We hope they won't say anything and plead ignorance. If they do say something, you might suggest that they not repeat what they said to anyone else, but don't push the point. If they ask why not, say something about, these aren't times to draw attention to oneself."

Zack made sure Collan agreed with his suggestions before continuing. "We'll take the saddles and packs with us. If you need a saddle, take one that doesn't have identifying marks. Can you take care of the bodies?"

"We can have the bodies cremated with their clothing. I want nothing of them left here!" Pennison said.

Zack nodded, then he and Currat rounded up the black stallions and placed long leads on them from their saddlepacks. They waved goodbye at the entrance to the yard. It took little time to secure the horses in the dell and collect the rest of the saddlepacks and purses. They left the saddles on the stallions and attached the leads to their brothers waiting along the trail.

* * *

AT midmorning the next day, they led the string of blacks down the road to the enclosure where Dartel hurried to open the gate. He looked glum.

"What's troubling you?" Zack asked.

"Yasho is ill!"

PROLOGUE TO PART III

ZACK looked at the list of accomplishments over the last year and a half since arriving with Ursel at Hagan's End. Overall, he was pleased. Yasho, after a long illness, worked mostly at the cheese factory now, which was running at full capacity. The innkeeper had left the Blue Sail to Ursel and Turlas to run, checking in once or twice a week, and seeming pleased with what he found.

The cheese factory was making a good profit, with the proceeds going to fund more operations against Ozlidians. Ursel had built a network of six groups, working the entire length of the north-south road. Several traitors had been dispatched to the Dark's Void. Adel's friend, the prostitute, had indeed developed a clientele of Ozlidian officers, and funneled information to Ursel through her.

After several trips to Arestead, he'd found a man his age, Argon Steadian, whose parents, wife, and children had been, tortured, mutilated, and killed by ten Men-in-Black while he'd been traveling for supplies. He told of a neighbor reciting the incident with tears of frustration streaming down his face. The man had some archery skills, but Cartel had greatly improved those, and also taught him how to use a sword. Chomping at the bit, Ursel had released him six months ago to return to Arestead and build his own network of spies and avengers, giving him seed coins to propagate his men, as well as a bird for communication.

All seemed well, and Zack contemplated soon returning to the Seven Realms. But the bird he received from Adel one morning stopped all such thoughts.

PART III

23

HIS expression grim, Ursel stalked through the adjoining door to Zack and Currat's suite of rooms. They looked up, and waved him to a seat at a table where they sat.

"It's confirmed by two more groups sending birds. A hundred Men-in-Black have crossed the border and are coming south, slaughtering anyone they suspect might be helping us as they go. Clearly, a new traitor or traitors are working with them. They know too much, and go directly to those who might know of us, asking about us by name.

"My parents had helped the village with some of the funds I'd sent them through Bryan. Friends hid them when Men-in-Black came looking for them. Still, the Ozlidians burned down their home and my da's charcoal factory. They have the coins to rebuild, but I will send them another gold coin. That should cover their cost, and it's not any less than we would do for anyone under those circumstances." He took a deep breath as the import of what he said sank in. "I'm a bit stunned."

Zack frowned, determination and anger filling him. "This is not spy missions any more; this is war! Send birds to bring in all the groups. I want them here safe and to make plans. Make sure all the men have weapons and the masks we designed. I hear that two of the northern groups won't wear them as some sort of show of bravado. I'll talk to them when they arrive. Wathdure surely knows what we look like, and he'll implant our likeness into his men's minds. Ursel, it's time Currat and I left for the Seven Realms, but not before we eliminate this mess."

"Have men you completely trust start carving out a tunnel from the cheese factory to a site nearby where we can buy and build a home. When we get through, everyone in Hamptor, except Adel and Turlas, will think you're dead. The bad part is that you'll have to act like you've gone to the Source's Light. You'll be highly restricted in your movements. Wathdure won't rest until the three of us are cremated and the route to that cremation will be extremely painful. You'll be safe hiding here. We'll establish a story that the man living in the home is ill and deathly contagious. The workers at the cheese factory must be constantly investigated for their loyalty. At some point, you'll be able to move about by going out through the factory. By then, Currat and I will be safe back in the Seven Realms."

"Is this really necessary? Are you over-reacting?" Ursel asked.

Before Zack could answer, Currat shook his head. "No, we're not overstating the problem. We've been expecting this for some time. Over the last year and a half, we've reaped over a thousand golds by trading the stallions to the garrison at Elizabethville. That also means over a thousand men killed. I'm sure Wathdure doesn't care about losing the men, but he does care about their numbers. Our killing those sent from the Ozlid's outlands saved him the trouble and cleared land for more political prisoners. We've lost only a handful, and that was due to their stupidity and wagging tongues."

Zack picked up the conversation. "Our ambushes work, and we learned a lot since starting them. We'll need to put that knowledge to work in all the groups. Now, we need to add war tactics to our responses. If Wathdure sent a hundred, they may only be practicing for a thousand. Also, Wathdure may not actually know about them. Saunderson or a man under him could have taken the initiative. Either way, we need to quell the effects of the force coming this way and destroy them.

"Ursel, please order lastmeal for all of us, and ask Turlas to join us as well. I wish Yasho were here. He knows so many men and their talents."

Ursel pulled the cord summoning a serving maid. "I may have some more information on those men. I found a chest, cleverly hidden, in Yasho's safe room, and he's been filling me in on other men not listed there. It contained a journal of the men he's dealt with, and their characteristics. It'll be useful going forward."

They chatted about everyday minutia while waiting for food and Turlas. The lastmeal arrived, with the spy close behind. "Ah, food, I'm starving!"

"Why are you in such a sweat?" Currat asked.

"I needed exercise, and I've been chopping wood for the inn."

Ursel chuckled. "We *do* have men for that duty."

"What can I say? The inn uses a lot of wood," Turlas replied.

Ursel spent the next few minutes bringing his partner their latest news. "We may need to ask Argon to pay us a visit. He needs to know what's going on here, and what may be coming to Arestead."

"I'll send a bird at dawn," Turlas offered. "The northern groups will make better time on the barge. Another bird will fly north to Adel. She can contact the various groups' leaders and have them ready. I'll contact Naz, and have the barge leave at first light. It would be nice if our priests could read a bird's mind. When Jasper left six months ago, I didn't think I'd miss him so much. He taught me a lot."

"Perhaps the Stones' energy will stretch this far one day," Zack said. "I wouldn't be surprised if some of your priests have the ability, if properly instructed. Once the tunnel and home are accomplished and Ursel has *died* you'll need a way of communicating in emergencies. Be thinking about making it happen."

Ursel looked Zack in the eyes. "You're really leaving?"

"Yes, I'm afraid so. Gaz has ordered us back. I'll send a coded message to him by the big bird asking to stay until we can see what the Men-in-Black's aggression means. Nonetheless, I doubt if he'll let us stay long. He hinted that the Zenith Lord wanted us."

"I understand," Ursel stated. "Actually, I'm surprised you haven't been recalled sooner. Not that I want to get rid of you two, but I knew it would happen someday."

"I think it would be good to send for Captain Tomwell," Zack said. "I'm sure his military background will help."

Turlas nodded. "I agree. Since we brought him in to the principal group, we've discussed several things he learned at the Hamptorian Academy, when we still had one. He taught me a war is defined as: when two opposing armies of a hundred men or more meet in combat. It seems this qualifies as *war!*"

"Wathdure attacked the Seven Realms with thousands of creatures from his necromantic army," Zack said. "The Zenith Lord defeated him. We're not sure how, but he did. I don't think Ozlid will use such a force against Hamptor or Arestead. He has his way without them. He sent a few of them when we last came here. I don't expect more than that, if any at all. Still, it would be good to apprise our groups of what to look for if the threat arises."

Ursel's gaze met Turlas's, and they nodded as one.

*　*　*

THE next morning, the barge went upriver and birds flew, coordinating the arrivals for two weeks hence. In the meantime, work began on the tunnel and the spies bought the property adjoining the cheese factory.

*　*　*

URSEL, Zack, Currat, Turlas, Yasho and the captains—Briggs, Branson, and Tomwell—met in a private dining room for lastmeal the evening before the first group leaders were scheduled to arrive.

"When the men arrive tomorrow, we're all clear on when and where we're meeting with them?" Ursel asked.

"Yes," Turlas answered. "I received a message from Collan that we are expected, and the family won't go near the dells. Sonkek, Eckert, and Bryan will guard the open dell from the trees. They'll send a signal at the first glimpse of Men-in-Black. We'll immediately see any incursion into the hidden dell and deal with it. The concealed trails leading back to the open dell were cleared last week. The groups are instructed to bring a full compliment of weapons. I almost wish the Men-in-Black would follow our men there."

"Be careful what you wish for," Captain Tomwell said. "If a hundred Men-in-Black fight us, we'll lose men, and it takes too long to find and train replacements, besides suffering the loss of friends and comrades."

"Crawford, will you be ready?" Zack asked.

Briggs nodded. "The *Sunbright Seas* will stand by for horses, and or prisoners to go to Elizabethville. This is one time I'm not looking forward to finding stallions ready to sail."

"I agree," Zack said. "Nonetheless, there are one or more traitors operating within our ranks. We need to discover who they are."

"You used the plural," Turlas said. "Do you believe more than one betrays us?"

"There must be, for the increased amount of incidents our people have experienced," Zack replied. "It will be interesting if one or more members of the groups don't come with the others. We expect forty men, plus Adel and the twins, if they can get away. The barge can carry half that number, and we've sent those instructions to the farthermost groups."

Captain Bronson leaned forward in his chair. "I have reports that the river has run at its normal flow over the last two weeks. It should arrive on time by midday tomorrow."

"Sonkek will meet and lead them to the dell using the lesser traveled trails and roads," Ursel said.

"I'll have provisions ready, Yasho said.

The knock at the door resulted in serving maids bringing in lastmeals and wine.

Before men left to rest, Zack gave out his last instruction: "We will leave for the dell at first light."

* * *

THE next morning broke clear and crisp. The men, minus Briggs, had met for firstmeal well before dawn. They started out with five pack horses full of supplies, including replacement weapons for the northern groups. Zack had sent for crossbows with stronger pulls and deadlier bolts from the Seven Realms to augment the long and short swords from the hoard brought from the Eastern Kingdoms.

Turlas surveyed the supplies. "It would be nice if the trail from below Ballrand's inn supported wagons."

Zack chuckled and nodded.

They mounted up, and each of the five men led a packhorse north. After they set the now usual pace of rotating gaits, Ballrand ended up with hungry men for lastmeal. Their rooms were ready, and the innkeeper had hired guards to watch over the supplies during the night.

Zack sat with Ballrand at a table in a corner. "You need to be extra diligent regarding your guests until we can sort out who the traitors are within the groups. I'd like to think, whoever they are, they'd be outside the groups, and that is a possibility, but the information leaked to Ozlid begs the opposite. Keep your family close and ready to escape if you see or hear of a large number of Men-in-Black coming this far south. Don't hesitate to close the inn and seek shelter somewhere away from here."

"I made those arrangements months ago," the innkeeper replied. "Not only will the bastards not find us; we have a place to comfortably spy on the inn and the road north. I know other innkeepers have made similar plans. Lately, I've heard tales about Spotfish practically discouraging guests from his custom. Normally he's proved somewhat driven for coins in the past, and has done all he can to get visitors. It's strange."

"Do you think he could be informing Ozlid of the happenings around him?"

"I've wondered more than once, but I have nothing to base any allegations on."

"I'll keep that in mind," Zack said. "Can you prepare firstmeal for us an hour before dawn?"

"That I can do, and I'll wake your group a half hour beforehand."

"Always the impeccable innkeeper! Now, I need sleep."

Ballrand nodded, and then escorted Zack and Currat to their room and left them with wishes for a restful night.

* * *

THE knock on the door roused Currat in the predawn darkness. He shook Zack awake, knowing he was only feigning sleep. Already packed for travel, they headed to the common room. Only Turlas awaited them, looking excited and eager. Zack and Currat sat with their back to the wall, facing the young spy.

"Don't be too enthusiastic for today's events," Zack said. "They could bring harm to any of us. I cannot believe this meeting of all the groups has escaped the notice of the Men-in-Black, especially if a traitor or traitors is hiding in our cabal. Hopefully, they won't have time to react with a large unit of men."

He tapped a finger on his chin, deep in thought. "I thought about stationing men along the trail to ambush any Men-in-Black coming through, but discarded the idea. They would be too far away, and after they faded into the forest, they would have trouble reaching the dell where they *would* be needed."

Turlas looked a bit despondent. "I guess I don't always see the possible problems that could arise. I need to work on that."

"It's a talent not too hard to gain. Think of the various scenarios that might happen; reject the ones that are not feasible or too outlandish, and plan for what remains."

"Outlandish?"

Zack nodded. "Oh yes! You'd be surprised what an active imagination can produce. Also, keep your plans as simple as possible. Most times, after the first arrow is shot or the first fight enjoined, tactics seem to fly away. The cleaner and clearer the strategy, the more effective it will be."

"We'll miss your guidance when you return to the Seven Realms."

"No, you won't! Ursel knows what we do, and how to keep you alive and our enemies dead. Don't underestimate him. He has a wealth of facts and fighting expertise."

The others filtered in, turning the conversation to more mundane subjects. Platters of steaming slices of pork with eggs and flatbread stopped most of those words. After eating their fill, they stepped into the stable yard, finding Tad and the guards loading the packhorses. None of the supplies looked tampered or disturbed to Zack.

The tallest guard approached him and Currat. "We saw a single rider wearing black clothes riding a horse like yours, Master Duval. He rode south around midnight and returned north a few hours before dawn. If I had had a bow, I'd have tried to bring him down."

With a rueful grin, Zack shook his head. *Two packhorses full of crossbows and bolts, and he wished for just one. As I told Turlas, you can't plan for all that might happen.* "Thanks for letting me know; it's valuable information. We'll make good use of it." The guard looked pleased and returned to helping load the last supplies.

"You think Spotfish is involved?" Currat asked.

"He or someone at his inn seems likely. Let's be sure and tell Ursel."

"Tell me what?" the big man asked from behind them.

"We'll tell you on the trail. We need to travel."

* * *

NO surprises came up on the trail. Zack led the riders into the open dell. Sonkek came out of hiding and reported to Ursel, Zack, Currat, and Turlas, who'd gathered in a circle, still on horseback. "We saw nothing out of the ordinary yesterday on our trip here. We took turns standing watch throughout the night and we're rested. When do you think the first groups will arrive?"

"It's hard to say," Ursel replied. "I suspect the men on the barge will be first, if they didn't have trouble on the way downriver. It depends how far up the north-south road the others stopped for the night. I don't think anyone will get here before midday, but you never know. We need to get the packhorses unloaded in the hidden dell. I would like to get that done before anyone else arrives."

"I don't think that'll happen," Sonkek said, pointing toward the trail with his chin.

Zack swung around and saw Cartel and his sons ride in.

"I invited them at the last moment," Ursel said. "I want them up in the trees, hidden and supported on a limb and able to shoot. I kept forgetting to tell you, and every time I thought of it, you weren't around."

Zack and Currat chuckled.

"Some of our best defenses against unforeseen problems come at the last minute," Currat said. "Let's get everything set up. I don't think we should distribute the weapons until the end, and I want to hide the packs carrying them."

"Is the bell in place?" Ursel asked.

"I instructed Eckert to put it high in a tree with the bell rope beginning several yards away, "Turlas answered. "If it's sounded, the noise will attract the intruders to it, not him."

Sonkek returned to his hiding place and the spies rode through the hidden pass into the second dell. Fires were started in the braziers, using charcoal to cut the smoke. The foods heated wouldn't produce much smoke, but Ursel wanted the extra precaution taken regardless.

At midmorning, Bryan led the two groups from the barge into the dell. The men were barefaced. After they settled their horses on the picket line, Zack called them to him. "The reason for this meeting is simple. There are traitors informing the Men-in-Black about who our men are and where they are stationed, and perhaps a lot more. Not wearing your masks could not only get you killed, but also your families. How many of you want to take that chance?"

Their faces fell except for one. "I *want* them to see who's killing them, and I don't have a family. Who put you in charge? I don't know you!"

"Do you know me?" Ursel boomed behind the man.

The man turned and swallowed. "Master Ursel," he said weakly.

"The man you spoke to so inappropriately is the person who arranged for my training in the Seven Realms, the man whose gold supports our operations, the man who arranged for our training and weapons." Anger filled Ursel's voice. "Besides that, he can kill you in more ways than I can count. He's Master Zack Stand, and his partner is Master Currat Duval, who matches Master Stand's abilities. If you show such arrogance again to someone you don't know, *I'll* make you wish you'd never heard of me. Hamptor owes them more than you'll ever know or guess. Now, get out of my sight before I become too angry to control myself!"

The offender took one look at Zack and Currat's stern faces and nearly ran to the latrine. He didn't come out for some time. The rest of the two groups went to their saddlepacks, pulled out their masks, and donned them without speaking.

Later, one of the masked men came to Ursel's side. "Master Ursel, I mean no offense, but why don't Master Zack, Master Currat, and you wear masks?" He went on to quickly add, "I'm just curious."

Ursel heaved a sigh. "They faced Wathdure and his second in command, Spercine, in Wathdure's palace and lived. While escaping, Master Zack was badly wounded and once, in Hagan's End, Master Currat was captured and tortured nearly to death. His father and friends were killed on their way out of the palace. Unfortunately, Wathdure has the ability to imprint their likeness in the minds of his men, and has already done so. There is no reason for them or me to wear a mask. Wathdure knows what I look like, where my family lives, and what I'm involved in, all through a traitor. We're trying to save all of you from this."

The man nodded and said, "I'll spread the word," before hurrying away.

Bryan entered the inner dell and whispered to Zack, "There is a lone rider wearing a cloak similar to yours, as well a mask, riding a black stallion, heavily armed, and sitting quietly in the center of the dell."

Zack nodded, flashed a hand signal to Currat, and the three men hurried to the mystery in the outer dell. A moment later, Zack's laugh broke the quiet of the morning and the distant warbling of songbirds. Currat joined in the merriment a heartbeat later. Bryan looked shocked.

Currat swiftly walked to the rider, held up his arms, and helped her dismount. "My Lady Adel, how good to see you! Did you come on the barge?"

"No, my coach is at Ballrand's Inn. My loves will be here shortly. They had to dispose of a few bodies on the way, and are bringing five black stallions with them. They used the elite guards' uniforms. My spies, I saw them! I counted closer to two hundred Men-in-Black. When I rode by their encampment, several came out and stopped the coach. They drew swords and were quite full of themselves. A Master of the Gold rushed out and ordered them to position. He apologized to me, and asked if I wanted the men who stopped me killed. I gave the impression of deciding and finally shook my head. He saluted. As we rolled away, I heard him berating his men. It seems our previous coach ride attracted some notoriety. I don't know for how much longer we can use the ruse before someone like Saunderson hears about it."

"First," Zack said, "it's very good to see you. Ursel will be delighted. Second, I think you're right about using the coach. I might go as far as having it repainted. Third, I want you and your husbands to wear your masks at all times. And lastly, continue impersonating a man."

"Speaking of that, how did you recognize me?"

"Not many sit a horse as gracefully as you do, and who else would know how to copy our leathers so well?" Currat answered.

"You said a Master of the Gold?" Zack asked.

"Yes. He is a handsome man, tall and well groomed."

"Where did you see him?"

"A day's ride north of Ballrand's Inn. The way their column had formed, strung out for almost a mile, it seemed they moved slowly. Some filtered in when they stopped us. I saw three Masters of the Blue among them as well."

"We have three groups not accounted for that are due today or tomorrow from the north. They'll have to circumvent the Ozlidians," Zack said. "I hope they have enough brains not to attack! Tomwell and his men are on their way from the south. It'll be interesting if a group that size travels south of Ballrand's inn."

* * *

TOMWELL led his men around a bend and reined in his horse. Approximately twenty Men-in-Black faced him with swords drawn. He and his men turned about and saw twenty or so more behind them. The captain drew his sword; his men followed suit."

"HOLD! Belay weapons." All the Men-in-Black sheathed their swords. The men in front parted, and the man giving the orders rode forward. "We mean you no harm. You're part of the men attacking the Ozlidian groups. I must speak to your leader." He spoke with a Hamptorian accent.

"What makes you think we are those men?" Tomwell asked.

The officer chuckled. "The masks give you away, and I suspect you're the leader. I have a message that must be delivered, or many will die unnecessarily." He rode toward Tomwell and extended his hand holding a parchment, folded and sealed.

Tomwell looked at the name on the document. "What makes you think I know this person?"

"*Please*, don't insult my intelligence. We will camp a mile north of the Running Bull Inn, and one of my officers and I will eat there each night. We can't wait more than a week." With that said, the officer wheeled his horse and rode north. His men followed.

Tomwell looked around behind his men. The Men-in-Black there were already fading back into the woods. Shaking his head, he continued north to the trail's cutoff without further interference.

* * *

ZACK was talking to Bryan in the outer dell when seven horsemen turned onto the grass. He recognized the lead horse and sighed with relief. He walked forward as Tomwell reined in his horse.

"It's good to see you. Did you have any trouble?"

"I don't know." He handed Zack the parchment, and told them what had happened on the road while Zack broke the seal and unfolded it.

The message read:

> *Currat Duval,*
> *Three Masters of the Blue, forty-two men, and I wish to go to the Seven Realms. Our fates are sealed in death if we return to Ozlid. We wish to fight Wathdure's evil.*
>
> *Master of the Gold, Duran*

"Thank you. Tell your men to keep their masks on while they're here. I'll explain when all the groups arrive. I'll show you through to the encampment. Find a spot for you and your men and rig your own picket line. If your men are hungry, there's fires going and ale, but keep them sober." A smile cut the sharpness from his words.

Entering the inner dell, Tomwell peeled off and took his men to a vacant area near the stream, but away from the latrines.

Zack went to Currat's side. "I opened your message," he said, handing the parchment to him.

"Duran! He is an honorable man with a strong character, and we would not have escaped Ozlid without his help. I think he wouldn't have changed much since then, and we should speak with him."

"I agree. He impressed me the same way as you. Unless something goes terribly wrong, we should be able to meet him three days from now."

"Zack, please don't talk about things going awry, and *terribly wrong* is out of my vocabulary at the moment."

* * *

AT midday of the next day, the last three groups rode in together. Everyone wore masks, which pleased all of the spymasters.

When everyone was settled, Ursel stepped onto a small boulder and addressed those gathered before him. "This meeting is highly irregular, and not without certain dangers. The reason is simple; there're one or more traitors among us."

It took several minutes to quiet the men's boisterous comments. Finally, Ursel raised his arms and called for their attention.

"Inns and people who've helped us in the past are being targeted by Men-in-Black traveling in groups of ten or more. The occurrences are too direct for happenstance. Now, there are reports of over a hundred Men-in-Black traveling along the north-south road. That is the reason for continuing to wear masks while we're here. Wathdure and his officers already know what Zack, Currat, and I look like, and our height makes us stand out. The need to wear masks identifies you even more. We'll stop for midmeal and afterwards, I'll talk privately with each group leader, and later with their men, one at a time, starting with the northernmost and working south.

"There's braziers burning, and food and ale available. You must limit the ale to one mug per meal. The stream runs unpolluted, sweet water. If you bathe, do it downstream and remember, other people use these streams, and we're guests in the area. For the time being, keep to your group."

When Ursel stepped down, the low murmur of voices broke away into individual groups.

"Nicely done," Zack said, with Currat nodding.

"I didn't tell them they'd speak with each of us separately."

Zack chuckled. "No you didn't...and you didn't tell us, either!"

"I know, I know. I just thought of it while looking out

over them. Do you mind?"

"Yes and no," Currat said. "We don't mind under the circumstances, but when you're working with your replacements of us, it's bad to spring surprises on them unless you're trying to keep them alert, and not on a subject as important as this one. I'm not telling you anything you aren't aware of already. Speaking of primary assistants, have you given any thought to who you'll select?"

"Only one. I'm greatly in favor of your suggestion for Bryan to take on more duties. He was my first choice when you brought up the subject. I'm thinking of asking Tomwell to promote one of his men to group leader, and work with me most of the time."

Zack nodded. "You're making good decisions."

"How do you want to work the men's interviews this afternoon?" Currat asked.

"I thought you two could listen in when I talk with the group leaders, and then speak privately with the members of each unit. We could be in private areas of the outer dell and rotate the men between us. Cartel and his sons would cover us from the trees. I think we should tell them we'll raise our hand and run it through our hair if we feel someone might be under a compulsion to do harm."

"Yes, I believe it *is* time for us to return to the Seven Realms," Zack said. You have our confidence to lead here.

Ursel nodded, but didn't look happy.

24

URSEL looked to the trees to see if he could find Cartel and his sons. He couldn't spot any sign of them. Pulling one of six lists from his pack on the ground beside him, he signaled for Zack and Currat to join him as the first group leader approached, leaving his men waiting at the entrance to the outer dell, talking amongst themselves.

He introduced the leader to Zack and Currat, who grasped forearms with him.

"Tell us about your group and any problems you see," Ursel said.

The man listed off the men's names and gave a brief background description of each one.

"Is there friction within the group?"

"Not now. I chatted both alone and with the two men together who seemed to have a problem. It all worked out, and now they go to the taverns with each other. I cautioned them about talking where others could hear and about the amount of ale they consumed. All my men have stated they have no more than two ales per visit."

"Do any seem unusually nervous at times?"

"No."

"Send your men to me one at a time."

The afternoon went without incident until the third man in the third group came alone to talk with Ursel. From the start, he shook and fumbled his words. Ursel calmly ran his hand through his hair and started asking routine questions. The man became more agitated, until he drew a hidden knife and lunged. He had taken one step forward, knife held high, when three steel pointed arrows protruded from his chest.

Ursel jumped back as the would-be murderer dropped face first at his feet. He looked over at the group leader's bulging eyes and motioned him over. Zack, Currat, and the two men they were interviewing all reached Ursel at the same time.

"You said you didn't see anything particular about your men. How did the one at my feet act?" Ursel said to the leader.

"He seemed reluctant to engage the Men-in-Black at times," the man answered in a strangled voice. "Once, I saw him change a death stroke to a wounding one. He assured me he only needed to become used to killing a man. The next time out, he performed the same. I'd planned to talk to him again when your summons came. He joined us before the order for using masks came to us. He knew the names of the other men in the group. I didn't want to kill him."

"Did any of your men react the same as he did?"

"No."

"And would you have shot one of those arrows if you saw him attacking me?"

"Yes," he said in barely a whisper.

Ursel waved the three remaining men of the group to him. They arrived looking shaken and nervous. Zack and Currat took one each to different corners of the dell and talked to them. Ursel sent the leader back to the entrance with an admonition not to talk to anyone else about what had happened.

Zack and Currat rejoined Ursel with men in tow.

Ursel motioned for Sonkek, who arrived with Eckert. "We've seen this before now. Wathdure would have had to visit him personally to place the craving for him to kill one of us and manipulate him to keep the compulsion in place. Or, at least, that is what we believe. As the Dark's power grows, eventually Wathdure may be able to accomplish the same without a visit. You need to stay vigilant for similar signs like this one showed."

He waved his hand in the general direction of the woods. "Take the body into the trees; we'll deal with it tonight. Return the arrows to the archers."

He returned his attention to the group minus one. "Talking about this to other men or where you can be heard will be considered treason! Do any of you we haven't talked to individually have anything to add?" The men shook their heads. "We'll talk to you again, informally. You may return to the inner dell."

Ursel gave a thankful salute toward the trees. A branch quivered in return.

They found one more, a lad of fourteen summers, too young for the actions his group committed. When Ursel came near, he drew a knife from inside his waistband. He tried to throw it, but dropped the weapon from his trembling hand and just stood there, shaking. Zack rushed over and pinned the boy's hands behind him. The youth's trembling worsened when he realized who held him, then his eyes rolled up, and he passed out.

Ursel, Zack, Currat, and the lad's father, brother to the group leader, sat in a semicircle before the limp body they'd sat against a tree with his hands bound in front of him. Currat patted the lad's forehead with a cool, damp cloth.

"He's not ready for the life he leads. Why did you bring in one so young?" Ursel asked the group leader.

The man, Derkson, hung his head. "He's my nephew, Narket. He followed me one day. My men encountered more Men-in-Black than we thought—a unit of twelve— and we were a man short. We took evasive action, but they followed and flushed us out toward the road and surrounded us. I thought we would all die. Suddenly, arrows flew into chests and necks at an amazing pace. I figured there must be at least three shooting from the trees. It gave us time to get our bows ready, and the Men-in-Black quickly died. Our rescuer, Narket, walked toward us, smiling. I had no idea he commanded such skills. My brother embraced him with tears forming. We didn't wear masks."

Derkson's eyes held regret and shame. "My brother finally told me Narket practiced archery for hours each day, and had done so for over a year. His mother died in childbirth and his father encouraged him to improve. Afterwards, Narket begged to become a member of our group, and said all the right things at the right time. I remained skeptical, but gave in a week later. The lad did well, and became a valuable addition. I closely watched him to see any bad attitudes forming in him. It didn't seem the missions harmfully affected him. A week ago, I heard he'd started having bad dreams and he'd awake screaming. I banned him from all upcoming missions, and then we received your summons. He immediately calmed, and the dreams stopped. He and his da wanted him to come with the group, and I allowed it. I've never seen him act this way."

Narket began to rouse. When his eyes focused on the men in front of him, the trembling started once more. He seemed to struggle with inner demons to speak. "I...I must kill you. You must...must kill me first!"

Sitting at his side, Zack firmly grasped the lad's bound hands. "There won't be anymore killing for you, giving or receiving. You're going on a long trip, and you'll find peace at the end. The dreams will go, and you'll no longer feel the torment."

The boy slumped, his eyes closed, his breathing becoming regular.

Derkson asked, "How?"

"He's under Wathdure's influence; probably a directive embedded in his mind. The farther away from Ozlid he is, the better he'll become," Currat explained. "There are healers in the Seven Realms who can remove the commandments buried in him." He looked at Narket's da. "It's either that, or someone will have to kill him."

Derkson and the lad's da blanched.

* * *

URSEL stayed behind. Zack and Currat arrived at the Running Bull an hour before lastmeal.

Ballrand showed them to a room upstairs with a table and four chairs. "The Master of the Gold is accompanied by a Master of the Blue and a sergeant most nights. They act the perfect guests. The Master of the Gold is much more a gentleman than any other Men-in-Black I've encountered. If he didn't come from Ozlid, he'd be welcome at any time."

"Between us," Currat said, "he may not return to his homeland. Nonetheless, someday he may return from a long trip."

The innkeeper looked surprised, but remained quiet.

"At least, that's what we desire," Zack said. "Bring only him up, and the three of us will have lastmeal here. After they arrive, have our horses saddled and stationed below the window. We'll make a hasty retreat if things go badly. If more Men-in-Black arrive later on, have Tad ring the stable bell."

"I understand. I'll send up some ale to enjoy while you wait, *if* that's possible."

Both spies chuckled. "It's possible," Zack said.

The crisp night offered cool breezes, but the spies made sure the window was unlocked and left slightly open. They'd finished half a mug of ale when a light knock sounded and Ballrand's low voice sounded under the door. "Your guest is here."

Currat opened the door and admitted Duran. Once inside, the Master of the Gold turned to Zack and offered his forehand to grasp. Zack didn't hesitate to take it as Currat closed and barred the door.

Duran turned back to Currat and they did the same.

"I never thought I'd see you again," the officer said.

"While we wait for lastmeal," Currat started, "please tell us the reason you and your men wish to leave Ozlid."

Duran looked sad. "It's not a particularly long tale. Wathdure became suspicious of my motives in giving some orders, or at least I think that's what happened. He had my parents killed. Of course, there's no proof, but I'm sure that's what transpired. Realizing I had no other reason to stay, and knowing either Wathdure or Spercine would have me murdered at some point, I started making plans. I knew two Masters of the Blue who were appalled at Wathdure's actions. One worked at the palace organizing the reports for Saunderson's review. He told me he'd destroyed several reports concerning you and your activities, and I believed him.

"I did all I could to feed Ozlid erroneous reports on your activities and misrepresent the number of losses you and your men caused. I didn't get any negative feedback until recently. I'm sure Saunderson is on to me by now.

"I knew another Master of the Blue at the fortress whose parents died mysteriously. He's quite bitter, and blames Wathdure, and I think he's right to do so. Men knew men with like attitudes and positions. Our faction grew. We vetted them as best we could, and killed four that tried to infiltrate the group. I must warn you; we may have not discovered all of the ones that might betray us, but I currently have no one in mind. We now number three officers and forty-two men, all of which are in my unit of one hundred and fifty men here in Hamptor."

Duran shifted uncomfortably. "There's one more Master of the Blue with us that I'm sure suffers under Wathdure's influence. Our goal was to find you and get to the Seven Realms. I'm fairly certain messengers have been dispatched, or soon will be, to the fortress—their missives containing most of our death warrants. Several of the men with me are away from their primary units. Some of them had leave, but many are away without permission. Can, or I should ask, *will* you help us?" Duran took a long swig of ale, his first since arriving.

Currat gave Zack a barely perceived nod.

"We will if you and your men will accept some precautions," Zack said. "You obviously would leave by ship for Elizabethville, in the realm of Stonecrest. You total forty-five men, possibly outnumbering the crew two to one. You would have to surrender your weapons and be confined below decks on the ship. I can promise neither ill treatment nor misuse. You'll have sweet water and good food. About twenty of your horses will travel with you, and the remainder will arrive a few days later. You'll be housed at a garrison in Elizabethville until our Zenith Lord decides how to proceed. I suspect you'll have your own area, but you'll be constantly guarded."

"At some time in the future," Currat added, "you'll be required to swear allegiance to the Zenith Lord and the Seven Realms. Whether or not you return to the three kingdoms would be nothing more than a guess, based on the need and agreements with your men. Once you commit to the Seven Realms and our Lord Greatstone, I imagine you'll be offered positions in the Guard or in one of the High Lords' Guard. I can promise you—you and your men will be watched for quite some time, no matter what vocation you and they choose."

The knock at the door cut some of the tension in the room. Ballrand identified himself and once the door swung open, he and two serving maids placed lastmeals and more ale on the table. When the maidens had left, the innkeeper said, "The Ozlidians are eating, and no others have arrived." He slightly bowed and closed the door behind him. Currat barred it.

The conversation turned to the activities at the palace while they ate. They finished the meal in reasonable time, bellies full. Pushing empty platters aside and after pouring more ale, Duran settled back in his chair. "So, how do we proceed?"

"I've been thinking of just that," Zack said. "I have a plan, but it depends on how you think it'll work. I suggest you divide your men into three groups. Of course, you and the men loyal to you would make up one group. Assign the two other units back north, one to spread out east of the north-south road and the other farther north and to the west. Order them not to hurt the residents they encounter, and do what they can to gather information on how they feel about Ozlid. It might be best to have them split into smaller units of ten or less when entering a village, explaining the need for the villagers to feel less threatened. Have them meet back in ten days to discuss what they found and how to deal with the information. Imply some villages might require further investigation, but for them to do nothing that would scare the villagers off, and that you want the village intact when you return in force. Will this plan placate those who might be under Wathdure's influence?"

Duran seemed to mull over Zack's words for a long moment. "Why would I insist on having two Masters of the Blue with me?"

"Tell them you plan on infiltrating Hagan's End, and you need their expertise," Zack answered.

"I can't see a problem with what you describe. You should be an officer in the high corp."

Currat chuckled. "What makes you think we're not?"

It was Duran's turn to chuckle, and he bowed his head in mock servitude, a smile creasing his face. "I'll give the orders at daybreak."

"Good," Zack said. "In two days, you and your men will be on the high seas *if* all goes well. I've prepared a map for where we'll be. Memorize it, and we'll burn it before you leave."

Duran smiled. "I glad you agreed to see me. I'm sure some of us will be murdered if we return to Ozlidian territory. And I appreciate you seeing me unarmed."

"Like our rank, what makes you think we're not?" Currat said to his former superior. "We each have four knives at hand if needed. I'm glad they're not required. Duran, I've received far more training in the Seven

Realms than anyone in the Ozlidian military. Zack and I know how to kill men in many ways, with or without weapons. One of the lessons I learned at the beginning is to *never* underestimate a person or situation."

Zack pulled a map from under him and gave it to Duran. "Our location on the map is a half-day's ride away. You'll travel for days after that. Be sure your unit is well supplied for at least a week."

Duran took the parchment and studied it for a long moment, then turned and tossed it into the fire. It sparked, flared, and slowly crinkled into white ash.

Duran left after again grasping forearms with his hosts.

"Cold camp tonight?" Currat asked after closing the door.

Zack nodded.

Several moments passed before Ballrand knocked. When the door opened, he looked confident. "Tad reports the Ozlidians are well up the north-south road."

The spies left with an admonition to Ballrand to watch for signs of trouble from the large contingency of Men-in-Black and added a silver to cover their costs.

The crisp, cold breezes from earlier in the night died down, leaving little discomfort in the mature woods when Zack and Currat rolled up in their cloaks. Sleep came easily, with Spellbinder and Snowflake tethered on long leads nearby.

* * *

ZACK woke Currat an hour before sunrise. They had a firstmeal of flatbread and cheese and as the first rays of sunlight reached the trail, they rode east. They kept a ground-eating pace and reached the dell shortly after midday.

Zack hurriedly called a meeting in the inner dell and described what would happen later that day.

Ursel looked please and said as much. He ordered the

weapons distributed, and gave orders for the collection of the Men-in-Black's arms collection. He ended with, "These men are risking their lives to leave Ozlid. We know the people over the mountains are nothing like the ones on this side, and we know nearly all, including the military, don't know the terror Wathdure causes. It would sicken them if—or I should say *when*—they find out. These are good men, not much different than us. I know it will be hard for some of you to believe, but they will help in the battles against Wathdure and the Dark."

Some grumbling whispered through the crowd, but it soon died down.

Zack stationed Cartel and his sons in the trees facing the outer dell. He ordered Bryan, Eckert and Sonkek back down the trail, each with a spare horse. "You are to let the unit led by a man with a gold stripe across his uniform pass. Do you remember the rise that allows sight of the bends in the trail below?" The three men nodded. "There are plenty of woods to hide in and still see who's coming up the trail. Using the spare horses, it'll take less than two hours to return. Run them as fast as you can, but change stallions often enough to keep them sound. Stay until that long before sunset before returning, unless you see another unit of Men-in-Black coming. If that happens, get here as fast as you can! Do you understand what you are to accomplish?"

Before their nods stopped, they raced to the picket lines and took two blacks each before bursting into the outer dell and racing down the trail.

Ursel then called the group commanders together. "Gentlemen, I don't expect any problems, but it's always good to plan contingencies. Arm your men. I want a line of three groups on each side of the outer dell. When the Ozlidians arrive, we'll order them to give us their weapons and to picket their horses on the west side of the dell. Have runners ready to take the weapons to the inner dell. Anyone being hostile to the Ozlidians will answer to me, and it won't be pleasant. At the same time, if any of the Ozlidians act threatening to you or your men in any way, report it at once to Zack, Currat, or me. We must and *will* treat these men with respect until there is a reason not to do so. You will be held accountable for the conduct of your men! Am I understood?" The six men answered affirmatively.

Ursel nodded, pleased. "In the past, you've operated as a close-knit and small unit. It's easy to forget we are in a war now, and part of an army. Albeit a small army now, but still an army. Like any army, discipline is important, and orders must be followed. Impress that on your men, and drive it deep into their minds.

"Another thing to make very clear to your men is that these men and the information they carry will be invaluable in coming conflicts. The Dark targets the Seven Realms at this time, but anything Wathdure does will directly or indirectly affect Hamptor and Arestead. We've told you of the necromantic army he used to attack the realm of Stonefire. I know some of you scoffed at the idea, and perhaps even thought we made the tales up. We did not! You know the terror Wathdure brought to your lands, and he will continue to punish you more and more.

"We are only an annoyance to Wathdure now, and we want to keep it that way while we find and train men. If not, *when* he attacks Hamptor and Arestead, he has the ability to completely destroy you and your families. Always keep that in the back of your and your men's thoughts. We walk a fine line. Don't cross it! Do you have questions?"

The tallest of the masked leaders said, "Sir, how do we handle these larger Ozlidian units coming south?"

Ursel answered, "Like we do the smaller ones, with our men hidden and shooting from cover in surprise ambushes. We'll also be building deadly traps, something we haven't done yet, but will soon. One of my biggest goals is to find a way of better communication when

Men-in-Black cross the border. Pass the word; if anyone has any ideas, I'll listen.

"Brief your men and get ready for the Ozlidians' arrival. You are carefully chosen leaders; you can take initiative action. Just be sure it's the correct deeds you order to be done. If there are no other questions, you're dismissed to your men."

After a pause, the commanders all briskly walked to the inner dell.

* * *

URSEL joined Zack and Currat for a midmeal of flatbread and cheese. A few nerves jangled his stomach. He asked, "Do you see anything we missed?"

"In planning, no," Zack answered. It's what we didn't plan for that I'm concerned might hurt us, which is always the case, as you well know. Currat and I trust Duran, but he's the only one. We have no history with the others, and neither did Duran with the majority of the men he vouchsafes."

The bell sounded once.

"It seems we have guests," Currat said.

The three walked quickly to the outer dell in time to see a masked rider dismount. When they reached him, he said, "Sirs, I got the signal that the man with the gold stripe across his uniform is coming. He should be about a half-hour behind me."

"Thank you," Currat said. Get some food and ale."

"Thank *you*, sir. The next time I go out like I did, I'm taking food with me; I'm starving!"

Ursel chuckled. "You've learned an important lesson today. Tell the men to form up here with their weapons."

"That I did, sirs, and yes, I will." He gave a mock salute and rushed toward the inner dell.

Within moments, masked men with short swords and knives attached to their belts rushed to find their positions. Many had short bows over one shoulder and a quiver of bolts on their hips. Thirty men, aligned with their back to the trees, faced an equal number ten yards away. Others stood ready to take weapons and direct the riders to the picket lines in the outer dell.

Ursel, Zack, and Currat mounted and rode to the entrance from the road, battle swords and cloaks in place. They didn't wait long.

Duran, leading his men two abreast, waved from thirty yards away. The three spies returned his greeting with a mock salute.

The Master of the Gold halted his men and came forward at a trot. "I'm glad to see you," he said, while looking at the men ready for their arrival. "I haven't noticed anyone acting strangely yet. The other two units should be far north or east by now."

Ursel said, "We haven't met. I'm Ursel."

"We have your description. You're hard to miss."

Ursel smiled. "That can be harmful at times! We're ready for your men. The picket lines are at the back of the dell on each side, ten yards before the stream. My men will collect your weapons as they enter. You don't have to worry; you'll eventually get better ones. Will anyone object to giving theirs up?"

"I talked with them. Some grumbled, but they all understand the reasons."

Zack said, "Have your men ride forward single file, dismount, and give their weapons to a man who'll approach them and walk their horse to a picket line. Once they'll all gathered by the stream, we'll talk to them."

Duran nodded and rode toward his men. Orders given, the Ozlidians followed them, and the operation started with Duran watching from horseback at the dell's entrance with Ursel, Zack, and Currat behind and slightly off his right side.

Their uniforms are relatively new, as are their boots. Overall, They are in good military inspection, but the horses need care for the most part, Zack thought.

Currat noticed two men staying at the back, letting others go before them. He pushed his hand through his hair. Duran also seemed to see their actions, and frowned. He started to draw his sword. Zack rode next to him and shook his head. The sword slid back into its sheath.

When the last man before the two lagging behind turned past Duran, the last two men spurred their horses into a gallop, pulling swords free. The Master of the Gold again started to draw his sword and once more, Zack stopped his hand with a slight smile. Thirty feet from Duran, they raised their swords and screamed, "TRAITOR!"

The galloping man on the right jerked backward with a bolt in his left breast, falling to the ground in two of his mount's strides. The horseman on the left received two shafts, one in his neck and one through his stomach. He fell off to the right, his boot catching his stirrup, dragging him ten feet before the stallion stopped, looking back at his former master. The animal reared up, dislodging the boot, then walked toward the other horses at the picket lines with a sigh and a determined headshake.

The spies couldn't help chuckling. After a few heartbeats, Duran joined in. He said, "I'll have my men bury them, and round up the other horse."

The four walked their horses toward the waiting Ozlidians. Ursel was the first to speak. "I'm Zack, as you probably know. I'm from the Seven Realms, the land you call Jewel." Pointing, he continued, "This is Ursel Glaston, a Hamptorian." Swinging his arm, he said, "This is Currat Duval from Ozlid. These things you know. Here are some facts you probably don't know and some of them Master of the Gold Duran can verify. I had an audience with Wathdure, where the lovely Spercine tried to kill me. Currat's father, a high administrator at the palace, and friends were killed in our escape from there. I was wounded at the border by a sergeant who enjoyed watching men on cross beams being tortured to death.

We separated. I was found and nursed back from near-death. Currat was captured and tortured by a Master of the Blue until most of us thought he wouldn't live. If you heard what they did to him, some of you would lose your last meal."

Currat picked up the theme. "I was taken to the Seven Realms and healed by men with far more abilities than our healers. I would have died here. Wathdure is part of the Dark's Source. He's already waged war on the Seven Realms. Many of you may not know the horrors he's perpetrated on Hamptorians and Aresteadians. Some of the men you left behind raped, murdered, and tortured men, women, and children in the foulest ways. I don't suspect any of you know Wathdure is a necromancer, or even know what that is. He raises the dead, overgrows their orifices with flesh, and implants directives in their dead minds to fight or kill. The messengers you've watched racing stallions at deathly paces are part of those creatures."

Zack said. "Wathdure and his superior, Shadure, second only to the Dark One, transported ten thousand of those creatures to the Seven Realms to wage war. Our Zenith Lord defeated them, but with heavy losses. You might like to know how I know what they are. I killed one escaping from the palace. Currat identified him as a sergeant who disappeared at the northern mountain pass."

Duran spoke. "Most of you don't know me, other than I'm a Master of the Gold. I commanded the east fortress at the border. I saw the torture on the crossbeams, but by Wathdure's orders, I couldn't stop it. My father *was* a Master of the Black administrator at the palace. He was kept at the palace to keep me in line. Wathdure made that quite plain. Have any of you actually tried to figure out how old Wathdure and Spercine are? Of course you haven't, because you're under their influence, and he blocks it from your questioning. How old is the palace?"

A man in the back raised his hand, and Duran acknowledged him. "It's over three hundred years old."

"How old is Wathdure?'

"I don't know," the man answered looking confused.

"Who built the palace?"

The man started to answer, but looked at some of his men with wonderment on his face before saying in a barely audible whisper, "...Wathdure."

Currat continued, "If you still doubt Wathdure's abilities, there are few in the three kingdoms living past seventy years. We suspect Shadure, Wathdure, and Spercine are over two thousand years old! The Zenith Lord has scrolls from that time that mentions them. Are these the same creatures, or something the Dark One recreated? We don't know. We do know they want to destroy the Seven Realms, and they'll destroy Hamptor, Arestead, and yes, Ozlid to reach that objective."

"You are all under Wathdure's influence," Zack said. You may not realize it, but the farther away from Ozlid you travel, the less he can affect you. Currat is one of your countrymen Wathdure couldn't control. Still, he told me that his mind also cleared the farther away he got from Ozlid. You'll be surprised at what you find."

Zack nodded at Duran, who said, "Get some rest, and start your preparations for lastmeal. From here, we'll eat on the road."

The Ozlidians broke up in groups to carry out their orders, most talking amongst them.

* * *

ZACK walked past the guards to the inner dell, and motioned Currat and Ursel to his side. "What do you think?"

Ursel replied first, "Surprise showed on most their faces, along with disbelief at times. As we talked and told about our past, I think they seemed to consider us more seriously."

"I agree," Currat said. He started to add more when one of the men stationed as a back guard scout rushed into the inner dell and to their side.

Ursel nodded for the man to speak. He said, "A single Man-in-Black rode close to our position. We shot him. Before he died, he said, 'Wathdure knows' and smiled. We took his body into the woods and buried him in a shallow grave. Here are his saddlepacks. We kept his purse; there wasn't much in it. The two-hour limit has been reached, and my partner will be on the way here. He's bringing the man's horse. Did we do good?"

"Yes, you did," Ursel said. "Get settled and find some food and rest. We have a long day tomorrow."

As the man moved away, Ursel said, "I don't like this!"

"We don't know *what* Wathdure truly knows at this point," Zack replied. "I don't think he knows about the stallions. It's something that would bother his ego; it's huge, from what I saw at the palace."

"I agree," Currat added. "He can communicate directly with some of his men. If one of those are in the hundred and fifty, we could be in trouble more than we think."

Ursel stopped a masked man walking by. "Ask Master of the Gold Duran to put one of his Masters of the Blue in charge, and then lead him to us." The man nodded and rushed toward the outer dell.

When Duran arrived, Ursel had moved away with Zack and Currat to a private location by the stream. Duran nodded and sat next to Currat. "You called and I came." A slight smile played across his lips.

"How would your men act when asked to fight the men you left behind?" Zack asked.

Duran shook his head. "I was afraid it might come to this. To answer your question, I don't know how they feel. The ones whose families suffered won't be a problem in most cases. The others, I have nothing to judge them on other than their actions and the things they said to me. I think they spoke sincerely, but that's not an absolute answer. I could explain the need."

"No," Ursel said. "I think it best to impress on them the fact of their immediate deaths if they return to Ozlid, no matter what their misgivings might become. You need to drive *that* deep into their consciousness. It is the truth, and it shouldn't take much for them to recognize its depth."

Ursel nodded. "We have forty men, and you have forty-three. Your former men number one hundred and five. Ours are experienced fighters. How many of yours are trained and how well?"

Duran answered immediately. "None of them are as good as they think they are, except the ones working administrative duties; they realize how badly they'd fight. Most never practiced weaponry after the basic maneuvers we all had when starting out in the army. There has never been much need. Wathdure controls Hamptor and Arestead without a reason to raise arms. The officers haven't been given orders to train men further than what they already know. Some officers trained on their own like I did; most didn't bother. Do you have an indication a fight is coming?"

"We aren't sure of anything," Ursel said. "A lone Man-in-Black followed you on the trail. He won't make it back. Nonetheless, we wonder what that portends."

"The one Master of the Blue remaining with them wants to kill all of you!" Duran said. "I have no idea if he's under Wathdure's influence more than any of us. Being the only officer left with them, he could stir them into a fighting mood. He's arrogant enough to believe he's talented and could bring it off. He's not and he won't, but that's not to say he wouldn't try. Delivering any of you to Wathdure would earn him much in rank and funds."

"Being in the dark, we can only acknowledge the danger," Zack said. "Ask your men to mind their surroundings on our march to the sea. There's not much more we can do to improve the situation. Rouse them an hour before sunrise. We leave at first light. We use a rotation of gaits to get the best speed without endangering the mounts. Let your men know to expect it."

Duran nodded, and left for the outer dell.

25

CURRAT rose to find Zack sharpening daggers by the light of a brazier where he also had their firstmeals cooking. He looked to the sky, finding it a full two hours before sunrise. "What disturbed your sleep?"

"Nothing much. I'm just anxious to get started."

"Me too."

Zack flipped over the bread frying in the pan. "I've been thinking; the trail is wide enough to ride two abreast for the most part. It'll certainly be wide enough when it empties onto the road. I'd like to see what Ursel thinks, but I'm in favor of putting our groups in front of the Ozlidians, giving our men time to take evasive action and prepare for battle. I'll have the Yowells hang back to watch the rear, both ways."

"Did you talk to the group commanders?"

"Yes, if trouble comes, they're to take to the trees and ambush the attackers as best they can."

Ursel walked over, rubbing sleep from his eyes. "I thought you'd be up early."

Zack explained what they had discussed.

The big man nodded. "I like the idea of the Yowells taking a rear position. They're smart enough and good enough to handle anything coming their way, *if* something happens."

"I don't think it will," Currat said. "The Ozlidians would have a lot of catching up to find us on the trail."

They chatted about non-war subjects while eating and having a mug of ale. Men started waking and rousing others close to an hour before sunrise. Ursel motioned Cartel and his sons to the side. "I want you and your sons to hang back. Leave before we start out when it's still dark so no one sees you hide. The Ozlidians shouldn't see you go if at all possible."

Cartel chuckled, "They won't see us."

Ursel looked down at the whip curled up on the weapons master's hip. "I don't remember seeing that before now."

Cartel's face took on a knowing smile. "It has its uses. I'll get my boys, and we'll shortly be gone." Grabbing cheese and bread, he hurried toward the stream.

Ursel went to the outer dell. Duran roused his men and some had the cook fires going. He saw the spy and walked over. "The men became sullen for a while last night, but when they realized their life would be better where they were going, and the only thing left for them back home was death, they came around. Still, there's a lot of apprehension."

"That's to be expected," Ursel said. "I don't foresee trouble, but if we're attacked, we won't know who's who. When we start out this morning, have your men roll their shirtsleeves up past their forearms. Word the order the best way for your men to grasp without upsetting them, if possible. You know them better than anyone, except maybe Currat. I don't think it would come over too well if he tried to explain our reasons."

Ursel's smile became reflected on Duran's face. "No, on that point, I think you're right. I'll explain it's just another way to prepare on the off chance something does occur."

Looking over Duran's shoulder, Ursel could barely see three men leading black stallions away from the dells. He smiled, nodded to Duran, and returned to the inner dell.

At first light, the camps looked settled with fires out. Ursel, Zack and Currat led the groups out. Duran followed, leading his Men-in-Black.

Bryan, Sonkek, and Eckert followed a good twenty yards behind.

Mostly black cloaks covered everyone, giving a ghostly effect until the sun gained height in the sky. Songbirds woke to dew-laden branches, wildflowers, and grasses; their songs filled the air.

"At least we're not riding into the sunlight," Zack said to no one in particular.

The trail gradually turned a more southerly direction. The column stopped to water the horses in a nearby stream. Men took bread and cheese from their saddlepacks to eat while riding or waiting for a spot to lead their horse to water. The whole procedure took nearly an hour to complete. They moved out into the warmth of the afternoon.

Zack sorely wished a priest with Jasper's talents rode with them. *Seeing down the road would make me feel a lot better*, he thought. Hearing a hawk's cry from far above, he chuckled at the coincidence.

When nothing untoward happened by midafternoon, Zack began to feel better. The campsite normally used for the trip wouldn't even begin to accommodate so many. Men spread out on each side of it, with Ursel, Zack, Currat and Duran settled down in the usual place. The number of banked fires grew along the trail.

Masked men and Men-in-Black went to the swift stream, collecting water for cooking and bathing. A few began talking among themselves. Ursel, not sure how it started, listened to some of the conversations, pleased in what he heard. The men began including others, de-scribing what the Ozlidians over the mountain knew of Hamptor and Arestead, and how many in the military didn't know what happened.

The Hamptorians listened with rapt attention about Wathdure's control of water under the palace, and the rivers leading to the mountains. Many of the Men-in-Black showed surprise at the degradation Ozlid heaped on Hamptor. Word spread; men began to look at each other differently. As midnight approached, the primary spies and Duran made the rounds, explaining the need for sleep to face a long day.

* * *

URSEL, Zack, and Currat came instantly awake, feeling a slight vibration from the ground. Using hand signals, they moved out of the glowing embers' light, silently drawing their swords. Duran slept on.

A masked man dismounted and stepped into the light, briefly raising his disguise. Sheathing their swords, the spies stepped into the light to face Cartel. His sons settled by the campfire. Duran roused and sat up, looking surprised.

Ursel asked, "What brings you in?"

"The training you gave our warhorses worked well. We traveled back toward the north-south road using rotating gaits. We saw no one for several miles. We turned around and came here. As night fell, we slowed our pace. The stallions, using moonlight, cantered around trail holes as if they didn't exist. I thought you might need us more traveling with you. There's no way a force of any size could catch up with us by tomorrow evening when we reach our staging area. What's happened on the trail?"

"Not much," Ursel replied. The Ozlidians and Hamptorians began talking together this evening. I would say it went well."

Duran nodded.

Zack said, "We should reach the sea by midafternoon tomorrow. I hope to see Briggs waiting when we arrive. Now, we need sleep."

The Yowells moved to the back of the campsite and bedded down. Soon, the only unusual sounds came from an owl in the distance.

* * *

SUNLIGHT sprinkled through tree limbs, changing the dew to vibrant colors as the Yowells ranged ahead, looking for trouble.

Ursel spoke to Duran. "What do you think of your men mingling along side ours at the staging area?"

"They seemed to talk well last night with no animosity after the word spread of our lands' dispositions. I think some understanding of each other's plight developed. It may do some good when they board the ship. Her captain might feel more at ease knowing their attitude."

Ursel nodded as he continued saddling Arrowsmith. He caught Zack's smile and slight gesture where Duran couldn't see him. Within a quarter-hour, eighty men followed the trail behind the Yowells' scouting mission.

At midday, Zack dropped his bread and drew his sword. Hand signals flew, and masked men took to the trees with short bows and full quivers.

Duran looked startled, but his hand dropped to his sword hilt. "What is it?"

Ursel replied, "Galloping horses, three minutes out."

Duran signaled to his men as well, and they moved off the wide trail into the woods, leading their mounts.

Three black stallions cleared the bend ahead of where Ursel, Currat, and Zack stood in the middle of the trail. The last one carried two men, one unmasked. The lead man executed his own signal, and the spies sheathed their swords.

Cartel reined in near Ursel as men dropped from trees and Men-in-Black moved back onto the trail. The four dismounted. Ursel signaled, and four other masked men came forward to lead the sweating horses to water. Cartel waved Jostel forward.

He bowed slightly to Ursel and spoke in a rush. "Men-in-Black at the staging area. I counted nearly a hundred, but they kept moving around, and I can't be sure of the number."

"Slow down," Zack said. "Continue when you're ready."

Jostel took a deep breath and continued, "They arrived

near nightfall yesterday. I heard them approaching and hid. They came through the boulder path. They found my supplies and searched for me, but soon gave up. I heard a man with a blue stripe across his uniform say, 'He's one man, and he ran.'" His laugh came with a sneer. He talked loudly about how Wathdure would pay them all a great deal of coins for what they did. He paraded around a lot. I couldn't tell if he was trying to convince his men or himself. I watched them until dark, after they went to sleep. They didn't even post guards, and they left the fire pit blazing. The area is crowded beyond belief with horses and men. Instead of forming picket lines on the road, they let them roam free with the gate closed.

"I worked around to the boulders and searched the area. There's another trail! You can't see it from the one we take, but it's there. I came back to the road and waited. They didn't wake until an hour after sunrise. What surprised me the most is they still didn't post guards, and I didn't see any scouts leave."

"The Master of the Blue you refer to has no military tactical training," Duran said. "He's not long from palace duty. To hear him talk, one would think he'd fought a hundred battles, winning them all single-handedly. His inexperience will work in our favor."

Zack answered, "Perhaps. A hundred and five men is still a hundred and five fighters; at least they think they are warriors. Our problem is your men are mostly the same. You admitted most of them have not practiced swordsmanship since their initial training. Nonetheless, we need to balance the odds from them outnumbering you more than two to one. Call all the men together when the trail meets the road."

* * *

MEN picketed horses in the trees on both sides of the road a mile from the rise leading to the waiting Man-in-Black. Masked spies walked east through the forest, keeping the road just in sight. Reaching the entrance to the staging area, Cartel crawled on his stomach the last yards to see below. He returned, looking pleased.

"Zack, it's the same as before, except the stallions have congregated at the stream. The whole area is very crowded. That Master of the Blue must be an idiot to keep the horses inside the enclosure. The place smells to the clouds!"

Zack looked at Currat and Ursel and nodded, flashing one signal. All three went to their assigned tasks.

Ursel mounted Arrowsmith and rode back down the road, stopping a few yards before Duran's mounted men. They responded to his signal and rode forward at a trot, with Ursel and Duran leading the way. "You, Zack and, Currat need to stay back. When the time comes, my men will fight Wathdure's men. It's the way it should be!"

Ursel started to speak, but stopped, and just gave a mock salute instead. Duran smiled. The spy signaled, and a masked man led two packhorses to him. He looked Duran in the eye, "Long and short swords. I suggest your men take one of each." Duran's smile stayed as Ursel trotted back toward the ridgeline.

Three group leaders waited on each side of the road. Zack's hand signals sent them scurrying into the forest. Currat joined Cartel and his sons. They crept silently toward the rise, covering the last few yards on their bellies.

An hour before nightfall, Zack's imitation of a hawk's cry sounded over the coming battleground.

Bolts flew.

Men screamed.

Stallions escaped.

Chaos reigned.

The chargers broke down the enclosure's gate, racing up the road. Clearing the ridge, the lead stallion locked legs, bringing the herd to a stop, staring at Duran's men mounted on their brothers a hundred yards away. He reared, then came back down and trotted quickly into the trees. His companions did the same. Duran and his men sat, waiting on Zack's signal.

It's difficult shooting bolts from tree limbs; balancing and not falling off takes skill. When bedlam strikes men, their moves are unpredictable, making targets hard to anticipate. Men fell, but more moved into the trees' cover. The one group shooting from behind boulders had a better shot into the trees on the east side. Duran's men moved farther back.

Zack looked down from his vantage point on the hill's crest. He estimated roughly half the Men-in-Black lay dead or wounded after several volleys. He sounded another hawk's cry, and then whistled for Spellbinder, mounting him when he arrived a few heartbeats later.

Duran spurred his mount forward, keeping it at a canter. He and his men stopped at the hill's ridge. Drawing swords. Duran swung his forward and he and his men galloped into the melee of death.

Zack stared at the horror below. Untrained men wounded more than killed. Screams carried across the battle and out to sea as the cruel brutality continued. Men's blood soaked the ground forming rivulets of gore, limbs slashed and missing, throats cut causing spurting blood to arc through the air, men vomiting, men crying.

With sleeves rolled up, telling the two factions apart came easy. The enemy Master of the Blue stood, staring back and forth as his men died around him, an expression of shocked disbelief on his face. One of his men ran forward, facing his superior; he calmly shoved a sword through the officer's gut. As the swordsman started to turn away, a bolt found its mark in the middle of his back. He went down, still smiling.

Suddenly, Men-in-Black on horseback rode through the boulders, their swords waving. The masked group taking cover behind the adjoining rocks, stood and shot. Zack counted ten men falling from their mounts. Another ten made it to the fight. Duran rallied his men and rode forward to meet the oncoming threat. Many of the Men-in-Black from both sides soon lay on the ground, wounded or dying. Duran wheeled his mount around as a man rose to a kneeling position and threw. The dagger hit the Master of the Gold in the right chest. He went down; his stallion sprinted away. Zack cursed.

Another hawk's cry sounded over the din. Zack, Currat, and Ursel sat mounted on the ridgeline. Drawing swords and knives, they guided their stallions with knee pressure, riding steadily with an ambling gait, downward.

Daggers again flew. Men-in-Black watched as man after man fell. Reaching the once grassy ground, now churned into gory dirt from the fighting, swords sliced through the air into men. After twelve more died, the rest lay down their arms and knelt on the ground.

Zack's hand signals sent Cartel and his sons racing toward Duran. A man stepped in Cartel's path. The whip sprang out like magic, looping around the man's throat. The arms master jerked, snapping the Man-in-Black's neck. Zack raised his arm, and more gestures waved the air. Steel-tipped bolts struck the remaining enemy. Cartel and his sons moved through the wounded, killing Wathdure's men and moving Duran's men aside for attention. He kept one man alive from the riders coming through the boulders. As the last sunrays dipped behind the trees, a relative quiet settled over the deadly field.

Ursel ordered the hidden torches found and lit. Thirty, spaced equally apart, encircled the killing ground. Another twenty marked the way through the boulders to the sea. Masked men began fitting the wagon's tracings to a stallion with long ropes leading to the rear. The dead of both factions, pulled ten at a time, scraped across dirt and rocks to the sea. Four masked men threw them off the cliff into dark waters. The moon and stars signified midnight when the last corpse sank below the waves. The body of the Master of the Blue and one other dissolved in the seawater within seconds.

Ursel approached the wounded Man-in-Black. "How did you find the trail you used coming here?"

"Why should I say anything? You're going to kill me."

Ursel looked at the man with a stoic face, his words sounding flat. "That's true, but there are different ways to die. One would be flaying your skin off your body, bringing you hours of agonizing pain, like your cohorts did at the fortress on the border. Or, I could simply cut your bones, one joint at a time. Or, I could make your end quick and rather painless. You decide."

Resignation seemed to dawn on the man. His voice came out dry and raspy. "We raided a farm ten miles north of Ballrand's Inn. The farmer's son jabbered on about they should have taken the trail when they saw us coming. It didn't take much to get the directions to the sea. Our sergeant put it together, and said this must be where the horses are going."

Ursel's sword sliced through the Man-in-Black's neck. He died almost at once. After cleaning his blade, Ursel headed toward the Master of the Gold.

Duran sat up with a white dressing wrapped over his shoulder and across his chest. He looked up at Currat's smiling face and said, "Yes, it hurts! How many of us are left?"

"Eighteen. Seven are wounded, but should recover." Currat took in the pain spreading across Duran's face that had nothing to do with his wound. "I killed five who lay unconscious with death injuries. They would've died very unpleasantly or never awakened."

"How…how do you do it?"

Currat spoke quietly, "You have no idea what Wathdure had done to me, and what I've seen done on his orders. It makes life black and white. The enemy is evil. The Master of the Blue and another Man-in-Black liquefied in the seawater, meaning Wathdure had more than a little influence in them." Little emotion sounded in his words. Zack came close, put his arm around his shoulders and led him away.

Duran brushed back a single tear.

* * *

THE midday sun bore down on the *Sunbright Sea's* deck as Briggs rode the captain's chair aloft. The spies awaited him. His jovial smile beamed at them not quite as intensely as the sun's rays.

Stepping out of the chair, he said, "I didn't expect to see all of you here. What do you have for me?"

"Eighteen men and one hundred and fifty stallions," Ursel replied.

"WHAT!" Briggs boomed in disbelief, and then his laughter filled the air. He stopped his merriment when the others didn't crack a smile. "You—you're serious?"

A half-hour later, the captain stood, deeply frowning. He shook his head before saying, "I'll take the men and twenty-five horses on the first trip, and then...five more trips with the remaining stallions."

Zack asked, "Can you manage two more stallions on deck and two more men on the first trip."

Briggs looked at the spies, gleaning the meaning and the sadness in Ursel's expression. "I can do that."

They loaded the black stallions first. The Men-in-Black came next, riding two men at a time in the captain's chair. Duran and one other rode alone.

Zack and Currat embraced Ursel and quickly said their farewells. Zack adding, "You've done well, and we love you like the brother in arms you are." Ursel smiled but didn't try to speak.

On deck, they helped Spellbinder and Snowflake out of the harnesses and led them to a place prepared for them. The crew jumped to obey orders, and the big ship slowly pulled away from the cliff.

* * *

ZACK turned from the window in Gaz's study at the Spires after summarizing his report lying on the spymaster's desk.

Gaz rubbed his chin before asking, "Does Wathdure know of Ursel's activities?"

Currat answered, "He recognizes some of it; I'd guess. I don't think he cares. As I see it, the Men-in-Black he sends across the border are of no import to his overall plans. I believe he's getting rid of dead wood, and those not fully committed to him."

"When will he take more decisive action?"

Zack and Currat both shrugged. They started to speak at once. Zack continued, "From the reports I've read, it seems Shadure and Wathdure are committed here and not overly concerned over the Western Kingdoms."

Gaz nodded. "The Zenith Lord concurs as do I. Much is happening here and I'm glad you've returned; you're needed.

EPILOGUE

SHADURE stood across from Wathdure on the Gray Plane, fixing his eye on his subordinate. "Are there problems in Hamptor or Arestead we should worry about resolving?"

"No, my lord. They'll be taken care of in due time." His smile matched Shadure's own.

"Good! Our plans are coming to fruition and we will destroy the Zenith and his offspring. We will please the Dark One.

CHARACTERS

Argon Steadian, Aresteadian Spy Leader
Arrowsmith, Ursel's Stallion
Ballrand, Running Bull Innkeeper
Bronson, First Mate
Bryan Daven, Fighter, Spy
Calbris, Elizabethville Spy
Cartel Yowell, Arms Master
Cerrit, Bargeman
Cerrol, Fighter, Spy
Collan, Hamptorian Farmer
Crawford Briggs, Ship Captain
Currat Duval, Zack's Partner
Cursong, Captain Brigg's Second Mate
Dackamo, Sis'on Slave
Darius Openhand, Ambassador
Dartel Yowell, Cartel's Son
Derkson Tomwell, Retired Captain from the Hamptorian
        Army
Eartel Yowell, Cartel's Son
Franc Horn, Innkeeper of the Silver Tankard
Franzt, Bargeman
Horance, Bargeman
Jadel, Sailor's Quest Innkeeper
Jarod Greatstone, The Zenith Lord
Jax Topin, Surveyor
Marcella, Seamstress
Massion, Member of Captain Brigg's Crew
Michael Gaz, The Zenith's Spymaster
Milfred Spotfish, Torrance's Wife
Naz, Bargeman
Obien Webster, Son of Family Killed by Bandits
Pennison, Farmer Collan's Wife
Rozbert, Farmer Collan's Grandson
Shadure, Second to The Dark One
Snowflake, Currat's Warhorse

CHARACTERS

Spellbinder, Zack's Warhorse
Synithy, Bryan Daven's Love Interest
Torrance Spotfish, Tankard's Delight Innkeeper
Turlas, Fighter, Spy
Ursel Glaston, Hamptorian Spymaster
Wathdure, Second to Shadure
Yasho, Innkeeper of the Blue Sail
Zack Stand, The Zenith's Spy

ACKNOWLEDGEMENTS

I once wondered why an author acknowledged so many people. Now, I know! I'll start with my writer's group founded by Sam Barone who brought a talented group together, although to my dismay, the group is disbanded: Sharon Anderson, Deborah J. Ledford and Thelma Rea. These folks gave of their talent, friendship and time. Besides that, they are nice.

And then there are the editors. One thinks they have written a masterpiece until an editor gets their head wrapped around a manuscript. Nonetheless, they found the writing, character and plot flaws I never thought of while writing my novel. Even with college training, this craft has a huge learning curve.

Fellow authors have given support, time and friendship. Chief among these is L. E. Modesitt, Jr. and Charles Fallon. They have become friends and good advisors of authorship over the years. Paul Genesse has been supportive and become another friend. Michael Stackpole gave me good advice and several tips about not only my novel but also the publishing industry.

Other friends in the industry have always been supportive and thoughtful in their counsel: Krista Wallace is one of these. For several years I've attended the World Fantasy Conventions held in a different city each year. Nearly all of the authors, editors and other industry professionals are approachable and helpful as are the wonderful people at the Miscon Convention run by Justin Barba every year in Missoula, MT.

I have been fortunate to know and learn from all these fine people. I wish them all the best in life and careers. Of course, the minute this manuscript goes to press, so to say, I'll remember someone who should have been included!

AUTHOR BIO

Born in Atlanta Georgia, Mr. Cox lived there until he joined the United States Air Force and served in Texas, France and Germany. Writing is his fourth career. He started in large mainframe computers, and then moved on to become a real estate broker. He returned to college to obtain a nursing degree and practiced as a Registered Nurse and also began writing his first novel, which he stated became his most rewarding work. He lives in Phoenix, Arizona.